Shattered

BOOK TWO

JADE AUSTIN

I'm Still Shattered

JADE AUSTIN

DEDICATION

I dedicate this book to people who grew despite
all the challenges that were cast their way.
You are an inspiration.
Thank you

PLEASE LEAVE A REVIEW

Thank you for supporting my dream of being an author. I would be honored to know what you think. Please drop a review on Amazon and Goodreads!

DISCLAIMER

This novel contains:

Bold/Capitalized Words
British Spelling and Abbreviations
Mental Health Awareness

The following are situations or themes throughout the book.
"Major" means that it is described in more depth,
while "Minor" means that there are either brief mentions of it
or that the situation may not turn out how it first appears.

Major:
Child abuse
Death
Gore
Violence
Suicide
Consensual Sexual Content

Minor:
Alcoholism
Infidelity
Attempted Sexual Assault
Genocide
Slavery

CONTENTS

Then

Two hundred and thirty-two bodies covered the cemetery above Loxley Lair, piling together in a mass of blond hair and empty blue eyes. All marked with the irreversible kiss of death.

There was a pounding in my heart I couldn't console as I scanned over each body, panicked, and ashamed that I'd let things get this far. I reached for Chad's hand and pulled him closer. My other hand landed against his chest, half from my own fear, half to protect him, and I could feel that his heart was wedged in the same predicament as my own.

We were staring at a massacre.

No one dared utter *his* name under the fog of impending doom. It swept in on us like frostbitten air. So foreign in the midst of the summer celebration where we had been ignorantly dancing below.

Hardly any shreds of clothing covered the dead. The crimson-streaked fabrics reeked of spoiled blood. Yet as the bile crept up my throat, I couldn't bring myself to look away. Curiosity bit at me. So I searched, weaving my way between the dead, looking for a familiar woman with long blonde hair. One who had delivered a letter promising *his* return. A secret I had yet to let slip from my lips.

It was possible her body was there, but as sirens sounded through the air and the mortal police came to investigate, as we watched from afar while they carted away the bodies, it was impossible to tell. If she was among the **MURDERED**, I didn't know. I had never seen her face.

Half of me hoped the bodies on the ground would be the end of it— the last of her—the last of *him*, but a horrid truth whispered in my mind: this was just the beginning.

"Prime Minister Alastor is going to be devastated by this," a detective muttered under his breath, and as his words flew over and into my ears, a realisation set in.

This was a plague of cruelty. One we couldn't erase from mortal eyes. Soon everyone would be wondering who was next—mortals, Casters, and Night Crawlers alike.

All because of Florence.

Chapter 1: The To-Do List

THREE MONTHS LATER

ଔ

*H*ands upon hands, offering delicious, sinful temptations. *Luring me. Curing me. Giving me the world. They caressed me in places I didn't know needed to be touched. They were the essence of heaven and perfection all wrapped in one. He pulled back to look at me, the intensity of his green eyes sending a wave of breathlessness to my lungs. I wanted him so badly at that moment.*

I wanted him, and I never wanted him to leave.

His lips parted and his warm breath sent chills through me. He looked at me with so much exultation, and whispered, "Are you ready?"

I was beyond ready. Ready to feel more of him, ready for him to enter me, but my body—my stupid, useless excuse of a body had other plans.

I woke up but it was too late. My hands flew upwards, sending Chad catapulting towards the ceiling, and a whimper left my lips.

No, no, no. Not again.

He crashed back down to the bed with a grunt of pain I was much too used to hearing over the past few months. I sat up with so much dread and guilt in my shaking hands as I examined him. How badly had I injured him this time?

"I'm so, so sorry, Chad! Are you all right? Is it your spine?"

"No," he said, clenching his teeth through each laboured breath. He lay flat on his back, eyes shut tight, a grimace on his face. "Not this time. Just a few ribs."

His hand drew a circular motion in the air above his chest, and emerald-green billows of smoke swirled around him, healing the physical damage I had done.

I closed my eyes and let relief wash over me.

Thank heavens it's not his spine.

That time had been the worst of all of them. I had sent him soaring into the stone wall, leaving him paralyzed from the neck down. All the panic in the world had flowed through me as I scrambled to use my purple magic to try and heal him. It took me a lifetime before I was able to fix him enough that he could do the rest of the healing himself.

Bits of stone continued to shower down on us, and I cringed at the falling pieces as I looked up to the ceiling and assessed the damage. The dent his body had left wasn't the worst one I'd seen, though the cracks spread all the way to the walls. With a struggling flick of his wrist, Chad sent the cracks travelling in reverse, hiding any evidence of the attack. It was an easy fix on the outside, but the true solution was figuring out what the hell was wrong with me.

"Did you dream about them again?" Chad asked, managing to sit up enough to prop himself on his elbows.

I winced. The small, frail children haunting my dreams of late. They were cursed with a situation so similar to my own as a child, the one my sister and I had been trapped in. They were children I couldn't save.

"Not exactly," I paused, heat spreading to my cheeks. "I may have been having a dream about us... touching, and we were about to... you know, do more, and I lost control." I bit my lip, but to my relief, he laughed.

"You know, if you can't resist me, even in your sleep, perhaps I should get used to all this pain. People all over the world are into all sorts of kinky mischief. Perhaps BDSM is more your style than you thought."

I whacked him in his stomach for such useless drivel at a time like this, but his breath left him again. He lay back down, clutching at his chest.

"Still... healing..." he said between desperate breaths, and I winced again, only *half* sorry this time.

When he stopped groaning, he said, "Perhaps my aunts have a spell or a potion that can help with these visions."

Ah, the devils themselves.

"I am *not* trusting them, especially when it comes to spells and potions," I insisted as I glared at him. Their bitterness towards me had always been prominent. "Not only have your aunts made a habit of poisoning and jinxing me, but they're also most likely in cahoots with Florence," I accused them for the thousandth time. Them and my singing ghost. It was the silver bullet that had pushed me over the edge—the part that stung the most. I'd trusted her and she betrayed me. She had lured us to Florence's hideout, right to where Florence ambushed us, right to where he told the Castwell sisters I'd be.

Chad's reply was predictable, exactly the same as it always was. Just as stubborn and in denial. "They would never work with a vampire, especially one like Florence."

I gritted my teeth in response. Of course he'd believe that. They were his family. They had raised him.

"If you won't let them help you, then maybe you could let—" Chad started.

If I had glared at him earlier, then this was the look of death. Any mention of the woman he was supposedly destined to marry—the woman his aunts adored so dearly—was forbidden. She was not going to help me overcome my visions so Chad and I could get back to our sex life. Over my dead body. Not that this *almost* mention of her was vastly different from any of the others. The first hundred times he'd tried to tell me about her, or reassure me that she meant nothing, I politely turned down the conversation.

She was the cold bite of autumn as summer waned to a close, a reminder of one of my constant fears before deciding to be with Chad, and a slap across the face as his aunts' voices played again and again in my mind, informing me that Chadwick had already spent a month with Mrs Prophecy, right before he'd vanished for another month to work with her.

Them, I corrected, forcing a deep breath. He hadn't been working all hours of the day with only her, he'd been working with his team of witches and wizards to solve the problem I couldn't: *Florence*. Regardless, I didn't want to know how clever she was, or how beautiful, or how she radiated with grace, and especially not how I paled in comparison. I wanted to know what I could do to help fight, not invent a fight in my head with a woman whom I had never even met.

"I don't need help," I said sweetly but firmly. I knew precisely how to solve this problem on my own. "All I have to do is go through my immense checklist. Once I save my sister, I can find the children to make sure they're safe. Then *that* will clear my mind and prepare me for destroying Florence. And all will be well. My nightmares won't plague us after that." Whatever lies I had to tell myself to get through it all. All I had known was nightmares. Why would they cease to be just because of a few victories?

"All right, but if you change your mind…" he began hopefully.

"I won't," I promised, cutting off his suggestion before he could get it out. I did *not* need Mrs Prophecy.

Chad stretched out his arms with an enormous yawn and then slid them around me, tucking me into him. In his arms—one of the few places I felt safe. His warm breath tickled my neck, and I leaned into him, running my fingers along his face, taking in every detail of the man I was so in love with.

"Do you want to go back to sleep?" he asked, and I could tell his eyes were soaking in all my features as well, like he was glad to have a moment together before the night truly began.

I nuzzled my nose against his. "And miss out on these moments with you? Absolutely not."

It was all work these days. No time to *just* appreciate him, but I honestly didn't trust myself to feel any pleasure, not with how my body kept reacting so violently to my own happiness. Especially since the warmth of his body was so tantalising, and memories of the dream I'd just had threatened to creep back into my mind. No, I wouldn't risk throwing him back against the ceiling, not when everything had been mended so nicely.

I shoved away the thoughts, the moment, and set my mind back to our mission.

"Up for an early training?" I suggested.

"Only if you promise to kick my arse as hard as when you don't intend to," he teased, knowing full well how lousy I was in magical combat.

"Perhaps a few kisses on my neck in the arena are exactly what I need to conquer you once and for all," I quipped.

A heavy breath from deep in his diaphragm left his lips, and I knew he was equally as tempted as I was to stay in bed and rip off each other's clothes, but perhaps the memory of his cracked ribs brought him to his senses.

"Save your sister, save the children, and destroy Florence," he said carefully, repeating my to-do list. "And then you're all mine." His hand slid like a feather along my hip, sending shivers through my entire body.

"Not if I have you first," I taunted, and then I forced myself out of the bed before I dared give in, ignoring the inevitably long wait that was sure to ensue.

6

Jade Austin

Chapter 2: Suggestions to Make You Shiver

We dressed in our usual training garments, which for me was a long, medium-blue tunic, a black belt around my waist, and matching black boots with trousers tucked into them that were tight to my skin but flexible for fighting. Chad wore a sage green tunic that brought out the green of his eyes, and loose-fitting trousers. I scanned the muscles of his arms as he rolled up his sleeves, and watched as they tightened, ready to cast his magic towards me.

We only had an hour or so before he'd be off to his aunts' castle in Lancaster. While I should have been used to the frequent absences by now, all I wanted to do was wrap my arms around him—beg him not to go. But he had duties, ones I couldn't be a part of.

Not only had I fallen in love with a wizard, but I happened to fall in love with the High Prince of the Casters. He ruled over all the Casters in the world, even the Caster kings and queens of the other countries. Sure, we had discovered that I was a witch, so technically I was part of his world, but I had been turned into a natural enemy the second Florence bit me, before I had ever laid eyes on Chad. Being a vampire made me an outcast. Thus, we worked together but separately. "We'll change all that," Chad kept telling me. Change, however, came very slowly when the vampire who'd turned me was leading a war against Casters and mortals alike.

"Armoury or maze?" Chad asked, tucking a dagger into his belt.

My mind flashed to last week when we had been training in his magical maze. The way it knew my weaknesses, the sunlight it could produce to char my skin if I wasn't quick enough to block it. If we were merely racing through it, that was simple. I had gotten to the point where

I could beat him to the centre every time now. Little did he know, I could run through the walls—a magic trick I had performed far before I knew I was a witch. However, if we were using the maze to train, that was an entirely different challenge I wasn't up for tonight.

"Armoury," I answered decidedly.

He grabbed my hand before whirling us off to the armoury. My heart stopped when a sudden movement in the room caught my interest. Three tall, heavily armoured figures, whose sweat permeated the room, lowered their clashing swords to bow down to Chad—added security measures I was still having a difficult time adjusting to. After nodding back at the men, they quickly exited to give us the room. Their blood was still pumping enticingly through their veins as they stood guard on the opposite side of the door.

"Defence or offence?" Chad asked, tossing a black leather vest my way. It was meant to protect me from the spells I pathetically let slip through.

I frowned at the leather as I strapped it on, remembering the poor cow whose blood I had failed to drink the day prior. How was I going to **KILL** Florence when I couldn't even **KILL** a cow?

"Offence," I replied. It was best if we started with less pressure, less green magic cast towards me, propelling me backwards after my failed attempts to defend myself.

So we began. Chad flicked his wrists, projecting a large, pellucid shape in front of him. It curved inwards on him like the cornea of an eye, reaching just above his head and extending down to his kneecaps. A shield.

"Do your worst," he called out, his skin shining behind the screen, but his definition of "worst" was vastly different from mine.

Energy built within the core of my chest, and what should have been his protection morphed into a target in my mind. The tips of my fingers tingled, and just before I allowed its release, I thrust my palms towards him. Jets of violet light erupted out, crashing into his circular plate and spraying sparks around him.

Only, he didn't even move an inch.

"You can do better," he encouraged, unphased by my power drain. "Push against me. Give me everything you've got."

I stepped forwards and pushed against him, envisioning his shield melting away to nothing, but no such result came. Attempting a different measure of attack, I took back my hand in a movement so quick only I could see, captured light from a candle nearby, and propelled it at Chad. Fire—my go-to since it had a way of bending until it became a part of me. It often fed off my heavy emotions, sending every nearby candle into a frenzy that scorched the ceiling and walls, often without my control.

But as I sent the flames spiralling towards Chad, they merely smouldered against the green shield for a fraction of a second before burning out. At least this time, he flinched.

"Try harder," he demanded eagerly, as though I weren't trying my damnedest. But I could see small beads of sweat running along his temple, ones that outweighed my own as I tried everything I could think of to break down his defences. At least I was doing *something*.

I sent another flame barrelling towards him, then another, and another, but each only produced the smallest of holes before his shield mended itself.

He wiggled his eyebrows at me, egging me on as my spell ricocheted off his shield again, causing little damage. My fangs threatened to bare themselves in my frustration. The urge to cheat and cast a rope around his ankles was conquered by a sheer wave of bitter truth: I was utterly useless.

"Let's switch," I insisted as thirty minutes' worth of sweat poured down my cheeks. As my magic disappeared, so did his shield.

Years of training gave him the endurance I yearned to have, and as he quickly began to attack with the flick of his wrists, I tried to produce my own shield, but I failed horrendously. He was simply better than me—faster, stronger, more focused. He had trained long and hard. I had been reduced to cowering in a corner and hiding my magic as a child. It was an unfair fight but a necessary one nonetheless.

Chad sent the most ridiculous attacks my way. Tickling charms, and freezing jinxes, and spells of every sort came flying at me, bouncing off my anti-charm vest and crashing back towards him before he waved a hand to redirect them to the side. With my shield method completely out the window, I switched to a repelling charm, but Chad took the opportunity to modify his attack as well.

Pulling the dagger from the clip of his belt, he flung it at me without a speck of mercy. I dodged it easily. Now, *this* I could work with. My vampire senses were a bigger, more relevant part of me. An emerald string appeared around the dagger's hilt and pulled the dagger back into his hand. He posed, ready to throw it at me again.

"Combine your vampire reflexes with your magic. You have talents as a witch. Use them," he called across the room, mimicking an emotionless voice his combat trainers had probably used with him growing up. Before I could roll my eyes or mention his lack of bedside manner, he cast another spell that would have hit me square in the chest if I hadn't dived out the way at the last second. Then he flung the dagger towards my new position, so I sprinted out of the way again.

I gawked at him from across the room. "*What* talents?" I huffed out, clearly not finding any at this particular moment.

"Come on, Azalea. Faster. Stronger." No emotion whatsoever. This was too difficult. Too soon for my subpar skills. "This is all still new!" I insisted, straining to project my voice over the sparks flying through the room. "Three months of training *clearly* isn't enough for these skills. Who knows if I was even fully aware I was a witch before Florence wiped my memory? With the way my father acts in my nightmares, I probably suppressed it from myself."

"Three months is plenty of time," he replied stubbornly, standing his ground with pride. "Stop doubting yourself. You have to believe you can do it for it to happen properly. It's like opening a door. It's not going to open unless you make it. Turn the knob, Azalea."

Easy for him to say. He was born into all this. He was a wizard prince with proper training. Not to mention he had additional, *extensive* training after his mum passed.

"I seem to remember a few kisses were promised to encourage my powers to come out," I struggled to get out as more thrusts of green magic crashed into me. The comment may have come off as sarcasm, but I truly was hoping for a kiss. Or more.

"I won't always be there to kiss you right before you're being attacked. Nor will we always have the time. You've got to find the strength within you. Wield it on your own."

As if testing me fully, his arms moved through the air in a fluid, sweeping motion, urging his magic to mix with the very air itself, and spinning it forcefully around like a boomerang. A violent tornado of emerald green captured me, and as I stood in the eye of the storm, I forced my powers against it, but my violet stream disappeared into the powerful vortex.

"I was thinking," Chad shouted through the green mass. "Suppose you didn't go home in the mornings. Suppose you didn't call the lair your home at all…"

"Meaning?" I called back, squinting against the winds and pushing against the swirls with all my might.

"Meaning I want to spend as much time with you as possible," he said shyly, even though he had the complete upper hand at the moment, "and perhaps you moving in with me would help."

Purple fire blasted through the tornado, causing the swirls to transform into a circular shield in front of himself as the flutter in my stomach weakened my knees. Bravely, he crept forwards, my sparks crashing off of his shield, the hint of a sly smile lighting his eyes as he silently approved my achievement and waited for my answer.

"You want me to—move out of Loxley Lair?" I asked, hardly able to keep the grin off my face. The idea was a whirl of fear and excitement, entwined seductively together. "And move in with you?"

He nodded, inching closer, a slight strain in his step as he pushed against my purple stream, which was now even more radiant than his shield. "Yes. I guess you could say I've grown quite fond of your company these past few months, and I crave having more of it." The reflection of the green and violet gleamed in his eyes. "And perhaps, now that your magic is improving, your sister could be safe at the castle too. You could protect her, and I could assist you in keeping her safe."

My heart lifted at the thought. Hydie, safe in Castwell Castle. Me, closer to both of them. But moving in…

"Aren't you a bit concerned it's too soon? Us moving in together?" I asked softly, but I instantly regretted the words. I didn't want to be afraid. I wanted to jump in wholeheartedly.

"We've known each other for a year now—" he started, but I cut him off with a laugh.

"I don't think that *finding* you and debating whether or not I should suck your blood should be considered our anniversary," I insisted, and his smile lifted me.

"We've been officially together since February—" he tried again, glancing to the floor, but I was grateful his smile stayed. A symbol he didn't find me a complete bitch for questioning his proposal.

"Minus the month you deserted me to go hang out with… *her*," I tested, biting my bottom lip and eyeing him warily to see how he'd react to the cheek I was giving.

"The month I was *preparing for a war*," he corrected, giving me a warning look before continuing. "So moving in together truly isn't that unreasonable."

Oh, how I loved that man. Every inch of me yearned to say yes, to shut down the idea it might be too soon in our relationship, or not as safe as it sounded with Florence running amok. But it could work. It truly could.

He was standing in front of me, my hands now pressed against his shield, his eyes blinking at me patiently, a smile waiting.

"I can't think of anything I'd like more right now," I said. Besides Florence's demise, of course. "But your aunts—"

The gleam suddenly died in his eyes, and his shield swiftly transformed into green vines that twisted me around and forced me to face away from him. His hands aimed my flames into a target on the wall that instantly began to smoulder. He nuzzled his face into my neck before placing a light kiss on my skin, and the target burst into a million pieces.

"I want to take you to my aunts," he said, his features fighting off a grimace as he admitted it. "We'll tell them together you're moving in, and nothing they do or say will change my mind."

The purple fire went out as if it had drowned in invisible waters. I turned around to face him. "Together?" What a traumatising occurrence that would be. I hadn't seen them since they had followed Chad to Loxley Lair and attacked my entire coven, choked me, and told me flat out they didn't approve of me for their nephew.

"Yes, but it'll be fine," he insisted.

"And if they show up to Castwell Castle? Discover Hydie?" *Hand her over to Florence in the inevitable case they're working with him?* I didn't bother saying the last bit out loud as I already knew his stance on the matter, yet he flinched regardless.

"She'll be safe from my aunts," he said reassuringly, "and if they try any tricks against her, I'll disown them. I'll tell them that myself," he added firmly, and my heart clenched at the sheer sincerity in his tone. He would do it too, and I loved him all the more for it. He switched to a lighter tone, taking hold of my wrists and keeping them aimed away, just in case. "Castwell Castle gets lonely without you. It would do my heart good knowing you were here. Knowing you were safe and happy."

I bit my lip to suppress the overwhelming glee that spread within me as I fully gave in. "I love you Chadwick Liam Castwell, and I'd be most honoured to move in with you."

The fire lit inside me once more, and I had just enough time to sneak in a kiss before shooting blast after blast of fire his way. He blocked all of them easily, regardless of my vampiric speed. Yet this time, I could feel the vibrant power in each violet blow.

I was going to move in with the amazing man before me, and I was finally going to get my sister.

Jade Austin

Chapter 3: Undeserving

After Chad went to Lancaster and I took an incredibly lonely shower, I settled on skipping the dull spell book studying I'd usually do, and instead decided to tell Abigail and the rest of the coven my news. Returning to the lair meant wearing vampire attire, so I slipped into a silky black dress that trailed down to the floor. The dark fabric enveloped my arms down to my wrists and ended in a pointed edge. It was light and airy, allowing for movement, with a gothic style that reminded me of the dress Abigail had been wearing when I woke up to find I'd been turned into a beast of the night.

Deciding that walking there would allow too much time to change my mind, I transported myself to my bedroom and immediately regretted it as the long-distance magic completely winded me. I stood panting and grasping the post on my bed as white lights twinkled around me. It was always like this, apart from the first time I had transported on my own, all those months ago. However, in that instance, I had been full of adrenaline, focused on saving Connor, and then immediately choked out by a wicked witch. I hadn't given the transporting the credit it deserved for consuming all my energy.

I appreciated the comfort of my bed as my legs seemed to crumple, and I placed my head on my red pillowcase. The crimson silks felt cool against my cheek. Silently, I thanked Fendel, the gnome who had once gifted me the pillowcase in response to all the times my crimson tears had stained the old ones. How often would I cry into my pillow once I lived with Chad?

I shouldn't have let my mind go there.

As if on cue, a scene washed away my room, and my senses were overwhelmed with death—the smell, the taste, the blood, and the haunting sound of a last heartbeat.

*You're going to **KILL** him,* one of Chad's aunts screeched through my head, and then I was back on my bed, panting harder than ever.

It was always so quick, never long enough to assess the scene for myself—to see how tangible it was, or determine if it was just a nightmare. Either way, one of Chad's aunts was sending more and more of these visions my way—scenes of Chad dying. And although they were just quick glances, the witches always made it abundantly clear that the source of his death was none other than me taking his final drop of blood.

I sat up and attempted to wipe the vile feeling from my mind. It was another problem to remind Chad of later. Gathering the fallen pieces of myself, I heightened my senses, eager for them to remain my own this time. Sounds from all over the lair slithered into my ears, filling my head with whispers. Heavy drops of rain cascading against the greenhouse roof, gnomes stirring boiling liquids in cauldrons reaching twice their height, and the flapping of manananggal wings until Abigail's sweet voice vibrated against my eardrums. There was a brief moment when I was pleased to hear it before any excitement was squashed by the voice of another.

Yet I couldn't run from her straight blonde locks forever. Sooner or later, I'd have to face her, regardless of the woman she or her wife might be.

Ingrid froze as I walked into the lounge, well before she turned her head to look in my direction, her eyes flashing red as they dug into me. Her wife, Irma, placed a caring hand on Ingrid's knee, and Ingrid jumped ever so slightly. In the four or so months that they had lived with us, she still hadn't forgiven me for the vision I'd had, revealing her lie that she knew more about Florence's plan than she had let on. She was afraid I'd tell the world that the man causing mass graves was the son of a German soldier. It should have been Florence she was afraid of, though, not me. For that reason, her opinion of me was listed as trivial. Her quivers and long blonde hair gave me reason to suspect her of more sinister dealings.

All blond hair haunted me these days. Not just because it was the colour of Florence's hair, or of all the victims he had dumped on top of Loxley Lair, but because of the mysterious blonde who was working with him. The one who had delivered the letter to me, insisting Florence would be back. I didn't know who she was or if she still breathed, but I knew the colour of her hair, and it was a colour that sent shivers down my spine whenever I saw it.

Thoughts of tricking Ingrid with one of the spells I had learned crossed my mind. I could grab onto her hand again on the off-chance I'd see another vision or clue that she was working with Florence. Perhaps he was blackmailing her. She came to us, claiming he had torn apart their coven in Germany. In my mind's eye, I saw her plead with him to spare Irma. The fear of losing a loved one could make people do terrible things.

Irma smiled sweetly, no doubt trying to make up for her wife's aversion to me. "Azalea, it's lovely to see you," she hummed in a soothing voice, as if I didn't live there and see them nearly every day. At least she was trying to be cordial, so I returned a graceful smile, hoping the I would be convincing.

"It's lovely to see you all as well. I was just here to share some news," I forced out.

"Oh?" Abigail said, furrowing her brows. "Is everything all right?"

Nodding at Abigail, with her perfectly trustworthy onyx-black hair, I released the breath I had been holding.

"Everything is fine. Great actually," I added in, not wanting to show any of my fear in front of the two blondes, but desperately wishing I could have the conversation privately with my best friend. I cleared my throat and gave in to the fact that they wouldn't be leaving any time soon. "Chadwick asked me to move in with him, and I've said yes," I spat out quickly, trying to get it out in the air before I changed my mind about telling her.

I half expected Abigail to jump up and congratulate me, but when her shoulders slumped and she gave an open-mouth frown, my stomach dropped.

"Oh," she let out, clearly taken aback. "But—" She looked around, trying to find the right words. "Don't you think it's a bit too soon?"

My fingers played together anxiously as my own fears spewed out of her mouth. *Of course I think it's a bit soon,* I wanted to tell her. *I'm frightened out of my mind.* But I wanted to move in with him so badly. The intense combination of fear and desire spun around me all at once. Keeping my thoughts locked shut, I shrugged, unable to think of a clever alternative.

Abigail threw a shifty look towards the other two women before asking me hopefully, "Do you think it'll help with your problem?"

My cheeks heated at her question. It was a topic we had discussed several times as I vented my sexual frustrations to her. The first time I had accidentally thrown Chad was the night after Florence's monstrous demonstration of power, when two hundred and thirty-two bodies had dropped like bricks against the cemetery above us. Chad had tried to console me after the sun had risen and sleep still hadn't graced me with its presence. I had just tossed aside my book, its pages landing crinkled against the floor, when he returned from reporting the news to his aunts and She-Whom-We-Never-Mention. When he had crawled in through my mirror, my chest had risen with anticipation. Ready for the distraction. Yearning for it. His green eyes glowed brightly as his palm cradled my cheek, and then his lips pressed hungrily into mine. That's when they entered my mind for the first time: the two children who had been haunting my dreams ever since. Starved, fragile, and broken.

I had lost all control and consciousness of my body, and Chad became my prey. My palms smashed up against him, propelling him through the door of my bedroom and out into the hall. Neither of us understood why it had happened when it did, but we learned pretty fast that our cravings for one another were the trigger to the pistol. We hadn't been able to fulfil those urges since.

My focus flitted back to the others in the lounge. Ingrid stirred uncomfortably, and I caught Irma's interested look, probably grateful to get rid of me, but the flick of her blonde hair took me back to the bodies as they cluttered the graveyard floor. Different from the woman with the letter, but each haunting me in my dreams. Something tugged at my insides, telling me the woman was still out there, and whispers down my spine told me I had run into the woman before. It told me she was the one who had been there the night Florence bit me, promising she'd take me to a place worse than Hell. The woman Florence told me didn't exist, but I could feel in my veins she was no figment of my imagination.

She was real.

Unidentifiable.

Haunting.

And too close.

As these tragic memories tightened their hold on me, a buzz from nearby pulled me back to the present once more. It was a sound I knew all too well as it was so often created by Florence. It was the sound of him running towards me, preparing to unleash his rage on me. Relief, however, washed over me as I heard the familiar, yet panicked breaths of my fellow coven-mates.

The trapdoor all the way in the entryway clanged open, followed by a rush of feet and frantic shouts.

"Leo! Charity!" a voice called out to the leaders of our coven. "Something's happened!"

The voice belonged to Riley O'Brien, the Irish vampire who lived at Loxley Lair along with his deceased family member, Grace O'Brien, the banshee. The urgency in his tone gave me shivers as I glanced at the three vampiresses in the lounge, and we quickly fled out to the entrance hall to find out what all the commotion was about. Part of me was thankful for the end of my conversation with them, but part of me dreaded what I'd be dealing with instead.

We reached the entrance hall at the same time as Leo and Charity Loxley, and our eyes quickly examined a rain-drenched O'Brien and a werewolf in her human form as they stood before us. Their chests rose up and down from their panicked run. Other coven members poured into the room, and tensions were strung tight as we awaited their news.

"The Downy Coven," O'Brien huffed between heavy breaths. "They're being ambushed by Florence. He—he appeared with a bunch of his followers while we were spying on them, hoping he'd show up— only, he isn't there for pleasure. He's there to **KILL**."

The word screamed out at me.

I remembered Downy Lair, the putrid blood fountain and moans of their group passion forcing their way into my mind, but an attack? It didn't make sense. Why would Florence attack Downy Lair? The leader, Elizabeth Downy, idolised him. Florence had returned those feelings towards her home and her sadistic, eternally red-eyed coven. He had dragged me there to show it off—nearly forced me to join in. He fit in so well with the immorality of it all, so why would he turn against them?

"They started slaughtering the whole lot of them," the woman werewolf continued. "We were able to hide in the forest, but I don't know what would've happened if they weren't so focused on the attack."

The woman's fear seeped out like a sickness, crawling across the floor until I was infected. We stood silenced by the news, unsure how to react.

Charity's feet twitched as though they itched to show her true, spider-like form. "Slaughter," the Japanese jorogumo repeated, her brown eyes somewhere far off in the distance. The word lingered on her tongue like a poison she was afraid to swallow. She looked at the two of them, water dripping off their bodies as they shook from more than the crisp September air they had travelled through. "And there's no way they can survive on their own?" she added.

"He's massacring them," he replied as he stared absentmindedly at the puddle they had created on the floor. "They all are, but this could be our one chance to help Downy Coven, convince some of them to join our side."

A silence filled the room, so thick you couldn't cut it with a knife. I didn't know what to do. I was frozen in the moment, without an ounce of concern for the horrid creatures who dwelled at the Downy Coven. But the smallest amount of guilt trickled in. I should care about blood being spilt. I should, but my memories there wouldn't allow it.

O'Brien's worried eyes whipped around me, pulling me into a memory where he had worn the same sullen expression, and my heart pounded louder. The memory of his worried eyes played through my mind. Florence had tried to force himself on me in my own bed. I had blasted him away, but my actions only made the fury build within him. If O'Brien hadn't walked in when he had, I could imagine exactly what Florence would have done to me.

Unlike Florence, O'Brien's soul was filled with kindness. He had a strong intuition and a natural urge to help others, but the banshee who had been in his family for generations had warned him that his good soul would get him **KILLED** one day. The thought screamed out at me, telling me he shouldn't go to Downy Lair. He shouldn't risk his life to save the beasts who didn't deserve saving.

I shook my head slowly, making a silent plea with him not to go, and his shoulders fell at my request.

"I think it all dwindles down to one thing," Leo began. "Would it be wrong to sit back and witness their demise, or should we go help them?"

Not one person rushed forwards. Not one person spoke in their favour. It was no secret what the Downy vampires were capable of. None of the other members had been inside the wretched lair, but in the days and nights spent spying on them, many had heard the screams. The kind that reached deep down into your soul and tore it to shreds. They could smell the fresh blood cascading out of the top of the enormous fountain, spilling down the three tiers like a monumental prize of the lair's immense cruelty. They had sensed the pain coming from the mortals within, whether it was from their **MURDER** or from being forced to partake in other vile acts with the merciless vampires who lived there.

Abigail cleared her throat. "I'll go," she declared, and Cristin immediately stepped forwards to join her, nodding in agreement. Of course she'd volunteer. She was always so brave, so fearless when it came to fighting Florence. And of course I couldn't let her go without me.

"I'll go too," I said, not sounding nearly as steady and confident as she had.

"We can help," Irma offered, but Abigail turned to them, and something inside me twinged.

"No, he's taken enough from you," Abigail told them sympathetically. "You should sit this one out. I doubt there's much we could do to stop him. We don't have the numbers."

I winced at the idea of the two women staying here. Perhaps it was a trap. It might be better to keep them where I could see them. But they heeded Abigail's caution and decided not to join us. I inwardly cursed myself for spending so much time with Chadwick. It was my fault I was absent so often, allowing the blondes to befriend my best mate. Abigail had once mentioned she had bad experiences with blonds. Between her ex-fiancé and Florence, one would think she'd stay away from them.

A few others volunteered to come, and after one more silent plea to O'Brien, who rocked anxiously on the balls of his feet, he turned his head away and I could finally think straight. He wouldn't volunteer.

"True heroes save all, even if they're undeserving of your kindness," Charity announced to the crowd of us, and I gritted my teeth to stop myself from rolling my eyes.

Stupid heroes, I'd say. Or perhaps we were selfish. If Florence was attacking, it was probably to gain followers for the army he was building. If we stopped him, maybe some of the detestable vampires wouldn't join him.

Attempting to look casual as I drifted towards the wall, I prayed I'd remain unnoticed as I positioned my hands behind my back. I flicked my wrists, willing my magic purse to appear in my palm. Chad should know where I was headed in case things went foul.

You need full confidence to make your powers work, Chad's voice sounded through my head. Confidence, however, tends to disappear when you are too ashamed to use your Caster magic in a room full of Night Crawlers, regardless of their acceptance of how you were born. Thus, my hidden hands remained empty. I gave another flick. Nothing. A warm air pushed against the folds of my dress, shifting It off to the left as Fendel magically appeared by my side. His small, porcelain-like body was posed with his hands up, offering me the small green bag I had been trying to summon.

I smiled before kneeling next to him. "You always know exactly what I need. Don't you, my dear friend?"

His lips curled upwards at the edges, ever so slightly, his delight radiating. He always had a sixth sense about me, and what I needed, all the way down to what I truly was: a witch. I knew the history between witches and gnomes was inauspicious, but still. One would *think* the porcelain I was unnecessary by now. Fendel and the other gnomes would have to warm up to me sometime.

I gave an affectionate pat on his shoulder before straightening my legs once more and pulling out a paper within the sage green purse. After quickly jotting down the summary of what had happened and explaining where I'd be, I carefully wrote his name in cursive swirls and replaced the letter in my bag, wondering if he'd be too busy with his princely duties to notice my location.

After a heedful look at Abigail and Cristin, together our eyes trailed over to the trapdoor, the sound of rain crashing into it like a plea for us to let it in. The steps were slick with rain as we trudged up them.

The others took off on foot, allowing me a moment to mentally prepare for the trip. Abigail and Cristin gave me encouraging looks before I grabbed their hands and closed my eyes. For a moment, it was like we were floating through space, weightless, and then as my feet touched the floor, all the weight of the world crashed down on my shoulders. Our linked hands kept me from falling forwards on my face, and Abigail and Cristin kept hold of me until I was safely propped up against a tree, my legs crumbling underneath me. I grasped onto the gnarled bark as it disintegrated beneath my palms, taking in deep breaths to try and reacquire my energy.

Downy Lair stood somewhere behind us, through the forest and out in the graveyard that stood a hundred yards away. I took in my friends' stances as they hid behind the other trees, ears perked, senses on full alert for any sign of danger, but it was silent. The screams and the moans were all absent tonight, just the trickling of rain masking the sound of the blood as it cascaded down the enormous fountain inside the lair. When Cristin's shoulders fell slightly, my body seemed to relax a bit as well. Florence wasn't there. There was no pull tugging me towards my creator, no moist breath creeping down my neck, his slicked-back blond hair was nowhere in sight. What was very present, however, was the smell of spoiled blood. It drifted into our nostrils like an abrupt warning, screaming at us to stay away. Yet as much as I wanted to obey, I knew we had to go closer.

A daunting gust of air and the crunch of leaves under boots met my ears as strangers slowly trekked towards us from somewhere up ahead. My eyes flickered back to my comrades, their eyes wide as they took in the sound too. It was too soon for the others to have caught up with us, regardless of how fast they were. These were not members of our coven. We were stuck between the unknown intruders and the dark lair I still had nightmares about.

Careful not to make a sound, we rounded to the opposite side of the trees. A crisp breeze rolled past, and a familiar scent reached my nose. I instantly felt relief.

Chad and Connor.

I peered beyond the trees and saw them slowly approaching the lair, not realising we were there. Trying not to startle them, I said softly, "It's just us."

They both jumped regardless, Connor's teeth bared and Chad's hands raised in front of him, ready to attack. As they realised who "us" was, their fighting stances dropped and they advanced towards us.

"Abigail and Cristin are here too," I told them as they reached us, and the couple came out from behind their trees, nodding in greeting. "I assume you got my letter?" I asked Chad, a faint smile spreading across my face, contrary to the grim situation we were in. "So nice of you to show up."

"You know I'd do anything to keep you away from Florence," he said with a slight jest in his voice, but I knew he meant it after all that had happened.

"Don't trust me to fight him without you?" I teased, trying to buy time before going towards the eerie silence of the lair.

"*You*, I trust. *Him*, I don't," he said, taking my hand and continuing towards the lair. The others followed along, carefully shifting their eyes through the trees to make sure we were truly alone. "So he attacked this coven?" Chad continued, and even though I knew he was right to get down to business, I really didn't want to. "He's been quiet for months. Why now? Why them?"

"I dunno," I said, casting a look back to the rest of them, wondering if they had any theories.

"'Tis the mystery," Abigail responded.

"More are coming on foot," Cristin stated. "Azalea took us here by magic, so we made it here before them, though it wasn't quick enough to catch any of the action."

"I can't hear much," Connor offered, lending his keen werewolf hearing to the situation. "It seems to be clear. I think Florence is long gone, but I can't be sure."

"It could be a trap," I said. It was always either a trap or a game with Florence. "He could be expecting us."

"Then perhaps moving quickly is our best bet," Chad replied, squeezing my hand.

I nodded, knowing he was right but also traumatised by all the other close calls and run-ins I'd had with Florence. For whatever reason, he didn't want to **KILL** me, but with enough rejections of his hand in marriage, that could always change. My friends, however, were vastly less safe. Abigail had continuously clashed heads with him, Cristin was always on her side, Connor had already been kidnapped and drugged, and of course Chad and Florence had their issues. They had gone head-to-head a few times, the worst being the night Florence had slipped me the love potion and Chad walked in on us snogging. There were several broken bones, Chad's body slamming into a wall of glass, and acid cast on Florence's face. Not a scene I wanted to recapture.

As we drew closer, we took in the gruesome sight before us. At the centre of the gravesite was an enormous crypt with Elizabeth Downy's name carved into its stone walls. The heavy entrance had been heaved open, with a single set of bloody footprints trailing out from inside. They led to their owner, who looked to be the only one who had made it out alive, even if only for a short moment. A young woman's body ended the trail, her bare frame laid out in a pool of her own blood. I could tell from a faint smell in her poisoned blood she had been a mortal. Shackles bound her wrists, and her wide eyes still wore the fear she had been subjected to in her final moments, if not long before too.

She had been one of their slaves. Bite marks covered every inch of her naked body. Some healed, some raw. The heel of one of her feet was severed off, and I had a dark feeling it was of her own doing to slip from her chains. The scars from the shackles she'd once had around her ankle were inferior to what she had done to escape them.

Chad conjured a blanket to cover her deceased body, and as I watched it float gently down upon her, I wondered how long she had been kept there, used for their sick desires.

There was still no sign of life as we approached the crypt.

"Should some of us stay out here to keep a lookout?" Abigail asked.

Chad and I exchanged worried glances. "It's safer if we all stay within arm's reach of one another," he decided firmly. "The second you hear anyone coming towards us, grab onto one another, and I'll haul us all out of here."

We all gave a nod. It would be a while before the others arrived to help, but the people inside could be hurt. If there were more slaves trapped down there, then these precious minutes could be the difference between their life and death. As we walked through the crypt door and down the long, wide staircase that extended several stories underground, the chances of anyone having survived became less and less likely. More blood trailed down the stairs, as well as more bodies. A vampire lay choking in his own blood. In too much agony to notice our presence, he moved his arms in small circles around the steps, trying to muster his last bit of energy to grasp onto anything, or distract himself from the pain. His eyes slowed, lingering on the inescapable void awaiting him as his death encroached upon him.

I didn't recognise him. I didn't know if he was from Downy Lair or one of Florence's followers, but either way, there was evil in this man's soul, and we could all feel it. I watched as Chad's eyes darkened, and I sensed the hesitation he felt as he stared down at the man. He was pondering the same dilemma I was: either help the man by healing him, or let him suffer for his sins. Saving him could mean information, but it could also mean lies. It was the person I expected least who came to put him out of his misery.

Cristin swooped in past us and cracked the man's neck in one swift go. For a second, a strange sadness draped over him before he looked back up the stone steps at all of us.

"Let God take him to whatever Hell he deserves," he said before continuing down the dim staircase, the torches on the walls casting his shadows in different directions.

I closed my eyes to block it all out—to void out the cracking sound of the man's neck. But after a faint, shocked breath fell from Abigail's lips, I reopened my eyes. She manoeuvred her way around the rest of us to follow after her husband. It was the first time Cristin had **KILLED** another person in nearly twenty years—nearly twenty years since he had fallen in love with Abigail and given up that life. He now fed on animal blood instead. I shuddered at the idea of the things war could do to even the best of us, and wondered if I'd be pushed to do the same—to **KILL**.

Remembering to stay within arm's length of one another, I took Chad's hand back in mine. I refused to take a last look at the dead man— he didn't deserve my pity. So instead, I followed the stairway down and didn't look back.

When we finally reached the bottom, the room opened into a giant, circular foyer that I remembered from before. The walls were lined with at least fifty doors, and in the centre of the morbid room was the same horrid centrepiece: the blood fountain.

Deep maroon liquid flowed down its tiers, falling at last into a large pool of blood, but this time, blood wasn't the only thing at the bottom. Nearly thirty dead bodies clustered together, tainting what had once been a freshly drawn food supply. Poison, fear, and rot only a vampire could sense drifted towards me, and I cringed as the smell warded me away. Cristin and Abigail stood frozen before it, and as the rest of us gathered around, I could see why. Among the floating dead bodies was another, one I had the greatest displeasure of meeting before. Only, this body was very much alive.

Chapter 4: Guilty by Association

Elizabeth Downy sat in the pool of blood, leaning against its edge. Her arms draped over the rim, and her head was turned away from us, so I could only see one side of her blood-covered face, but I could instantly tell it was her. Her soaked hair shone crimson in the firelight, and her sullen expression grew to a wicked smile.

"How kind of you to join us," she said, not even turning to face us. Her Welsh accent brought back a plague of memories, and her smile made her faint crow's feet crinkle even more. She crossed her long legs, one now protruding out of the blood—a I of ease and leisure in the face of this horrible situation, to portray her intense obsession with being seen as sexy and tempting. "Whatever brings you here on this lovely day, Azalea?"

The sound of my name sent chills racking down my spine. Of course she'd be addressing me. Out of the five of us standing together, I was the only one she had ever met.

"We heard Florence was here," I stated with a steady voice, not knowing what to give away. "It was quite a shock to us to find out you were no longer on his side."

She gave a short laugh. "Yes. He was indeed here."

"Didn't seem to turn out so well for you now, did it?" I tested, and she gave another wretched laugh.

"No, it didn't. *Clearly.*" She wasn't giving away anything.

"Well," I tried again, a bit of my frustration ringing through, "not to encroach on your own hopes for how this conversation plays out, but perhaps you can tell us more. Perhaps you could explain why Florence would attack you and your coven. If I remember correctly, you're one of his favourite leading ladies, not an enemy."

The implied question broke the last thread holding her sanity together. She violently whipped her head to look at me, piercing draggers through me with her eyes. I took a step back, my breath hitching in my chest. She was no longer the Elizabeth Downy I recognised—powerful, strong, prizing her beauty above all else. This Elizabeth was broken inside and out. I stared at her face as the blood trickled down the drooping, scarred atrocity it had become.

She glared straight into my soul. "Favourite..." she repeated, drawing the word slowly between her gritted teeth. "Perhaps once, but not anymore. Pity. It seems as though you've fallen from his graces too," she said as if it were a threat—as if *I* were next on the list of people he'd like to mutilate and throw acid on. She looked exactly as Florence had when Chad cast acid on his face, only hers wasn't healing.

My mates around me stood just as tense as I was. There were no words for the pain it must have caused. The pain it might still be causing her.

I closed my gaping mouth before opening it once more. "And what did you do to fall?" I asked slowly, not daring to rush it. "You're on his side."

"His side," she laughed, staring at me dead-on, lowering her chin to appear darker, more intimidating. "*My* coven doesn't fraternise with the likes of *them*," she said, casting Chad a disgusted look for being a Caster before tilting her head back arrogantly. "Or at least we didn't until Florence stole some of my coven away and shredded the rest of us." Her eyes flickered over the dead bodies floating around her, but I couldn't tell from her expression if it was sadness that swept over her or agitation from having lost all of her followers.

"Do you mean to say that there are Casters on his side? Working with him?" I asked urgently. My eyes flew over to my friends, but they looked just as taken aback by the news as I was.

"Obviously," she spat, a bit of blood spraying out. "He's always had an obsession with them—envy that often turned into lust."

I couldn't understand. She wasn't talking about me whom he lusted for. Florence had been as shocked as I was to find out I was a Caster—the part of me that had been suppressed from childhood fears and the potion that had taken away my memories. He hadn't known what I was. But if she wasn't talking about me, whom was she referring to?

Before I could ask, Chad took the lead. "Who is he working with?" he asked. "Which Casters?"

She hissed at him viciously in response, attacking him with her eyes, before turning back to me. Chad and Connor took the hint and slinked a half-step back. They weren't her kind.

"I don't know," she said as if I were the only person in the room. "But it cost me everything. My home, my coven, my face…" Her voice trailed off, vividly portraying the misery she felt. "Working with filth was the breaking point of our alliance. I couldn't agree to it. So he made me pay."

I wondered if her face would ever truly heal. She had looked older than the rest of us, perhaps twice my age when she had been turned, but she made it clear how much she prided her looks. Now that her wicked face matched her personality, I wondered what she'd find to live for.

"Surely you can tell us more," Abigail tried, slipping her hand into Cristin's for support. "If he's no longer on your side, then help us get your revenge. He's ruined everything you've worked so hard for. Tear him down. Tell us what he's planning."

The smile returned to the woman's bloody face as she rested her head along the edge of the fountain, an image of pure relaxation. For a moment, I thought she was done talking to us, but when she looked back into my eyes, I felt we were the only two people in the room.

"For now, he's laying low, but when he strikes it'll be big. He's trying to outdo his father, and I dare say, he's doing a *fantastic* job," she hissed.

"And who is his father?" I dared. My chest felt as though it were being compressed. The information dangled in front of me, so close. We'd tried searching for anything on his father, or on him, what his plan was, or what had made him the way he was, but we'd been unable to find anything.

She merely laughed, shaking her head at me as if it was just all too easy to draw me in.

"The number of things you've failed to find out is pathetic," she laughed, but then her face turned stern. "I'll tell you if you promise to **KILL** the son of a bitch for me."

Again, the word screamed out at me. I wanted to do it, but when it came down to it, would I be able to? I swallowed down my doubts and nodded, hoping I was more convincing to her than I was to myself. Apparently, it worked as she continued on, the gleam still shining in her eyes.

"After his mother died, he was raised by a Nazi soldier, beaten brutally every day to the point that his soul seemed to break. He gave into that hateful way of life," she told us, glancing away as though she was suddenly uninterested. "But the one who raised him was not his father. Not by blood anyway. His true father denied him in every way, claimed he wasn't his, and I'll bet you can imagine just how well that sat with Florence."

She took a long, exasperated breath before continuing on. "You see, Florence was very keen to make his birthfather proud at the beginning, but as the war went on, he grew very dark indeed. He took life after life in his father's honour, yet none of it was enough. His father still didn't accept him as his own son. At Florence's lowest point, well, that's when he met *her*."

My throat tightened. I didn't have to ask *who* she was referring to. It must be the furtive blonde. But her name... I needed to know.

"What do they call this woman? This friend of Florence?" I questioned steadily, not wanting to seem too desperate for any information.

But her reply was a shrug. "I don't know her name, I only know *of* her, but let me tell you this. This woman is even darker than Florence, and the deal they made, well..." She paused, reeling me in further. "It was like making a deal with the devil herself."

"And what was the deal?"

"She said if he promised to help her **KILL** his father, then she would bite him, turn him into a vampire like herself. Make him stronger than he ever imagined possible. And Florence took her offer. When everyone thought the war was over, when everyone presumed his father to be dead, Florence and this girl found his true location. Hunted him down and tore him to shreds, piece by piece, and feasted on his body for celebration."

"And—and his father?" I asked. "Who was he?" But I already knew the answer. It was a suspicion that had whispered out at me ever since our hunt in Germany. One I was too afraid to voice. And her hints all but confirmed it.

"Why, the big man himself," she said coolly, letting the suspense stretch out. "The one in awe of the Aryan race. The *Führer*, the beloved Adolf Hitler."

I closed my eyes, letting it all sink in. *Of course.* How could Florence come from anyone less treacherous?

Sharp breaths sucked in behind me but were quickly hushed by one look from Elizabeth.

I steadied myself, running over the information in my mind. What was next? How could this help us get to him?

"And what does he plan to do that will overshadow Hitler?" I asked, incapable of imagining worse.

"I don't know, darling," she said, her voice dropping down to a whisper. "But I can promise that whatever Florence does have planned will be much, much worse.

"Now," she started again, changing the subject as she sat up straight and waded through the blood as if she enjoyed it. "If you and your friends will be so kind as to leave me, I believe I've met my part of the bargain."

I looked back at the rest of them, grasping at all the information she had given, the lack of it. We needed more. We needed everything to stop him before he could fully start. But when I turned back to the vampire and her miserable, droopy face, I saw true sadness in her expression for the first time. Her eyes danced upon the dead body of one of her comrades as the trickling stream of blood caused it to float her way. When it reached her, she gently slid her fingers along his pale skin. It was almost seductive. Hunger burned in her eyes, tempted by the meal in front of her.

"*Boed i Uffern fy nghlywed ac agor wrth i mi puntio ar ei ddrysau,*" she breathed out in Welsh, helplessness swallowing her up whole.

I could feel it before it even happened. I watched in slow motion, running to stop her as her teeth dug into the corpse's skin. Poison crept through her veins, turning them as black as night. As they protruded from her head, her neck, her whole body, her eyes rolled into the back of her head, and death took her as its own.

Chapter 5: The Itch of the Full Moon

There were no survivors in Downy Lair. Just rooms upon rooms of dead vampires and mortal captives alike. Corpses of every size, shape, colour, and sex littered the floor. Their slaves were attached to chains and tubes with crimson blood that crept up the walls, all the way to the ceiling, and eventually connected to the fountain. More blood stained the ground—putrid, spoiled, wasted. So much death for nothing except a show of dominance.

When backup arrived, we inspected all the rooms in the circular lair, and after much too long being in that dreadful place, we went back to Castwell Castle.

Chad and I lay out on his bed, trying to absorb it all. He was on his back, running his fingers over my hair as I absentmindedly played with a button on his navy shirt. Scars etched their way into our hearts from the memory of this new massacre. It felt as though all the emotions were crashing down on me at once, holding me underwater as my lungs prayed for air. When the water finally drained out, it took with it all the energy from my body. I was left with my own thoughts and nightmares, and only a touch of information to distract me.

Blonde hair and blue eyes crashed into my vision as they so often did. All those bodies.

"An Aryan race," Chad breathed out, breaking the silence with his solemn remark.

"What a sadistic way to get back at his father," I replied, hating Florence with every ounce of my being. He had always fed on the people his father seemed to treasure. Yet even though Florence shared those features, he was never prized by his father himself.

I wondered if Elizabeth's words were true, if she really didn't know more, but the truth had died with her in a pool of blood, vanity, and despair.

"It just happened so fast," Chad said, feeding off of my dark emotions. "I couldn't even see it happen until it was done."

I wish I could say the same. Her black veins, her lost eyes circled my mind on replay.

I blinked, clearing the dismal thoughts from my head. "It's good she's gone," I decided, but the raw emotion slipped out with it. "The world is better off without people like her in it."

He nodded but his arms still held tension. He was even less accustomed to watching death than I was. "Up until a few months ago, the only person I had ever seen dead was my mum," he said softly, his mind trapped in a distant memory. "I held her in my arms and watched the light fade from her eyes."

My heart felt his pain so thoroughly as it clenched and then shattered, blowing off into the winds as though it were no more than ash. I tilted my head up to look at him, but he wasn't truly there. His eyes were focused far off in the distance. Wrapping my arms around him, I nuzzled in closer. He rarely talked about her, or her **MURDER** over two decades ago at the hand of a vampire. Someone like me. I couldn't heal him, nor would he ever fully mend from such a loss. Even so, I yearned deeply to ease his pain. My own mum was gone, or perhaps a dubious ghost, but I didn't remember her in life. All I knew of her was her ghost form. I couldn't even remember the horrid scene Hydie had written to me about, the one where my father **KILLED** our mum and somehow managed to turn the table around and blame me. But as Abigail had once told me, perhaps not remembering was a blessing.

"I should go," Chad said in almost a whisper, as though the hushed tone would make it less true.

"Stay," I insisted, sitting up to look at him, but I knew my automatic response was unfair, even as the word spewed out of me. He had so much weight on his shoulders, and strong as they were, they were starting to buckle from the new pressures. His recently accepted princely duties, the war, the prophecies, and now more death pushed down on him. Not to mention, the sleeping schedule that the scalding sun forced me to have that took away much of his slumber. "You haven't slept and I haven't seen you eat anything all night," I told him, taking in the exhaustion on his face.

He couldn't go back to his aunts' castle so soon. He just couldn't. He needed to find time to put himself first, or he was bound to explode from the pressure.

"I'm afraid I don't have a choice," he said, rubbing at his worn face before taking in a deep breath. "Circumstances with the prime minister are getting out of hand. The sweeps, the broadcasts... His daughter has been missing for nearly a year now, and he's almost lost it completely."

The guilt in my stomach wouldn't rest at those words: the prime minister's daughter. It seemed like a lifetime ago that I had seen the woman's death, yet I remembered it vividly. The *crack* her skull made as Florence smashed her head into the alley wall. The way he tore a bite right out of her neck. And what made it all worse was I had helped bury her in the ground. It was a better solution than the alternative—leaving her corpse in the alleyway to rot as Florence had suggested—but a dark sin nonetheless.

There was a time before Chad and I knew what each other were, a time where I had accidentally admitted that the case of the missing woman was indeed a **MURDER** instead of an abduction as he had presumed. But the first time he had ever brought me to this castle, the one I'd soon call home, he had pieced together that vampires were involved.

As for the woman's distraught father, we all thought he would have stepped down from the position by now in order to focus on the search, but he was using all the power of his position to raise hell. It was too late for the Casters to modify his memory, the case too widespread. There was one idea, however. Something vastly immoral, but it could work.

"We could frame someone," I let slip, hardly able to look at Chad when I said it.

He looked at me intently, his head tilted in a slight angle, his dark brows furrowed. As I stared into his green eyes, I could almost see the motion beyond them, the gears spinning around one another in his mind before he uttered a single word. "Who?"

I shrugged, not knowing if I meant it. Not knowing if they deserved such a vile accusation. "One of the men in the prison."

He nodded slowly, the gears still turning. "It could work."

I refrained from cringing as I remembered my one trip to the prison owned by the Loxley Coven, where I'd been meant to feed on one of the despicable men but had failed to find the courage.

"I mean, of course it's the *wrong* thing to do. Florence should be getting all the blame. He's the one who—" I paused, horrified by the word I had been surrounded by lately. "He **KILLED** her. I can't help but think he's seeking attention. He wins if the mortals know it's him. The prisoners, though, they're already in prison for life. Perhaps we could make a truce with one of them. They're frightened of us anyway. They don't know what we are or what we're doing to the inmates, they just know that every so often, another one of them disappears. We could promise one that we won't take him."

"You know what I think?" Chad asked, his tone suddenly perkier. "I think I have a very diplomatic, brilliant girlfriend."

I blushed. "Or perhaps just one who feels guilty for helping Florence cover up the poor girl's death in the first place."

"I don't believe a new vampire can be blamed for the doings of their—" His tongue stumbled over the word. Sire? Creator? They all suggested I belonged to Florence. "Well, you can't be blamed for the workings of a right arsehole," he decided, and then let out a deep breath. "Fancy a shower before I go?"

The seduction resonating in his throat made me forget about all the horrid things these past few months had brought—Florence, the nightmares, Elizabeth's death. My eyes traced his fingers, up his arms, and to the dragon tattoo whose tail slithered out of view and under his shirt. Part of me grew warm, anxious in the best way until the cold hard truth pulled me back. I wanted to join him, let his body distract me from the current events, but I knew precisely what would happen if I did.

"Save my sister," I told him, reminding him of my to-do list.

"Save the children," he continued.

"Destroy Florence."

"And then you're all mine."

But oh, the way he said it…

He placed a quick kiss on my cheek.

"Will you at least eat before you go?" I pleaded with him. If he was going to forgo sleep, the very least he needed was a source of sustenance.

"Anything to make my Azalea happy," he said as he unbuckled his pants and pulled them off in preparation for his shower. "But I do have a favour to ask of you. Do you think you could go down to the pub tonight? Give Connor some company? The night before the full moon's always the hardest for him."

I nodded. Of course I would.

Chad edged his way back to me, taking his time to undo each button carefully, attempting to give the intimate interaction one more go, on the off chance my abrupt reflexes had decided to take the day off. I bit my lip to hide the smile peeking out at him, but it was enough to make it bleed. I licked the drop of crimson liquid from my lip and threw myself back on the pillows, no longer able to look at the man who knew how to tempt my mind, my body, and my soul. He let out a small laugh before disappearing into the bathroom, and I sent a thin stream of purple magic after him to slam the door shut. I knew exactly how eager my eyes would be otherwise.

ભ

An hour later, I was walking to the pub for a chance at fresh air and clearing my mind. At night, people were scarcely outdoors these days. I was glad for the earth's tilt away from the sun, but since the days were shorter than they had been in the summer when Florence had made his first mass attack, people cleared out of the streets by early afternoon. Even as a vampire, walking alone at night didn't feel like the sensible thing to do with Florence lurking only God knew where. Only the presumption that he was far away from here, hiding or laying low as Elizabeth had mentioned, made me feel a bit more hopeful. For now at least.

If business at the pub had been bad when the prime minister's daughter went missing right outside of it, it was laughable compared to the steep slump the business had taken when everyone knew there was a madman on the loose. As I walked in, I saw Connor alone behind the bar, absentmindedly staring down at his hand as he wiped down the counter. Not only did he have Downy Lair on his mind, he also had the full moon to consider. The potion Chad had created to give him control over his transformations worked wonders, but the urge to change on the full moon still clawed at him from inside.

"Did the old man send you to puppy-sit me?" he asked, finally breaking his trance to notice me.

A smile broke out over my face at the transparency of it all, how well he knew his mate. "It's almost like he cares," I replied, smiling.

"Is he too busy saving the world to join us?" Connor asked, continuing to clear the counter. His tone played with hurt and jest all at once, as though he couldn't decide if he wanted to be in a foul mood or find happiness. "I mean, I knew I wasn't pretty enough to keep him all to myself, but I thought you were," he said with a laugh, and my smile widened, joining in on his humour. Bickering back and forth was a joyful hobby of ours, even in the darkest of situations.

"When isn't he busy these days? It's *almost* as if he's a prince in the midst of a war."

"Perhaps one of these days he'll trust us enough to bring us along instead of his stupid witch-friend," he huffed, crossing his arms childishly.

Even though the mention of her pinched me, his phrasing left me quite satisfied. "See, this is why you and I get along, Connor. We have a common enemy," I told him.

Connor hadn't met Mrs Prophecy either, and it was clear that he wanted to just as little as I did. After getting rid of Florence, it was our common goal to rid her from our lives, and get Chad back to ourselves.

"Now you know how I felt when he started dating *you*," Connor laughed, no doubt trying to bicker even more to distract himself, but it was too far. His words bit at me. It was like a sharp prick in the wrong spot, and I winced. Chad being with Mrs Prophecy reminded Connor of dating? "Not that she and him are—" he tried quickly, but I waved my hand, brushing the matter under the rug. I knew what he meant, yet it still left a pit in my stomach.

"Could we not talk about her, Connor?" I asked, my usual cheekiness gone. Instead, the words came out as a sullen plea. "I'm meant to be here cheering you up," I said, plopping my disheartened self down onto a barstool, "not going off into my nightmares."

He laughed again, showcasing his warm, contagious smile. "Fair enough. So I hear you're going to speak to the old witches soon, off to tell them the big news of you two lovebirds moving in together. And then you'll be off to rescue your baby sister."

Not what I meant by "cheering" him up. Instead, this would much better be defined as "bringing up things I'd give anything for my mind to cast aside for a moment." All I wanted was for the thoughts to stop eating away at every bit of bravery I still managed to possess.

"And tell me," I quipped, leaning towards him from the other side of the bar. "How is it going to feel tomorrow night, Wolfie? The itch, the burn to change forms even though the potion won't allow it?"

"Okay, okay, I get it," he said, throwing the white flag into the air. "What a vicious bite you have. Moving on from the dreadful circumstances to boring small talk instead. I assume recent vampire suicides are also off the table?"

"You do realise that if I leave here and you're in a more depressive mood than you were before I arrived, Chad is going to be livid, don't you?"

"It's not my fault he's so positive all the time. He was born a Caster, not turned into a dark creature like we were. We can't help being so down in the dumps sometimes."

"We all have our own tragedies, regardless of how we were born," I told him softly.

"I know," he said, dropping his charismatic smile for a moment, and I took in the dark shadows underneath his eyes. "I'm just in a foul mood."

I nodded understandingly. Connor, Chad, and I could start our own group therapy circle based around the trauma of our parents, their deaths, and how they could eat away at you from the inside.

"How's business?" I tried, but looking around, I could tell this wasn't going to be the end-all topic to the dreary discussions we had started off on. The crowd had never been so sparse.

"Well, horrible, isn't it?" he asked, taking a look around at the people sitting at tables, drinking quietly as if the night had taken away all their spirit. There were a few cheerful conversations going on, but nothing close to what it should have been on a Friday night. "It's better than last week at least. The less disappearances, the more people are willing to come out at night, but have you seen what the prime minister has been broadcasting all over the news?"

I hadn't seen it, but I had heard of it. Due to my relationship with the Caster I called my boyfriend, technology was now technically allowed at the lair, but the entire coven was still hesitant to use it. I supposed that came with generations of hate towards the Casters and the knowledge that all electronics were actually magically driven. Either way, I still didn't turn on the telly at Chad's castle. It was depressing knowing what was going on out there. Knowing that mortals had no explanation for the disappearances, and that anxiety around the world was running high. If ignoring their end of it made my life a smidge more peaceful, regardless of the slight ignorance that came with it, then so be it.

"Prime Minister Alastor wants to initiate curfews at night," Connor continued. "He says we'll all end up like his daughter and the others if we don't comply. I mean, I can't blame him, but think what'll happen to this place if those regulations do go through," he said, waving a crazed hand around at the pub. "And I heard America's closer to a complete shutdown than we are. The riots going on over there are getting out of hand."

"Just like you Americans to fight first, ask questions later."

"Hey! I resent that. Besides, I'm barely American," he said, his accent proving him wrong as he placed a falsely shocked hand against his chest. "I've been here for enough years to wash it all out."

I rolled my eyes at him, but before I could say some snarky remark, I felt a rage that did not belong to me. The roars of one of Chad's aunts, and the fear coursing steadily through both of the old crones, crashed into me as though they were there, striking me across the face, but they weren't. A second later, I felt my purse grow warm, and a stream of light gleamed out of the seams. Knowing Connor couldn't see the light that was only intended for me, I looked up at him.

"That'll be Prince Charming checking in on us," I told him, patting the purse.

"Ah, I remember the days he used to write me secret love letters," he said with a sigh before going off to check on some of his customers.

I laughed as Connor walked away. I was horrible at putting people in a good mood. Thankfully, the werewolf put up with me anyway.

Opening the letter, I stared down at Chad's neat scrawl, happy to have a small piece of him while he was away.

Dearest love of my life,

The aunts of mine have agreed to meet with us. I told them we had some news to share with them, but I haven't given away the surprise. They said we can meet with them in two nights' time. My schedule is clear a week after that, on 30 September. Perhaps you could give your sister a bit of heads up that we can retrieve her that night.

Sincerely,

The best lover in the world

PS If Connor ends up even more down in the dumps, I'll know exactly which vampire to blame. No pressure.

My whole body turned warm as I took in his letter. The formality of it. The silliness. I knew he'd be cross if Connor wasn't happy. Or not truly cross but solemn nonetheless. The rest of the letter, however, was harder to digest.

I watched as the letters magically disappeared, allowing me the proper space to record my reply.

Of course. Hyping up your aunts' anxiety and giving them more to worry about will put them in a grand mood. Brilliant idea. As for my sister, I'll write to her and tell her the news. I can hardly wait, even though the thought gives me shivers all over.

I love you. Stay safe.

PS Connor was apparently tasked to bring my mood down with him, but I'll do my best. For you.

I half expected him not to reply, but I was happy to get one more letter before he went back to his tasks.

I suppose I can stay alive for you. Knowing that you'll soon be there every time I get home will keep me going.

I can't wait.

After placing my last letter safely back into my purse, I rounded the counter and situated myself behind the bar. Almost instantly, Connor was speed walking to get back there with me.

"No, no, no, no, no," he insisted. I flashed him a look of pure innocence, but my smile uncovered the lie. "Get out," he pressed. "We're not trying this again."

"Connor," I said, tilting my head down at him. "I can help, I know I can. Plus, it'll help me with my potion-making skills."

"I've seen exactly how your potions turn out, Azalea Kroge, and I'll tell you, the word 'skills' should be stricken from your repertoire. Not to mention the last time you tried to help me behind the bar..." he exaggerated, but I took a glass from the counter anyway.

"If someone gets overly sloshed again, it'll only be your fault for not teaching me properly," I told him, turning around and reaching for whatever bottles my hands felt like grabbing down from the wall and attempting to balance them in my arms.

"Trust me, he didn't throw up because he was drunk. He threw up because it was disgusting." He laughed before muttering under his breath, "A vampire making drinks? You can't even appreciate their taste."

I laughed and moved aside. The rest of the night was spent with me bullying him into teaching me different concoctions until we shut down the pub. When Connor retreated to the flat above Castle on the Rocks, I transported myself to my bedroom at Loxley Lair. Even though the sun was far from rising, the trip was enough to wear me out. As soon as my head touched the pillow, I drifted off into a deep slumber.

Nightmares plagued my dreams as they so often did. The girl, hardly even school age, clutched tightly onto her younger brother as they peeked out from under their bed. Bruises, tears, and pain coated her face. Her lungs controlled the pace within mine, her heart pumped at the same terrified rhythm, and her thoughts became my own.

She's coming.

Her arms wrapped even tighter around the small boy as footsteps drew in close. Grotesque, clammy, bare feet were visible as they rampaged around the room, searching for the scared children, but suddenly they halted, and horror ensued.

Hands clawed at the girl's feet, dragging her out from the one place that was meant to be secure. As she let go of her brother to scrape her nails against the hardwood floors, her eyes gazed right into my soul.

"Help!" she screamed, but as I sat up straight, waking from the dream, her eyes stayed ingrained in my mind. Those sweet, innocent eyes of a child afraid of the monster her mother had become. But as always, she was just out of reach.

There was no one next to me to throw—to send crashing against the wall. So I sat alone in a pool of my own sweat, hugging my knees close to me, wishing I could hug the small girl instead.

Chapter 6: Unsoothable Storms

*T*here aren't any prisoners willing to take the fall," Vincent, the warden of the Loxley Prison, told me the next night, and my shoulders fell. So much for my plan. I was about to leave the lair when he told me the bad news. "We fed them the truth serum you gave us, and they all either admitted that they would pretend to comply and then reveal the lie in the courtroom, or that they were too frightened it would ruin their chances of getting released early."

I bit my lip to let the pain distract me from my disappointment. "Of course," I told him, giving my best attempt at a firm nod. "It was worth a try. Cheers for testing out the theory," I told him with a small smile.

"It was a good idea while it lasted," he told me, "but perhaps we could capture Florence and feed him one of your boyfriend's potions to restrain his superhuman strength. The court could pass him off as certifiably insane if he tries to tell them vampires exist, and then after he admits to the woman's **MURDER**, we could stage his death."

"Mmm," I agreed with a nod, "that sounds ideal anyhow, doesn't it?" And it truly did. I couldn't wait for Florence's capture. "Well, I must be going. Thank you so much for all the work you've done."

He nodded and then I was off.

Now that Chad's aunts knew he had befriended a werewolf, he no longer had to disguise the fact he was suddenly unavailable every time there was a full moon. He took the night off to keep Connor company, which left me free to visit the end-of-terrace house in Brighton, the one I had called home in some other life.

I ambled through the city, letting the glow of the moon shine on my face. Mortal officers decorated the streets—added safety thanks to the prime minister. As I neared my childhood home, I watched an old man in his garden, eyeing me with what must have been suspicion. Glancing away from him, I ignored the magic at my fingertips. I didn't want to transport there. I wanted to walk. I craved the fresh air.

When I arrived, I bent down and crawled to the secret spot in the flowers, a sacred hideout my sister and I had used when we were little. The familiar scent of the azaleas and hydrangeas welcomed me in, as well as a letter written with my sister's usual boxy print. Carefully, I slit the letter open and read it, my heart racing the way it always did when I read one of her letters, hoping she was okay. Praying she didn't completely hate me for abandoning her there.

> There's talk of postponing the start of the term, and I'm completely distraught. Our father, on the other hand, smiled when he heard the news on the telly. Yes. Actually smiled. It was sickening really. He wants me to be miserable. Keep me locked up here with him so I can become as pathetic as he is. But honestly, I think my mind will perish if I have to stay with him much longer.

The clasp on my purse opened on its own accord, and I stared at it warily. Chad knew me too well. He knew I'd give it all a second thought. As I slipped the envelope out of the small bag, I wondered what spell Chad had placed on it to will it to open at the exact moment my anxiety kicked in, or even when he had done it. Nonetheless, I pulled out the stationary inside and reread the letter I had written to her months ago yet never had the courage to deliver. The ending was magically wiped from the bottom, courtesy of Chad, so I could add in the update of my story. It had everything, nearly the entire tale of what had happened to me. The potion that had taken my memory. Florence. Chad. The creature I had become. Everything up until the point I found out I was a witch.

Up until then, it had been as if Hydie and I were casual pen pals, writing back and forth. To her, my memories were lost due to a bump on my head. If she questioned the sorry excuse, she never let on, and for that I was grateful.

I swallowed down the fears of her reaction, the doubt she'd even want to come with me when she read the truth of what I was. I was exactly the thing my father had feared I was: a witch. But did she know? Had I known what I was before my memories had been lost to me? Question after question sifted through my mind. Was Hydrangea like me? Was my mother? Had she been the one who taught us to hide it all away from our father?

The pen moved rigorously under the weight of my worried hand, careful not to tremble as I finished out the autobiography. I wrote what I was, and although I had so many questions for her, I felt it was only fair to let her ask her questions first. At the end, I let her know I finally had a place she could stay, a place away from our father, if she was willing to take it.

> Be ready.
> 30 September.
> Nine at night.

All if she was willing to run away with me. Perhaps she felt she knew me already, but the truth was, she didn't. She didn't know the new Azalea, the one plagued with nightmares, the one who surrounded herself with creatures of the night. It was entirely her choice, and I swore to never guilt her if she chose not to come.

I love you, I wrote, and I meant it wholeheartedly.

It was a slow walk back to Castwell Castle that night. My ears were open for any threats, any buzz through the air, but none came. I walked into the castle, propped myself onto the sofa with Chad and Connor, and laughed along with them as we watched some fantasy film I had never heard of before. After a while, our laughter settled into a strange focus, but it was clear by the dazed and distracted expressions we all wore on our faces that the focus was not on the film itself. There were other things on our minds. Storms the fictional world that played before us just couldn't soothe.

Chapter 7: A Dream, a Letter, and Hundreds of Slaves

Where are you? Where are you? Where are you? I called out into the night and bolted upright from the bed. Air rushed into my lungs as beads of cold sweat trickled down my body. My hands clutched to the silk sheets underneath them, grounding me to the present even though the echo of my own screams reverberated in my ears.

I was at Loxley Lair. I was home. It was a dream. But the last reaffirmation felt like a lie. It wasn't a dream. Those children needed help.

I drew my knees to my chest before clutching them tightly and whispering to the small children I knew couldn't hear me. "Just tell me where you are," I pleaded, but no response came. They were somewhere in England, or at least I could tell they were from here based on their accents, but there simply weren't any more clues.

Giving up on sleep, I dragged my feet to my bathroom mirror. The curtain that usually covered it hadn't been drawn shut in ages, and as I stared back at my face, the bronze skin a paler shade than normal, I decided I'd take Chad's blood duplication potion a day early. Today was the day I'd come face to face with the aunts who hated me, all to tell them I was moving in with their nephew. As if I yearned for more stress in my life, I was also going back to the flowers by the fence to see if Hydie had accepted my offer. Clearly, I was going to need the pick-me-up.

It was four in the afternoon, much earlier than I'd typically wake up. My ill-tempered state of mind and the sun that streamed into half the corridor as I trekked my way up to the kitchens informed me I should have done better to fight off the nightmares and gone back to sleep. After managing to down an entire quart of the potion Chad has so generously, or idiotically, stocked our fridge with, I went up to my bedroom to find the perfect outfit for such a miserable day. I tried on twelve. Twelve hideously *imperfect* outfits before settling on one. It was made from Charity's fine silk, with short sleeves and modest, full-length coverage, and it was a lovely shade of lavender that matched my magic. A stone necklace decorated my neck before I deemed myself presentable to give Chad's aunts the news that would surely infuriate them to no end.

Before meeting up with Chad, I made my way back to Hydie's house. When I crawled back to our spot, careful not to muck up my evening dress, two waves crashed against me: one of horror and one of relief. There was a letter, different from the one I had placed there, waiting for me. I used a finger to slit it open, and the short reply gave me chills. Three simple words, scratched out onto the parchment. Jotted down in such haste, I wondered what it meant.

I'll be ready.

There was a lot of necessary mental preparation on the journey back to Chad's castle. Each step forwards took an effort and a will I didn't know I had. I made my way up the stairs to the bedroom I realised would soon be mine. Chad stood in front of the vanity, attentively buttoning the cuffs of his shirt, and I just stared at him, happy to be his. For him to be mine. When his eyes met mine, his charming smile lit up his face, and I bit my lip back at him.

"What?" he asked, his tone coming off incredibly cheeky. "No excuses not to come? No urgent coven matters to take care of or dentist appointments you forgot you had?"

Such a clever jest at the teeth I could so easily use to tear him apart.

"Was there an option not to come?" I asked, tossing my thumb back towards the door, ready to go out the way I had just come in. "Because if there was, I can gladly find something else to busy myself with. Something more enjoyable like listening to nails get dragged along a chalkboard or stabbing pencils through my temple."

"You always have an option," he said, moving closer to me. I loved the pounding of my excited heart, the way he made me feel as he looked into my eyes. "But I'm glad you came."

He was so close. Close enough that I could feel his minty breath as he looked down at me.

The air around us seemed to hum as his green eyes danced with the same excitement I felt within. And as if he could read my mind, he took a hand and placed it so close to my cheek, not daring to touch but satisfying nonetheless, as he whispered, "I'd kiss you right now if you'd allow it."

I almost let him try. I yearned for his soft lips to press against mine, make my heart whole, take my mind to another world entirely, but I knew my body simply wouldn't let him. Not with how passionately I felt about him at that moment.

I glanced down at the ground before taking a deep breath and looking back up at him through the curls that swooped down, shielding half my face. "Let's go before I lose the strength to do this."

Perhaps "strength" was the wrong word as I felt absolutely none. Not one ounce of bravery, moxie, or willpower to face the women who were so abhorrently against me. We weren't even there yet, and I could somehow feel their disappointment, the fear they carried as they waited for us to tell them our news. I supposed it was more a feeling of duty to help him that convinced me to go. I could help him with so little these days, but I could support him through the challenge he was inevitably going to face with his aunts because of what I was.

"I'll transport us there. You'll need all your energy," he stated.

"Think I need to keep my wits about me, do you?" I asked, batting my eyes innocently as if there were no risk in the endeavour.

"Oh, most definitely. I know how hard it is for you to hold your tongue," he said, the smile shining bright in his eyes, knowing full well I couldn't keep in my temper when it got the best of me. But I couldn't let him win that easily.

"You know, there are quite a few things I won't be able to stop my tongue from doing when my body allows me to have my wicked way with you," I teased.

Any joy in his eyes turned dark with hunger as he stared back at me, biting at his lip to stop himself from reaching out to me. He let out a hot breath, not daring to say a word, but I could feel his want for me radiating off him. Either way, he shook his head, coming to his senses once more.

"Now," he started again. "I know you don't like them but—"

"I don't *not* like them, I just—"

"Despise them?" he said, filling in my blank.

"No," I said stubbornly, but honestly I wasn't sure if I had the right words to describe how I felt. I let out a heavy breath, trying to let any hatred for the witches escape with it. "I want them to like me so badly, and not just for my own sake, but for yours."

"It doesn't matter if they like you or not. I'll still love you all the same."

My heart fluttered at his words. "I know," I told him gently, "but it would make life easier, wouldn't it? Easier on you. You wouldn't have to be so torn between the two worlds. If they didn't hate me—"

"They do not *hate* you," he insisted, but he had no retort for the stern look I gave him.

They most definitely *did* hate my existence, so I tried again. "If they didn't hate my kind, then perhaps you might not feel inclined to work so hard without me..." My voice tapered off pathetically, and his face slumped, portraying the sort of guilty look that could only mean he was sorry, but there was no change in sight.

He took my hand in his, moving his thumb against the back of it. The solemn feeling in my chest kept my magic at bay.

"I don't mean to shut you out of it all," he said, his voice soft and sweet like a lullaby.

I nodded my understanding. "It's the way it has to be for now, but I just hope that one day it will be different."

"One day," he agreed before taking my other hand in his and bringing them both up to his lips. His warm breath, his lips, the light kiss all gave me a small glimmer of hope, but before that sensation took off on a quest of its own, Chad's green swirls encompassed us, and we were whirled off to a castle in Lancaster.

I took a single look at the castle and had to cough to hide my scoff. The grandeur was just as showy and obnoxious as his aunts. There were golden turrets atop creamy, marble towers. At first glance, it looked as though it was covered in far too many windows, but when my eyes focused, I saw that several of them were mirrors, the stars in the night sky displayed across them. The reflections became overwhelming as they bounced off each other with a sickly, dizzying effect. The chaos continued down to the ground, which lay torn up in a right mess as if every single flower and hedge had been uprooted in the midst of the gardener's tantrum. To make matters worse, if not much, *much* worse, there were hundreds upon hundreds of frozen gnomes littering the garden, leading all the way up to the golden front doors.

Chad's wince was substantial enough for me to feel as I stood next to him. His eyes scrunched up as he looked at my gaping mouth, and then grimaced back at me apologetically.

"Fuck," he let out as panic encompassed his eyes. "I swear I was going to warn you about those," he said, his voice straining against his own throat. "I'm so sorry. It *completely* slipped my mind. They've been here ever since I can remember."

Regardless of his sincere apology, I huffed out an angry breath at his slave-keeping aunts before remembering I "did not hate them."

"Anything else I should be aware of before entering their domain?" I asked, sarcasm coating my tongue, but an honest request nonetheless. "Perhaps I should've prepared better for the information they'll cast out at me, as well as the spells and poisons."

If it were possible for him and his princely stature to cower, I honestly think he would have. Instead, he awkwardly itched at his raised brow, letting out a strangled sigh. "There are so many things in this world that you don't know, but I can't think of a single one you'd want to find out." He tightened his grip on my hand encouragingly, yet the goose pimples still spread across my skin like wildfire. Perhaps it was meant to relax me, but it had the complete opposite effect. "Knowing might be more of a curse than it's worth."

Ignorance is not better.

Terrified eyes stared back at me as I tiptoed through the wards, up the path, and past the tiny prisoners to the grand entrance. It was a different feeling from the feigned frozen act the gnomes at Loxley Lair would play. There was an eerie silence that echoed with fear. I crept forwards, scared I'd terrify the poor souls, but also ignorant to whether or not their senses were still intact after being frozen. I prayed for their sake they were truly unaware of how much time they had been wrongfully imprisoned here. Perhaps it would make the matter less traumatic.

When we approached the entrance, the doors flew open to reveal a room decorated in gaudy gold accents. That was about the most welcoming event that happened, for as soon as our feet touched the slick marble flooring, the two old lions Chadwick referred to as aunts swept in on us, dressed as the hags they were.

Chapter 8: A Catastrophe

O ne of Chad's aunts gave him a kiss on the cheek, making sure to intercept our hands and cause me to take a step back. She looked so similar to her sister, both with peppered grey hair and wrinkles, draped in long, medieval-looking witch dresses I had once mistaken to be extravagant Halloween costumes.

"Chadwick," she greeted curtly. Her tone was all down to business. "Forgive the front gardens. They're quite a mess. You see, there was an urgent need to remove all the azaleas and replace them with lilies. So many dreadful potions need azaleas for whatever reason. They all had to go into it."

Azaleas for lilies. Insult to injury.

You will not roll your eyes, I sang cheerfully to myself. *You will grit your teeth and bear it.*

The other witch, however, crept along the far wall next to another doorway, half-hidden in shadows, a sharp fear radiating off of her as though it would lash me across the cheek at any moment. She gave a firm nod to Chad by way of a greeting but became rooted to her spot a good twenty metres away. Even through the dim lighting I could see her eyeing me suspiciously. Her muscles were tense, ready to spring into action if needed, as if I were a predator hunting down her cub.

I had expected their exhausting back and forth dialogue, but it was as if the one who had nodded wasn't entirely up for it. In fact, all she seemed to be up for was attempting to punish my presence with her dark stare. Her eyes told a story of her own nightmares, her suspicions of everything I'd do to tear their lives apart.

Whispers began to bounce off the walls, but they were indistinct, so quiet yet so prevalent in the large hall. Then as quickly as they had come, they were gone. An awkward silence forced my eyes from the brooding aunt, onto her more vocal counterpart, and then to Chad to find him also staring at me.

Apparently having missed something, I summoned the most polite voice I could manage and said, "Pardon. Could you repeat that please?"

The witch sucked in her cheeks, half amused by my ignorance, half annoyed and repeated, "Of course you don't mind having dinner with us. Chadwick here seems to think you'd be opposed to it."

"Not entirely what I said Aunt Mallory," he replied, his head held high like a prince, but irritation still ringing through. "I merely suggested it was a bit rude to prepare a dinner you know she isn't able to eat."

"Nonsense," Mallory insisted, her hand waving away his comment as if it were a puff of smoke clouding her view. "We shan't starve as a consequence. If she's any sort of proper guest, she'll be delighted to join us. Besides, what's 'rude' is keeping our other guest waiting."

Chad's muscles pulled in tight as the wicked witch linked her arm through his and dragged him towards the door that stood guarded by the other witch, who must be Morgan. For a moment my feet were fixed to the ground, terrified at the idea of this other guest. Another unpleasant surprise—but how many more would there be?

Mallory pointed her finger at the door, and it flew open to reveal a seemingly empty dining room, but the slow beating of a heart announced the presence of another. My own heart moved along faster, clashing with the calm one. I met Morgan's eyes once more, still glued to me as if I were the villain in the scenario. Willing my legs forwards, I set one foot in front of the other to follow the Casters into the room, only breaking eye contact with the second witch when I passed through the threshold. But as I did, I could hear another one of her whispers, just barely audible, yet enough to send chills down my spine.

*You're going to **KILL** him.*

My eyes flew back to her, wide and horrified. Even the feeling of being deeply offended didn't mask my own fear of the thought she'd just sent my way. Her eyes were intense, yet she made no motion to speak again, so I turned around, in a partial daze. I could sense her presence close behind me, closing the door as if it would slow down my escape. With one last glance at her, my attention was drawn all the way down the long, formal table, set with shining gold plates and steaming foods, and straight to the most beautiful woman I had ever seen.

Her pale face was as smooth as porcelain, her cheeks were flushed with a delicate rosy hue, and she wore an elegant, pink dress that made her breasts pucker out admirably. She looked to be a few years older than me, draped in confidence and success. Her hair was a long, shimmering, magical shade of blonde. But the image of a mysterious blonde flickered across my mind before it froze me in horror.

No, no, no, I repeated in my head as I tried to mask the shock on my face. She-Whom-We-Never-Mention could not possibly be the woman who had handed me Florence's letter. She was too close to Chad. Working with him. Learning all that the Casters had planned against the other side. This was a nightmare. But as my eyes flew to Chad, desperate to warn him, he gave her a warm smile she didn't deserve.

"Ah. I didn't know you'd be joining us," Chadwick said. His tone bordered on unease, yet it was still much too friendly.

She stood soundlessly to her feet and moved to bow her head in welcome. I fought hard not to roll my eyes at the formality of it all, the I she was clearly putting on to shield her true identity.

"I hope I'm not intruding, my prince. Your aunts were so generous with their invitation," she said sweetly.

"Not at all," Chadwick replied. "You know your presence is always welcome."

"Ah, and Azalea!" she exclaimed as her whole body seemed to follow her eyes over to me, and she wrapped her slender arms around me for a hug. "I've heard so many wonderful things about you. Prince Chadwick speaks very highly of you, you know?" She pulled back to look at me, a warm smile on her face, her hands gripping my arms as if waiting for consent to touch me hadn't crossed her mind.

"I'm sorry," I said, putting on what I hoped would be an innocent smile. "I *so* wish I could return the sentiment. I don't exactly know who you are." Snarky yet subtle, I hoped. Yes, I knew exactly who she was, but her name I did not. And honestly, I would have been quite content to never find it out.

Chadwick gave an awkward laugh before attempting to rectify the situation. "That's not *entirely* true. We've just been a bit busy with Azalea's training is all. She knows how much help you've given my family in the past few months. But I do suppose a formal introduction is needed."

Traitor.

"Of course," the beautiful blonde said kindly, letting go of my arms to offer out her hand. Another form of touch I desperately didn't want. "I'm Lili, and it's an absolute honour to meet you."

My stomach clenched at the mention of her stupid name, a flower just like mine. Mallory's voice echoed through my head, and I tried very hard not to bite into any of their necks. *"An urgent need to remove all the azaleas and replace them with lilies."*

You do not hate them, I quickly told myself over and over to rein in my temper. *They're just old and set in their ways of blatant slavery and mistreatment of creatures they deem beneath them... But. You. Do. Not. Hate. Them.*

"Ah. It's a pleasure to meet you," I said, reluctantly shaking her hand.

Her smile brightened, and she swiftly changed the position of our hands so that she could lead me to a spot at the table. I watched the back of her hair as it shone in the light, trying to remember the head of the woman who had given me the note, but it might have been possible that she looked identical to Irma and Ingrid from behind. It was quite unfair that her face was so exquisite and flawless, yet the one part that could convict her was perfectly ordinary. It would be so convenient if it were her, if the woman his aunts believed to be his future bride was in fact the one working with Florence. Two birds. One stone. But I'd have to gather enough evidence first.

"You must sit next to me," she instructed gleefully, and I hated how perky and completely un-evil she came off. "I have the feeling we're going to be the best of friends. I just know it!"

His aunts looked just as happy as I felt by that statement, but we took our seats around the large table, all grouped towards the end of it. Chadwick sat at the head of the table, an aunt on either side, with She-Who-Unfortunately-Had-A-Name-Now placed between me and the aunt who had apparently taken a vow of silence for the night. The lack of symmetry at the table succeeded in making me feel like the odd man out, but I should have felt a fragment of appreciation for having a barrier between me and the old woman who looked quite inclined to **MURDER** me.

At another point in time, it would have been refreshing to just hear one of them speak instead of their exhausting banter back and forth, but if one witch was inclined to make me feel awkward with her stare, the other was insistent to petrify me with her words.

Mallory placed a frilly cloth napkin onto her lap, instructing everyone with her body language to tuck into the meal as well. Then she flicked her wrist, and a bowl of steaming squash soup adorned with pumpkin seeds magically appeared at each of our place settings. In a past life, I'm sure I would have been eager to dive into such an embellished meal, but the stench that now rose off of it seemed to activate my gag reflex. Instead of taking my spoon, I noticed a pitcher of water in front of me and reached for it.

"So," Mallory began, dabbing her mouth with her napkin and pivoting her head towards Chad. "What is this news you've come to tell us? If she's pregnant, I'll go straight to my grave."

I clumsily knocked the pitcher into the wine glass I had been filling as I choked on my own spit. The glass clattered onto the table, spilling all of its contents. The pure shock I had in response to her comment was enough to catch me off guard, and my vampire reflexes came in a tad too late. I quickly righted the glass, but the damage had been done. I had made a right mess, and I had managed to rub it in their faces that I was a vampire all in one go.

Chadwick laughed, placing his napkin politely over his mouth as he did so. "No, no," he insisted as if it were the funniest thing in the world. I wished I could find some humour in it. "No one's pregnant, Aunt Mallory, but we do have some exciting news to share. I hope you two will act graciously in response."

He flicked his wrist, and a translucent bubble surrounded the muck I had made on the table. An image of my hands spilling the water played in reverse within the clear orb, and when everything was back to the way it had been, the bubble vanished with a *pop* before he flicked his wrist again to fill my glass with water.

"That was really excellent, Prince Chadwick," Mrs Prophecy commented. "You've been getting much better at the time bubbles. I'm still rubbish at them."

Chadwick bowed his head in thanks, his eyes closing a fraction of a second longer than they normally would have before he turned back to his aunt. "Perhaps we should finish our meal before discussing the matter, however. I'm famished and I'd like to eat."

I tilted my head down, a sliver of guilt coursing through me. When was the last time I had seen him eat? Not that we had much time together these days, but hopefully he wasn't avoiding food in my presence to spare me the discomfort.

The Casters sat, eating almost soundlessly. Not a clink of a spoon or slurp of their drinks. I imagined all of them had attended some finishing school that I had no doubt missed out on, full of proper things to do and say. It was like an unspoken language, and Lili seemed to be a master at the craft. A polite comment about the meal, a gentle laugh at her hostess's joke, the flip of her blonde hair, the tidying up of her plump lips with a napkin after every bite.

It was sickening.

I was thankful to be left out of most of the conversation, though. I prayed Chadwick wouldn't find a way to invite me in. At one point our eyes met and he flicked his wrist. The water in my glass turned to a rich crimson hue. I picked it up eagerly, casually checking to see if any of the witches had noticed, but they were all perfectly content with ignoring me for the time being. Mouthing a word of "thanks" to Chad, I took a deep sip of the blood duplication potion and smiled at him gratefully. He gave me a wink in return, and I glanced away, the grin growing on my face as I remembered exactly why I was here and how much I loved him.

Like claws on a chalkboard, the blonde witch piped up excitedly. "Prince Chadwick, you'll never guess the news! The Warlocks of the South have decided to speak to us. They're willing to hear us out, let us convince them not to sit idle during this war."

"That's excellent," Chadwick replied with so much glee towards the witch that my stomach twinged with jealousy. "When have they agreed to meet with us?"

"A week from today."

My eyes quickly flashed up to Chadwick, and he was staring right back at me, clearly having noticed precisely which day that fell on.

"30 September?" he asked her, and she nodded happily in response, completely ignorant to what she was asking of him. "Is there any way we could reschedule? There's already something very important I'm supposed to take care of that day."

"There's nothing more important than finding alliances, Chadwick," Mallory chuckled dismissively before taking a sip of her wine.

As the witches continued on to the next topic, my heavy-hearted boyfriend gave me a miserable look. I shook my head, attempting to soothe his mind with my smile. As much as I hated the idea of admitting it, Mallory was right. I could handle the meeting with Hydie and my father on my own. The war came before that, and Chad had a very important role in all of it. He gave a meek smile before turning his attention back to his aunts and the blonde who was most definitely out to get me, whether she realised it or not.

They continued to chat, mostly small talk all royals and higher-up witches must have been coached on. Probably a class on how to magically extend nonsense into a twenty-minute conversation. I had enough to focus on without attempting to use my words—keeping a pleasant smile on my face as I forced down each disgusting bite, secretly rinsing the bad taste from my mouth with the blood, politely smiling and declining as tiny little fairies offered me spoonfuls of various meats and sides and vegetables. But I wasn't the only one who was hardly eating. Morgan had hardly touched her plate. She was staring off into the distance, dark circles surrounding her eyes as if she had lost a lot of sleep in a short period of time. The younger witch who sat in between us was hardly eating either. She was in the middle of taking the daintiest bite possible when Mallory spoke up about it.

"Please *do* eat some more, Lili. There's plenty of food," she insisted with a sweet tone she had never used with me.

"It truly is delicious, but you know I'm watching my figure," she laughed girlishly.

"And what a great figure you have too!" Mallory exclaimed, and I couldn't help but notice as her eyes flickered over to me disapprovingly.

I looked down at my lap, unable to help but feel slightly ashamed of my own body in comparison. Not that I was by any means unhealthy, but I did have a rather sizable bum. Warmth spread back to my cheeks, however, as I remembered just how fond of it her nephew happened to be.

"Being in good shape will help keep you protected out there," Mallory prattled on. "More and more Casters are missing daily. Those wretched vampires are doing heaven knows what to them."

My mind travelled back to what Elizabeth had said about Casters joining Florence's side, and my impulsive mouth opened up, acting entirely of its own accord. "Are you sure they're 'missing' per se? *We* were told there are Casters joining forces with Florence."

A fork clattered against a plate and they all stared at me. Apparently, that was the wrong thing to say.

"Oh my," Mallory breathed out, crinkling her nose in disgust. It seemed to be the most preposterous thing she had ever heard in her ripe old age. And that was all she managed to say. I had somehow succeeded in taking the words from her overly chatty mouth.

"That—er—doesn't seem very likely," the blonde tried, politely shutting down my hypothesis. She angled her body towards me in what I took as a very condescending manner. "That's quite unheard of, you see. Casters don't interact with Night Crawlers, let alone join forces with them."

"Well, Chad joined forces with me, with my coven. We're working together to bring down Florence. Why wouldn't an alliance go in the opposite direction?"

"If Casters are joining the other side, which first of all is a *ridiculous* assumption, then they're being forced into it," Mallory said, unfortunately finding her voice.

"Surely you don't expect everyone to follow you without question," I suggested, hardly able to suppress a surprised laugh, but I would have been better off shoving my foot in my mouth.

"Of course we do," Mallory huffed stubbornly. "Our system is run in a much more traditional manner than the way these modern mortal fools run their governments. Our people may believe they have a say in whether or not they join the fight, but when it comes down to it, they'll do as they're told."

I furrowed my brow at such an arrogant thing to say. The muscles in my mouth twitched, ready to respond to the tenacious witch, but I focused my eyes on Chad, hoping he'd either give me advice or the will to keep my mouth shut. His expression, however, was far from helpful.

He leaned back in his chair, his face nearly blank except for the smallest twinge of intrigue, as if he were watching a game he was pretending to be disinterested in.

Letting the air fill my lungs, I ignored the foul stench from the food and simply nodded. "As you wish," I said politely—a lame, generic way to give her the impression she had won. It wasn't worth the fight, not when we were here for their blessing to move in together or whatever it was we were after.

She looked far from satisfied, though. Taking one last bite of her meal, she pointed a finger to the plates, and with a puff of red smoke, they all vanished, including the forkful of food Chad had been in the middle of lifting to his mouth. He gave a frown before closing his mouth and examining his flustered aunt.

"Now," she said, as if I had taken all of her energy just to spite her. "What is this news you must tell us? I simply cannot wait a moment longer."

My heart skipped a beat. Part of me wanted to negate the part of the night where we'd tell them I was moving in, while another part of me wanted to get it over with, but as Chadwick cleared his throat, my body tensed, waiting for the inevitable wrath that would follow.

He moved back in his chair before declaring, "Azalea and I are moving in together. She'll be coming to live with me at Castwell Castle, and we're very excited about it. I hope you all can share in our joy." His tone, however, suggested his hope was already diminished by their initial reactions to me.

Every single heart in the room seemed to quicken its pace at the mention of those words, mine included. Lili sat with her mouth slightly ajar, perhaps the only time tonight I'd seen her look anything but positively graceful. Mallory sucked in her cheeks in frustration, but it was Morgan who looked the most appalled by the news. The faint whispers started up again, echoing through the long dining room, but as my eyes trailed along everyone in the room, it seemed that no one else either heard them or was bothered by them.

"No," Mallory said simply, dropping her royal act and scraping her chair across the floor to make her point abundantly clear. "I will not have a vampire defiling our ancestral home more than she already has. This is ridiculous."

"I don't believe I posed it as a question, Aunt Mallory," Chad growled back, and I almost dropped my jaw at the curtness of his response.

"And what would your mum think of all this?" she continued hurriedly, completely ignoring his comment. "You know that was her favourite castle."

"I don't know what she'd think, and if you haven't noticed, she's not exactly here to ask," he said dismissively and took a sip of wine.

I couldn't look away. It was a trainwreck, but I couldn't help but appreciate the sheer amount of stubborn determination he was putting into it.

"You can't just *move in* the same *thing* that **KILLED** her," she enunciated.

"I'm not asking for your blessing, Aunt Mallory. I merely came to inform you and warn you there will be extra wards around the castle to keep the two of you, or anyone without my explicit permission, out."

My mind raced to catch up as I engaged in a staring competition with my lap, twiddling my thumbs anxiously. *Okay, so* not *asking for their blessing, and we're adding more wards to keep them out.* At least Hydrangea would be better protected. Perhaps this was some of the information he mentioned I was better off not knowing. At least not until it was absolutely necessary.

"And what's next?" the witch asked, standing to better portray her anger. "Are you going to run off and join the vampire's side too?"

"If you haven't noticed, it's no longer Casters versus Night Crawlers. The sides are changing. This is a war between those who wish to remain hidden to mortals and those who refuse to."

His aunt brashly continued to argue, but her shouts of protest transformed into background noise in comparison to the echoey whispers. I looked over to the witch who had sat so silent for most of the night and jumped when I saw her staring directly back at me. Her whispers crescendoed but her lips stayed absolutely still. It was then that I heard what she was communicating.

*You're going to **KILL** him. You're going to **KILL** him. You're going to **KILL** him,* was running through her head over and over. My heart tightened and my chest rose up and down at an impossible rate. It was as if I could feel her sadness, her rage, her fear all wrapped into one.

"This is the most reckless thing you've ever done!" Mallory shouted.

"Don't be so dramatic. Moving in together is the best—"

*You're going to **KILL** him.*

"You know what the council expects of you. What your people expect from you—"

"And I couldn't care less about what anyone expects from me!"

*You're going to **KILL** him.*

"And what is Lili supposed to do?"

"She's a grown woman. Ask her yourself!"

*You're going to **KILL** him.*

"What about your poor Aunt Morgan?"

"Her dreams mean nothing but a reflection of her own fears. That's not going to happen."

You're going to **KILL** *him. You're going to* **KILL** *him.*

"She has never been wrong about her visions."

"Well, there's a first time for everything."

You're going to **KILL** *him. You're going to* **KILL** *him. You're going to* **KILL** *him!*

It was as if I could feel it, hear the colour red screaming out at me as it had done so many times before. Over and over, her words echoed through my mind, the stress, the inevitability growing louder and louder until I could hardly take it any longer. Green slowly seeped into my consciousness like a soothing whisper, a mutter of consoling words of, "No she won't. That's not her true character," but the red violently overtook it, washing it away like a tear dropped into the sea.

YOU'RE GOING TO **KILL** *HIM! YOU'RE GOING TO* **KILL** *HIM! YOU'RE GOING TO* **KILL** *HIM! YOU'RE GOING TO* **KILL** *HIM! YOU'RE GOING TO* **KILL** *HIM! YOU'RE GOING TO* **KILL** *HIM! YOU'RE GOING TO* **KILL** *HIM! YOU'RE GOING TO* **KILL** *HIM! YOU'RE GOING TO* **KILL** *HIM!*

It grew louder and louder until I was blinded by the violent colour, and then screams from nowhere overpowered it, saying, "No, I'm not!"

My voice swallowed every other sound, and I found myself on my feet with every set of eyes on me. My lungs struggled to accept the air that was trying to fill them. I looked around to everyone in the room, even the small fairies who had entered to announce dessert. Then my eyes darted back to Morgan's, and even though they were haunted, hollowed, and frail, I spat back at her once more. Partially to calm her aches, partially to prove her wrong, I said, "I will not **KILL** him, so you can keep those *grotesque* thoughts to yourself."

The silence burned like dry Ice. Chad's eyes darted back and forth between me and his aunt Morgan.

You can hear her? He asked, and our eyes both widened when I could hear him as well. I gave a nod before Lili cleared her throat, and we all looked at her.

"Oh dear," Lili said, patting off her mouth with a napkin one last time and then setting it on the table. She slid out of her chair with hardly any noise and stood up. "Perhaps this lovely dessert should be adjourned for now. Prince Chadwick, why don't we show Azalea to our workroom?"

The question did nothing to soothe my anger. "Our" workroom? Did I miss the part where she suddenly owned the place?

Chadwick cleared his throat. "I believe Azalea and I have overstayed our welcome." A breath of relief swept out of me but was quickly the last bit of air I could manage to let in as the blonde gave a smile.

"I'm sure your aunts will insist you stay longer. Oh, don't you?" she asked, looking between the two women whose faces had weathered several years from the stress of the conversation. To my surprise, they both nodded.

"Stay," Mallory said, a command for a dog. "Might as well make yourself a bit useful while you're here, Chadwick."

He gave a very uncomfortable look before casting his gaze towards Lili—a cross between hesitation and full-fledged panic in his eyes—but she didn't wait for an answer. The blonde witch gave me a look of upbeat satisfaction as she grabbed at my hand. It wasn't my intention to pull my hand away quickly, but either she didn't notice or it didn't bother her. She merely linked arms with mine and dragged me out of the room, leaving Chadwick the only option of following. I craned my neck back and watched as he gave both aunts a look that communicated how frustratingly disappointed he was with the events that had just played out before he followed soundlessly after us.

The passageways we took to get to that sacred workroom of theirs were just as overly showy as the outside of the castle, and Mrs Prophecy jabbered on about all the details of its history, blissfully ignoring the fact that my entirely tense body was signalling to her just how desperately I wanted to run away.

"Prince Chadwick has been working so hard, yet we still have so much to do," she said to me before turning round to a less-than-enthusiastic Chad. "And you're still coming back after you deliver Azalea to London, aren't you?"

I don't know why shock seemed to gut me. He was always here, with her. Why would today be any different? It didn't stop him from wincing, however, as he glanced at me apologetically and then back to the blonde.

"Yes, of course. Especially if we have to prepare for the meeting with the southern warlocks." I flinched at the word "we."

"Excellent!" she said.

I, on the other hand, was seriously over this whole ordeal.

"I'm actually quite tired," I tried, giving her the sincerest tone I could muster through the agitation that radiated from me. "Perhaps I should retire as Chadwick suggested."

"And miss out on a girls' chat? Nonsense," she rejected before moving on faster than a dog distracted by a rogue rodent. "I love your dress by the way. Purple looks fabulous on you. Although I must admit, pink was always more my colour," she said, gesturing to her gigantic bosom that was popping out over the top of her dress.

Faint puffs of purple magic threatened to transport me away from the hell I had walked into, but the opening of a set of double doors was the distraction I needed.

The room oozed with power from its magical mirrors to the wireless tech that was strewn around the room. Books flew across from the west wall to a table in the east, organising themselves and flipping to certain pages before thinking better of it and returning to their shelves. A floating, transparent map took centre stage in the room, with curves and mountains that rose up from it. As Lili hopped over to it, dragging me with her, she snapped her fingers and the map rotated to face us.

Something eerie prickled at the back of my neck. Something off, but I couldn't quite place my finger on what it was.

The woman finally let go of my arm to point her finger at a place that lay at the very top of it.

"This is where Chadwick and I will be travelling next week," she said importantly. Her delicate fingers fell through the mountains, and beads of silver flickered at her touch. "It's very cold there. I don't know how people without magic manage to live up there. Thankfully, we'll have warming charms to keep us heated."

My lashes attempted to blink away the image of the two of them canoodling together for body heat if they didn't have "warming charms" to keep them comfortable.

"This workroom is where we do all of our research. We hold brief meetings over there," she said, gesturing towards the mirror, "and all the azaleas have been going towards the potions we make over there. Very busy work. Prince Chadwick tells me you've been dabbling in potion-making yourself."

Of course Chadwick had told her that.

"Yes. Just a dabble," I replied, careful to control my tone as I mimicked her choice of words. "But I'm not very good at it."

"But he says you're a natural," she said, sounding genuinely surprised before turning to Chadwick. "Don't you, Prince Chadwick?"

Chadwick coughed awkwardly in reply, and I couldn't help but roll my eyes around in a big circle. *He* felt awkward? Did he have any regard for how I felt?

"She's more skilled than she knows," was his reply before he conveniently busied himself with a pile of papers that stood half a metre tall. Turning his body to give them his full attention, he flicked his wrist over the papers, and the words instantly levitated off them, page after page disappearing as the words melted into a tablet nearby. An interesting way to type out the work.

The witch, having proved her point, turned back to me happily and gave such a sweet smile that it made me sick. "See? He's very proud of you. He's told me all about you. I feel like I know you already. Like the truth serum!" she gasped. "I can't believe Duchess Morgan and Duchess Mallory slipped one into your drink when you first met them. It makes me slightly fearful they'll do the same to me. They haven't, of course, and to be honest, I don't have much to hide, but the breach of privacy alone is worrisome. And then the frog in your throat at the annual Saint Valentine's Ball! That sounds ghastly. I'm so sorry you had to go through that. I wish I had been there to help in some way."

"Why weren't you there?" I asked. She had suddenly piqued my interest. "They discovered you just before then, hadn't they?"

Perhaps Chadwick didn't believe she was the prophesied sorceress. Perhaps he originally didn't want to give her the time of day, but then the war decided otherwise.

"Oh," she said, strangely surprised by the question. She cast a sideways look over to Chad before saying, "Well something very important came up resulting in my absence, but everything's fine now."

I grimaced at the idea of her being at the next ball, whenever that would be, but before I could ask, Chadwick turned around and walked over to me, apparently having lasted as long as he could.

"I'm sorry, Lili," he said, sliding his hand into mine. "But we must be going."

"Oh, you mustn't," she replied, sounding quite disappointed, but Chad remained firm.

"We must," he replied solidly without even looking at her.

"Well, cheers for finally bringing Azalea along with you," she said, placing an appreciative hand on his biceps before turning to me. "I've been dying to meet you."

My eyes trailed from her hand, back up to her eyes, perhaps a bit too slowly. I could have sworn her eyes flashed a look of satisfaction as she lifted her hand away from him. "It was a pleasure to meet you," I told her dully.

"The pleasure was all mine. Perhaps next time we can discuss your theories on what that vampire of yours is up to."

I pressed my tongue up against the roof of my mouth to lock it in place, and Chad's grasp on my hand tightened. Florence. *My* vampire? How dare she. The blonde bitch was about to get a right earful of my suspicions if we didn't hurry up and get out of here.

"Goodbye, Lili," Chadwick told her, already pulling me out the door.

As I glanced back at her, she gave a little wave, and whispered back to him, "I'll see you in a few."

Chapter 9: Pink

I was enraged—enraged to the point I couldn't even speak. Chadwick pulled me down the corridor as heat fumed around me. She was evil. She didn't look like it with her stupid pink dress and her puckering breasts, or sound like it with her polite, princess-like pitch, but I knew what she was—a traitor.

Chad dragged me back the way we had come as if he could sense I was going to bite her if I had to spend one more moment there. We rushed down the stairs and all the way back to the gaudy, golden front doors. His aunts were waiting in the foyer, but they didn't mutter a word to us as we entered. They exchanged looks with their nephew, curt, agitated, and controlled all at once. Not one glance was spared in my direction until my foot caught on a faint cloud of red smoke and I stumbled clumsily through the doorway. Then Mallory's gaze met mine, gleaming with guilty pleasure as she tilted her chin up at me, and as my eyes wandered over to Morgan's glare of death, I wasn't sure which bitch had tripped me. I had a feeling it was the more vocal one. Either way, it caused my spark of fury to fully ignite as we walked back out the grounds and were surrounded by the still faces of their other victims. For a moment, I fully lost it.

As soon as the doors shut behind us, I slipped my hand out of Chadwick's and let my purple magic seep out, covering the ground like an eerie Halloween fog. He turned his head to look at me without missing a step. There was a strange sense of shock and added stress coated on his face as he realised what I was doing. The sound of hundreds of unfrozen heartbeats filled my ears as the once enslaved gnomes were given a second chance. Their small bodies moved frantically about, intercepting our path with quick feet, but Chad didn't slow. He kept his eyes straight ahead.

The wards shimmered as we crossed through, just enough for my trained eyes to notice, and to my relief, several of the gnomes passed through the wards as well. They chattered excitedly to one another before dispersing towards their freedom. A small victory in this disaster of a night.

Chadwick finally stopped his stride to turn around and face me. His brow lifted as though I had been a very naughty girl. I smiled mischievously as he grabbed onto my hip, but in actuality, I was too immersed in my pissed-off daze to feel true pride for freeing the creatures.

Green magic surrounded us, yet Chad's intense eyes never left mine.

When we landed in his bedroom and the smoke cleared, I cocked my brow back at him.

"Yes, Prince Chadwick?" I asked, taunting him with my feigned innocence.

"When they find out you've freed all of those gnomes—"

"It'll be too late to round them all back up," I finished for him, justifying the whole scene that had just sped before our eyes. I turned to the vanity, removed my earrings, and then laid them on the surface as I continued to argue my point. "They were keeping them as slaves and trophies, and it was despicable. And you'll defend my honour, won't you? Or will you merely sit back and watch as you did at dinner when they were on about how obedient every one of their subjects is?" I asked.

"Oh, I was quite keen to take a step back and enjoy the show. See if you could handle all their madness. It's not every day they have someone brave enough to stand up to them."

"I've noticed," I said, with too much cheek for my own good. "Mrs Prophecy was a master at twirling all of you around her dainty little fingers."

"Is that jealousy I detect?" he asked with intrigue.

"Never," I lied, tilting my head up to hide my wounded pride.

"I'm sorry," he said hurriedly, sensing an impending row. "I had no idea they were inviting her."

"Well, it's lucky they did," I scoffed, thinking of the horrors that could have arisen if I hadn't met her, "because she's vile."

"How so?" he questioned, unconvinced.

"She's working with Florence. I know it."

"You think everyone's working with Florence."

"I do not!"

His hand flew up so fast, immediately ticking off the numbers as he went. "Missouri, your mum, Aunt Mallory, Aunt Morgan, Ingrid, Irma, Lili—"

"Arg! Stop saying her name," I screamed out. "I've heard it enough times tonight to last a lifetime. Besides, the last three you mentioned are all blonde, so they're obviously suspicious."

"Why? Because Florence is blond?" he asked, momentarily dropping his charming stance.

Panic slammed into me as I realised the bit of information I had put off telling him for far too long. "No…" I started cautiously. "Suspicious because of a letter I received."

"A letter?" he asked. His eyes searched my face for answers.

I nodded timidly. "There's something I need to tell you."

I didn't know why I hadn't told him. I really didn't. Whether it was saving him from worry or attempting to save myself from more stress, it hadn't worked either way. So I told him. I laid out every detail of the night he had passed Castle on the Rocks Pub down to Connor, the blonde-haired woman, and the letter. Florence had written out his promise to return and insisted that next time he wouldn't fail, but I wasn't sure what that part was referring to. Did he have a plan to **KILL** Chadwick, a plan to kidnap me, or a plan to force me to be his wife? I simply didn't want to think about it for long enough to find out.

Chad's eyes grew wide with anger. Perhaps it even bordered past that, straight on to full-blown fury. "How could you not tell me that?" His voice was at a volume only I ever reached when patience had completely deserted me.

"I dunno," I said hurriedly, eager not to make him cross. "Perhaps because I'm a coward. Perhaps because I knew you had too much on your shoulders that I felt I should bear this one alone."

"Well, that is about the daftest reaction you could've had," he yelled back, throwing his hands up into his hair and pulling at it.

The sound of my own teeth grinding together to stop me from yelling back filled my ears. Good. At least I could control my tongue through a breaking heart if not for my hot temper.

"I'm sorry," I managed to let out, even if I choked over the words. I couldn't deny it. It wasn't the smartest reaction. "It was the wrong way to go about things. I know that now. But that hair. I know it's *her*." I still couldn't bring myself to utter the witch's name.

"You just told me you only saw the back of that lady's head, and Lili's head looks the same as any other blonde woman out there."

The corners of my mouth almost lifted at the words as if he thought she was ordinary, easily lost in a crowd, not the beautiful, almighty sorceress I always pictured her to be. Almost, but not quite a smile as he still threw daggers of disappointment at me with his eyes.

"I knew you wouldn't believe me, at least not right away," I said bitterly, "but think about what Elizabeth Downy said before she went and offed herself. There are Casters working with Florence, and that *girl*," I continued, refusing to let her name fall from my lips, "she's a spy."

Chad shook his head, far from believing me, but I couldn't blame him really. I *was* jealous. I missed him, and even the bloody stars thought he should be with her.

"Azalea, you literally said yourself that Ingrid and Irma are both blonde. Not to mention the tens of thousands of other people out there with blond hair, several of which Florence already **KILLED**. What about that night at Loxley Lair with all the dead bodies? That happened *after* this letter of yours. Perhaps the woman with the letter is already dead. Perhaps the note didn't succeed in scaring you enough so he went and offed the messenger."

"I thought about it but—"

"But your plan to hate Lili was too strong to resist accusing her?" he asked calmly, his face worn with exhaustion, but I just gawked at the audacity of what he was saying.

"You know what?" I said decidedly. "I don't care that you don't believe me. I know what I saw, and that blonde bitch—"

"*Witch*," he corrected at a decibel only a vampire could hear, but I turned on him so fast and pointed my finger right at his nose before completely snapping.

"No one asked for your opinions or your coddling fantasies of how perfect she is," I growled back.

Chad sighed as if the conversation was too much for him to handle. "She's not perfect, nor did I say she was, so don't put words in my mouth. She *is* my friend, however, and she's done a lot of work against Florence. Slow down and think of this logically. Don't you think you might be overreacting a bit?" he asked timidly.

Any "reacting" within me swelled up way beyond "overreacting" from the sound of the word as it left his lips. "Overreacting?" I snapped back, and he winced. We were on the verge of a war, the spy was right before us, yet I was overreacting? I could feel—literally *feel*—my eyes turning red. I needed to calm down.

"Okay, wrong word! Wrong word," he said in a panic, retracting his previous statement by drawing an X with his arms. "We're stressed—both of us, and we're being put into really difficult situations that aren't fair, I know that, and I'm sorry. I'm so, so sorry," he said, placing his hands on my upper arms to display his sincerity. "I'm tired—I'm tired all the time, and I constantly have a million things going on in my head, or a million things to do, and none of that's fair to you. I wish we were in a place where I could spend every moment with you, and away from her, to make you feel all the love I feel for you, but I always have to run off to handle something else instead of giving you the attention you deserve. And of course I have to bloody run off again tonight, but I want so desperately not to muck things up with you."

I took in a deep breath to let it all soak in, to soothe my troubled mind. His words wrapped around me like a warm hug, yet tears still brimmed in my eyes. I looked around his bedroom, too stubborn to let the tears fall, and willed my eyes to shift back from red to blue. But jealousy seeped in again, regardless of how his words squeezed me tight. My tongue swirled around the roof of my mouth as I glanced around, trying to fight off the self-destructive thoughts, but I couldn't help it. I couldn't help but wonder if she had ever been *here*. Had she been to Castwell Castle? What had she touched? What had she defiled?

But Chad took me into his arms, and I let him hold me there, praying he wouldn't leave. "This is going to be your home. It's a place she's never been and never will be. It's all ours," he said softly into my ear, and I nodded against him.

The air slowly deflated from his chest as he rubbed my back gently. I wanted to give in to his touch, to relax, but the thought of it made me fear for his safety. Fear swelled inside me as I wondered how far my body could throw him now that this familiar sense of love ran over me, so I softly pushed myself out of his arms to get a good look at him.

"Let's talk about this later," I suggested, "when we're both not so overwhelmed and anxious. Just be careful," I started calmly, before adding, "for me." Nothing was fixed but there was no point in arguing it now.

He nodded. "Of course, my love," he purred, leaning into my neck.

"Casting a spell to shield her boobs in that damn pink dress wouldn't hurt either," I teased to lighten the mood, testing the waters as he leaned back to look at me once more.

"'Oh, but pink is more my colour'," he mimicked, and I rolled my eyes at the mere memory of her facetious comment. At least Chad recognised the ridiculousness of it all. He laughed as his hands grazed my arms that were still carefully tucked behind my back. "You look beautiful in this purple dress, my dearest Azalea, and if anything, pink is more your colour than hers. The flowers you were named for are the most beautiful shade of pink. I don't know why she would say such a thing."

Warmth spread through my chest as I stared up at him through my lashes. For a moment, I felt I had nothing to worry about. Perhaps I could be the girl the stars told of. The one with powers so strong they could hold the attention of the High Prince of the Casters. The one who could help him win the war, and he could be eternally happy alongside. But that feeling seemed to diminish when the smile in his eyes faded away and his lips spoke of the business he must handle.

"I'm really sorry about the thirtieth," he whispered sweetly. "If I can get out of it, I will. I want to be there for you. Freeze the son of a bitch for all he's done to you. Aid you. Protect you."

Even though I knew I could face my father on my own—knew I didn't need protection—I still wanted Chad there.

"I'll be fine," I assured him regardless. "It's probably good to do it on my own—face my demons. Besides, I know you'll be there afterwards to come and piece me back together."

"Of course," he said in a hushed voice, his breath tickling my neck, tempting me to touch him in ways my body wouldn't allow, not without harming him.

"Are you sure you don't want to stay?" I asked in the sweetest, most luring manner I could manage. "Perhaps work out our to-do list a bit more?"

He laughed at the memory. "There's almost nothing I'd like more right now," he insinuated. The word "but" hovered on his lips without even slipping from them.

"I know," I whispered back so he wouldn't have to voice his reasoning for needing to go. "But I'll miss you more than you know."

"I have a feeling I'll know exactly how much," he said, as if his own heart would replicate the feeling entirely.

Placing a hand over my mouth, he cast a warming charm over me, and I closed my eyes to imagine his lips over mine.

"I love you," he murmured, and when I opened my eyes, only his green swirl of magic was left in his wake.

Loneliness swelled within me, amplified by the memory of her touching his arm so intimately. Then my eyes fell down to my purple dress, and her words echoed through my mind. *Pink was always more my colour.*

My sorrow swirled around and was cast aside and replaced by a strong distaste. Then I did something I was not proud of. I lost myself. All alone in his room, my eyes flew to the few pink things that sat out, and each of them burst into flames. Pink jewels, pink pen, pink hair tie. Power radiated through me, hot, welcomed, and I looked into the mirror, hating every piece of me, and grabbed at my hair. Long locks of dark brown turned to purple, and I glared at my reflection, bitter that she got him in that moment, not me.

Chapter 10: Intrusions

I burst into Abigail and Cristin's room an hour later, completely
disregarding any rules of privacy, and plopped down onto their bed.
Abigail was in the corner painting a dark, abstract scene that
screamed hopelessness and despair.

"So things went horribly, I'm assuming?" she questioned, wiping
her hands on a tan cloth before coming over to the bed. As she sat down,
I placed my head on her lap, and she began to stroke my hair, ready to
console me. I internally blessed her for her kindness.

"Not 'horribly,' but not wonderfully either," I sighed.

"At least your hair looks stunning," she commented, taking in its
new colour, and I laughed. "So how'd they take the news?"

"Well, it's not as if I expected them to welcome me with open arms,
but it didn't make matters any better considering the surprise guest they
invited along." I paused, waiting for her to catch my drift.

"No," she gasped, already knowing precisely who I was talking
about. "They invited *her*?" she asked, and I felt comforted in the fact that
she felt as I did about the once nameless witch. Not to mention, she still
felt disgruntled towards the aunts after having been a victim of their red
magic. "How malevolent."

I nodded before covering my face. There was a fine line between
venting about the witch and flat-out whining, and I had already crossed
that border. It was hopeless fighting against it after the flood gates had
already opened, and I was drenched by a pool of self-pity.

"And she's fucking gorgeous too," I let out pathetically. "She's so
polite, thin, big-breasted, and his blasted aunts are in love with her. And
she's blonde."

I hadn't dared remind Abigail the seriousness behind the blonde
hair, and she didn't seem to pick it up on her own. I had told her when I

initially received Florence's threatening letter, and it felt like I was overthinking the whole ordeal, especially considering Chad had just brushed off the matter so effortlessly. Not to mention, she was team Ingrid and Irma already.

Abigail's face scrunched in discomfort, teetering between speaking her mind and keeping her question locked tight behind her lips.

"Go on," I insisted. I could feel her question anyhow. How could she *not* wonder with the prophecy hanging over like an impending storm?

"Is she powerful?"

My shoulders rose helplessly in a shrug. "I don't know, but she must be if those old crones think she's the one," I murmured, thinking back to Germany when they had looked Chad in the eye and insisted she was the girl the stars spoke of.

"And how did Chad handle the intrusion?" Abigail pressed further.

"Graciously," I reported, sullen misery still sounding in my throat. "I mean, he got us out of there as soon as he could, told me I was beautiful... All that rubbish," I spat out bitterly, not truly meaning it. I was grateful for him, just hopelessly broken for reasons that had little to do with him.

"That's how you know he's a keeper," she told me, and I nodded, knowing full well she was right. I'd fight to keep him no matter how many blonde damsels got in the way.

"I'm throwing a 'going away' party for you," Abigail added, her tone lifted as though a farewell party would wash away all my sorrows. "I was thinking it could cheer you up, so you have the strength to collect your sister."

I nodded in agreement. "Cheers, Abigail."

"Can't have you leaving without us letting you know how much you'll be missed," she told me sweetly.

My eyes explored the dark room and then took in the painting that seemed to be a still life of my own distraught emotions.

"Where's Cristin?" I asked, forcing myself to move on from challenges that weren't truly in my way.

"Off in Africa again, trying to convince the Day Walkers to pick a side. Our side. Any side besides sitting by and watching the world crumble," she said, referring to the darker-skinned vampires that could last longer in the sunlight thanks to their melanin, which was even more protective than mine. "It's hopeless though," she went on. "They believe the rest of the world should be left to deal with their problems on their own after everything we've taken away from them. Honestly, I can't blame them. I'd be in total agreement if the situation weren't as dire as it is."

I bit my cheek at the thought of it. The Day Walkers. The war. All of it felt too real. Too close.

A knock at the door took me out of my thoughts, and I turned my head as Irma walked in, nearly as comfortable as I was to barge in. I hated it.

"Oh," she said in her German accent, jerking her head back as if she were surprised to see me, Abigail's best mate, there. "Sorry. I didn't mean to intrude."

I fought not to roll my eyes.

"No, not at all," Abigail assured her in a sweet tone that seemed to poke at my patience. Why did she have to be so kind?

"Are you still wanting to join us for a hunt?" Irma asked before turning her eyes to me. "You're more than welcome to come along, Azalea. It would be so good to get to know you better."

Abigail threw me a look of guilt, and I couldn't help but let my heart falter. Why was everyone so trusting of blonds these days? Even my best friend. Between Florence and her ex-fiancé, Abigail had freely admitted to despising blonds, yet here she was, traipsing through the lair with them.

I sat up and gave Irma a kind smile. "No, I'm in a rather foul mood, but cheers for the offer."

"Oh no," she gasped. She strode over to the bed to sit and placed a hand on my shoulder—a gesture meant to comfort—but it only resulted in taking me aback. She had no fear for me, regardless of knowing I could see into the past—see if it was she who had delivered Florence's letter. But her touch seemed to speak volumes for her innocence. Either that or she didn't care. "What happened?" she continued on.

Abigail patted my lap consolingly before unnecessarily explaining to the slightly less-suspicious blonde vampire. "She's just met the mysterious witch who the elder witches seem to believe is Prince Chadwick's soulmate."

My stomach gave a heave when hearing the words out loud. Did she really have to say all that in front of Irma?

But Irma's face held nothing but sympathy. "I've seen the way he looks at you, Azalea," she declared. "He has eyes for you and you alone. Don't let anyone convince you otherwise."

"It's kind of hard," I said with a bitter shrug, "when she's got her full chest out and she's touching his arm."

God, even I could hear the bitterness roll off my tongue, and I felt ashamed of myself. It was time I got over the perkiness of her breasts. Sure, mine were small in comparison, but who cared? The touch, however, well that was a different story.

"What a bitch," Irma uttered, true affection in her voice, and I stared at her. Perhaps I could like this vampire. At least, I could like her better than her counterpart who still quivered in a corner every time I walked into the room.

I gave her a smile before looking away. "You two go. I'll be fine here, I promise. It'd do me good to search for Florence anyway. I've been meaning to test out a few skills." No need to mention there was magic involved. They already knew even if I was too penitent to say it.

"Perhaps next time," Irma sighed, and I nearly laughed as I gave her a reassuring nod.

Not in a million years.

ೞ

Hours later, I sat atop my bed, hunched precariously over a map of the world. I stared at the magically enchanted terrain, desperate to get a sense of where Florence was. A tingling, an inkling, a pull, or anything, when Chad climbed in through my mirror. How he managed to slip in so gracefully every time, I'd never understand. Despite his elegant movements, exhaustion consumed his face. I wouldn't have blamed him for curling up in his own bed and falling asleep straight away, but it meant the world to me that he had come here instead.

When he had fully passed through the portal, his lips parted to greet me, but he froze at the sight of my purple hair and let out an airy laugh.

"Get it all out of your system?" he quipped, and I bit my lip to suppress the smile he always managed to sprout.

"Nearly," I teased back.

"Good, but you do look rather gorgeous. Purple is very becoming on you."

I let out a truly repulsive snort before gathering up the map and setting it aside so Chad could join me on the bed.

"So how'd it go?" I asked as he lay down next to where I sat, and I propped my head up on my elbow so I could give him my full attention.

"It went brilliantly, to be honest," he said as though he couldn't believe his luck. "We have a really solid plan in place. There's no way those warlocks will say no to joining forces with us."

"That's wonderful!" I said sincerely. "I hope it all goes well."

We talked for a while, him telling me more about his plan, and me threatening to turn his skin purple if he didn't come to the farewell soirée with me. After less than thirty minutes together, yawns drew more air to my lungs, and Chad began to sing me a sweet lullaby. And then I was carried off to sleep.

The skies were lit with swirls of pinks and oranges, not a single cloud blocking the view. The warm, deep voice that had just caressed my ears slid to a higher octave. A woman was running towards the horizon, her voice unwavering even as each foot hit the ground, her long blonde hair flowing playfully in the wind. The gentle breeze rolled her song to my ears, sweet and soft, a child's happy tune—but as I ran after her, the song slowly turned to a minor key, and I could finally hear her lyrics.

> *Oh, how low you'll sink*
> *To blame those innocent people*
> *When the real enemy stares back at you*
> *Right through your mirror.*

Ashes began to fall from the pink sky, and the pleasantness in the air turned to the stench of death. As I drew nearer to the woman, she turned around, flinging her soft yellow hair over her shoulder.

I sat up straight, waking from the dream. Chad was fast asleep next to me, his magical dragon tattoo snoozing across his chest, but his presence provided little comfort. Her eyes were still engraved in my mind. Her crooked smile. Her pointed teeth. Her hair. Only she wasn't who I expected. Not any of my suspects. The woman who had looked back at me was me.

Chapter 11: Spies

I didn't bother mentioning my dream to anyone. For once it wasn't of the children, and it hadn't made me throw Chad against the wall. This one was just a dream, yet it seemed to wreck my mind more than any of the other nightmares would have. And as much as I wanted to dismiss it, it was my sole companion as I readied myself for the party that was meant to be in my honour.

My violet hair was curled up into a chignon with loose strands to frame my face. The style partnered with my strapless dress to leave my smooth skin bare. Dark green silk fabrics, courtesy of Charity and her French-based clothing line, wrapped tightly around my chest before flaring out at my waist.

Chad came in through the mirror, looking dashing in dark purple robes. And the sly smile he gave me as his eyes roved over my whole body told me he thoroughly approved of my outfit as well.

"The things you make me want to do to you," he whispered. If he had asked, I would have let him whisk me off to his bedroom and forget about the silly party, but for once I was a good girl. He slipped his hand into mine and led me out of the room, up the stairs, and across to the ballroom as I stayed lost in my own fantasies of the two of us.

We walked together at a mortal's pace, enjoying the privacy of one another's company. The double doors opened to reveal the grandeur of the ballroom, and after thanking the frozen gnomes hidden behind the doors, I examined the room in awe. In place of the gothic I were sheets of white silk draped on the ceiling and walls, curving inwards like a gorgeous tent. The candlelit chandeliers had been replaced with twinkling fairy lights. It was hard not to gasp at the surprise—electricity—a once forbidden treat.

As the gentle hum of magic played in the air, my gaze shifted down to meet several smiling faces. My heart lifted with joy, thankful for having met each and every one of them. Vampires, manananggals, a jorogumo, a banshee, and a few ghosts. All happy to see me. All there to wish me the best. I couldn't help but notice two who were missing. Missouri, the ghost, had been absent for months, no doubt chasing after Florence. She was perhaps the only one here who had truly liked him, although there were definitely a few women he had charmed at one time or another in the six years he had been a part of the coven. The second missing person was my singing ghost, but a shimmer in the corner of my eye caused me to look over at the beautiful woman as she drifted in through the wall—my mum.

A mixture of sadness and fear settled in her eyes as she stared back at me. She knew precisely why I no longer trusted her or longed for her presence. She had led me straight to Florence's trap. But I didn't care how she felt. I hadn't seen her in months, and it wasn't right for her to turn up now, on a night I already felt so anxious about.

Stubbornly, I turned away from her, eager for her to leave. She hadn't taken me away from my father, she had let him keep hurting me and Hydie, and she had never given me any of the answers I needed. I longed to know whether or not she was like me, or why she had stayed with my father, or let me know if my father was right. Was I really the one who had **KILLED** her?

My heart sank even lower into the abyss. Perhaps that's why she had led me to Florence. Perhaps that was why she was still here, a spirit left with unfinished business, to get revenge on me. But after at least half an hour of mingling and small talk, I let my mind wander away from her, and when my eyes aimlessly ended back to where she had been, I discovered she was long gone. A pit grew in my stomach—a missing piece I thought she could fill, but as the party carried on, I resolved to deal with that matter another time, and my attention went back to the people who were present. The people who were living. The people who actually cared for me.

Chad's warm laugh filled the room, and I looked across to where he now stood conversing happily with Cristin and O'Brien. Each held a glass filled with red liquid. I let out a laugh of my own, shaking my head at how comfortable Chad felt with my friends, my family. Not to mention, how adorable he looked trying to fit in, drinking merlot as though the other two men were drinking the same.

Apparently in too much of a euphoric daze, I was caught off guard when I was swept into a hug. Blonde hair, surprise, and the smell of Irma overtook me.

She leaned back and began gibbering away as though we were old mates, but it took me a moment to catch up as I studied how completely unafraid she was of me, to touch me as though she were innocent and there was nothing my visions would see to deem her as a traitor.

"—and although I'm sad we haven't known each other very long before you're moving out, I know we'll still be friends," she ended, and I blinked at her a few times, still attempting to catch up.

"Yes," I said politely, remembering to give her a smile instead of merely staring at her blankly.

"Anyway," she went on, her eyes travelling over to Ingrid, who was unabashedly staring at us, "I'll check in with you later."

So friendly, so innocent, but in these times, surely it was important to stand my ground—be cautious. Yet as she pranced away and gave her wife a sweet kiss on her cheek, I couldn't help but realise how sincerely she acted.

From behind me, I could hear Abigail's soothing breaths, and she stopped at my side, watching the two women with me. "We've all made mistakes in the past. It's whether or not we grow from them that matters, isn't it?" she asked before taking a sip from her glass, but when I turned towards her, something in the intensity of her eyes made me question if she was merely referring to Ingrid. Or perhaps there was something more. Either way, Abigail's words made my cheeks heat in embarrassment. Had Irma been centring her hearing on us, she would have heard proof of my *almost* accusation. Was anyone bothering with discretion these days?

Eager to change the subject, I cleared my throat and said, "Thank you for throwing this party. It's bittersweet in a way."

"Isn't it?" she replied, sadness resonating in her voice. Her eyes diverted mine, and she bit her lip as we noticed both our partners walking towards us. "I'll miss you very much, just—be careful," she added. "Especially with his kind. And remember, you always have a home here if things go awry."

I furrowed my brows ever so slightly, wondering why she'd say such a thing, but the two men were too close for me to press further. At least Chad's hearing wasn't as enhanced as ours.

"Thanks for all your help with these decorations, Chad. I couldn't have done it on my own," Abigail said, gesturing around the room. She gave him a smile that looked so genuine, though I knew it was forced.

I gave Chad a look of surprise. When had he had time to help?

"It was mostly your hard work, Abigail," he replied.

"I was just filling Chad in on our troubles locating Florence or any of his people," Cristin informed us, sounding more pessimistic than usual. "We thought Downy Lair was a sign he was coming out into the open again, but apparently not."

"We need more spies," I sighed, sounding just as hopeless, as though it were contagious.

"That would require having more people on our side," Cristin came back. "There are too many struggles when it comes to recruiting the other covens."

"Which we'll get through, it's just been difficult," Abigail commented. "They're too afraid right now. Most of the covens nearby are either in hiding or have already joined him. The attack on Downy Lair seemed to be a tipping point."

"Why do you think he hasn't attacked *us*?" I wondered aloud. Was Florence too frightened? He was nearly captured the last time he was here. Chad's green magic had been wrapped around him. How he had escaped, we were still none the wiser, but if he could flee once, surely he wouldn't be afraid to combat us again.

"For all we know, he could've tried already," Chad put forwards. "My royal guards and the wards here might've been enough to scare them away."

"Guards?" I blinked. The wards I knew of, but the guards I didn't. I hadn't seen them. I had been practising transporting every time I came or went from here.

Helping with party decorations, placing guards outside, what else was he doing to care for me that I wasn't aware of?

His eyes seemed to contract at that. "I *did* tell you, didn't I?" he asked as if he were being scolded. "I meant to tell you before I coordinated things with Charity and Leo, but I must've forgotten."

Not wanting him to feel he had done something wrong, I gave him a smile. He was sweet. He did so much for me, and what did I do? Add to his stress by accusing his greatest ally, Lili?

I let out a small laugh to ease the tension in his shoulders. "You've been busy. You're fine," I told him, running my hand along his back. "Anyway, you think Florence may have tried but not been able to get past them?"

"Perhaps," he continued, sounding much less subdued. He let out a deep breath. "The guards stand just within the wards as an extra layer of security. You don't think I'd leave you unprotected while I'm away all the time, do you?" he asked sweetly, and I could feel my smile brighten in response. "But I only have so many guards, and I'm still working on gathering allies, so unless we want to spread ourselves out thin, we've got to come up with a better solution until we build up an army of our own."

"You mean to tell me witches have control of all the magic in the world, yet there isn't a secret trick to destroying vampires?" Abigail asked with a sense of sarcastic humour on her tongue.

"I mean, there's plenty. Stunning spells, jinxes, potions, acidic magic—" Chad started.

"Sunlight, beheading, a stake to the heart—" Cristin continued on.

"—but none of it matters if we can't even find the son of a bitch," Abigail added, sounding defeated.

"And what about us *good* Night Crawlers? How are we going to **KILL** his entire horde without magic? Break their necks one at a time?" Cristin asked, with a bit of rage brimming from his eyes.

The scene of him ending the vampire on the stairs at Downy Lair flashed before me, and sadness swelled in my own eyes at the thought of how war could unravel years and years of sparing people. How many would I **KILL** by the end of this? Who *wouldn't* I **KILL** if they tried to hurt Chad or Abigail or my sister? I shuddered at the thought.

"Are there potions *we* could use to help even the odds?" I asked, gesturing to the rest of the Night Crawlers in the room.

Chad let out a cough. "Magic is… tricky," he started slowly. His hand rubbed the back of his neck as he chose his next words carefully. "It's not something we give away to Night Crawlers, at least not traditionally."

I nodded, understanding. We weren't even technically supposed to use technology, although some covens, such the Chateau de Rouge, used it without permission. And I was caught between the two worlds— tainting their witch magic with my vile vampire blood.

"I'm sure we can come up with something different," I declared with optimism, but the rest of them didn't look as assured.

The whole lot of them scanned the floor as if the answers were there. But then a thought struck me. Something Abigail had mentioned a lifetime ago, back when Florence was just *one*, not an entire army.

"Holy water!" I exclaimed, my volume much too loud for a formal ballroom. Their faces didn't light up as mine had, so I tried again. Turning to Abigail, I urged her to remember. "You know. You said holy water could destroy evil souls, and if Florence isn't evil, I don't know who is."

"But how would we get it?" she asked. "We can't exactly go up to a Catholic priest. They know something's wrong with us. They can sense it. Not only that, but I'm Jewish," she added, exasperated at such an idea.

"She's right," Chad said, unconvinced. "They can sense something with witches too. It's likely going to be the same with anyone who isn't

89

a mortal. And we can't steal holy water. Our magic only works to transport it if it's been given to us willingly."

"Well, then have the priests test it on us," I returned stubbornly. "Tell them to throw the water on us to prove ourselves worthy."

Abigail flinched at the idea. "Then there's the matter of catching Florence," she added timidly, "before he disappears again. We were too slow at Downy Lair. They all vacated the premises before we even arrived."

"That's because we didn't know their plan until they were already there," Cristin said thoughtfully. "We need a way of tracking them as soon as they leave their hideout."

We paused for a moment, internally searching for solutions, when a thought piqued my interest. "The mortals. They use facial recognition software, don't they?" I asked, and Chad nodded. "And you say all technology is truly magic, so can't you do a spell of some sort to search for his face?"

He tilted his head forwards, filled with intrigue, before placing an arm around my waist. "That's brilliant," he commented proudly. "It would take a substantial amount of magic, but perhaps several of us together could do it. Well, as long as we have—" He stopped short and cast me a look as though he had toppled over a fountain of champagne-filled glasses, and any warmth I felt from his compliment diminished as he stumbled over his words.

He needed a strong witch. A powerful sorceress that the stars prophesied. He needed *her*.

I swallowed down my self-wallowing pity and forced a smile before telling him, "Anything to find Florence."

The corners of his mouth lifted into the most unconvincing smile I had ever seen.

Cristin gave Abigail a thoughtful look before she nodded to him. "We'll do it," her husband said, accepting the quest. "We'll get the holy water if you'll be in charge of the facial_recognition task," he cast towards Chad, who nodded in agreement.

"And what will I do?" I teased, wrapping my arm around Chad's side and leaning into him. "Continue to be the brains of this whole operation?"

Chad's chuckle vibrated against me, and he kissed the top of my head. "You have enough on your plate between collecting your sister from your father, figuring out where those children are being kept, and yes, coming up with more brilliant ideas."

I rolled my eyes, unable to help feeling a bit useless on the whole war front, but I supposed he was right. One task at a time.

"Dance with me," I practically demanded, wanting to escape my troubled mind for just a moment longer, and he gladly obliged.

Giving Abigail and Cristin a smile as they held their glasses up to us in farewell, I let go of Chad's waist so I could hold his hand, and he spun me out onto the dancefloor. The music, played by the usual quartet of aged vampires, was slow, passionate, and moving.

"I love you," I told him, my face against his chest as he held me tight.

"I love you too," he whispered into my ear, and my chest filled with a glee only he could produce.

For a moment we just danced, but my anxious mind kept lingering back to the horrible things going on in the world above us. Just as my thoughts were about to trap me, Chad placed a light kiss on my neck, and all my worries seemed to melt away.

"Distract me," I told him.

"I think we passed by a nice supply closet," he commented, his voice highly suggestive. "There's few things we could do in there that might suffice as a distraction."

My brain heavily weighed it as a viable option. I could picture his hands holding my wrists, items falling off the shelves, my lips being unable to contain my cries of passion. Something pleasant occurred in my nether regions before reality crashed back into me. My chest heated as I placed my forehead on his chest, too horrified to glance around or see who had heard.

Chadwick merely laughed at my response. "Don't worry," he whispered into my neck, sending shivers down my spine. "Soon we'll have a whole castle to ourselves—more or less," he added, referring to his humble servants who had already had quite an earful of us, I was certain.

If only he was right. If only we could be together without my infuriating visions meddling with our sex life.

A shadow approached us, and I looked up to see Charity smiling at me. Unsure whether it was because of the conversation Chadwick and I were having or due to something else, my face heated uncomfortably.

"Azalea," she said softly. "Can I borrow you for a moment?"

"Of course," I replied, looking up at Chad before I let go of him.

"But just you," she told me, giving the wizard an apologetic look.

Such mystery to it all. I didn't know whether to be frightened or intrigued.

"All right," I replied, sending Chad one last look of confusion before following Charity across the length of the room to the closed set of French doors.

I turned my head towards her, hoping she'd say more without any prying. To my relief, she complied. "A certain gnome has a bit of a surprise for you." Her joyous grin lit up her face in a way that informed me everything was just fine.

As I turned back to the doors that were now open, I glanced out into the corridor and spotted a curious-looking Fendel. The doors eased shut, and as soon as the gap in between them disappeared, I saw something spectacular. Fendel's skin morphed into a soft texture I had never seen it as before. It was elastic rather than hardened, matte rather than shiny, and his lips curled into a smile right before my very eyes. He waddled towards me in full motions he had never let me witness.

"Sorry, milady, but we still can't trust the witch-boy," he said in a squeaky voice, and I nearly jumped right out of my skin. He wasn't bothered by it, though. He simply stood on the tips of his toes to reach my hand. Pulling me away from Charity's side, he led me into a room I had never entered before: the gnome's quarters.

My shock was far from over, for as I walked in, there weren't just the twenty or so gnomes I had seen frozen around Loxley Lair, but hundreds of them, all happily crammed into the space, all smiling at me brightly. Not only that, but they were all moving—waving, clapping, jumping up and down on their toes as though I was the most interesting being in the room.

"We overheard you talking about how you need spies," one said in a strangely deep voice as he appeared on my right, causing me to jump once more.

"We're tiny—" said another, who was in fact quite small compared to the rest.

"Nimble!"

"And can fit into small places."

They all nodded in unison, and I had to blink a few times to ensure it wasn't a dream.

"How—er—where did you all come from?" I questioned, hardly able to hide my curiosity, my fascination with their tiny faces, pointed hats, and skin that was now much less like porcelain and more like my own. I was amazed by how real they looked, how they were actually letting me see their true selves for the first time.

"You freed us," one said.

"Remember?" asked another.

"The rest of you are all from those witches' front gardens?" I clarified.

"Well, most of us," one with a particularly large belly offered.

"But some of us got picked up along the way," another piped in.

"After you freed us, we knew we had to find you."

"And while we wandered around, other gnomes had heard of you."
"The witch who saved Fendel."
"Yes! From the same witches."
"And we knew it had to be you."
"My," I let out, truly not knowing what else to say.
"Every gnome in the whole world must know about you by now," one squeaked from the back as he craned his neck over the crowd to see me properly.
"And we truly want to be of service."
"We can help."
"We can fight in the war with you."
"Be the spies you need."
"Station ourselves everywhere."
"Until we find the evil man who hurt you."
I blinked, overwhelmed to say the least. I couldn't believe they'd risk their lives for me, someone most of them had just met. "I can't have you going and risking yourselves," I insisted, swallowing down the sadness, the reminder of the pain I felt when Chad's aunt had frozen Fendel. I had thought he was dead. "Fendel could've died because of me, and I will not have any of your deaths on my conscience. I won't allow it."
"But vampires are easier to battle than witches."
"They're quick, but they don't have magic like us and the witches do."
"You freed us. We'd do anything for you."
I fought back the emotion that swelled in my throat. Their sweetness, their bravery, it was all too much as I tottered back and forth between the choices one only has to make during a war. And then, against my better judgement, I nodded, accepting their offer.
"But how will I ever be able to repay you?" I asked them, and they all squeaked out their refusal in unison.
Fendel's smile lit up the room as he looked up at me with hopeful eyes. "You already have," he said, taking a step towards me. "You're the only witch who's ever shown us kindness."
I couldn't keep my legs from jittering beneath me, so I crumbled to the floor, puffs of air trapped under the poofs of my dress, and I let my tears fall freely over my ugly-crying face. But the gnomes didn't turn away from me or freeze up. Instead, they hurried forwards, a few holding out tissues to me as they clambered over the folds of my dress, and they wrapped me up into one big hug.
Then and there I decided that by the end of this war, I was going to free every single gnome out there, regardless of any witches who tried to stand in my way.

Chapter 12: Our

The day after the party, Chad helped me pack, taking way too much time holding up my lingerie and teasing that he was imagining me wearing it... Not wearing it... The undergarments lying on his floor... It took my mind off most of the challenges that typically cluttered it, but he refused to let me forget about one of the things I couldn't solve: touching him in the special way I so yearned to do.

Charity had been in earlier and announced that the French lair had tentatively agreed to fight against Florence with us. She added that I could take all the fine clothing from my wardrobe to Castwell Castle, a celebratory gesture in light of the good news. So I bustled around, going full speed, handing Chad armfuls of clothes. He would disappear and then reappear with empty arms, ready to transport more. When my bedroom was empty of the few items I had collected over the past year, we said one last goodbye to everyone before he transported me off to my new home.

Landing in his bedroom, I nearly tripped over all of my clothes that were strewn about everywhere. Gawking at Chad, I couldn't help but let a small, surprised laugh leave my lips, but all he did was shrug and say, "I swear I was getting to it."

"Well," I said with a heavy breath. "I don't know how all of this is going to fit into your wardrobe anyhow."

He laughed in response before he stalked over to his wardrobe and flicked his wrists. Instantly, the wardrobe began to grow, like a pufferfish filmed in slow motion, until it was nearly three times as large as it had started out. A buzz whizzed past my ear, and I ducked as the articles of clothing went zooming into place, each hanging themselves precisely where they ought to go.

When the floor had been cleared, I turned to face him. My mouth gaped open, and he walked up to me, putting one arm swiftly around my waist. Using his other hand, he tilted my chin up, shutting my mouth.

"*Our* wardrobe," he corrected, and I laughed back at him, still amazed at all the magic he was capable of.

"You couldn't have done your wrist-flicking thing to get all those clothes *out* of my wardrobe?" I quipped, but he nuzzled his head against my neck, tickling it with his warm breath until I gave in. "All right! All right! *Our* wardrobe."

"And this is *our* bedroom," he displayed, waving his hand out to show it off before wrapping his arm back around me and transporting us to the back gardens. "And this is *our* lake," he introduced proudly. The green swirls didn't even get the chance to fully dissipate before our feet landed in the library. "And these are our books…" *Poof!* "Our astronomy tower…" *Poof!* "And our ballroom."

My feet struggled to keep my balance as the green smoke disappeared for good. Apparently, he had decided this was our final destination before he held me in the waltz position and began tracing the formation around the room. I couldn't contain my laughter, and it began spilling out uncontrollably.

Oh how I loved him—loved all we had, every moment, every hope for our future.

"We should go salsa dancing soon," I suggested, though I didn't know if I'd even be able to dance with him that way, that sensually, without shoving him away. "Keep Connor company," I added on.

"I quite agree," he replied happily, and we spent the rest of the day wasting the time away before reality would force its way back to us tomorrow.

༄

The girl sat on her bed, facing away from the door and towards a wall as her small fingers worked diligently to fold a piece of parchment against her bony thigh. Her feet dangled over the edge as she folded the square into triangles and then reopened it to fold it into a smaller square. She kept working until it was a neat little arrangement that she could slip her fingers into.

Her arms tensed as her brother's cry came from the other room. As the cries and heavy footsteps drew nearer, her heart quickened. She hastened to hide her creation under her pillow when a woman barged into the room, her hair a mess as she held the crying toddler. The mother's mouth opened to spew commands, but abruptly closed as her eyes went to the pillow.

Before the girl could distract her or climb onto the pillow to slow the woman down, her mother grabbed it and pulled out the paper fortune teller.

"What is this?" she demanded, ignoring the way the boy screeched in her arms.

"Liz—Lizzie from school showed me how to make it," the girl stuttered.

"Well, maybe Lizzie is a form of the devil too!" she hissed at the child, and the girl cowered deeper into her bed in response.

Without another remark, the woman flopped the crying toddler roughly onto the bed before fleeing the room. The girl scrambled to follow the woman all the way to the fireplace that burned sadly in the other room. As sorrow swept over the girl's features, the flame in the fire turned purple, engorging, and the woman gasped before clawing her fingers into the fire and grasping the smouldering paper she had just thrown into it. It crumpled to ash within her hand, scalding her palm. Slowly her gaze travelled back up to her young daughter, rage filling her eyes.

"You. Little. Witch!" she screamed. She screamed it over and over until I could take no more.

I sat bolt upright, the sound of my own panic filling the room in the form of pounding heartbeats and laboured breaths before realising Chad was sitting on the edge of the bed next to me.

"I'm sorry," he said instantly, worry stricken across his face. "I didn't mean to wake you."

It looked as though he was just getting home. No sleep clouded his eyes, just caution.

I mumbled, "It wasn't you," but he stared at me apprehensively.

"Another dream?" he asked, squinting and trying to focus on me through the veil of darkness his human eyes hadn't yet adjusted to.

As exhaustion slammed back into me like a violent wave, I plopped backwards onto my pillows, letting out a deep sigh. I was tired. Tired of the uncertainty of my dreams. Tired of everything. Pressing my palms against my eyes, I nodded. Why did these dreams always plague me? Why couldn't I be normal like everyone else?

"You know, my aunt Morgan has special dreams too?" he told me softly. "So did my mum. Most of the time nothing bad was going on so their dreams weren't as horrid, or as frequent, as yours," he looked down at his hands before looking back at me. "We'll figure it all out, okay?"

"Okay," I replied. Normal dreams would be quite pleasant when all of this was over.

I smiled over at Chad to reassure him I was all right, but his expression was uneasy. Something was on the tip of his tongue, begging to come out.

"What is it?" I asked, turning to prop my head on my hand so I could look at him better.

His mouth shifted to the side as he bit his cheek, making my heart beat quicker.

"Well, I've been struggling with defining the line between keeping things on a need-to-know basis, so I don't distract you from your tasks, and withholding too much."

"Go on," I pried slowly, waiting to hear more.

His gaze avoided mine, instead following his hand as he began running it up and down my arm. His fingers tingled with magic as he cast a warming charm on me. Light, pleasant, soothing. He continued on, stumbling over his words as if they were too hard to admit. "And with your dreams, and it being the day before you go get your sister—I—"

"Chad," I said, placing my hand on his. "If I can take a weight off your shoulders then let me. What is it?" I tried again.

"There are some things I should tell you before..." He paused, trying to find the words to say. "...before others do," he finished, his fingers fidgeting anxiously together. "Things I should've told you sooner but I was afraid to..."

How could so much fear and anxiety derive from so few words? Why should he be afraid? Should *I* be afraid?

"Tell me before I fully wake so I can pretend this is all a bad dream," I suggested cheerfully, trying to lighten the mood as I leaned in towards him. I desperately wanted to ignore the sinking feeling in my chest.

"There's something important I have to do," he tried, and my heart kept sinking lower and lower.

He was going to leave again. I just knew it. He was going to go on one of his month-long hiatuses—disappear with little to no contact—but I wouldn't have it. I hardly had time with him as it was. He'd have to take me with him, or I'd pack myself in his suitcase and he'd be forced to bring me.

"I'm going with you," I declared, suddenly very awake. It wasn't a question. Sitting up, I gave him an intense stare, not bothering to push away my curls as they draped messily over my shoulder. He leaned back to get a good look at me, my own stubbornness radiating off of me like an intense fire. "I don't care if your aunts turn me into a pumpkin or if What's-Her-Face insists on putting her hands all over you. I'm coming with. I refuse to sit around, useless, waiting to hear back from you to see if your bloody heart's still beating, wondering if you've been coerced into marrying that witch while you're away. I won't do it." And I meant it wholeheartedly. "I don't care who you have to talk to, or convince, or curse for all I care. We're a team. This is *our* problem. *I'm* helping, and *they* can deal with it."

For a moment, everything stood still. My body tensed for the smallest fraction of a second, my stomach pulled somewhere else. My face creased in confusion as I noticed Chadwick's body. He was now laid out next to me instead of sitting on the edge, his arms positioned behind his head. His eyes grew intense with admiration and his lips curled into a warm smile.

"What just happened?" I asked, searching his face for an answer. "Something changed. There was a pull and then I was back."

"I'm *so* sorry," he let out quickly. Surprise coated his face, but when he didn't explain further, I arched my brow. "Your worried expression was just about the most adorable thing I've seen. Too precious to resist, so I gave you a kiss, and apparently, I'm too irresistible."

A bit of humour seeped into my own consciousness as I realised what had happened. The consequences of having a boyfriend who could turn back time within a magic bubble. And I didn't even get to remember the kiss? That was hardly fair.

"How exactly did that work out for you?" I bit my lip, imagining his mouth on mine, wondering how much damage I had done to the interiors of the castle in this alternate timeline.

"Not well at all, unfortunately," he said, fighting against his own smile. "Let's just say, the wall didn't entirely make it."

I sucked in air around me, suddenly hot at the thought of the physical contact. "And how long did the kiss last before my powers royally kicked your arse?" I teased.

"Is that sass?" he asked, feigning interest. "Good thing I needed practice with my time bubble. Who knew you'd grow to get such a big head?"

I took the liberty of smashing my pillow against his head.

"Now tell me these secrets of yours before I blast you into the wall on purpose," I threatened. "Where are we off to and for how long?"

"We're not off to anywhere—"

I glared intensely at him.

"—because that's not the news," he added quickly. "Not because you wouldn't be allowed to come."

I frowned at the lack of information. "Then what is this mysterious news that 'others' might tell me before you do?"

"Well, you know how things were before we met. Before Florence. I was running the pub. I had very little intent or motivation to hurry back to the world I was born into, to really take charge as a prince. There was always the occasional ball or gathering, but I was perfectly content in my time off."

I nodded, urging him to continue.

"Now that Florence has started a war, and I've been forced to accept my duties once more, there's something that is expected of me."

Too many ridiculous things ran through my head as he gave pause, and I willed him to go on before my mind could run even more rampant.

"Well?" I urged. "What is it?"

"My mother was the eldest, you see. Even though she and her sisters are fraternal triplets, she was born first, so she took on the reign of queen when she came of age. And because of the current events taking place, it's expected that I hurry and accept the role as a king."

I blinked at him a few times, not fully comprehending. "So, what exactly will the difference be? Between your princely duties and becoming a king, that is."

He coughed awkwardly, staring up at the ceiling instead of meeting my eyes.

"Just... more," he said quietly.

Chills covered the surface of my skin, and I realised the tasks that might be considered *more*. More time away. More travelling. More decisions. More stability in his personal relationships.

"And tell me," I asked before fear could silence me. "Are kings supposed to take on prophesied queens?"

I heard his saliva claw its way down his throat, and his heart quicken its pace.

"That doesn't matter," he deflected, a sense of helplessness radiating through his voice.

I blinked pointedly, not believing he could say such a thing. "It matters to me," I told him flatly. I knew he was trying to dismiss the question so it wouldn't add to my list of worries, but that's not how my mind worked. I wanted to know—to be prepared for the worst.

The silence screamed in my ears as I watched him lay there, staring at the ceiling, my insides crumbling as he said nothing. Taking a deep breath to summon my inner patience, I opened my mouth to continue, but he cut me off.

"I want you to meet them," he blurted out. "Everyone."

"Them?" I asked sceptically.

"Witches, warlocks, elves, even the mermaids," he went on. "All the Casters. You can convince them you're not evil—show them how wonderful you are."

Hell fucking yes, I can, I coached myself, knowing full well I was an enormous bloody chicken. But I had been around them once at the Valentine's Ball, and I could do it again. March right in there and scream, "I'm not evil," until I was blue in the face. And then when they finally found out what I was, I'd tell them to shove their mythical prophecies right up their—

"You're brilliant," Chad spat out, interrupting my absurd and impotent train of thought. For a moment, his sweetness caught me off guard. "You're brilliant, you're kind, you're powerful, you're passionate, you're beautiful, and you're everything I need. They'll see that in you, and they'll all come round."

Blood swirled up to my cheeks, and I focused my eyes to get a good look at him in the dark. Forcing myself to accept the compliments was challenging. It was my natural reaction to reject them, to refuse to accept them as truth because I didn't feel that way myself. But I choked down the words that crept up my throat and settled on a more positive response.

"I love you, Chadwick." Yet it only succeeded in making him wince. "What?" I asked.

"You use 'Chadwick' when you're cross with me. Are we all right?"

I rolled my eyes, wondering if he could see it in the dark room or if my dramatic efforts were futile. "I'm not cross. Chadwick just seems posher, and you'll have to keep up appearances, what with you getting promoted and all," I teased.

He smiled, leaning into me and finally trailing his eyes to mine. "I love you too, Azalea, and no one will convince me otherwise. We've come a long way since any trickery with love potions."

Horrid memories of Florence took over, and I pushed them away, instead, thinking of Chad's lips once more.

"You still haven't given a fair explanation for why I had to miss out on the kiss in this timeline."

He shrugged. "Honestly, I think I've been practising my timing bubbles too often. It was a natural reaction," he said earnestly. His eyes ran along the walls, smooth and absent of cracks. "It served as pretty good damage control though. Quite efficient."

Giving me a quick peck on the forehead, he got out of bed and straightened out his clothes, ones he had been wearing all day as he worked hard, planning for the Caster's next steps. Typically, we'd use this time for my training, but after that dream and such intense news, I was hardly up for it. I fought back the urge to tell him to come back to bed, and as I started tossing my hair in a high pony, grappling with the idea of training, a question dawned on me.

"When will it be official? You becoming a king," I clarified. I was so overwhelmed by the title that I couldn't quite wrap my head around how I felt about all of it.

The smile he gave didn't meet his eyes. It was nervous, unspoken fear.

"The coronation will be in a month," he announced, and I dropped my hair, causing it to fall back down in a messy array on my shoulders.

"You really don't give a girl time to prepare, do you?"

"Procrastination is something I'll work on," he said with a warm smile. "At least you have less time to have your knickers in a twist over it."

"Less time to plot your **MURDER** for being so cheeky," I quipped, resuming the work on my hair. "Any update on the facial recognition strategy?" I asked eagerly, hoping there would be good news, but he merely shrugged.

"Neither good nor bad, I'd say," was his response. "We have the scans. They're fully operational, but Florence hasn't triggered them yet. Not too surprising though. He's had decades to practice avoiding witch magic, and as daft as I'd like to think he is, he seems to always have the upper hand."

"But hypothetically, if he were to slip up, we'd be alerted right away, wouldn't we?"

He nodded, running his fingers through his hair and causing it to stick up in all directions. Exactly what I needed at the moment to keep my worried heart out of the deepest depths. It was the perfect combination of silly and sexy. "Yes, we'd know," Chad confirmed. "You should take a look though," he suggested, sounding slightly more upbeat. "I've set up a station in the library if you wouldn't mind working your own talents on it."

I let out a harsh laugh. The pull I felt from Florence was the furthest thing from a "talent" there had ever been, but I nodded nonetheless. "Of course. I'll have a look."

"Have Abigail and Cristin had any luck with the holy water?" he asked.

"Not since I spoke to them last," I said with a sigh.

Stretching out a bit, I glanced over to the clock that sat on the bedside table and resolved it wasn't too early to end my slumber, not that it was likely I'd be getting more sleep anyhow. The sun had just set, and if I wanted to avoid keeping Chad up into the late hours, we'd have to start our training soon. I sat up and swung my feet over to the floor.

"You should take the day off from your training. Just relax a bit before you go," he proposed.

"At this point I feel like overthinking the whole scenario with my father and sister will make matters worse than if I were to just... wing it. You know?"

"Are you sure?" he asked, creasing his brow, and I nodded before fully clambering out of bed. "Such a hard worker," he told me admiringly, and I laughed, knowing he worked harder than anyone. Not to mention the immense duty that hung heavily over him like a storm cloud.

"Whatever you say, my king," I quipped, still unable to fully come to grips with it all, but he sent a slick stream of magic that gave me a quick zap on my bum before joining me to get into our training garments.

We trained for nearly an hour before exhaustion overtook Chad. I gave him a quick kiss goodnight before he retired to our bed, then I trained a bit more on my own. After a good, long shower I retreated to the library to do my studies. A vision from Chad's aunt clouded my sight as it often did, and I closed my eyes tight, willing it away.

Please not tonight, I begged no one in particular. I couldn't stand to watch myself dig my teeth into Chad right now, and to my surprise, the vision silenced itself.

After a few hours of studying spells and the history of witches, and too long staring at the facial recognition screens in the library, I decided to practise my transporting from room to room to wear myself out a bit. I only made it to three chambers before my body decided it had enough. I crawled into bed next to Chad, cursing our opposite schedules, the fact it was nearly his turn to wake, and that he'd be gone when I awoke.

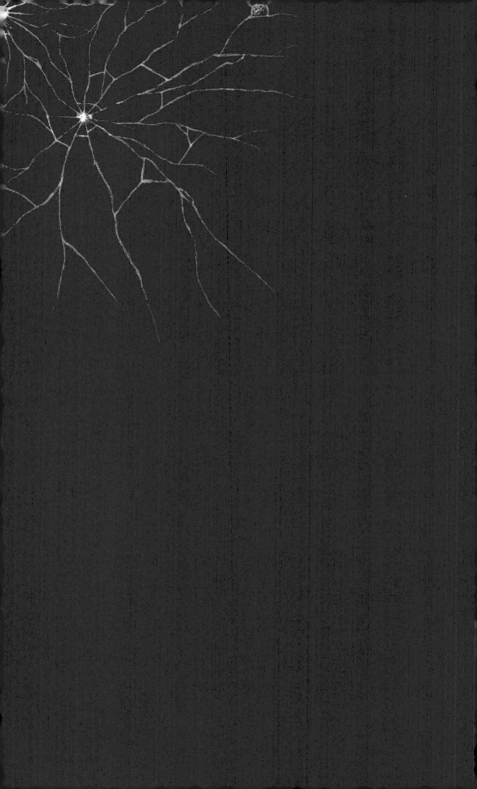

Chapter 13: Save Your Sister

When I awoke from another nightmare of the children, Chad's side of the bed lay empty and cold. My hesitant body was pulled down, further into the bed, as though the earth's gravity weighed more than usual.

It was 30 September. The day I'd get my sister. And preparing for the day took a lifetime.

I was staring into the mirror, wondering how in the hell my ruined mind was going to get me through this, when there was the faintest of shimmers in the reflection, and Chad's eyes replaced mine in the mirror.

With the most endearing look, he leaned forwards, poking his head through the portal, and whispered, "You've got this," before placing the sweetest kiss on my lips.

I memorised the feeling, the softness of his lips, and instantly regretted not keeping them against mine longer. When I opened my eyes, he was completely immersed on the other side of the mirror, grinning wildly at me. Then he turned to look at something over his shoulder and looked back at me. With an encouraging wink and a wave goodbye, another shimmer turned his reflection back to mine.

I am strong, I told myself with the added strength Chad had gifted me. I could handle my father on my own. And even though the man I loved couldn't be at my side, he was with me in spirit. Besides, there was a young woman I was dying to get to know once more, and she was waiting for me.

With one last glimpse in the mirror, I whirled myself off to a special place, hidden amongst magical flowers of blue-violets and pinks.

When I arrived, already crouched down in the precious hideaway of my childhood, I forced my stubborn arms and legs to crawl out to the back garden. I yearned to cower there, to wait for my sister to come out so there was no risk of meeting my father, but I could hear hurried voices from within the end-terrace house.

"Why would you even say that?" I heard Hydrangea ask, and my heart went into panic mode. "Of course I want to leave. I hate it here," she stressed to our father, whose furious breaths rasped in my ears.

I stood up and brushed off the skirts of my dress. A dreadful decision to wear a dress. How could I expect to crawl across grass and deal with a madman in a bloody dress? How could things already be going so horribly?

"This is your home!" our father roared back, and every nightmare I had ever had of his treachery seemed to be a lead weight, slowing me down as I neared the back door.

"This was never a home," she replied solemnly. "Not to me, not to Azalea, not to mum."

It was as if his rage ignited from her words, and the power behind his hatred shook me. My feet were glued to the pavement. My whole body immobilised from memories that should have stayed forgotten but were unleashed in my sleep. A monster. A torturer. A nightmare.

Before my trembling feet could agree to bring me nearer, before my father could intervene, Hydrangea slammed through the door. Her rattled breath caught as she took sight of me, and she ran to me, her heavy trunk clattering to the ground as she wrapped her arms around me in a warm embrace.

The impact caught me off guard, and I stumbled back a step before returning the embrace. For a moment, we were small girls again. Alone. Safe. Happy. But the moment was short lived. The man who had clawed his way back into my consciousness flung open the door after her. As his deep brown eyes took me in, I heard his cold heart skip a beat, and the blood drained from his face. I was a ghost—a bad memory to him.

His mouth dangled open stupidly as he gawked at me, taking in my presence and staggering slightly until he leaned against the doorway to help prop himself up. The smell of his boiling blood mixed with a heavy dose of alcohol drifted over to me, and as if unable to form a concrete thought, only a single word slipped from his cracked lips. "You."

My disturbed mind that had always teetered between fight, flight, and freeze decided it had been too long since I had been given the opportunity to stand my ground.

"That's no way to treat your long-lost daughter, now is it?" The words seemed to flow out of me automatically, vibrating with anger as I stared back at him.

His face was overgrown with a matted beard, and his eyes blinked away the confusion, mostly caused by the lagers he had no doubt downed earlier that night.

"Ha," he clicked, a crooked smile extending on his face, his arms folding as his eyes travelled the length of me. I couldn't fight off the cringe it produced. "Should've known you were in charge of her sudden interest to leave," he sneered.

"I've always wanted to leave," Hydie insisted, holding on tightly to my torso. She was roughly the same height as me, much taller than the tiny girl I had tried to protect in my memories, but just as loving and strong-willed as I knew her to be.

"And little Miss **MURDER** is going to take care of you now, I suppose?" He phrased it as though it were the utmost ridiculous sort of joke. His eyes shifted dangerously to mine, and my heart was suddenly a lump in my throat. "Well, don't leave on my account," he huffed dramatically, losing his footing as he spoke. His face turned to satisfaction as he caught his balance, but he bent over slightly, turning his stance into a ridiculous bow that urged us like a hunched-over servant to come forwards. "Come in," he insisted, a false kindness in his throat. "I'm sure there's *loads* to catch up on."

The back door screeched, and he disappeared into the house, the sound of his clumsy steps clattering against the floor. I stared at the door as it swung shut—a bear trap ready to spring if he successfully lured us inside.

Hydie and I exchanged hesitant looks before her eyes wandered neither directly at me nor away, just around my frozen form.

"You need closure, don't you?" she asked me, furrowing her brows as though trying to understand precisely how I felt.

I didn't need closure, I needed to get her out, but a vindictive claw ripped at my aching heart, dying to know the things my sister couldn't tell me, the *why* behind all the pain he had brought me, and I found my feet moving towards the door and stepping over the threshold, as if lured by a piper's song. The decision was no longer mine.

Hydie closed the door behind us as we crept in. The corridor was thin and dim. Papers crunched and bottles clanked as our steps couldn't help but collide with the littered mess. A smell of putrid mould and amber liquid that would've knocked any mortal off their feet choked my lungs. The blaring sound and glow from the telly led me to the man I was ashamed to call my father.

He sat in a large chair, aged yellow stuffing protruding out of blood-red leather. The chair creaked under the weight of him. As he turned to face me, he folded a leg casually over the other, as if he were the most relaxed he'd been in years. When his lips parted, my arms tensed, aching to cover my ears, to run, to hide as if the little girl I used to be was still inside, but I stood my ground. I was stronger than him. Faster. Better in every way. No fear of him should ever conquer me again.

"So…" he drawled, his tongue slipping lazily over the word. "What brings you back here, after all this time?"

I fought the urge to yell, to scream how much I despised him, how much he had taken from me even without remembering half of it. But bitterly, I swallowed it all down. It wouldn't change him. It wouldn't make him care.

"I'm here to get my sister, and I pray I'll never have to look into your eyes again," I declared, but his answering laugh made my body cringe in displeasure. How could he find humour? How could he enjoy this?

"Well, I'm afraid to say she's not going with you, love," he stated in the most cunning of ways. "In fact, I will not let any of your sadistic sins rub off on her, you witch." The word "witch" flew off his tongue with so much disgust, it sent a twinge of pain to my heart.

"And you think you're going to stop me?" I asked, fire burning brightly inside of me, and it succeeded in pissing him off even further.

He looked at me with the same fire that now burned through him before spitting out, "You **MURDERED** your own mother. Why would I let you take the only daughter I've ever cared about? Why?" he screamed at me. "So you can **MURDER** her too?"

Everything in me shook. I wanted to deny it, to tell him he was wrong, but the void in my memory screamed at me.

I don't know! I don't know! Panicked thoughts slammed into me just as rough as his words, but as tears started buckling, threatening to fall, to accept his words as truth, Hydie called out to him, defending me when I hardly knew whether or not I deserved it.

"She did not **MURDER** her," she hissed at him. Each word rang out in fury. "You did. You **KILLED** mum and to this day you can't admit it to yourself."

"Shut the fuck up," he demanded, but she didn't hesitate to respond.

"Yes, you did!" she screamed and then her eyes flew back to me. My heart raced in confusion, yearning to trust her, to believe she had seen the truth for herself, not just assumed or invented the story in her head. But she told me, "Don't listen to him, Azalea. You know the truth. I know you've forgotten but the truth is still in you. Trust yourself."

I gulped down the guilt, the doubt I felt, and fell into her dark brown eyes. I could do this. I could do this for her.

"Let's go," I decided, and as I went to grab her hand, a dark red smoke crept towards us. The hair on the back of my neck stood on end as I turned around, withdrawing my hand from hers. An eerie feeling settled in. Familiar. Dark. Haunting. I knew what it was as soon as I saw it.

The red, shimmering cloud swirled around my father, his hair blowing in the winds it created, but his heart didn't fluctuate from the power. It fluttered in fear.

"Stop!" he yelled as that fear flashed across his eyes. Anger swiftly flooded in to replace it, and he glowered at me. "Stop it right now."

But I knew this feeling. I had felt this too many times in my life. Too many dreams of red that haunted me to my core, but it wasn't just from a nightmare. The red was from him.

"It's you," I let out, slowly taking in the truth. "Our mum wasn't the witch. You are."

His eyes glazed over, and he stumbled back half a step before shaking the drunken confusion from his head.

"You're the devil with all your lies you wicked girl." But there was a glint of a different kind of fear in his eyes. One that hinted he had buried this truth down, yet it was clawing its way up to the surface. Only, how could he deny it when it was so plainly in front of him?

Is he doing it? Hydie's voice sounded through my head, and I jerked my neck to stare at her unmoving lips.

H—how? I started without letting the question come out of my mouth, but her thoughts were hurried.

Is he doing it, Azalea? Can you see the red? She asked, her urgency ringing through my head. *Let's go before he traps us.*

But it didn't make sense. How could she not see it? How could *they* not see it?

"Stop!" my father yelled. Sparks of electricity darted out of his hands, and before I could cast myself out of my own confusion, his magic thrust her into the corner.

There was no air in my lungs as I looked at him and then back to Hydie as she slowly pulled herself back up, groaning in pain. In pain, but okay.

Spit rained out of his mouth with every syllable. "Stop that bloody thing you do," he demanded, his hands gripped onto his hair as though he was going mad. "Stop doing that thing in your fucking heads!"

Only, he wasn't *going* mad. He *was* mad. His red storm was brewing, twisting around him and growing into something terrifying, but I was ready to defend us against him. To stand up to his magic.

I could use it.

I could use my magic against him, and no one was there to stop me. Not my mum or my own trained suppression of my powers in attempts to keep him satisfied.

"You're a wizard," I told him stubbornly, prepared to act, prepared to knock the wind clear out of him if I had to. "You have magic and you passed it on to me, but you're too much of a drunken coward to see it."

He growled as though my words were burning him, and his hands wandered down from his hair to cover his ears. He decided, "I should've **KILLED** you when I had the chance." His eyes were a pool of rage, and a throbbing vein popped aggressively from his temple as beads of sweat rolled down his face. "But I will not make that mistake again."

He moved so fast. If I were still mortal, I wouldn't have been able to stop him. His hands stretched out in front of him, ready to grip my neck, ready to crush it until I choked on my own blood, but what came from his hands was even more terrifying.

A blast of red electricity shot towards me—a speed so quick that only my eyes could see, only vampire reflexes could react to, and only my fear could produce enough of my magic to fight back. My arms were a blur as they pushed out in front of me, and with the one spell I had failed at over and over again in my trainings with Chad, I thrust my father's red power back towards him. But instead of feeling any satisfaction from accurately performing the spell, I felt a wave of his blood splash onto me, and when I opened my eyes, there was hardly anything but the taste of his blood on my tongue to identify him by.

Chapter 14: His Rightful Place

Warm and wet, the perfect mixture of savoury, sweet, salty.
Yet the only thing I could think of was that I had just
KILLED him. It was my father's blood on my tongue.

Shivers racked my body. My hands slowly descended, no hope of
controlling their violent shakes. I couldn't stand to look at them. What
they had done. What *I* had done.

Teeth chattered. A soft *drip, drip* as the remnants of my father fell
to the ground. Hearts pounded, but now there were only two of them left
to fill my ears.

My eyes scanned the floor, finding fragments of flesh, unidentifiable
until I found a hand convulsing in a puddle of crimson.

No. No, no, no, no, no, no. "No!" I screamed, and even the sound of
my own voice sent shivers down my spine.

A faint whimper sparked more fright within me, and I jumped as my
eyes flew over to Hydrangea. She blinked through the liquid that coated
her lashes, blocking part of her view but not concealing what had
happened. I couldn't feel my own body as I watched her. Helpless.
Traumatised. Shattered. And it was entirely my fault.

"I—I didn't mean to!" I stuttered out at a decibel I couldn't lower.
"That's not what I wanted! I—I want to undo it!"

Before I could stop, I bent over, and vomit splashed out, right into
the mix of everything.

"It's—it's—all right," she stammered out. "It wasn't your fault—"
But it was. It *was* my fault.

I couldn't even wipe my mouth, or bother to rid the taste from my tongue, blood and vomit alike. I couldn't handle it. I couldn't breathe, I couldn't scream, I couldn't do any of it. I had to fix it.

"I can change this. I'll go back," I let out.

But before Hydie could answer, before my brain could catch up to the meaning of my own words, purple magic flowed out of my hands.

And everything moved backwards.

A reverse of movements, both small and large followed. My words slammed back into me. The bile flew up into my mouth and back down to my stomach. Hydie's forced reassurance of things that would have never been all right. The shakes, the drips of blood floating away from her eyes. The cries of *no, no, no*, the twitching hand, and then all of the blood flew off of me and into the air. Twirling around, colliding with all the bits and pieces of flesh until they formed the solid, heated figure of the man who was about to cast a spell to **MURDER** his very own daughter.

The rage was back in his eyes, the pure hatred he felt for me was back, but a breath full of a sad relief left my chest, and for just a second, I closed my eyes to feel the moment—to take everything in. Time slowed as the air around his arms whooshed from his sudden movement. The thud of his next step took an eternity to follow the first, but when I opened my eyes, this time I was ready.

I slid onto the floor, my foot stretched out in front of me before colliding with his shin. A crunch of his bones met my ear just as his stream of red magic shot out from above me. His scream filled the room as he flew into the air, his arms waving around from the shock of it all. I ducked my head down to avoid his flailing body as he tumbled towards the floor. In a blink of anyone's eyes but mine, I was back to my feet, casting a trail of purple magic into the air in circles before roping it around his entire body, just in time to bind his hands and stop him from breaking his own fall. Blood and spit sprayed out as his cheek hit the hard wooden floor, and I pulled the rope taught to ensure he'd have no chance of escape.

"You little bitch!" he called out, spit still streaming out between his clenched teeth as his beady eyes darted around, eager to find me. Brown eyes he had once given me. Brown eyes I no longer had.

Being the generous soul I was, I circled around him until my feet were level with his face. I crouched down, just as eager to look into those eyes.

"Trust me," I told him sternly. "This is *much* better than the alternative."

Hydrangea's body shook as she stood in the corner, but the small vibrations were nothing compared to how her body had shaken moments before. What they could have been if I had deflected his spell towards him. Spell or not, he had meant to end me. To **KILL** me. Instead, he'd endure a long life, and I hoped to God he'd learn to feel regret for what he had done. And with that, I knew exactly where to put him.

"There's a place for people like you," I told him as I examined every part of him. "Your rightful place." How could he hold such hatred, such evil feelings towards his own flesh and blood? "You once told me I'd go to Hell," I continued, the memory of his voice echoing through my mind. He somehow didn't know what he was. He was too drunk, too terrified to accept that he was the exact thing he hated me for. "But it's really you who will rot there. And not because of what you are. No. But because of what you've done."

"I am not one of you!" he yelled out, the vile stench of his breath staining the floor, but I no longer let it bother me.

"You are," I told him simply. "And believe me, it takes one to know one, but until Hell swallows you up whole, I know where to keep you."

I straightened back up and met Hydie's eyes as they scanned over me. She knew something had happened, something different than it may appear, but the slight lines that were marked between her brows revealed she didn't know quite what it was that had happened.

"There's a prison," I told her. "One owned by the people I've been living with, and the warden knows all about our kind. He won't be able to escape," I said, hoping the information would give her comfort.

When she gave an understanding nod, my shoulders, which had been so tense, fell in relief.

"That'll be perfect for him, Azalea," she confirmed. Then her eyes lit up with a smile that inspired hope.

A wave of reality washed over me, ridding me of the adrenaline that had coursed through me only a moment ago, and a harsh exhaustion nestled itself in its place. But I didn't have time to feel the loss of energy, or hope, or anything in between. I had a task—to put my father where he deserved.

I crept over to Hydie, ignoring my father's struggling body, and took her hand. "I'll be right back for you," I assured her.

She nodded, much too brave and too innocent for the horrors she had just seen in another life, another timeline. With a gentle squeeze, I released her hand and then stalked back over to our father. His mouth parted to spew hatred, but my emotions allowed a spell to clash into his head, knocking him out cold. With ease, I lifted his warm body from the ground and gave my sister a firm nod before violet swirls entangled around my father and me. A moment later, my feet met the jagged pebbles that paved a trail up to the heavy iron gates of the prison.

115

It was only a few precious minutes before Vincent found me. His arched brow invited an explanation.

"This one's blood is off limits," I insisted, but then a flutter of my stomach made me pause. "At least for now," I added.

The warden gave a firm nod before drawing closer to retrieve the unconscious body. Lifting my father into his arms as though he were as light as a pillow, he asked, "Did he deserve whatever it is you did to him?"

I nodded, a smile almost breaching my lips, but cold, cruel memories pushed it back. "Wholeheartedly," I responded, and I let out a breath. "He's a wizard, so he'll need to be subdued. Often." Then with another nod in farewell, the purple magic swallowed me up again, and I was too distracted to care what Vincent thought of me, of my magic, of any of it.

Stumbling back into my childhood house, the thought of how brown the floors looked without all the blood crossed my mind. But as Hydie's eyes took me in once more, white lights clouded my vision. My consciousness had overstayed its welcome, it would seem, and as white turned to dark, I watched as my sister's arm flew out towards me. Yet before her skin could meet mine, I was gone.

Jade Austin

Chapter 15: The Photograph

A warmth overtook me as a voice filled my ears, yet it was so far away. I reached out through a silky green haze before my yearning hand grasped onto a shirt, and my eyes fluttered open. Chad and my sister stared down at me with worry stricken upon their faces. Only when they saw me staring back at them did both their faces split into smiles.

"You're up," Hydie breathed out, relief radiating in her voice.

Chad's hand found its way along my forehead and my hair before he kissed my brow. "I'm glad you're awake."

I frowned at the two of them as I fought against my exhaustion to sit up. I was laid out on the sofa of my father's house, his presence still lingering unwelcomed. Trash was strewn across every surface except for the one I laid on. Hydie and Chad knelt on the grimy floor beside me.

Propping myself onto my elbows, I ignored the looks of caution they cast at me, urging me with their eyes to move slowly so I wouldn't faint again. But I had more pressing matters to address. I wanted information.

"What—what are you doing here?" I asked Chad.

I watched as he rubbed some of his own exhaustion off his face, and he stretched back a bit, readying himself to explain what in the bloody hell happened to me.

"Well, I hadn't heard back from you, and I grew worried. I mean, I know you said you could handle things on your own, and clearly you can," he added, gesturing to the space around to signify the lack of father figures in the room, "but I was able to rush through a few things and came here to check on you. Hydie, here, was just catching me up on everything."

Hydie beamed back at him before turning her head towards me. *Good pickings sis,* she messaged through the strange connection we apparently shared. *He seems very nice. His aura is a lively orange. Not to mention, he's quite handsome.*

I blinked at her a few times, unable to answer, unable to decipher whether or not this was some bizarre dream or a reality where my sister was complimenting me on my choice of boyfriend via messages in my head. The dream theory seemed the more viable option.

"And does anyone want to catch me up on what's happened?" I asked, referring back to what Chad had said aloud. "Why am I laying here? How long have I been out? And why can I hear your voice in my head?"

Hydie shrugged at the last question. "I dunno. That's just how we've always communicated with one another. Mum thinks it's why it took me forever to actually talk when I was younger."

Mum, I repeated in my head. I furrowed my brows once more, not an ounce less confused.

"You two are telepathic?" Chad asked, almost mirroring my own surprise at the news. His lips twitched to the side as though it all made sense to him. "Explains how you heard my aunt Morgan back at their castle."

My lips parted as I stared at him in utter bewilderment before I decided on rolling my eyes at him. Of course it made sense to him and not me. It was just my own brain we were referring to.

Seeing the frustration on my face, Chad jumped in to explain. "You overworked yourself. Hydie said you transported your father somewhere and almost immediately returned. No wonder you fainted. You can't go transporting when your mind is in whatever fragile state your vile father put it in."

I let out a deep breath as the whole scenario came back to me. "If only that were the half of it," I let out before diving into an explanation of what had happened. My father's magic, exploding him into a million pieces, and then somehow reversing it all and taking him to the prison. By the time I was done, I felt more drained than I had before. Chad and Hydie, on the other hand, seemed to have a worldful of energy as they spewed out questions left and right, their faces slowly morphing from confusion to amazement and back again.

"Your dad's the one you got your powers from?" Chad asked. "I had always assumed it was your mum."

"Same," I replied, but Hydie shook her head.

"No, it's always been him," she told us. "He can't see his own magic. It only ever manifests when he loses control of his emotions, and that always happens when he's too sloshed to realise or remember. What I don't understand is how I don't remember him dying."

"Well, you can't have," I replied, truly not understanding it myself. I turned to Chad. "I reversed it all. Undid it like you un-spilled my drink at dinner with your time bubble."

"That spell is really advanced," he told me. By now, I was sitting up properly, staring back at him. "It's really tricky to create a small bubble, let alone one as large as a whole room, which it must've been if Hydie doesn't remember any of it."

"And good thing you don't," I told my sister, trying to manage my own expression at the memory.

"Only really powerful sorceresses can reverse time by more than a few seconds," Chad said, his lips splitting into a grin, and I gave a glare to ward it off. Now was *not* the time for him to hint that perhaps I was the prophesied witch he was destined to marry.

"And our mother," I started, turning back to Hydie. "Are you sure I didn't—" I hesitated. I didn't want to know, yet I did, all at once. I swallowed, braving the words. "Are you certain I didn't **KILL** her?"

I held my breath as Hydie glanced down, her curls falling into her face as mine always did, before she looked back up at me and nodded. "I'm sure," she confirmed. "I remember it all too well. It was him. He was furious with her. It was one of the only times she had ever defended you and your magic, and he completely lost control. Sent a blast right at her that couldn't be undone. That's the only time I've ever seen sadness in his eyes. It only lasted a second before he rounded on you. He grabbed you by the hair and dragged you up to the bath. He began drowning you, and shoved your nose into the bottom. You were bleeding, but then there was this song and he—he stopped."

I couldn't blink, let alone breathe, as her story came to a close. That moment. That memory. That dream.

Chad's hand caressed my cheek, and I closed my eyes, immersing myself in his warmth. This was all too much. "Let's take her home," he whispered, and I nodded, lulled by his voice before my eyes widened with another horror I had managed to forget for just a moment.

I turned to my sister, fear leaking in once more. "And you—" I began. "You're truly okay with what I am? Both parts?"

Staring into her eyes, I tried to take in everything about her. Her small movements, any thoughts she might try to throw my way, but she placed a light hand on my leg and smiled. "I'd follow you wherever you went, Azalea. You're my sister."

I gave her a small smile in return. "But a vampire…" I said, urging her to take in the gravity of it all.

"I mean, of course it was a shock, but honestly it makes more sense. The whole memory thing, you being away for so long, your eyes… I'm just happy you're in a place where you can take me in." She beamed at the both of us.

Chad smiled back at her. "It's our pleasure. I'm sorry I can't stay long. Now that I know you two are safe, I have to get back to finish some business, but our friend Connor is there, and he's eager to meet you, Hydie," Chad said before helping me up to my feet.

A bit of green clouded my vision as I stood up too fast. I needed a nap. Another one.

Once the dizziness disappeared, I studied my much-too-brave sister out of the corner of my eye before testing out the waters a bit further. "And Connor's a werewolf," I added, trying to see if she'd flinch. She merely snorted.

"We always used to talk about that sort of thing, remember?" she said, but of course I didn't. "You'd read these books about magical creatures when we were little to try and figure out what was happening to us—to figure out what we were. And you'd read about all these other creatures and we'd wonder if they existed like we did." She shrugged at me, an innocent spark behind her eyes. "Now we know."

"And you're not afraid I'm going to bite you?" I asked, knowing I had explained my diet in the letter, how I hadn't ever **KILLED** anyone. At least not until tonight.

"Azalea," she began, looking at me as though I were slightly ridiculous. "You do realise you were a vegetarian before that man turned you, don't you? Of course you turned out to be the type of vampire you are. You wouldn't even harm an animal when you were normal."

Well that was news to me.

Hydie went to retrieve her trunk. Once she returned, Chad offered an arm out to her. Then he gripped my hand tightly and gave an encouraging nod.

"Ever transported before?" he asked her.

"No, but now that I've seen Azalea do it, I can hardly wait to try."

And with that, his green magic swirled around us and carried us to the front steps of Castwell Castle.

When Hydie took in the sight, she gasped.

A castle? She asked, sounding quite impressed. *You didn't tell me your bloody wizard boyfriend was rich too.*

I gave a small wince. *Did I happen to mention he's a prince?* I asked.

Her eyes widened even more, and I looked up at Chad. A small gleam sat in his eye as though he knew we were conversing without him, and I smiled, glad to be away from that house, away from my father, and away from the nightmare that almost was. As Chad took Hydie's trunk and led us up the steps to show off our home, I tried to bury all the horrors of the night and cast them far, far away.

The doors to the entrance hall flew open for us, and I watched as Hydie completely lit up. Her eyes danced across the hall before they landed back on mine, and I gave her a smile.

"I'm so glad you're here," I told her, and she nodded happily.

"Me too," she replied, taking my hand in hers and giving it a squeeze.

"And me!" Connor chimed in, sounding much too chipper as he slid into the room. His eyes seemed to glow as he took in Hydie, and he instantly pranced over to her, grabbed her hand away from mine, and kissed the back of it. I fought the urge to growl at him.

"You are beautiful," he said smoothly, staring into the eyes of my eighteen-year-old sister. "You know, I passed your sister up because I had a dream her better half would soon appear, and here you are."

I let out some horrendous sound that was a cross between a laugh and a scoff before linking arms with my sister and taking her trunk from Chad. "Perhaps we could save these lovely formalities for a different time," I decided. "It's quite late and we've been through an ordeal tonight. Besides, she's not used to our odd sleeping schedule. How about I show you to your room?" I asked her before sending Connor a scathing look that I hoped would send his tail between his legs. "*Away* from the mangy mutt who's drooling all over you," I added.

Chad stifled a laugh, but his face immediately dropped into a stern expression towards Connor as he saw the fire behind my eyes.

Pursing my lips at the two wankers, I began escorting my little sister up the grand staircase. She willingly followed, and it was no wonder. A grandfather clock on the first landing read three in the morning. I had been out for quite some time.

"Don't be jealous, Azalea," Connor shouted after me. "You had your chance!"

I took the liberty of flashing him a rude gesture before we rounded a corner. Hydie merely laughed as we wound our way up the stairs and to her new bedroom.

Such a haughty American, she told me silently, and I rolled my eyes again.

Tell me about it, I agreed without hesitation. I smirked at how natural it felt to talk to her.

03

As I left Hydie alone to get some rest, I had half the mind to lock Connor out of her room in case he had the bright idea of going in to talk to her. But as I perked my ears to hear if Chad had gone, I heard Connor in one of the drawing rooms watching the telly. All his flirting aside, his presence gave me an odd sense of security.

Hydie's room wasn't far from mine, another thing that eased my mind, knowing she was close. My room was empty when I got there, but there was a note laid neatly on my pillow, waiting for me.

She's amazing, and I'm so glad you were able to bring her here. Get some rest. I love you and I'll see you as soon as I can.

-Chadwick

When I woke, however, it was to an empty bed. I let the sounds from all over the castle rush into my ears, but Chad's soft, soothing breaths weren't there. Letting out a disappointed breath of my own, I went down the corridor to check on Hydie. Her light footsteps sounded from behind the door. They travelled back and forth, and the sound of drawers opening and closing told me she had begun to make herself at home.

As soon as I knocked, her sweet voice called for me to enter. When I walked in, she gave me one of her bright smiles.

"Sorry I slept so long," I commented, briefly looking over to the clock on her bedside table. It was already night again. A bit of guilt swept through me as I realised she'd be yet another human I'd be forcing to adapt to my sleep schedule. "Did you sleep well?" I asked, and she nodded.

"The best I've slept in quite some time," she reassured me cheerfully. "This place is amazing, Azalea."

"I can't wait to give you the grand tour," I said, giving her a smile.

I watched as her delicate fingers folded the shirt in her hands, the way she bounced around as though a weight had been lifted off her shoulders. It was so nice to see the joy sparkle in her eyes. Hopefully, it'd be something I saw in her more often.

"I can't either," she decided, placing the shirt into the drawer before closing it and turning back to me. Her shoulders lifted excitedly. "Let's go now," she said. "I can finish unpacking later."

I nodded back at her, unable to wipe the smile from my face at the thought of finally having my sister.

We made our way through most of the castle, but not even I had ventured into every room. Hydrangea reminded me of myself as she took in the library, the maze, the stables. The only difference was the way she lit up when I showed her one of the kitchens. It hadn't occurred to me she'd be hungry, but Poppy and the other fairies delighted in feeding her to her heart's content.

When she'd had enough food and magical excitement, we strolled back to her room and plopped down on the bed, laying down to soak everything in.

She was here. She was safe. She was loved. And not even rewatching that treacherous man's death could take me off the cloud I floated on.

"You should stay while I finish unpacking," she insisted as she sat back up and hopped off her bed. "Have I told you how much I missed you?" she asked.

I laughed, staring up at the ceiling. "Well, my heart missed you so much it wouldn't let my brain forget you. And thank heavens it didn't," I added, emotions welling in my throat.

She smiled as she took another shirt from her trunk before shaking out the wrinkles and folding it neatly. I turned onto my side to look at the few belongings she had. I wanted to get a better sense of who she was, what she was like, but my eyes fell almost instantly upon a framed photo she had set next to her bed. As I stared at it, the muscles in my body froze, and the world around me seemed to crack right down the middle.

Forcing my chilled body to sit up, I took the frame into my hands. I couldn't tear my eyes from it as my mind raced to comprehend the sight. There was a woman holding onto the younger versions of Hydie and me, but her face—

"Who's this woman?" I asked timidly, bumps prickling my skin. "The woman in this photograph."

Hydie's busy body slowed to a stop, and the breath she let out was filled with the utmost sadness, confusion, and pity. "That's our mum," she said softly, trying to ease the pain of my lost memory.

But even as I shook my head at her, I couldn't blink. The woman's eyes, her cheeks, her smile, her everything—it was all wrong.

"No it isn't," I told her stubbornly, the words coming out as a weak resistance. My voice resonated much firmer this time as I said, "That's not our mum. I've never seen this woman before in my life." My heart was a hammer my chest couldn't control. There was nothing in this woman's face that I knew. Nothing.

"Yes it is," Hydie replied softly, drawing in closer to me, sensing something was wrong.

My heart sank as crimson tears brimmed in my eyes.

If this was my mum, this woman I had absolutely no recollection of, then there was only one other person my singing ghost could be.

Chapter 16: The Singing Ghost

My singing ghost had to be Chad's mum. There was no other possible explanation. As the realisation crashed into me, it suddenly made sense she would betray me—lead me to Florence's hideout in Germany only for Connor to get abducted. The trap had been meant for me. She wanted to get rid of me. Perhaps she thought I wasn't powerful enough for her son. Maybe it had all been a test and I had failed. Her sisters were against me. Why shouldn't she be? But then why was she there? Always in my life. From the time I was a child, to the times she had urged me to write to Chad when I had been avoiding him. Protecting me from my father. Why? What was her motive?

"Are you all right?" Hydie asked, and I jumped up from the bed.

I was there, in her room, my hand shaking as if my brain had lost control of it. Snatching my hand with the other to calm its seismic waves, a small laugh left my lips, desperately willing the tension to break. Hydie's brow furrowed with worry and I couldn't blame her. She had known me her whole life. But I was the eldest. I was meant to be the one protecting her, not passing out on the floor of her bedroom and completely losing it at the sight of a photograph.

"I'm fine," I insisted, but the quiver in my voice gave me away. "I just—need a quick lie down, that's all. Give me a shout if you need anything."

I tried not to run from her room, to walk slowly, to concentrate on my breathing and not have another fainting spell, but it took everything in me. Backing out of the room, I gave a meek smile, a lousy response to her gaping mouth. But I found myself in the corridor, closing her door. The sounds around me were muffled. My sister standing on the other side of the door, fairy wings, the breeze outside, everything… All noises that normally would have been amplified to my ears were hushed as I found my feet carrying me over to my bedroom, saw my hands moving on their own accord, grabbing out some parchment and a pen. The pen swirled around in my hand, forming the letters and words of the request that burned within me.

I need a picture of your mum. I need to know what she looked like.

He was going to ask questions. He was going to avoid a prompt response, but I didn't have time. My sanity was slipping away. I could feel the tears beginning to buckle and my own questions cluttering the chaos in my head, seeping their way down to my throat like a scream ready to terrorize anyone in my way, but my purse glowed, and I took out his reply.

The statue in the garden. You know the one.

The rest of his letter lay forgotten as I set down the parchment and whirled myself off to the spot just between the double staircase that led up to the main entrance of Castwell Castle.

The waning crescent moon shone brightly along my skin. The chilled night air swept in on me, but even as bumps covered my skin, I couldn't look away from the statue.

I avoided that statue. So many times I had passed it—refused to look at the three witches out of pure spite for his aunts, but as I curved my way around to the third stone figure, a bitter cold poured into my lungs, and it hurt to breathe. Staring back at me was the stone form of the woman who had sung me to sleep countless times.

She was beautiful. Her skin was smooth, her smile pure, and when my eyes drifted shut, I could see her in the flesh. I could feel her warmth. I became mesmerised by her green eyes—the twins of Chadwick's—as they stared back at me, creasing with merriment.

My eyes reopened to gaze back at the statue before me, but the warmth vanished and was instantly replaced by a chill. Prickles slid down my spine, and the hair on every inch of my skin stood on end. Without knowing why, my eyes drifted up to the castle. The stones towered high above me, and I watched as a translucent grey hand curiously closed the drapes to one of the windows.

She's here.

The mix of nerves and frenzy kept my hesitation at bay, and I stormed up the steps to the entrance of my home. I couldn't transport. Every bit of my energy went towards placing one foot in front of the other. She was avoiding me. Anger blinded my will to soothe myself, and all I could do was focus on discovering which room the deceased witch was hidden in.

Purple electricity smashed into the tall front doors, slamming them open. I didn't care which one of Chad's servants observed my temper as I flew up staircase after staircase until I was sure I had reached the floor the ghost was on. Panicked sweat congregated on my chest as if I were ill, but I shouted down the empty corridor, with not a soul in sight.

"What do you want from me?" I yelled. "Why do you follow me? Why?"

My voice bounced off the walls, travelling all the way down, but the silent response swallowed me whole. My teeth gritted together as I stormed down the passageway, opening doors and peering inside the rooms. But it was to no avail.

She had to be there. She had to give me answers.

"Why did you trick me?" I called out, cracks within me breaking me down slowly. "I trusted you, and you led us straight to Florence. I don't get it. Tell me why!" But I was shouting to no one. She was either ignoring me or long gone.

I choked on a sob. She couldn't leave. Not now. Not when I needed her.

I plunged my hand forwards onto another doorknob and jerked it open with not a shred of hope, but I jumped as her lifeless eyes met mine.

All the breath left my body, and my throat closed. Her face was filled with sorrow as she took me in—sorrow for what, I didn't know. Before my wits came back to me, she glided through me and the world turned to ice. Too many seconds passed as I struggled to overcome the frost, and when I did, I turned on my heels. The corridor was empty, save for old portraits on the walls, but an invisible string wrapped around my torso, and I bent to its will.

"Wait," I called after her, running in the direction I was being pulled. I rounded the corner, and she waited at the end of another long hallway. "Talk to me," I demanded, continuing after her. "If you can sing, you can talk. Tell me what you want from me. Why are you in my dreams from when I was a child? Are they true memories?"

But she didn't answer. She just kept her eyes locked on mine until she drifted around the corner and out of sight.

My whole body itched to follow. I yearned for information, but some clever part in the back of my brain remembered her trickery, remembered what happened the last time she led me round corners to some unknown location. Yet my heart was in mourning, and any common sense was overridden. I had just **KILLED** my own father and somehow undone it, and now I had lost the hope I held in my heart that my mum was out there, watching over me even in her death. But that woman, that ghost, she wasn't my mother. She belonged to Chad, and I didn't know what to make of the whole situation. The pull yanked at me harder, and my feet ran after the woman who held on to so many secrets.

I rounded the next corner just in time to see her disappear again, and I cringed at the eerie sense of déjà vu. But she couldn't be leading me to another trap. This was my home now. My home with her son. Surely she'd give up her odd, wishy-washy vendetta against me. I could have used my vampire speed to catch up to her, but I was too hesitant. I wanted to be able to run the opposite direction if need be, focus my ears to hear if the other two Castwell sisters were lurking nearby, but as she led me higher and higher through the castle, to a tower I had never set foot in before, I felt as though we were more and more alone. Hydie, with her perfectly human ears, wouldn't be able to hear me from up here. Perhaps the odd fairy or guard could' but who knew?

One last curve up a spiral staircase took us to a door, and as Chad's mum turned to face me, I reached out for her, only for her to pass through the closed door without a word.

I swallowed down all the fear that was rising within me and reached towards the circular latch. It gave a loud click before creaking open to reveal a dark room. As I forced my terrified feet forwards, I realised which room I would be entering, the one at the uppermost part of the turret: the attic. Chad's voice echoed through my memories—a joke he had once told about there being a ghoul who dwelled here. Now that I was here, it was the ghost of his mum I feared more.

The attic was much larger than it appeared from the outside, as if a spell had been placed to transform it into a mystical, hidden realm. It was dark, and the hundreds of mirrors throughout the room made it infinitely more petrifying. As I stepped closer to the ghost, I could see her reflection playing out in each of them, beautiful and calm, but haunting.

"Talk to me," I let out in a quivering whisper, but her ascending arm with a single finger held out was her only response.

I let my eyes wander to a chest that lay at the hem of her floating skirts—the item she wanted me to find. I could see a key, carelessly left in its lock. My eyes trailed back to hers, and she slowly drifted back as if clearing the way for me

Tears breached my eyes. I wasn't brave enough to trust her fully. How could I?

"I don't understand," I pleaded with her. "Just tell me what it is. Tell me what you want from me."

When her lips lifted into a sad smile, and she pointed to the chest again, I gave in to the falsely mute ghost. Eyeing her warily, I edged closer, my reflection cast upon all of the mirrors now. Kneeling before the chest, I anxiously turned the golden key, closing my eyes as it clicked, and then pushed open the top of the chest.

Hundreds of pictures, documents, and newspaper clippings from various papers stared back at me. My eager fingers sifted through photographs of bruised and abused children, stumbling upon reports of their deaths. It felt as though my chest were caving in on itself. Their faces—their tiny little faces—were helpless. All those lives taken, and for what purpose? I tried to sniff back the emotions, but it didn't help. Blood tears trickled down my cheeks as I took in their sad eyes.

I looked back at the ghost. "Why are you showing me this?" I asked, my voice cracking alongside my heart, but she simply pointed back to the chest, and I continued my search.

My fingers brushed against a cold surface. Shifting the papers out of the way, I uncovered a small hand mirror adorned in a tarnished, silvery frame. I gripped its handle and looked at my reflection—the image interrupted by long cracks that fractured the glass. From the corner of my eye, I saw the ghost shaking her head, and I laid down the mirror, feeling even more defeated. Shifting over another newspaper clipping, I uncovered a diary bound in a soft, navy velvet. Shuffled between its pages were more photographs and articles peeking out, but as soon as I opened it up, the younger version of myself stared back at me.

Shock rattled me as I took in my brown eyes—the eyes I had before I was changed. I couldn't have been more than two years old, but I was sure it was me. Large, cursive words that must have belonged to Chad's mum were scrawled neatly next to the image. They read a single name followed by a question mark: *Detective Harrison?*

I flipped through the pages quickly, picking up key terms and phrases as I went.

Father
Abuse
Suppressed powers
Witch?

Alas, I stumbled upon a page marked by a thin blue ribbon, and my eyes flew over the entry, taking in each and every word marked on its surface.

I want to help the child, but this one is harder to find than the others. I can feel her sadness so powerfully, yet she won't speak to me. It's almost as if she's too young. Perhaps she doesn't know how. I will save her from her horrid father though. I must.

My heart fluttered and my eyes flew back up to the ghost. She had been trying to find me. She wanted to help me.

I turned the page, yearning to know more, but the rest of the pages in the diary were blank, and I could feel in my heart why. She must have been **MURDERED** soon after that entry.

The word sent chills down my spine. Death. To take someone's life. I had been so close to taking my father's life—someone who may actually deserve it—yet it still felt so wrong. How could anyone take Chad's mother away from him?

My mouth hung open as I turned back to the ghost, searching for the right words to say, but I had none. I was desperate for more, but a faint breath that didn't belong to either of us sent the diary toppling back into the chest. Instantly, I was on my feet, but all I could see was the ghost and hundreds of my reflections playing out across the mirrors. I gave his mum a questioning look, wondering what she had led me to now, but her eyes were just as wide and fearful as mine. Her hands flew to her ears and she leaned towards me, her eyes flickering down to my hands before shaking her head and drifting away. Her back touched a mirror and she sank through it, disappearing from the room.

The foreign breath sounded again and my eyes flew around the room. My hands reached to cover my ears as the ghost had silently instructed, but it was just me in that room. Me and an invisible person whose slow breath was far calmer than mine.

I circled around, searching for whoever was there with me, half expecting to see the ghoul, but that wasn't what caught my eye. It was me. One of my hundreds of reflections. But this one wasn't mirroring my fearful stance. This Azalea wasn't holding her hands over her ears at all.

My hands slowly fell, and my wide eyes studied the eyes across from me, but an eerie smile spread upon the figure's lips. My heart raced dangerously as she motioned me forwards with a single finger, *my* finger, but when I took a step away, the temper of the reflection seemed to burst. Suddenly, all of the reflections were her—identical to me in every way except the purple hair that slowly morphed into straight, blonde locks. I was staring at the version of me who lived in my dreams.

"Fancy seeing you here," it said in a voice I knew all too well.

I stared at the woman, willing myself to wake up, pleading with my own mind, but this time I wasn't trapped in a dream.

"Who—who are you?" I stuttered, but my fear seemed to please the woman in the mirror.

"I am you," she said happily as if it were a song—a sick, twisted game.

"No, you're not," I told her, wishing I hadn't uncovered my ears, but it was too late. Invisible vines seemed to hold me still, locking my hands and feet in place.

"What? Because my hair isn't purple, I can't be you?" She let out another laugh. "Oh, but the winds tell me there's a colour you hate more than blonde these days. One you despise because a pretty little witch decided she fancied it."

The figure's hair glimmered in every mirror before pink replaced the blonde at its roots and travelled down the full length of it.

"Dreadful, isn't it?" the reflection asked, and I gritted my teeth at her.

"Release me," I demanded, stubbornly struggling against the vines as I tried to appear calm, or just as collected as the figure in the mirror seemed to be. "Release me and then tell me your purpose."

"But that's no fun," she declared, her brows raising in earnest.

This wasn't funny. This was horrifying. Why the hell didn't I listen to my intuition as it screamed at me not to come up here?

"Tell me why you're here," I tried again, finding some fiery part within that yearned to hide behind my crippling cowardice.

"Don't worry," she said, waving her hand out in front of her calmly. "Your little ghosty didn't know I'd be up here waiting for you, so don't get all teary-eyed on me now. Besides, I promise I'll let you go after we have a nice little chat," she insisted, and her finger moved to trace along her bottom lip, forcing it to pucker outwards in a feigned pout. "Now," she went on, a smile brewing from behind her eyes, "tell me about your views on this Florence fellow. Word has it, you despise him, but honestly, I think you two would work well together," she commented. She removed her finger from her lip to check her nails before they too flashed to a bright shade of pink.

I stared at her, completely lost as to what her intentions were—her motive. She'd scared the singing ghost off to talk about Florence?

"He's vile," I replied, playing along. Curiosity whipped me across the back before Florence's body flashed in my mind, climbing on top of me, undoing his trousers, but the woman in the mirror spoke, swiping the memory away.

"Oh, he's not all that bad," she insisted, widening her eyes at me as though I were being ridiculously childish. "You should really try him on for size. He's handsome, powerful, and great in bed," she added, and my stomach lurched.

I choked on the new, poisonous images she trapped in my head. Her—*me*—in bed with Florence.

I gritted my teeth to fight it all away. "And just how is it that you know him?" I growled at her.

She clicked her tongue at me. "You can't expect a lady to tell all her secrets, can you?" she sneered, but I pressed on. She had to tell me something—anything I could use to get to him.

"Do you work for him?" I asked, my voice too eager, but she acted as though she hadn't noticed.

She shrugged her shoulders indifferently. "For him, *under* him, it's all the same thing really," she said with a mocking sweetness.

My nostrils flared, my temper rising as she deflected each question towards a meaningless answer. This was getting absolutely nowhere, yet I couldn't help but press her for more on the off chance she offered something helpful. "And why is it that you have my face?" I snapped back. She giggled in response.

"Sorry, I didn't know you had already claimed it!" she laughed.

"What are you then?" I screamed out at her, fighting against my invisible restraints.

"Oh, just a humble servant to her master. A magician, a weapon, and the deliverer of Florence's warning letter all wrapped in one," she said, rolling her hands around as though she were truly wrapping the concepts together. My breath caught at her words. "What? You don't remember me?" she asked, frowning from the sting of being forgotten. It all but clicked. Her hair had just been blonde, only moments ago. *She* had been the one who delivered the letter, months ago at Castle in the Rocks, whatever *she* was. "Well," she scoffed, looking thoroughly agitated, "perhaps this time, I'll have to make a longer lasting impression, won't I?"

Blonde hair flashed before my eyes as I strained them harder, reining in the memory of her nudging into me, sliding Florence's letter into my hand, and then slipping away into the crowd.

"That was you?"

"Yes, not long after you had burned the whole place to the ground. Lovely reopening by the way," she added as though it were a pleasant afterthought, but I just stared at her. What the hell was she on about?

"*Florence* burned down Chad's pub," I corrected.

"Actually, that was you, darling," she said simply. There was no smile across her face, which frightened me even more. There was no joke behind her eyes.

I nearly rolled my own eyes at the accusation. "No. It wasn't," I huffed out.

"Ah, but you did," she said, her eyes piqued with intrigue. It was all just a game to her, to me, to whoever she was. She gave a snap and a white candle appeared in her hand. "You see, you have this *thing* where you let your emotions control your magic, my dear. And tell me, when Florence and his warriors were outside that pub that night, what did you feel?"

Fear, anger, anxiety, I thought, refusing to satisfy her request for me to speak, but it didn't matter.

"Yes," she hissed out as if she were in my head, listening to my very thoughts. "And what happens when you let those emotions get the best of you?" she asked, then she pursed her lips and blew on the candle, magically lighting it. Its orange flame flickered wildly even though her breath no longer crashed into it. "What happens to those little flames?"

I didn't have to say it out loud as the images of all the flames I had ever engorged came to the forefront of my memories. The night I was turned and Florence forced his first kiss. The day Cristin had shaken me awake from my nightmare. The time my singing ghost had led me to Florence's hideout.

The flam' in the woman's hand grew as my thoughts passed by. But I couldn't have set the pub on fire.

"Oh yes, you did," the figure in the mirror whispered seductively.

Stretching the candle towards me, the part of the mirror where her fingers seemed to touch rippled like a stone plopping down into water, and her hand pushed past the barrier, right towards me. Her real flesh. A real flame. It blazed taller as my eyes grew wider, but there was nowhere to turn. Every single mirror portrayed the hand and the candle, and hundreds of them surrounded me. The flame flickered in the reflection of her eyes. I watched as her smile grew, and then all of a sudden, all the hands turned over, dropping the candles onto the wooden floor.

And the entire attic went up in flames.

"Until next time," the voice cooed, but all of the mirrors reflected my curly, purple hair, and my horrified expression.

The invisible chains broke with a snap, and my body moved without thought, without hesitation as purple swirls crashed into the chest that still sat on the floor, unprotected. The force of the magic sent the top of the chest slamming down, shielding its contents from the flames. As I swirled my arm around, a powerful spurt of water cascaded into the room, extinguishing the fire. Sizzles and steam filled the attic as I fought to replenish the air in my lungs, and with the last bit of magic I could muster, I grabbed the handle of the chest and whirled away to my bedroom.

Chapter 17: Who Is She?

I was dripping from head to toe in the water I had somehow conjured in the attic. After sauntering over to the bathroom, I stared at the mirror to ensure the image that stared back at me was my own. The reflection mirrored my movements as I scrubbed away the mascara that streaked down my face.

I was a wreck—inside and out.

A deep voice crashed into my eardrums, and I jumped before my frantic mind could quite place who it was.

"Azalea?" Chad called from the bedroom, his steps edging nearer before his knuckles rapped on the door. "Azalea, are you in there?"

Quickly hoping to appear presentable, I wiped the black muck from underneath my eyes, but it was like removing a single ash from a fire. It was no use. I still looked like a right mess. Trying to compose myself, I replied, "Yes. I'm—I'm in the bathroom. I'll only be a minute," but he entered the room anyway.

Chad's brows heightened and his eyes flashed with worry when they took in the sight of me, trailing from my soaked hair down to the scorched hems of my dress. "Er—what—" he tried, before landing on, "Are you all right?"

My lips forced a smile. My head bobbed aimlessly until reality set in and broke my will to pretend. A magnetic force pivoted my head from side to side, revealing the truth. "No," I sputtered out. "No, I don't think I am."

Before any means of an explanation left my lips, Chad wrapped me up in a hug. His warmth spread against me, washing away the very edge of my worry. The feel of his breath travelled down my neck, and he gripped my hair, drawing me in closer to him. It all made me wish he'd never let go.

"Tell me," he whispered lightly in my ear. "What happened? Is Hydie all right?"

I nodded into his chest, my hands tucked in between us, holding onto his shirt. "Yes, she's fine. I just—" Where to begin? Bring up the mother he yearned to have back? Drudge him through his own horrid past as well as my own? Or perhaps start with the reflection that spoke with its own mind? I'd sound completely mad if I didn't already.

No longer feeling as though I deserved his warmth, I pulled back from him, dragging my hands along my face, taking out a bit of my frustration on it as I went. My mind was a melting pot of information, blurred together as though I'd never be able to see straight again. Untameable thoughts boiled from within, rising up with violent bubbles peering over the edge, ready to spill out.

"There was this mirror," I started. "In it was this woman from my dreams, but this time she was real, and she was me, but *not* all at once," I blurted out, my hands raised in front of me as though they were trying to push away the confusion that swirled inside of me, but it didn't help. "And—"

"What *mirror?*" he interjected. His gaze held mine intently as though the mirrors were the most pressing detail I had listed. Yet before I could stumble my way through a clumsy response, something shifted in his eyes, and whatever it was told me he knew precisely what mirror I had been referring to.

A sense of shame crept Its way up to my stomach as I realised that I shouldn't have gone into that attic. Not just because I had been led there by a mysterious ghost, but for a lack of preserving Chad's privacy.

"It—it was several mirrors actually," I admitted, guilt brewing in my stomach.

"In the attic," he finished for me through an airy breath. His shoulders slumped as though his fear had become a reality. I nodded nonetheless. "You shouldn't have gone up there," he said solemnly. It wasn't a command but a sad reply. "It's—haunted you could say."

"Haunted by your mum?" I pried, but his head snapped up to look at me, and his eyes grew wide.

"No," he said, taking a tentative step towards me. "Why would you ask that?"

My heart faltered a bit. If it wasn't haunted by her, what did haunt the attic? Perhaps there was a ghoul after all.

I chewed my tongue, searching for a gentle way to tell him, and then decided to start over. "I was led up to the attic," I told him, wanting desperately for him to not be furious at me for it. "I was led to this chest, and inside—"

"You looked in the chest?" he asked abruptly. Anger flashed in his eyes, but his lids shut, suppressing the fire. When he opened them again, the sadness had returned. "That stuff is meant to be private," he explained in a voice that stood on the border of patience and pain, as though my action had insulted him. An insult or breach of his trust was never what I had intended.

"I was led there," I repeated quickly. "I was *told* to open it—"

"By whom?"

"Well, by the owner," I replied cautiously, dreading the way this information would disturb him.

Shaking his head, he started, "But I didn't tell you to—"

"By the *original* owner," I told him, choking on the words. I wanted to undo everything and never go up there in the first place, to never see her face, but it was too much to try and undo. Too much time had passed in between. "Your mum." I let out. "Or her ghost to be exact."

Chad stared at me. His mouth hung ajar, trying to grasp onto some unknown clarity. His hand furrowed up his hair as he dragged it back in disbelief. "My mum? You saw my mum's ghost?" he asked softly. My heart clenched as I nodded, unable to imagine what he was feeling at that moment. "I haven't seen my mum's ghost in over a decade, and you just happen to see her all of a sudden? Is that why you wrote to me?"

I winced and turned away from him slightly, my eyes skimming my reflection in the bathroom mirror, hoping we were truly alone. "The thing is," I went on hesitantly, turning back towards him, "it's not 'all of a sudden.' You see, Hydrangea was unpacking and I saw a picture of her, and me, and our mum, only I had never seen that woman before. Or at least I don't remember her face," I corrected. "Then it hit me. The woman I've been seeing, my singing ghost… She's not *my* mum. She's yours."

Chad's jaw clenched shut. For a moment, all he could do was blink at me as shock turned to confusion and confusion turned to denial. His mouth parted, a question at the tip of his tongue, but as if he thought better of it, he turned to walk back out to our bedroom.

Chills covered me at the idea of him leaving, and my legs followed him as I prayed he'd stay. He plopped down on the chaise as though the weight of the world were on his shoulders, but his stillness only lasted for one heated second before he was up again, eager for more information.

"*My* mum is your singing ghost?" he asked anxiously. "The one who led us to Florence's hideout in Germany? The one you've been seeing since you were a child?"

Scepticism clouded his face. I nodded, scared to hurt him, yet knowing I had to tell him the truth.

"I swear I didn't know it was her," I insisted.

"But that's impossible," he said, his eyes darting to anything but me. "Why would my mum be going to you before we ever even knew each other, and—and not even bother to see me?" he finished.

Sorrow for the man before me swept through like a winter wind. Moving closer to him, I took his hand to ease his shakes—the same shakes mine had done the moment I realised the ghost was not my own mum—and his cold hand made my breath catch. I lifted my palm to his cheek and pushed out purple swirls of calm, trying to ease his sadness as he had done for me when I most needed it. I yearned to ease his pain. His eyes went slightly out of focus before they met mine and steadied.

"It was not my intention to steal her away from you," I told him. "I didn't know. But I think I know why she's been following me. There's a diary in the chest," I dared to admit, "along with the photos and newspaper clippings of—"

"—child abuse cases," he finished, knowing full well what was in the chest.

"Yes," I confirmed, eyeing him carefully to see if I should continue on, "and in the diary, her last entry mentions a child she was trying to help. I'm pretty sure that child was me." His silence swallowed me whole, and I slid my hand away from his cheek. A question burned inside that begged to be let out. "Why was your mum watching over me?"

Chad stared back at me, his eyes glazing over ever so slightly, lost in a memory. When he lifted his head up and down, a newfound realisation brought his eyes back to the present. He let out a heavy sigh before he started to explain.

"Witches and wizards possess different types of power," he started, and I waited patiently for him to continue. "Some have visions of the future, some have visions of the past like you, but some specialise in the *now*." He took a deep breath before continuing. "See, my mum was like me. We can feel or hear things that are happening in the present, things others can't possibly know. For some, that sixth sense is soft or hidden, and for others, it's more powerful, but you can only ever be granted one of those sights. My mum's gift, well... hers was strong."

My mind worked furiously to catch up, attempting to hold on to all of his words, following them like a road that led to understanding, but the destination remained out of reach.

"I was young at the time," he went on, "so I didn't quite understand it fully, but she would hear voices in her head, voices of small witches and wizards who needed help or who were having their powers suppressed by someone in their lives."

"Like my visions of the boy and the girl," I said, not really asking, but laying it out on the table to digest.

He nodded back at me. "I've wondered if you have the same calling my mother had, only different. You have visions from your childhood. Perhaps these children's cries for help are from the past as well."

My heart seized at the thought. He had wondered that? Why wouldn't he say something—mention I may be cursed with hearing the voices of those I could no longer help? Plagued with the cries of children I was too late to save? A nightmare. I couldn't handle the thought. Chad's features resembled agony, as though he didn't want it to be true either.

I shook my head, clearing the thought from my mind. "In the last entry of your mother's diary," I went on, trying hard to focus on its pages, "she mentioned a child. A girl. But she couldn't hear the child's voice because the child might not have been able to talk yet." Chad swallowed and gave a nod to indicate he was following along. "And your mum, when she passed, you were eight. That would've made me—"

"Two," he finished and I nodded.

"Maybe I was a late bloomer. Perhaps I couldn't talk, but she could *feel* my cries for help. Maybe she was writing about me."

"The odds," he said, his voice conveying the gravity, "they're astronomical."

"Hardly," I insisted, tears beginning to brim in my eyes. I didn't know how to feel, but apparently, my eyes were choosing for me. "I lived in Brighton, not too far from here, and my magic was most *definitely* being forced into suppression by my father."

"And my mum was called to you," he said before staring up at the ceiling and letting out a breath that hinted at a laugh. "All this talk about prophecies, and who I'm meant to be with, and it turns out that we were connected far before either of us knew it." His green eyes fell back to mine before he said, "It appears we might have been destined to be together after all."

I looked down to the floor as the blood rose up to my cheeks, my head instinctively shaking from side to side, embarrassed or unworthy of such a proclamation. "Or something like that," I said, still not believing in myself enough to think I could be the powerful sorceress of the prophecy. "Either way, I'll fight to keep you."

Chad inched closer and gently placed his hands on my hips, stirring feelings of strong admiration in my heart, but he knew better than to tempt me into a kiss by now. There was something, however, that just didn't sit right.

"Chad," I went on. "Your mum, she—"

"Mm-mmm…" he interrupted, his forehead brushing against mine to halt my words. Sadness soaked his eyes, but as he tilted his head back, the sorrow nearly disappeared. He seemed to suck in his cheeks a bit. His eyes drifted away from mine, searching for an escape—a way to leave this haunted memory he wasn't quite ready to speak more of.

"You mentioned mirrors, and a woman from your dreams," he said, finally grasping the exit. His gaze swept over me, suddenly remembering I was drenched in water, and he flicked his wrist. As his green magic swirled around me, drying my clothes and hair, it brought a warmth that would have otherwise been taken away by the mention of the woman in the mirror. "Tell me," he said softly. "Who is she?"

My tongue pressed to the roof of my mouth, too stubborn to willingly voice how insane I was. But to hide it would be far worse. My hair fell across my face as I tilted it down in shame. His aunt's nightmares clouded my visions as I opened my mouth to spill the little I did know.

"It's as if it's my own reflection, but it's not. It can talk. It has a mind of its own," I told him, realising I sounded as mad aloud as I did in my head. Perhaps worse.

Tell me it's a cruel trick the mirrors play, I pleaded with my eyes. *A mirror to display my dreams, not a reality*. But I could hear his heart accelerate.

"That's—" he paused, frowning at me. Then he landed on one of the few words that fit. "That's very bizarre."

Shit. Yes. That much I know.

Another idea pricked my fingertips. The idea that I wasn't as evil as his aunts made me out to be. "Maybe I have a twin," I suggested. Anxiety and the need to find answers overtook my hesitation as I studied the fine carpets of the room. "Perhaps I have another sister I didn't know about. What if she's the one your aunt dreams about... hurting you," I decided, too terrified to say the real word of what she saw me doing. "I mean, we could stop her. We could save you if those visions are a true possibility."

"I don't know, Azalea," he said, and his face confirmed precisely how uncertain he was. "I'm still not sure her visions are real and not just some manifested fear of hers. You're not going to hurt me, and as far as a twin... Wouldn't you know?"

"Of course I wouldn't." I rolled my eyes as exasperation rang through my voice. "I don't know a damn thing about anything in my life except for how seriously we should take this threat."

"Azalea," he said, shaking his head, "I don't—"

"Her hair," I realised, way too invested for my own sanity to let him finish out his thought. "Ask your aunt what colour my hair is in her visions. This—this other 'me' changes it. When the reflection first shifted from me to her, her hair was blonde." *Blonde*, I stressed with my eyes. He knew the importance of the colour even if he refused to take it seriously in Lili's case.

The flash of blonde hair in the crowd.
The letter crumpled in my hand.

Guilt crept in as I realised my accusations of Mrs Prophecy may have been unwarranted, but I quickly brushed it off. I'd save that for another time when I wasn't so intimidated by her.

"Then the reflection's hair did this whole—shimmering thing," I explained, flinging my hands around as though it would help paint the picture in his mind, "and then it turned pink."

"Look, Azalea," he resumed, and I could scream at the doubt portrayed in his voice. Why wouldn't he believe me? "The mirrors in the attic are portals to thousands of other places in the world. I think someone's preying on you—playing a trick," he decided firmly. "By all means, talk to Hydie about it. See if she knows about another sister, but honestly…" He took a deep breath, pity tainting his features. "I don't think there's another *you* out there. Twin or not."

My face dropped. He didn't believe in the woman in the mirror. He didn't believe there was an imposter. He thought his aunt's dreams were only dreams. Or worse. Perhaps he thought I was capable of acting out her dreams yet wasn't voicing it.

The echo of Morgan's dream sounded through my head, and I closed my eyes, a silent prayer attempting to override it.

*I am not going to **KILL** Chad. I am not going to **KILL** him.*

"I don't know," I said out loud. And I didn't. I couldn't see the future, I couldn't do much of anything. I let out a defeated breath. "But she feels real, and if she is, *she's* the one your aunt has been having visions about, not—" I stopped myself. What? Not me? For all I knew she could be me. She clearly could no longer be construed as a dream, but what was she? "Just be careful," I warned, and a flood of sadness washed away the confusion. It didn't matter if I had an evil twin, it didn't matter if Florence was on the loose, or if Lili was working with Florence. All that mattered was that Chad was safe.

Chad's eyes seemed to understand the pain that crashed into me. He wrapped his arms around me, squeezing me tight, silently agreeing that he'd do his best to stay unharmed.

His mother's green eyes floated back to me before fading into their grey, ghostly form as they had before. My heart ached for Chad, but it ached for me too. I didn't want to bring her up again. He hadn't wanted to talk about her anymore, yet I still needed to find out more about my past.

"You should rest," he said lightly into my ear before pulling back and letting go. "You and your sister have been through enough. Take things slowly or you'll drive yourself mad. Embrace this moment. You finally got her out of that wretched house."

He was right, even though his phrasing about me going mad made me cringe. But I finally had my little sister.

I nodded and he let out a deep sigh, his fingers brushing back through his hair. As his dark brown locks fell into random places, my eyes lingered back over to the chest, and Chad stiffened, taking it in for the first time.

"The reflection tried to burn the whole place down, but I extinguished the flames," I explained.

He took in the burnt hems of my dress. I watched as the gears cranked in his brain, the way they moved so slowly as though the tragedy from his past was reining them back. His features were draped in uncertainty, probably trying to decide how he should feel about his mother, about me, about anything I had spewed out without taking much heed of the precious few memories he had of her.

"I'm going to take the chest back up to the attic," he breathed out.

The idea took hold of my heart and squeezed so tightly, it made my eyes widen. I had just saved it from the attic. It shouldn't go back, but it wasn't mine. I wouldn't be the one to decide its fate. Chad's eyes didn't leave the chest as he trailed over to it, carefully placing his steps as though it might attack. "I'll make sure it's protected."

I nodded, but a bit of acid churned in my stomach. Did he mean safe from that reflection, safe from fire, or safe from me?

"Do you want me to come with you?" I offered, a drop of premature hope rising in my chest, but the shake of his head washed the hope away.

"No," he replied decidedly, still mesmerised by the chest. "I'll handle it."

I nodded once more as a feeling of regret and sorrow boiled in my centre.

He bent down to the chest, running his hand along the bloodwood curves, lost in a time from long ago. It was so rare he spoke of her. This was the first time I had ever truly tried to pry, and I still felt like I didn't have enough, but it wasn't worth completely breaking him down to find more. I just hoped more information would come in time.

"I'm sorry, Chadwick," I tried, a sense of gloom hanging over me. It wasn't my intention to push him into such a dark place.

His eyes finally looked into mine. "It's okay," he said, but I couldn't tell if I was grateful or terrified he was looking at me again. "I have to go," he told me, "but I'll be by tomorrow to check in on you and Hydie."

Something caught in my throat at those words.

Tomorrow.

I hadn't expected him to stay, but to be gone overnight?

"Tomorrow? Is everything all right?" I asked.

"Yes, there's just a lot of negotiations and events coming up that require extra attention," he said, "but I love you."

"I love you too," I said back, trying to fight away the disappointment in my tone.

He gave me one last smile before grasping onto the chest's handle and disappearing with it in a cloud of green smoke.

His words played through my head—negotiations and events that needed extra attention. I just prayed Mrs Prophecy wasn't one of the *things* requiring said attention. Yet as her perfect features and proper mannerisms sent a cringe through my body, I seriously doubted my prayers would be answered.

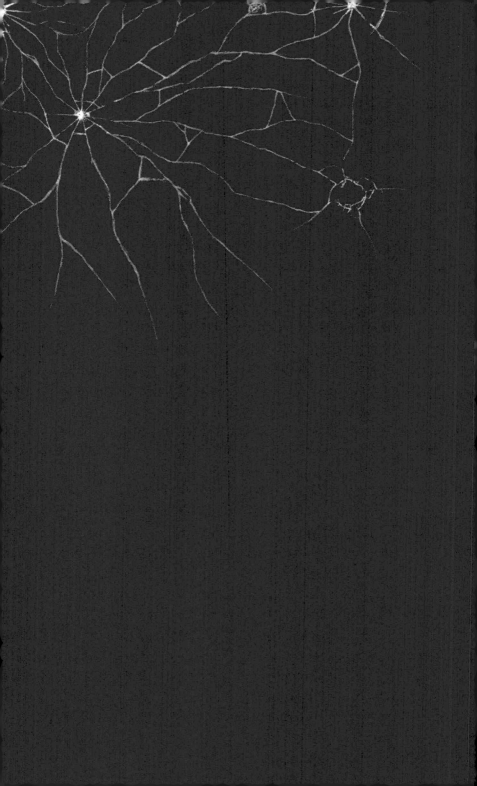

Chapter 18: Detective Harrison

I sat at a large dining table, watching Hydie as she ate a hearty supper, disgusted by the smell. I had deserted the poor girl for an entire day as I slept my misery away, yet I still felt completely exhausted. A melody played loudly in my head to occupy my thoughts, to wash away the confusion or worry.

"You can sing out loud if you want," Hydie mentioned softly before taking another bite of bangers and mash.

My eyes fluttered as I stared back at the young woman. My thoughts were her own. So strange, so unfamiliar, yet the feeling of home and comfort all swirled around simultaneously. Her innocent lashes batted back at me as she tilted her head, observing me as I observed her.

I shook away the offer with my chin before straightening the slump in my back and leaning in towards her. There were more pressing matters than a song to fill the air, and now was as good a time as any to bring them up, no matter how ridiculous they sounded.

"Hydrangea—"

"Hydie," she corrected simply, an effort to bring the past back to me, and settle into our old ways.

"Right," I accepted. "Hydie, when we were younger," I started again, shifting uncomfortably in my chair, "did I ever mention a woman who would come to me?"

Her mouth twitched as though the idea were disagreeable before opening it to say, "You mean your singing ghost?"

A jolt of excitement coursed through me. She knew. She knew me even if I didn't know her. But the joy dissipated as quickly as it had appeared when I took in the tension in her shoulders. A slight cringe, a small twinge of discomfort as she forced her eyes back to mine. Her heartbeat changed as microscopic beads of sweat began to congregate above her brow.

"Yes," I confirmed, shaking the eerie feeling off and looking down at my hands as they picked at the folds of my dress. "My singing ghost. Was I very fond of her when we were growing up?" My eyes travelled back to hers.

Her shrug only increased my desire for knowledge. "I'm not quite sure how to answer your question," she said honestly. "I'm not really sure she was real. I never saw her. I always had the feeling she was more of a bedtime story you used to tell me to make it seem as though things were going to get better."

I leaned in, silently pressing her for more information.

"Well—when I was real little, you'd speak of her—a 'see-through lady' with a beautiful voice who was going to take us away from our father, away from all of it. But one day I saw you crying in our garden hideout." Sadness or some type of pity seemed to fill her, brimming in her eyes. "You had changed your mind, I think. Said it was impossible for her to come. You had given up on the idea that a ghost could save us."

I nodded. She was dead. Of course she couldn't truly take two small girls away.

"But she was kind to me, wasn't she?" I asked, refusing to let tears spill out. "Never led me towards harm?"

"Azalea, what do you mean? She wasn't real," she insisted, but the look I gave her all but confirmed the singing ghost was very real, not just some imaginary playmate of mine.

"Yesterday, you remember when I left your room after seeing the picture of our mum?"

She nodded hesitantly.

"Well, I've been seeing my singing ghost recently, and I thought *she* was our mum. That photograph proved otherwise."

"Then your ghost is real?" she asked me before a flitter of the word crossed her mind. *Ghosts*, she thought, horror stricken across her face as though she had truly seen one. I nodded to her, confirming such beings existed in this world. She gave a small grimace before saying aloud, "I don't know why I'd be surprised, really."

Nothing should surprise either of us at this point.

She glanced around the room as though making sure no one watched her eat her food, a meal that was now growing cold as her fork lay useless, stabbed into a bite that hadn't yet met her lips. Swallowing down whatever she was feeling, she gathered the courage to press further. "And have you figured out who she is?"

I nodded. "It took until yesterday to realise she was actually... Chad's mum," I told her, braving the words I had struggled to accept yesterday.

I could feel her mind as it processed the information, running the idea back and forth, forcing it into a box that made sense. "Then Chad must've been the weeping boy you dreamt of," she discerned suddenly, and my heart stopped as I took in her words. "The one you said missed her as much as you loved her."

Chad. I had dreamt of him. A weeping boy I had forgotten along with the rest of my memories, coming back to me in another life.

Hydie's lips curled into a kind smile. "It seems as though the two of you were meant to be," she said softly, and every part of me tensed in response, remembering the bloody prophecy—the strength I couldn't possibly be capable of, and the power Lili seemed to ooze out of every pore by comparison. I did what my mind was best at. I avoided the topic completely.

"Is it possible I had a twin?" I spat out. "Had or have?"

She sputtered out the word, "No," without a second thought. "There's no twin," she said confidently. "No twin or other sibling. Just the two of us."

"Are you sure?" I pressed. It was entirely possible she didn't know. Perhaps she had been too young to realise.

"I'm positive," she said earnestly. "I'm sure we would've heard in one of dad's fits of rage. There wasn't anything he'd hold back if it meant incriminating you or casting some dark shadow on you," she decided. She was sure of it, I could tell as much from her tone, her posture, her everything. Yet it still didn't make sense. "Why?" she pressed, worry absorbed into her, but my heart fell.

I wished, just for once, that my life would make sense.

"Nothing," I told her. "It's just a dream I have."

But she could sense the half-lie as it slipped off my tongue.

"A dream and a what?" she asked, and I realised I both loved and hated her gift, the bond we shared.

It's too mad to admit, I let escape into my thoughts, and she nodded slowly, staring into me as though she could feel everything I felt: the confusion, the stone that sat in my stomach, and the terror.

Mirrors, her thoughts breathed back at me, and I closed my eyes. She could see into me. She could feel my worry over my reflection. "No," she continued softly. "I don't think you have a twin, but it wouldn't hurt to research it just in case."

Hydie carried the remnants of her meal over to one of the kitchens, and we set to work. She hadn't brought her laptop. It was just another thing she thought our father would hold over her head if she took it with her. He was the one who had bought it after all. She had only brought the bare minimum—the essentials to make it through to when school would start at the end of the month. Of course there was no computer room in the castle, no endless supply of cords and cables when the owner could make a screen appear from thin air. I stumbled through the spell, failing several times to produce a computer of my own as my nerves shook me, before giving up and deciding to venture to the library. My powers were too unsteady to conjure a screen, let alone transport us both there, but the conversation of explaining how everything electronic was truly magic was more than enough to fill the time as we walked all the way there.

When we arrived through the library's revolving doors, we logged into two adjacent computers. The usual wave of confusion crashed over me as I typed in chemwizwy448 as my password, wishing I knew what it meant. Perhaps it referred to how gifted I was in chem class, but that idea hardly made sense when I was so rubbish at potion-making. We settled ourselves into the chairs and began researching the unknown— something I had grown quite accustomed to in the past year.

Nearly an hour passed before we found anything of use.

"This is that name you mentioned. The detective," Hydie told me.

I yawned and stretched in reply. All the time-bubbling and transporting was still taking its toll on me, and I knew that if I were to try and adjust to Hydie's schedule, the sleep deprivation would only grow worse.

I scooted my chair closer to her computer, resting my head naturally on her shoulder as I muttered the headline under my breath. "Detective Retires After Over A Decade Of Investigating Mystery **MURDER** Case."

What a bloody mouthful, I thought, and Hydie nodded in agreement.

"It says here," Hydie went on, pointing to a line further on in the article, "that he poured his entire career into proving it was the father who **KILLED** the mum, not the child." She turned to me excitedly and I straightened up in the chair. "This has to be referring to you, doesn't it?"

A bit of hope sparked, but the mystery overwhelmed it.

I shrugged my shoulders. "It's worth a shot," I told her. "Does it say where to find him?"

"Not exactly," she said, shifting her lips off to the side before continuing. "But it does say he was part of the Brighton Police Department. This article is quite recent actually," she added, sitting up straighter in her chair. "We could go there. Snoop around a bit for more information."

The intensity and immediacy of it all put knots in my stomach, but I nodded anyway. Better to go exploring before I chickened out of the whole ordeal. Peering up at the clock that sat at the peak of the tall, slanted ceiling, I checked the time to make sure the office would even be open, and then thanked the earth's autumnal tilt for allowing dark to come earlier this time of year. Yes, the office would still be open.

As I lowered my eyes from the clock, I spotted a librarian with bone-straight auburn hair, and found her eyes were already piercing into mine. Her heart quickened as she diverted her attention to a pile of books that lay before her, and a rosy hue itched at my neck as I remembered the day she had caught Chadwick and me kissing between two shelves in the back of the library. A time when we could get hot and intimate without nightmares plaguing me. Only, I didn't have much time to reminisce about the feel of his lips on my neck as I felt Hydie's eyes bore into me instead. The blood rushed further up, coating my cheeks in embarrassment as she shook her head at me, an equally embarrassed smile on her face.

Nasty. Your red aura is shining louder than your sexual thoughts, she iterated through our connection, and I rolled my eyes at her.

It's not my fault you're a mind reader, I responded bitterly, but nonetheless, a smile split across my face. Childish, sisterly bickering that felt so much like a safe haven in my shadowy past life.

I had never been to the police station in Brighton, so I couldn't transport us there. Instead, my purple swirls took us to the nearest location: our childhood home. Even with our father safely tucked away in a prison cell, the house sent an eerie chill up my spine, and bad memories rang through my head. Hydie, however, diligently tried to get my mind off of my trauma by asking me questions about the magical world all the way there. When we finally arrived at the station, my nerves were soothed more than I thought possible.

As we stepped into the station, whispers of the latest missing person case and vicious deaths filled the air. Important looking officials bustled back and forth, pushing us closer to a mousy-looking receptionist. Strands of grey explained the style choice of her unapologetically large, feathered hair. She stared at us over her bright orange spectacles as we made our way past the disgruntled officers to her tall desk.

"G'day, ladies," she said in a thick cockney accent. She eyed us suspiciously, though her wide smile worked hard to cover it up. "Not e'ry day youngin's like you pop in. What can I do for ya?"

Hydie and I exchanged glances, trying to force our tongues to say the right thing. Anything to get the information we so desperately sought.

"We were wondering if you could help us," I told her, putting on my own faux smile. "We heard Detective Harrison retired, and we were hoping to get in touch with him."

I didn't know which was more rambunctious, her teeth as she chomped onto her gum, or the dark look she gave us as she peered over her glasses. Either way, I felt silly for not having a better plan. The vampire in me wished to bite her neck and steal a glance at the information she kept on her computer, the witch in me wanted to blow some magical dust at her to knock her out cold, and then the mortal part, hidden deep down inside, was fighting to keep the other sides at bay.

"And jus' what is it you were hopin' to tell 'im?" she asked blatantly, and I fought back an eye roll.

This was completely pointless. Did I expect her to just hand over his address and we'd be on our merry way? I couldn't exactly say we were his family. Family would already have his address without snooping around his former workplace.

I looked to my younger sister as though she'd know better—as if she'd be able to offer me guidance of some sort—but her eyes weren't on me or the lady, but *around* her.

Taking in a deep breath, Hydie folded her arms and placed them on the counter. With her best and brightest smile, she finally looked past the woman's strange glasses and into her eyes. "There's this case he was interested in, and we're going to uni to become detectives ourselves," she lied bravely, lowering her voice as other workers crossed back and forth around us, all uninterested in what we had to say. The woman's back straightened, and her ears perked ever so slightly, most likely at the idea of a secret shared between just the two of them. "We'd love to pick his brain, offer a few details we've discovered along the way as we're interested in the same case ourselves."

The woman's lips tightened from curiosity. I bet she knew precisely which case we spoke of. Her eyes darted to her computer, lingering over the screen that held the information we sought.

"But I heard a rumour," Hydie continued, getting even closer to the woman, and the woman leaned in even closer in response. Her posture oozed with an eagerness for gossip. "Word has it that he was interested in the small girls far before their mother died..." The way Hydie's words lingered in the air provoked thoughts the woman couldn't help but think.

Yes. Always a mystery, it was... I heard her think to herself, and Hydie turned briefly to give me a satisfied smile before turning back to her.

"Do you think he knew something was amuck with the girls' father?" Hydie asked, continuing her low, luring tone.

"Well," the woman started, her rear shifting anxiously as her beady, brown eyes darted around the room at the people who were far too busy to pay any mind to us. "He always said the father was harmin' the girls, yet he never had any proof. Just an odd suspicion that none of us could ever quite place. But he wasn't wrong, was he?"

"What do you mean by that?" I pressed her further.

"It was such a mysterious case," the receptionist said quietly, her long nails tapping against her keyboard, her fingers itching to search for his information in her system. "Harrison was always goin' on about that house, saying there were strange things none of us had ever been privy to, 'n' then one day the lady of the house dies," she whispered, her brows raising, satisfied we were hanging on to her every word. "Such a mysterious case, it was. A woman was reported dead in her own home, leaving behind a husband and two daughters. Only the husband claimed his eldest daughter was the one who done it. Nearly ruined the poor girl's life. But when they'd run the autopsy on the mum, they couldn't figure out the cause of the death."

"Is that normal?" I asked. "To not find a cause, that is." My heart was pounding in my chest. No known cause of death. My father had used his magic to **KILL** her, and his magic hadn't left a trace.

"Oh every once in a while," she said slowly, "but this one was pretty peculiar. Eventually, the case grew cold. Everyone left well enough alone. Everyone 'cept Harrison, of course. He was always goin' on about those two little girls, left to live with a father like that."

"And the girls. Do you remember their names?" Hydie questioned.

"How could I not with Harrison goin' on about it all the time? Little Azalea and Hydrangea. Odd names if you ask me."

I gulped. It truly was our mum's case.

"He tried getting someone at child services to do something, place the girls in a new home, but there was really nothing they could do. Not enough evidence for anything there either. But the detective kept on it for years up until the point he just up and left. 'Retired' the papers say. But I say the case drove the poor man mad."

I forced myself to breathe as Hydie leaned in even closer.

"And what's he up to now?" Hydie asked. The purposeful, careful phrasing was replaced by genuine intrigue. Even though all her memories were intact, she still yearned to know more about our lives from an outsider's perspective.

The woman suddenly sighed and leaned back into her chair. "That's all I'm sayin', deary," she declared, her itch for drama apparently soothed. "Sorry to have wasted your time, but I can't go about giving out his information to every stranger that stalks in here. You think you're the only one askin' for him? No, a sweet man came by earlier today askin' for him. Quite a handsome chap. Blond and dreamy," she said lightly.

My shoulders fell and my heart dropped down into a deep pit of panic. *No*, he couldn't be on to the detective as well. Blond, yes.

"Dreamy", perhaps in some eyes. But sweet? Florence was anything but sweet. What were the odds that this mysterious stranger was someone else?

"But I'll tell you the same thing I told him," she went on, her volume much louder now that she was shooing us away. "You leave poor Harrison to rest. He's in need of it after this whole ordeal. Even decades later, mind you. Now," she pushed her orange spectacles back up the brim of her nose, shifting her bum from side to side in her chair. "I can leave him a message for you if you'll just give me your phone number."

"That won't be necessary," Hydie chimed in politely. She glanced at me, a sparkle shining brightly behind her eyes, but her chest rose and fell just as quickly as my own. "Cheers, but I think we've heard enough to help."

But had we? We had to get to the detective before Florence could— if it wasn't already too late.

"Come to think of it," the receptionist said slowly, rising to her feet. Her eyes pierced into us as though truly seeing us for the first time. "The girls would be much older now, wouldn't they? Just about your age…"

"Ta!" Hydie interrupted in farewell.

With that, we fled the station, hearts pounding loudly. Cold air bit at my already chilled body as we pushed the doors open and practically ran outside. Florence was going to get to him first. But why? Why would finding out about my past life help him when he was the one who had erased my memories in the first place? And how the hell had he asked earlier today when the sun had been out? The reflection I had seen in the attic had to have helped him. She had to be a witch like I was, producing a protective charm on Florence so he could travel by day. What spell was she using to intercept the cameras and the facial recognition software we had searching for him?

What did you mean when you said we've heard enough to help? I asked Hydie eagerly, leading the way around the corner of the building and into the shadows of an alleyway.

She thought of it in her mind, she replied silently. *It was almost a whisper, but I heard it.* My heart seized from the anticipation, and she stopped in the alleyway to face me, her wide eyes staring into me. It made sense that I hadn't heard the clue if it was a faint whisper. *She remembered Detective* Harrison *explaining how he found out about us in the first place. It makes complete sense too,* she said as she took my hand. *He lived in one of the terraced houses across from us. No wonder he was investigating our parents. He probably heard dad shouting loads of times. Of course he'd be eager to get us out of there.*

My breath caught from all the excitement, both good and bad. We were close to finding him. Perhaps even closer than Florence if the receptionist hadn't divulged the address.

I reached around her waist, praying we weren't too late. Then I gripped her tightly and transported us back to the house of traumatic memories.

We landed safely in our floral hiding spot, and I had to rest for a few moments before I could get up. Hydie was spewing out words and theories at a thousand kilometres per minute, but I focused my ears, listening for Florence's buzz, or any pull, and was thankful when I found none.

Perhaps it wasn't too late.

When my legs were ready to hold my weight once more, we crawled out of the azalea and hydrangea hedges and crossed the dark street to investigate the house right across from our own.

We made our way through the gate and up the path, only the wind caught me off guard, and any hope was snuffed out like a candle. I stopped dead in my tracks. A cold, putrid whiff of air entered my nose, and every single part of my body tensed with dread.

That smell, I thought, panic floating through me freely, shredding apart any pleasant feelings. *Death*.

Hydie folded her hand into mine, confirming she had heard me. Her thumb traced along the back of my hand as her eyes travelled around my outline. *Black*, her voice whispered through my mind.

I stared at the door of the house, anxiety anchoring my feet to the pavement. I couldn't go in. I already knew what lay before us. I could see the whites of the man's eyes, hear the absence of his breath, and taste the remaining spoiled blood as it deterred my taste buds.

"He should be laid to rest," Hydie breathed aloud, and even though every inch of me wanted to run, to pretend we had never come across his existence, I held my breath and forced my heavy feet forwards.

I rattled the front door handle, but it was locked. There was no sign of forced entry, or entry of any kind really. My magic swirled stubbornly along my palm, urging me to let it out. The lock clicked, and the handle allowed its pivot. The harsh smell slapped my face as the crack in the door widened to reveal a mucky room. We walked in tentatively, our eyes rolling over endless stacks of crinkled papers. Thin, tweed rope crossed from pin to pin, running along the walls, connecting facts and timelines the detective had pieced together. Newspaper clippings and scribbled down notes littered the floor, along with drawings of eyes that stared back at me. Eyes I'd seen a thousand times. My eyes. The work was arranged in its own organised chaos. The words "death", "abuse", and "mystery" assaulted my eyes.

The smell drew me past the kitchen, down the corridor, and into a bedroom where a cold, pale figure lay in its bed. A sharp breath left Hydie's lungs. Her free hand flew up to cover her nose and mouth, and my grasp tightened around her other hand.

The blankets were drawn tightly around him as though he were ready for a deep slumber, only it was death that had taken him instead. And not just death from anything. Bloodied fang marks pierced into his neck, confirming my dark suspicions about who was after him.

Florence.

How had he found out about the detective? How had he reached him so quickly?

Every nerve inside my body spun into a frenzy. My mind was a swirl of incomplete thoughts, all colliding together and rising to the point that I was going to explode if I didn't move—if I didn't peel my eyes away from the corpse that screamed out dead ends and lost hopes.

Then part of me froze. A numbness spread within me, detaching myself from the present and leaving only the slightest part of my consciousness behind, my brain's way of protecting itself from the hurt it couldn't stand to endure.

"We have to phone the police," I sputtered out absently.

Hydie positioned her body sideways, cringing away from the bed, itching to flee the horror, but her eyes were still glued to the dead man. "What if the police think we did it?" Hydie asked quickly, her heart accelerating to a dangerous speed. "What if—"

"He could have a family," I let out automatically, but my mind didn't truly process the gravity behind it. My fingers flew up to pinch the bridge of my nose, attempting to ward off the headache sprouting from the chaos within me. "He could have loved ones who deserve to know what happened to him."

Unable to stand it any longer, I spun on my heels and left the room, Hydie trailing close behind. My fingers itched to find a phone or anything to help. They moved frantically as though they had completely lost control.

I ran down to the dining table and sifted through the clutter from all his research. Papers floated their way down to the ground, but I still couldn't find his phone anywhere. Thoughts of having to go back to his bedroom—standing next to the proof that he was gone forever—caused a crack in my mental shield, and my feet moved towards his sitting room. The drawings sent my shivers over the edge, and I squeezed my eyes shut, willing the phone to find me instead.

A *whoosh* sounded through the air, and I opened my eyes just as a cell phone flew into my hand.

I looked at Hydie, whose young eyes were wide as she stared down at the phone. She gave me an encouraging nod, and my fingers dialled 999 with record speed. The single ring extended for an eternity before the operator's voice echoed through the speaker. I kept my focus on inhaling through my nose and exhaling through my mouth.

"999 operator. What's your emergency?" the woman said calmly from the other line, yet my heart leapt with fright.

"Yes," I said, hastily trying to gather my thoughts and push away the blur that had obstructed my mind. All the eyes on the wall and news clippings of child abuse cases crashed into me, and a flash of the small boy and girl from my dreams blinded me before I blinked it away. Clearing my throat, I dug my nails into my palms and forced myself to stay in the present. "I'd like to report a death," I told her, though my voice was hardly more than a breath before I refined my definition. "A **MURDER**," I added, and my whole world came crashing down.

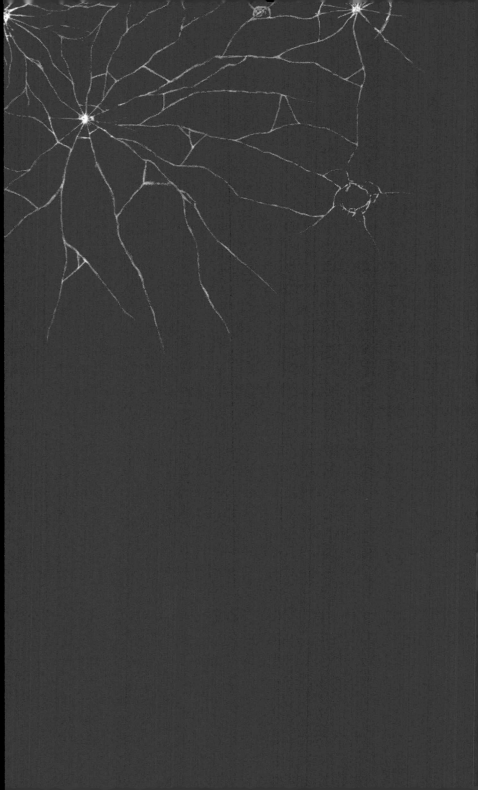

Chapter 19: Laid to Rest

I ensured that any video evidence of you two being at the police station is erased, and slipped something into the receptionist's tea. Her recollection of the day is too foggy to place the two of you there, let alone incriminate you," Chad said as I paced back and forth across the entryway of Loxley Lair. Knowing that my sister and I wouldn't be suspects for the **MURDER** only scraped the surface of the pressure that weighed down on me. Chad attempted to give me a comforting smile. "She really should watch what people slip into her tea," he added, but I simply couldn't find the humour in anything.

I should have felt relieved that there was an ounce of good news, but there were a thousand things poking and prodding at me, a thousand more questions filling my head like a swarm of bees. Matters were only made worse by the present company we were in as we reported the death to my old coven.

When I told Chad the news, he thought it best we inform the Loxley Coven as it was obvious Florence was responsible for the detective's death. There was no way in hell I was going to leave Hydrangea anywhere other than in my direct eyesight, so we brought her along with us. It turned out that bringing her to an underground den of monsters wasn't the best idea I had ever had. Several members of the lair were present in the entryway, including a handful of vampires, manananggals, and werewolves, who all stared at Hydie as though she were a tasty treat. I believed they could resist attacking her. They had chosen to live here after all—a lair where taking innocent lives was frowned upon—but resisting temptation to feed on her flesh and blood would be a challenge nonetheless.

Pacifists not saints, I reminded myself as Hydie retreated even closer to the path I paced. The Night Crawlers couldn't be expected to make their natural urges disappear any better than they could expect me not to be part-witch.

A manananggal met Hydie's eyes, and as Hydie did the decent thing by looking away from the woman's severed torso, the bat-like woman licked her lips. It confirmed the rationality of my decision to not have invited my sister to live here with me, and I very pointedly halted my pacing to put myself in between them.

"I know Florence did it," I said aloud, panic rising in my blood as I thought of the teeth marks in the detective's corpse. I hadn't wanted Hydie to witness death. I didn't want her to be part of this world where slaughter was just another customary sight to take in. I gripped onto my own hand, twisting it anxiously as I went on. "I don't know why he'd do it, or how he found out, but it's got to be him."

"How long do you think the detective had been dead before you found him?" Abigail asked, and Charity and Leo's gazes penetrated through me as they listened closely for my answer.

"Not long," I told her. "Judging by the smell, it can't have been more than a few hours." Guilt crashed down on me. I could have stopped this. I could have gotten to him sooner.

"It would've been daylight," Chad pointed out, his green eyes steadying me. "It wouldn't have been safe for you to go out."

But that just ignited a headache. "This just further proves my point that Casters must be working with him," I insisted, shying away from admitting to the Loxley Coven that I had seen said Caster in the mirror, and that she was, in fact, identical to me, just with stupid, straight pink hair now.

I glanced at Hydie from the corner of my eye, realising she could hear all my thoughts, and she stared back at me, her eyes squinting as she added that bit of information to her collection of things I wasn't telling her outright.

"Missouri left us to join Florence's side," Leo said, referring to the miserable teenage ghost who had a foul attitude towards me but somehow found love in her cold, dead heart for Florence. "Is it possible that Casters close to you are joining him as well?" he asked Chad.

Chad's eyes flew over to me, probably remembering the times I had claimed Lili must be working with Florence, but a bit of guilt pricked at me. Lili hadn't been the blonde to deliver Florence's letter warning of his return. The witch whose body mirrored mine had been, and any hope of finding out if she was a long-lost twin fizzled out with Detective Harrison's abrupt death. Not that Lili was *completely* cleared. Jealousy aside, I still had an eerie feeling every time I thought of her.

"It's fully possible that some Casters are switching sides," he told them, "*likely* even, so I've been reigning in how much information I share with them."

My breath caught, both surprised and relieved he was taking my worries about Mrs Prophecy seriously.

"Abigail and Cristin were informing us of their progress," Charity said, glancing over to the two members who were in charge of collecting holy water.

"We're still working on gaining the priest's trust in order for him to hand over the holy water," Cristin informed us. "It's as if he's torn between trusting us now that throwing the water on us had no effect, and wondering if the water even worked in the first place. Maybe we could catch one of Florence's followers for him to test it on instead."

Chad nodded firmly as an idea sparked in my mind.

"Perhaps you can test it on one of the prisoners," I suggested, looking back and forth between Abigail and Cristin, whose features piqued with interest at the idea. I cringed, thinking of my father who sat in that prison—his skin producing boils, melting away completely, or whatever the bloody hell holy water did to people with evil souls. "Just not my father," I added quickly. "At least not yet. I think I'd like to talk to him one day when I've gathered enough courage. But you could interview the other prisoners. Listen to their stories, find someone who isn't pure at heart or even halfway," I stressed, remembering the prisoners I had watched months ago as they sat in a therapy circle. "Not all of them are evil, just very misfortunate."

Abigail gave me a firm nod in response, and I turned towards Chad as he slipped his hand in mine.

"Cheers for meeting with us," he said, nodding to the leaders of the coven, and Charity and Leo nodded in return. He looked at me carefully, taking in the bags under my eyes, the tight pull of my mouth, and he gave me a warm smile. "It's been a long night. Ready to go home?" he asked, and I gripped onto Hydie's hand so we could all transport back to Castwell Castle.

With a final goodbye to the coven, Chad's green smoke swirled around us and dropped us into the entrance hall of our home.

We all let go of one another, and I realised how hard it was to stand without their support. Dealing with all the death Florence left in his wake was exhausting. There would be an eternal scar on my heart from it.

"Hydie and I should probably eat," Chad suggested, "and then we should all get some sleep." We silently agreed to his plan, but he shifted his jaw around, thoughts from the events of the night still weaving their way through his mind. "His funeral is in three days," Chad told us. His words made the detective's death feel all the more final. "Something tells me we should go."

I nodded as I leaned against him, and he wrapped me in his arms. His embrace was precisely the blanket of security I needed just then. He placed a light kiss on top of my head before letting out a deep breath.

"In the meantime, perhaps you two could focus on staying safe," he suggested with worry in his voice, yet the request was firm all at once. "The two of you should stay inside the wards. I'll produce computer screens for you to use whenever you need them. Hydie can read some of the books you've studied on the history of witches, and you can help keep an eye on the facial recognition software," he suggested further, pursing his lips and wincing a bit as though afraid I'd think of him as condescending or controlling. But honestly, with the sheer exhaustion I felt, the idea of staying inside the castle, far away from death, was a welcome one. Even if it was only for three days.

I nodded before pulling away and giving the two of them a small smile. "I think that sounds like a perfect plan," I told him, and Hydie's breath radiated relief as she nodded beside us.

☙

The day of the detective's funeral arrived. I stood alone in our bedroom, dressed from head to toe in black, when Chad appeared, his green swirls revolving around him. As the smoke disappeared and he took me in, sadness cloaked his features. It lapped around his eyes, crashing into guilt, and my heart sank as I looked away from him. He was wearing all black, ready to attend, but his posture screamed something else.

"You can't come, can you?" I asked, and even though I didn't want to believe it, his shaking head confirmed it. Something larger had happened that required his attention.

"I'm so sorry, Azalea," he let out, hardly above a whisper as his voice cracked at the truth.

I let out a rough, laboured breath, steadying myself so I could hold back the tears. "It's okay," I told him, and I gave what I hoped was a convincing shrug. "It happens. I'll be fine. I didn't truly know him anyhow."

"That doesn't excuse my absence," he told me, walking towards me. He placed his hand under my chin to aim it towards him, and I saw the sorrow in his eyes once more. "Forgive me," he pleaded softly, and I nodded.

Of course. There was no point in wallowing over things that couldn't be helped.

"There's nothing to forgive," I explained. "You haven't done anything wrong. You're working so hard to stop Florence. Your people are counting on you. There's no time for small things like this to distract you."

"Death is not small," he insisted, but I waved my hand to brush it off.

"Tell me you have a lead, at least," I insisted, and I was grateful when he gave a nod.

"Florence has been spotted close to Brighton," he told me. "We're going to track him from there."

My eyes widened at the thought of the **MURDERER** being captured. "I'll go with you," I sputtered out. "I can help."

Chadwick shook his head, and he grasped the back of my head to lay a kiss across my brow.

"No, you should go to the funeral," he replied after his lips parted from my skin. "I don't think you'd forgive yourself if you missed it."

I bit my cheek, knowing he was right, yet still wishing I could be in two places at once. Ironic, considering the mysterious reflection of mine. Flushing the thoughts of worry out of my mind, and swallowing them down, I nodded.

"All right," I told him swiftly, "but promise me you'll write if you need help."

He nodded back in response. "Of course," he said firmly, but I wasn't entirely sure he was ready to put me close to Florence so soon. "I made you a present," Chad said, reaching into the pockets of his mortal wear and retrieving a bottle of purple liquid to hand to me. "I made this a few days ago, just in case you ever needed it. It'll protect you from the sun since I won't be there to cast the protection spell, but it's not perfect. It doesn't completely halt the burning process, but it'll slow it down drastically," he explained as I took it from him and examined it. "The weather will be cloudy, and the potion should help with the rays that come through, but it'll be safest if you hide in the shadows."

"Cheers," I told him, and then I placed a kiss on his cheek. "And good luck."

"You too," he said back, and I closed my eyes as he softly kissed my neck, but when I reopened them, he was gone. Just a touch of green magic left to remember him by.

Ↄ

We weren't attending the first part of the funeral, the indoor church service, but we watched from afar as they drove him and his coffin to the cemetery site. A crowd of at least a hundred people gathered to give their condolences and see him laid to rest, including the receptionist we had met days before. She appeared genuinely sad to see her former colleague gone. Even though I knew Chad had made sure she wouldn't remember Hydie and me, I was glad her eyes never lingered towards us as we hid in the shadows, safely under the cover of a tree.

Light peeked through the cracks of the orange leaves, threatening to turn me to stone. Thanks to Chad's potion, the burn was faint, yet it was nothing compared to the sorrow I held in my heart. Harrison was a man I had never met, but it still felt like a great loss, for he was a man who actually cared about the wellbeing of the small girls in the end-of-terrace house. A man who worked to save us, but couldn't. He, along with Chad's mum, had died before they could help, and I continued to pray history wouldn't repeat itself. I refused to believe that the small boy and girl were in the past, out of reach. I would save them. And I would not die trying.

Long after the crowd of relatives and friends dissipated, long after the shovels patted the last layer of dirt atop his grave, and the sun had disappeared behind an array of dark clouds, Hydie and I neared closer to where Harrison's body lay underground. Sitting on the earth next to the freshly placed dirt, I picked at the folds in my black dress while Hydie stared intently at the stone.

Is anyone near? she asked.

I closed my eyes and let all the sounds crash into my ears.

No, we're alone.

A gust of golden wind shimmered around us, and from far off in the distance, azaleas and hydrangea flowers drifted towards us before circling into a decorative wreath around the pointed top of his gravestone—a thanks for all he had done for us. As the wreath rocked against the cold winds, Hydie let out a long sigh.

"I'm not very skilled at using my magic," she said softly, "at least not in powerful ways that could protect me. Just small matters with the mind. And I know Detective Harrison had less than that. He didn't have *any* powers, or a means to protect himself from people with cruel hearts. So, I've been thinking a lot," she told me, her voice conveying a serious tone I hadn't heard from her before. "I think it'd be best if I deferred from school for a bit. I was wondering if you and Chadwick could train me," she asked before breathing out, "I don't want to be caught off guard, you know? Just in case."

My heart clenched at the idea of her going toe-to-toe with a vampire. Of course she needed training. Hell, if *I* still needed training against Florence and his cronies, she would be an easy target. They would hurt her so violently. Physically, mentally, emotionally—or worse.

"I think that's a brilliant idea," I told her, looking back down at the flowers she had arranged as they continued to sway in the wind. I let my purple magic stream out of my hand and onto the flowers, memorialising them, frosting them into place so the wind no longer threatened to knock them away. "I'll teach you everything I've learned, and you can join in my training with Chad."

Thoughts swirled around her head like a halo, whispers that were as quiet as the winds. Not meant for me. When she finally opened her mouth to speak again, she said, "I've never been very good at physical magic. Just telepathy and auras. I can do a bit, like with the flowers and secret hiding places, but the physical part has always been more your expertise. That's why our father didn't mind me as much. My powers were easier to hide."

Such a gentle way to put it.

She gave me a hopeful smile before placing her delicate hand into mine and squeezing it tightly.

"Let's go home," she said, and I smiled back at her before gathering my long dress to stand up again.

There was a lot to catch her up on, and little time to do so while Florence was lurking somewhere out there. Not to mention, having another witch on my side sounded comforting when all the other witches had it out for me.

165

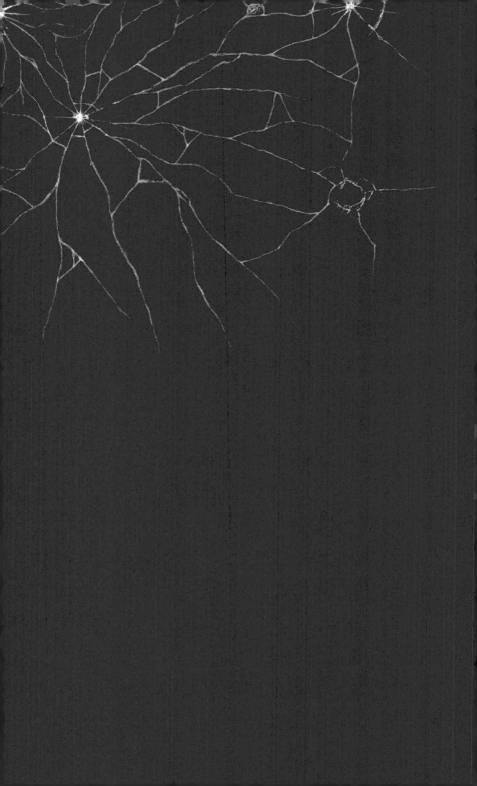

Chapter 20: Prying

Make a shield," I instructed Hydie, placing my hands in front of me to demonstrate. I pushed out a translucent, purple shield. It was larger, sturdier than when I had begun my own training. Its light didn't flicker or fizzle out before me.

Shields would be the most valuable lesson to teach her. It was more important for her to master protecting herself than fighting. Fighting could get her **KILLED**.

Hydie blinked at me. "You never wanted me to practise any magic when we were younger," she said from across the armoury, my protective vest strapped around her. She stared down at her hands as if realising she had them for the first time. "You thought it was better to keep my powers secret. I don't understand how to do it," she explained, her volume lowering slightly from embarrassment.

Poppy's wings flittered somewhere nearby. Her company served as moral support for my sister's first training lesson. I hardly knew what I was doing myself, let alone how to teach it. And as a fairy, Poppy had her own type of magic. Not to mention, she had spent years watching over a younger Chad as he practised for the battles of his future.

I shrugged, truly not knowing how to describe it—how to unleash the powers that itched to escape my hands. It was just as Chad had said. Now that I knew the power was there, now that I knew it was part of me, it longed to seep out and play.

"Dunno," I muttered, wracking my mind to try and think of a way to explain. I let my shield disappear into nothing. "Usually I just flick my fingers outwards, and half the time, my magic does what I want it to.

Chad sort of twists his wrist a bit like this," I explained with a quick demonstration.

"And Duchesses Mallory and Morgan use their pointer fingers," Poppy chimed in.

The thought of the two witches and their crooked fingers caused me to grit my teeth. I was just glad the small fairy hadn't mentioned how Mrs Prophecy wielded her magic.

"Who aren't we supposed to mention?" Hydie asked, and I flinched. She had heard my previous thought.

"No one," I insisted, stubbornness rolling off my tongue, but she pressed further.

"Clearly *someone*," she commented, doing that squinty-eyed thing she always did when my aura changed.

I clenched my teeth before casting a sideways glance at Poppy. The fairy merely stared at me with intrigue.

Purple sparked at my fingertips, and I let out a hot breath. There was no point in hiding it.

"There's a prophecy that says Chad's destined to fight in a war— *this* war most likely. But to help him win said war, he's supposed to marry the most powerful sorceress of all time," I said mockingly, trying to brush it off as complete rubbish. Hydie saw right through me.

"And you're worried that's not you?" she asked, squinting her eyes at me again.

"I mean, of course I'm worried. Wouldn't anyone be?" I asked irritably, not truly expecting an answer. "It's not as if I'm very powerful, and there's this witch who his aunts are convinced he's destined to marry. Even if I wanted to believe in myself, I have this voice in the back of my head reminding me how spectacular she is."

"Now," I announced, wanting to forget the pitiful looks they threw my way, and focus on the current task. "No more talk about prophecies. Let's start your training."

Poppy and I spent nearly half an hour walking her through how to compel her magic before anything remotely exciting happened. Finally, a hint of gold shimmered from Hydie's fingertips before disappearing in the air a few metres in front of her. Her eyes lit up with equal parts of joy and magic.

"Did you see that?" she asked excitedly, and I nodded eagerly as I smiled back at her.

Poppy clapped enthusiastically as her wings fluttered in the air. For being four inches tall, she sure could hold a lot of happiness.

"I mean, it wasn't much but it's a start," Hydie added, her contagious smile infecting me.

After a while longer, Poppy went back to her daily chores. Hydie and I laughed, giddy when her magic started building up to the size of a small plate.

"Something else has been bothering you—a lady in a mirror or something," she pried, continuing to work at her magic as though she were merely making small talk, but the smile was washed off my face. "Talk to me, Azalea," she urged. "Tell me all these things that keep bothering you."

I cringed as the pink-haired Azalea clawed her way to the front of my mind. I didn't want to think of her, much less tell my sister about the whole ordeal. I'd sound mad.

"You're not mad," she enunciated, her tone portraying the annoyance she felt from me keeping it from her.

I glared at her before sending a purple shock across the room to her. It hit her vest, knocking her back a few metres. "Stop reading my mind," I growled.

"I'm your little sister," she called out, trying to produce a shield with her magic again. "Barging my way into your private business is, in fact, my job."

Hydie's gold magic fizzled out, and I arched a brow at her. "Clearly, the topic is too distracting," I quipped, but she promptly halted her shielding practise altogether.

She walked across the room before crumbling to the ground in front of me, exhausted and sweating from all her hard work. I joined her on the ground, knowing she'd refuse to let the matter go. Grudgingly, I told her all about my nightmares of the children, the nightmares of the woman with my face, and all about the woman in the mirror. Both her words and thoughts assured me that she didn't think I was mad.

"So that's why you asked about the possibility of having a twin?" she asked, careful not to push too far.

I nodded, my eyes trained somewhere far away. *Yes,* I whispered in my mind.

"Have you thought about going up to the attic again, and trying to ask her?" Hydie asked, but a shiver slithered down my spine, and my head snapped up to look at her.

"No," I admitted, and then bit at my cheek. "She felt too dangerous. Part of me wonders if she can appear if I'm not up there to cast my reflection into the mirrors, and part of me thinks she's a figment of my imagination." I shrugged, looking into my sister's brown eyes. "I'll figure it out though," I tried to reassure her, and I hoped it would be sooner rather than later.

So much had happened in my life as a vampire. So much yet so little at the same time. I had discovered powers I didn't know I had, brought my sister home, learned about Detective Harrison, and found out who my singing ghost was. Yet there were still so many questions that remained unanswered. Perhaps the only question Hydie knew the answer to trickled its way into my mind.

"What was our mother like?" I asked.

Hydie tilted her head down before peering up at me through her lashes. Giving a shrug, she said, "For a while, she was there physically, but not mentally. I think dad really ruined her—tore her down until she was nothing more than a shell." She fidgeted her fingers in her lap. "She wasn't a mum, or even a person, at least not from what I remember. She taught us how to speak French, and that's all. That picture in my room is the only image I have where she's smiling. It's the only time I remember her looking happy. When she died, I think we were more fearful dad had no one else to torture than saddened that she was truly gone."

I bobbed my head, lost in thought. *What a horrible childhood*, I thought, and she nodded back.

Chapter 21: It's Coronation Day

L *et's build an army. Let's just go right up to each Caster and say, "Yes, I'm the bloodsucker created by the son of Adolf Hitler: Florence, the insatiable,* **MURDEROUS** *vampire you've all come to fear. Want to work closely with me? Want to be my bloody friend? Oh, and by the way, I'm dating the man who's to be crowned your king tonight."*

What a nightmare.

I paced around our bedroom, stress boiling my insides, thwarting me from adding the final touches to my outfit for the night. Thoughts crashed into my head like bombs. Would the Casters at the coronation know what I was by now? Would they know the intimate relationship Chadwick shared, with not just anyone, but with a vampire? Had he unleashed that can of worms, or would it be like at his Valentine's Day Ball, where I got to float around in a pretty dress and meet all of the souls who were completely ignorant to the fact that I was tricking them—lying to them one by one, and making them think I was only half of what I truly was? Chad had told me he wanted more of the Casters to meet me. He wanted the ones who had already met me to like me even more. Perhaps that was his plan before telling them what I truly was—a ruse to make them believe I was trustworthy before pulling the rug from under their feet. Or perhaps his aunts had already revealed my identity, now that they knew what I was. Was producing a frog from my throat child's play compared to the world of pain and suffering I would endure tonight?

I took a deep breath. It was all I could do to hold it all in—to rein in the anxiety, and snuff it out like a flame. I thanked the heavens there weren't candles in our bedroom as there had been at Loxley Lair. The ceilings would be scorched from all the emotions that raged through my body. Thoughts of flames, however, reminded me of the wretched words the pink-haired Azalea had uttered—words I was eager to force down and prayed were lies. I hadn't been the one to burn down Castle on the Rocks. That was rubbish. Whatever trick she was, I couldn't let her, or *it*, win.

My feet stopped their nervous trek, and I focused my thoughts back on all the hard work we had done in the past few weeks. We had spent hours training, preparing for our next collision with Florence. I was becoming quicker, stronger, and my magic was growing to the point that even I believed I could **KILL** Florence. If I could outpower and outwit the evil man, then a few grudge-holding Casters at a coronation would be nothing by comparison.

We had saved my sister, but the rest of our to-do list remained unchecked. And now the pressures were accumulating one by one.

Argh. *God, please calm my mind and get me through this wretched night.*

I took another deep breath and then walked as slowly as possible down to the entrance hall of the castle. Connor and Hydrangea were waiting for me, wearing lavish clothing and the same apprehensive expression I wore.

"We can all pretend to be sick," I suggested. "If we stick together, there's no way he can drag us all there."

"Unless he walks in on us while we're plotting," Connor stated, nodding his head over to the green cloud of smoke forming by the grand front doors.

The cloud cleared to reveal the devilishly handsome wizard, dressed in expensive robes and a smirk that stirred something inside of me. He sauntered over, spreading his arms in greeting.

"What?" Chad asked, feigning innocence as though he didn't know how sexy he looked in his white robes with golden accents. He cocked an eyebrow, and I bit my lip to contain myself. "Why so glum?"

"You've interrupted our plotting," I replied bitterly, glaring at him for his impeccable timing.

Placing an arm around Connor and me, he placed a kiss on my temple. "Pity. Pray tell, what were these excuses you lot concocted?"

"Chickenpox," Connor blurted out.

"The plague," I insisted.

"Really bad dandruff," Connor put in, enunciating each syllable to express the devastation of it all.

"I just don't want to go," Hydie admitted flat out.

Chad let out a laugh before angling his head smartly. "As it just so happens, I can brew potions to remedy all of those," he quipped, smiling at the three of us. "Aren't you all lucky?"

"*Luck* is an antonym," I told him with a sour look on my face. "Don't pretend it's synonymous." But I knew we could only procrastinate for so long before we'd make the man of the night late to his own celebration.

I took Hydie's hand in mine and gave it an extra tight squeeze. The thought of being surrounded by hundreds of Casters, not to mention Mrs Prophecy, made my stomach lurch. Just because the other "me" had admitted to being in cahoots with Florence didn't completely clear Lili of all her sins.

"I won't let you out of my sight," I promised Hydie, and she squeezed my hand back.

"Everything will be fine," she assured me, and for a second, I almost believed her.

"I don't know why you're all nervous," Chad laughed. "I'm the one who should be trembling. I'm about to hold the highest political position in the world."

"There are a few Night Crawlers who would beg to differ," Connor challenged, and I rolled my eyes at Chad.

"You were already in the top three," I teased Chad. "What's another tier or two?"

"A whole lot," he replied, but for the first time since his arrival, a bit of unease seeped into his voice. Before I could console him, however, he gripped onto us tighter, and swirls of shimmering emerald magic eclipsed us.

A moment later, we appeared in the throne room of the Castelo de Lisboa, one of the many castles Chad owned in western Europe. Hundreds of chairs faced a stage, with a navy blue aisle splitting the section in half. At the centre of the stage sat a large throne with blue cushions, adorned in a frame of silver swirls. Several magical creatures bustled to and fro, carrying trays of the most putrid-smelling human food, tidying up, or doing a bout of last-minute decorating. But apart from them, we were the first to arrive.

Chad's arms fell off of our shoulders and back down to his sides. He tucked his hands into his pockets, and even though his posture remained perfectly upright, his heart hammered loudly. He pulled his face into a calm expression that seemed to pain him. I rubbed his arm to try and comfort him, anything to take a bit of his tension and wash it away, but I'm sure it hardly helped. How could it? He was about to take on such a powerful role in the midst of a war.

"You'll be brilliant, Chad," I told him sweetly. "There's no one I'd choose to reign, save for you. You love your people, and I've watched you busting your arse to protect them. It's *them* who should be working hard to deserve *you*."

His face seemed to brighten at that. The corners of his mouth tilted upwards ever so slightly, and his eyes shone brightly, but the hope disappeared from them as he looked down to the grey tiled floor.

"Cheers for coming," he said bashfully, connecting his eyes to each of us in turn. "I couldn't do this without you lot."

"Does that mean we have to stay the whole time?" Connor piped in, and I elbowed him in the stomach. "Only asking!" he said loudly, as he rubbed where I had hit him. "I mean, they'd want us to go if they knew what we were, wouldn't they?"

"Perhaps, but don't let that idea scare you off. Stay, have a dance or two. Mingle," Chad suggested. "But if it grows to be too much, you can leave. Azalea, will you be good to take them back home?"

I nodded. "If need be, but I'm sure I'll convince Connor to suck it up and stay for you."

Chad gave half a laugh. "Trust me. I'll be fine. I'd be eager to leave, too, if I were you. Just check in with me before you go?" he posed, and we all nodded in agreement.

"We wouldn't dream of leaving early," I insisted, but he shook his head, his mind still off in a distant land.

"Might want to wait before deciding that," he said, more to himself than any of us, and I was too afraid to ask what he meant by it.

"Good luck," Hydie wished.

Chad gave her a warm smile in return before he nodded in farewell. Then he and his elegant white and gold robes disappeared.

"So," Connor said abruptly, clapping his hands together as a hot, nervous breath left his lips. "Shall we sit in the back where we can slip out if things go south, or in the front where we can throw spitballs at him in the middle of his first speech as king?" he asked, much too loudly.

"How about in the back where no one will notice us pulling your ear for all the rude comments you make?" Hydie suggested calmly, not even giving him the satisfaction of glancing his way.

Connor gave a small *woof* in reply as Hydie walked off to the back row of chairs. "Damn," he called after her. "Have I told you how much I love your feisty spirit?" he asked with a flirty air to his voice, and I grabbed onto his ear before dragging him forwards and sitting between the two of them.

After half an hour of high tension to keep me company, an ornate clock chimed five o'clock in the evening. A set of double doors slid open, and hordes of Casters poured into the room. Each witch and warlock chatted happily, but as soon as they set eyes on us, the talk died.

Every one of them stopped in their places to take us in, their eyes daggers, and I turned back around quickly to avoid their threatening gazes.

Shit, I thought. *They know. They all bloody know.*

I felt Connor sink into his chair beside me right as Hydie grabbed my hand and squeezed it.

"Change of plan," Connor whispered to us, panic penetrating his usually cocky voice. "No spitballs. No staying. Just leave, leave, leave," he hissed, shrinking even further against my arm.

But this time, I didn't hit him. My magic itched to poof us right out of there. I could understand Chadwick being beyond busy, but not fully warning us that they knew what we were? What a complete and utter prat!

The murmurs picked up again, as did hesitant footsteps nearer, and as I fought to ignore all of the whispers and avert my eyes, their insistent words fought back in full force.

Dangerous.

Bloodsucker.

Cursed.

Doomed.

Dead.

Evil.

Their thoughts of hate and fear crashed into my head like a chaotic storm. I forced myself to sit upright, commanded my hands not to cover my ears, and willed the clock to move faster. As they filed into the seats furthest from us first, I wondered if I could speed up time without completely ruining Chad's special day.

A familiar voice drew my attention, and without thinking, I looked up, meeting a set of eyes I had seen many times before. The first time I had seen her, her face had been lit up with a giddy smile as Chadwick had sweet-talked her. I remembered teasing him, saying she'd do anything for that charming smile of his. In fact, that was the last time I had seen her smile. Her face seemed permanently etched with anger every time she looked at me, and I had assumed it was because she had caught Chad and me snogging, but seeing her here confirmed that it was something deeper than that.

Abomination, she hissed in her mind, but it was in a voice I had heard several times over the intercom, urging patrons to come to the counter before closing. It was the librarian.

She stuck her nose into the air before finding a seat far away from me, and my eyes sifted through the rest of the crowd, eager to see if there was anyone else I didn't know was a bloody witch. Several witches, wizards, warlocks, fairies, and even a few floaty creatures with sage green skin that reminded me of genies stared back at me before diverting their eyes. I recognised some from the Saint Valentine's Ball, but most of them I had never seen before. Eventually as more chairs were filled, a circle closed in on us, and there were very few empty seats left separating us from the Casters. But if they were relieved not to sit next to us, I was even more grateful.

A deafening roar filled the hall as a heavy thud resonated outside. Warm air swept in, yet none of the Casters seemed taken aback by whatever beast had just arrived.

"That'll be the elves," Connor whispered. "They travel by dragons."

I shivered in response, my body immune to the fiery air they had blown into the hall. Part of me was glad I couldn't see the large monsters. Chad's dragon tattoo was the only glimpse I'd ever need of one.

After a few more minutes, tall blue elves drifted in and took their seats, and the hall was filled. The doors closed, and I felt Connor let out a deep breath.

"Maybe that's the worst of it," Hydie whispered with a shrug. "They'll be busy watching Chad the rest of the time, won't they?"

Looking around, I confirmed there were fewer eyes on us, but just I was about to agree with Hydie, I heard a familiar breath. My eyes searched the room to see if there were empty seats other than the few around us, but there weren't, and my heart hammered in my chest as a perky witch squeezed her way past the other Casters in the last row, and stood right next to us.

Mrs Prophecy, I thought to myself, not even bothering to look over at her, but I felt both Connor and Hydie stir uncomfortably in their seats beside me, and I couldn't help but look at her. Only I really, truly wished I hadn't, for it wasn't just her blonde hair and full breasts that made me want to drive a stake into her heart, it was also her dress. She was decked out in a big white dress with golden accents—nearly identical to Chad's robes.

The fucking audacity.

Connor turned his head quickly, staring right at me as though he was afraid I was going to **KILL** her right then and there. Hydie's voice whispered in my mind, sending an endless pour of reassurances, but they were interrupted by the intruder's poisonous tongue.

"So good to see you again, Azalea," she said, gracefully smoothing the fabrics of her dress as if I hadn't already noticed it, and took the seat on Connor's other side. "And this must be your sister, Hydie, and Connor. I've heard so much about you all."

"Hydrangea," Hydie corrected curtly. She pivoted her body towards the woman to give her a small smile, and then silently observed the area around the woman's golden hair.

I glanced at Connor, hoping he'd either speak so I didn't have to, or for the ceremony to start and put me out of my misery, but Connor was no help. He sat there with his mouth slightly ajar as he took Lili in, his gaze dropping for just a second down to her chest. I could tell he felt the heat I threw at him, because he gave a sudden jolt before shifting his fearful eyes up to mine and then back to her before muttering sheepishly, "Um, yeah. Heard about you too."

I rolled my eyes at him and he gave a small grimace. Regardless of whether or not it was his first time seeing the witch we always vented about, couldn't he remember we hated her? What good would ogling at her do when it came to getting rid of her?

But honestly, it was as if she didn't notice. She sat with the straightest, most proper positioning at the tip of her chair before continuing on in her sickly sweet tone. "From prince to king," she commented, a dreamy expression on her face. "The poor bloke was in shambles when I went back to see him just now. He's so lucky his best mates came to cheer him on."

To say I wanted to wring her neck would have been an understatement, but fortunately for her, for me, and for everyone around us, a full orchestra of enchanted instruments began to play. Though it did little to calm my nerves, the music was enough to hide the sound of my gritting my teeth—teeth I'd gladly use to tear into her.

An old wizard dressed in fIne robes hobbled his way onto the stage, a scroll positioned importantly before him. He peered over his spectacles and began reading aloud. His raspy, low voice was enough to put even the best of us to sleep as he rambled on and on about prosperity, transition, and honour. At what the clock marked as the fortieth minute, Chadwick and his aunts appeared in a bloom of red smoke. Everyone in the hall stood, causing me to jolt before exchanging glances with Connor and Hydie, and following suit. The formality of it all never ceased to amaze me.

I took several deep breaths, pretending Lili wasn't there, and tried to focus on Chad. His chin was held high as the elder wizard continued his speech. Then the old man placed a crown of gold and emeralds on Chad's head and pronounced him "King Chadwick, High King of the Casters."

A chorus of echoes followed as the whole hall repeated his words, and as the new king took a seat on his throne, the intensity of it all began to set in.

A king. I was created for a vampire, but I had fallen in love with a Caster king. How the hell had that happened?

Chad's green eyes gazed over the crowd until they landed on mine, and I smiled at him, pride swelling in my chest. As the old wizard blabbered on, Chad's eyes never left mine, and his smile only brightened. From the corner of my vision, I noticed Lili sitting up a bit straighter in her chair, something I hadn't known was possible, but Chad remained focused on me, and I loved him all the more for it.

The dispersing crowd caught my attention, and as they gradually made their way out of the throne room and into the great hall for the feast, Chad gave me a wink and disappeared amongst a cloud of green smoke.

Connor coughed to gather my attention and offered me his arm, which I linked into mine. Turning his back to Lili, he offered Hydie his other arm, and for once it made me feel relieved. Better my eighteen-year-old sister than Lili.

"Shall we join the festivities honouring the pompous king?" he asked in a whisper, putting on his best snooty British accent.

I nodded with a smile, and he began to lead us out.

"Save me a seat, will you?" Lili asked from behind us, peppering her voice with a honey we couldn't refuse. "I just want to check on the duchesses to see if they need any assistance before the meal."

Allowing me the moment to be petty and ignore the bitch, Hydie replied for me, giving her an unconvincing nod. As we continued into the other room, the putrid smell of a grand feast floating into my nose, I heard a puff of wind, signalling Lili's disappearance.

"I'd much sooner be imprisoned for her **MURDER** than have her sit next to us again," I told them, and Connor quickened his pace.

"Oh, we know," he said anxiously. "Just pray we find a table for three."

We didn't.

I rolled my eyes. There were ten long tables, each with at least a hundred chairs surrounding them in the great hall. Even though several parties had already taken their seats, each empty set of chairs provided far too large of a gap. My heart picked up speed. The spacing all but confirmed the inevitability that there would be an empty seat next to us for a big-breasted blonde with no decency to get her own wizard and leave mine alone.

As though that were his summoning charm, Chad appeared in front of us. His smile was so bright, and his brows rose excitedly in the air as though to say, "I did it!"

He rushed forwards, and the three of us unlinked arms so he could give us each a hug. When, at last, it was my turn for his embrace, he wrapped his arms around me and placed a quick peck on my lips. My body froze and my throat clamped shut. Immediately leaning back from him, I scanned my eyes around to all the Casters who were unmistakably glaring at me.

"Chadwick," I gasped, looking back at him. I didn't want to scold him when he was so jovial, so I kept the rest of my warning behind locked lips, but *honestly*! Was he trying to cause an uprising? At least it answered my second question of whether or not they knew we were dating, but how did he expect any of them to warm up to me? Surely not by rubbing it in their faces.

He laughed, clearly deflecting anything that could dampen such a substantial occasion. "Oh, I can do whatever I want," he insisted, doing his best to sound important but remaining quiet enough that only we could hear him. "I'm the king now. They have to follow me."

My lip fell down to gawk at him. "That's precisely the cocky attitude that's going to get you dethroned, or worse, assassinated," I hissed, apparently unable to keep from scolding him for longer than a few seconds. "How are witches doing it nowadays?" I challenged, pure sass slipping off my tongue. "A curse to the heart? Beheading? Setting your body on fire?"

"Apparently, death by being unable to bed their gorgeous girlfriends," he whispered against my ear, and I could not control my arm fast enough to resist whacking him in the stomach.

My eyes grew wide when I realised what I had done. The gasps a few witches gave sank my heart into a black pit, and the sudden appearance of navy smoke as a heavily guarded wizard appeared before me shot my heart right back up, where it promptly lodged itself in my throat. The sound of scraping metal sounded around me, and I turned to see several more guards, each with their own colour of magic dissipating around them. Chadwick raised a slow, much-too-casual hand to dismiss the men before laughing and wrapping a reassuring arm around my waist.

"God, I love you," he said, pulling me further into the great hall as if I hadn't almost been annihilated for hitting the High King of the Casters.

Panic ran through me as I realised I had let Hydie out of my sight, but as I craned my neck around to search for her, I found her and Connor following closely behind. They were eyeing all the strangers who were keeping a close watch on us. The expression of disgust was unashamedly stricken across the other guests' faces.

Chad led us to the table down the centre, parallel with the rest, and pulled out a chair for me. I sat, not quite understanding he was placing me next to his own seat. As he sat at the head of the table to my left, and Connor and Hydie filled the spaces to my right, I shook my head at the whole lot of them.

"We can't sit here," I whispered frantically to Chadwick. "It's not proper. There should be more important people sitting next to you. Higher-ups."

"You three *are* the most important people to me. Besides," he said pointedly, careful to speak so low that only we could hear him, "if a vampire-witch, a werewolf, and a teenage witch all sit next to me, it's less likely anyone else will want to join in our conversation. Perhaps they'll all grow bored and find their way home sooner."

"I seriously doubt that, Your Majesty," Lili said, popping out of nowhere. "Azalea's all the rage, you see? They're all here to see the mystical vampire-witch you spoke so fondly of at the last council meeting," she told us as she sat down in the seat next to Hydie. "And thanks for saving me a seat. So very kind of you all."

As soon as her eyes left us so she could neatly place her napkin on her lap, I glared at Connor for sitting next to me, leaving my poor sister to be subjected to the blonde witch. His eyes widened in a silent apology.

"What do you mean, they're all here to see me?" I asked her, looking around at all the people who very clearly looked as though they didn't want to see me right now.

Lili looked at me with a glimmer of amusement. "Well, your boyfriend fought very hard to have you here without everyone declining their own invitation. He must care about you immensely," she told me, and I looked over to Chad, who wore a very timid expression from his place at the head of the table.

"They wanted to see you, and they have nothing to worry about, nor do you," Chad assured me. "They see vampires as harmful creatures, and you merely being here proves them wrong." He shifted awkwardly towards Connor. "They also know you're a werewolf."

"And here I was, thinking people were staring because I smelled bad," Connor replied, shaking his head as though he were relieved it wasn't the latter.

Hydie laughed quietly under her breath, but I was too concerned to see any humour in the situation.

My eyes travelled around the room, and sure enough, nearly every eye in the room met mine. Fighting the urge to slink down in my chair, I gave Chadwick a grave look that he conveniently avoided before I turned my attention to Connor instead. "Why aren't they staring at you?" I asked, full of resentment. "You transform into a whole other being. Why aren't they more fearful of you?"

"Well, *he's* not threatening to take place as their queen, is he?" Lili chimed in with a smirk.

"Neither am I," I flustered automatically, but Lili laughed in response.

"Maybe not directly, but still. They're intrigued by you," she said with a smug grin, "but also terrified."

They were terrified? *I* was terrified. I was the one surrounded by the whole lot of them.

I wanted to glare at Chadwick, to chastise him for not warning me at the very least, but between his attentive bodyguards and all the eyes glued to me, I knew I shouldn't dare. The thought that Mrs Prophecy was in on the secret only made matters worse. I gave Connor and Hydie a look that I hoped communicated wanting to leave as soon as possible. It no longer mattered that I was the one who had insisted we should stay the whole time. That was before I knew I was going to be picked apart, piece by piece by Casters whose eyes radiated fear and threats all at once.

I was about to reply to Lili, to say something especially snooty, but my eyes glanced down and noticed her dress.

It was pink.

I blinked a few times to let it all click. She had changed her fucking dress.

I looked over at Chad's outfit and then back to hers, my mouth open dumbly, but I couldn't close it. She was doing this on purpose. She hadn't worn the other dress for Chad to see. She had worn it for *me* to see, and now that she had caused that ripple, she was free to wear her favourite colour again.

She glanced down at the empty plate in front of her, her jaw stretched downwards a bit as though she was fighting to hide her smile, but it shone far too brightly in her blue eyes to keep it a secret from me.

I was going to **KILL** her. I was really going to **KILL** her.

My back straightened as I sucked in a bit of air, trying my best not to explode.

It's okay, Hydie told me, her urgency ringing through my head. *Just breathe*. But breathing was so hard.

Connor coughed awkwardly, and I looked back over to Chad, whose intense green eyes were staring deep into mine. The look on his face was a cross between embarrassment and hope that I'd keep whatever it was I was thinking to myself.

Air finally slithered its way into my lungs, and I forced a small smile. Bickering with one of his allies, today of all days, would be wrong. Regardless of who it was. I would save it for a different day, one where there weren't so many witnesses. Instead, I trained my eyes on anything else apart from the people in that room. I hoped the night would be over soon—that I could endure what was left of it. Only, I wasn't so lucky.

Chad's aunts appeared with a pop of red smoke. Mallory propped herself importantly in the seat across from me, her snout held high in the air. Her silent sister, on the other hand, flopped into the chair next to her with a slouched back, staring at me with hot vengeance in her eyes.

"Ah, if it isn't the vampiress herself," Aunt Mallory sneered, not bothering to look me in the eyes. She fluffed her napkin in the air and placed it on her lap as Lili had. Her eyes tore into me, and I instantly wished they hadn't. "Have you freed anything *here* that doesn't belong to you?" she growled through her teeth. "The guards? Or perhaps the fairies this time?" she listed off, still bitter about all the innocent gnomes I had freed.

I couldn't hold in my temper any longer.

"If they're being held here against their will, then you can be damn sure I'll be setting *them* free as well," I snapped, but the spiteful hag didn't even bat an eye. She merely glowered at me harder.

"As lovely as this chat is," Chad chimed in, cutting off his seething aunt as she opened her mouth, "I do believe it's time for my speech."

He stood up and cleared his throat, and the whole room instantly hushed. The seats had all been filled, and although the Casters seemingly took turns to glare at me, most of them gave their attention to their new king.

"It is my great honour to have you all here tonight, sharing this moment with me, but it is not just me we should be celebrating; it's you," he called out to the crowd.

He flicked his wrist, and there was a puff of green smoke before an empty champagne glass appeared in his hand. Hundreds of other glasses followed suit, placing themselves in front of each person. Several floating bottles popped open loudly, and then sped around the room, filling each glass.

"These past few months have been long and hard, but many of you have done wonders, pulling long, strenuous hours, and filling our once empty cups with hope." The bottles disappeared into thin air now that every glass was filled, and Chad smiled as he swirled the pale, bubbly liquid in his own glass.

"There was once a time where the lines between good and evil seemed very clear, but times are changing," he announced as the white linen tablecloths turned to green. "Some of you already know this, but there are Casters in league with the vampire called Florence."

A few people in the crowd gasped, and the lights in the room flickered.

"There are Casters who wish to make us known as superior to mortals, and they're sinking as low as **MURDERING** innocent mortals to bring our existence into the light. As a result, word is spreading in the streets. Panic is rising. While many of us have agreed to try and keep our existence a secret, our main goal is to keep the peace between mortals and beings like us who they don't believe exist. To do that, we must tear down this terrorist organisation. The lines between Night Crawlers and Casters have become blurred, but as we step into this new worldview, I urge you to jump in bravely, and leave your old ways behind you. Fear will leave us weak, knocking us off our feet like a storm," he said firmly, and several beings in the room leaned in towards him. "But we will not fall down. Sticking together and growing beyond just Casters will keep the good that's been scattered around our world strong," he finished calmly, and a bountiful surplus of fresh food appeared on each plate.

Chad took a steady breath and raised his glass into the air. I reached for my own glass as everyone did, and copied his gesture.

"Now," he continued a bit louder, "I welcome you all to make this toast to the capable, brave individuals like yourselves, who have either already chosen to join me in my quest to fight against the **KILLERS**, or those of you considering it, or even those of you who just came for the food," he added, and a few people laughed at the break in his serious tone. "I would not be where I am without you, and for that, I am indebted to you. To us," he exclaimed, "for fighting for peace, and believing in the good souls who are truly worth fighting for."

"To us," the voices in the hall echoed.

"Tuck in," Chad invited, and as he took a sip from his glass, he smiled at me fearlessly.

Chapter 22: Fair Blue Skin

I stared at Connor, envying the way he tucked into the meal—a mortal's appetite. He was turned into a Night Crawler, just as I had been, but his werewolf senses were vastly different from mine as a vampire. He was not sick to his stomach at the smell of the food or the thought of being the most hated creature in the room.

Lucky tosser.

"Azalea," Lili started, causing me to jump. Half the dining hall went stiff from my sudden movement before cautiously returning to their meals. "Your new hair colour is absolutely marvellous by the way. Purple is very becoming on you." She lifted her napkin to pat off her already perfectly clean lips as though she were trying to gather attention to them.

I smiled at her while the reminder that nobody had asked her opinion on my hair ran through my mind. "And your dress," I pointed out, hating her for matching Chad and then switching to this pink one, "simply breathtaking."

"Thank you," she said, sweetly. "I was wearing a different one earlier, but it got a small tear so I decided to change out of it."

"Were you?" I asked casually. "I hadn't noticed."

"As you probably all inferred from my speech," Chadwick interrupted, ending our petty banter, "there are more and more groups of radicals who are protesting in the streets. Not just in England, but all over the world." He shifted uncomfortably in his seat before gaining eye contact with each of us closest to him, eager to draw us back to what truly mattered. "Thanks to our interventions, the news reports have extracted the gory details of the drained blood and the fang marks in the victims' necks. Word has still managed to slip out, somehow, and there are mortals who believe the **MURDERERS** are vampire-like creatures."

My heart sank as he continued on. "For now, no one noteworthy is a firm believer that vampires exist. For all we know, it's just a bunch of loons protesting, but we're working diligently to keep it that way."

Mallory let out a small, seething laugh. "If only there was a prophecy with *instructions* on how to eliminate this new power," she sneered, raising her brows and flattening her lips into a straight line.

I rolled my eyes. It was no secret that the same prophecy about the war mentioned Chad marrying the most powerful sorceress in the world to help them win. It was also far from a secret that his aunts believed that witch to be Lili, but I reminded myself that I hadn't witnessed anything that proved her fit for the position.

"No one's stopping anyone from fighting in the war, Aunt Mallory," Chad chastised.

His other aunt momentarily broke her eyes off of me to look at Mrs Prophecy herself, and then continued her penetrating gaze into me. I yearned to glare back at her but thought better of it in case it encouraged her to start screaming accusations of **KILLING** Chad once more.

"I'm merely saying," Mallory continued, "if you were to marry Lili—"

"Do not embarrass yourself and everyone else at the table just because you lack the gift of foresight or good manners," Chad interjected, staring her down with a heated expression that I could feel on my very skin.

Is this always what family dinners are going to be like? I asked myself. The pit in my stomach was growing again at the thought of Chad marrying Lili, but Hydie replied.

Depends. What's the average life expectancy of a bitter old hag? she asked, staring straight at Mallory.

Apparently six times as long as a normal human, I told her, remembering my studies with Poppy.

At least you and Chad are likely to outlive them, said Hydie, shifting her eyes over to Morgan. *Although this one seems to think otherwise.* I noticed Morgan's glare was no longer on me, but on Hydie instead. It was the same look of pure infuriation, just a different target. *She's trying to send you morbid thoughts, but apparently she's figured out that I'm blocking them.*

I gave Hydie a frown, itching for her to tell me if she could hear Morgan's screaming in her head, but Mallory's panicked voice interrupted my thoughts.

"We can't win the war unless—"

"There are a thousand ways to interpret every prophecy," Chad cut off in a tone that relayed it was a claim he had laid several times before. He kept his voice in a harsh whisper to avoid the prying ears of his other guests. "The stars are always changing. Stop acting like you're the wiser."

"*Shifting slightly*, but not completely rearranging themselves," she pontificated, clawing at the napkin on her lap in frustration.

Chad gritted his teeth back at his aunt. "You said you weren't going to do this tonight." He stared down at his half-eaten plate with a crinkled nose as though he had lost his appetite.

"Well, I decided that I can't just sit here while you go and pretend your relationship with *her* isn't revolting," she jeered, tilting her head in my direction. "You can't just go around kissing her in front of everyone like it's a game." Her throat threatened to relinquish her voice to its full volume, but I frowned at her. How the hell did she know he had kissed me? She hadn't even been in the room when it happened.

Chad let out an airy laugh to magnify the ridiculousness of her statement and leaned in towards her. "I'll kiss the woman I'm in love with in front of the whole damn world if I want," he told her boldly, "and it still doesn't give you the right to try and ruin the evening."

I looked over at the guards who were spread around the perimeter of the room. Each of them had their eyes glued to me, watching my every move. No doubt a request made by the duchesses. I quickly looked down at my fingers, twiddling them together awkwardly. It wasn't me they should be staring at. I wasn't the one in a row with the king. His aunt was.

I couldn't look at the other Casters in the room out of fear that they were all watching, but several unrelated conversations and the sound of masticating teeth flew to my ears, informing me that most of the guests weren't paying us any mind. About bloody time.

Connor nudged me in the side just as Mallory spat out some other line. *So, you wanna go now?* he mouthed, his thumbs pointed towards the door. His eyes followed suit to enunciate the plea. His plate was nearly licked clean of the food. Apparently, we were free to leave now that he was done stuffing his face with their disgusting mortal food.

Fighting the urge to roll my eyes at him, I shook my head. I couldn't leave Chad now. Not when he was fighting in my honour.

We could excuse ourselves to go to the bathroom, Hydie suggested, the heat of the row scorching her as well. *Perhaps they'll make amends when we're gone*, she added, but I shook my head again and gave her a smile.

No. Part of me wanted to hear more about the prophecy, and part of me didn't want to leave the dress-switching witch alone with him, so I stubbornly stayed posted in my chair.

Morgan switched back to glaring at me. Mallory whispered urgently to Chad, something about how perfect Lili was, and Lili widened her eyes at me apologetically. I couldn't stand her long enough to pretend she meant it sincerely, so I quickly looked away and glared openly back at Morgan. It didn't matter that I couldn't hear her accusations of **MURDERING** her nephew. I could feel them.

Hold your tongue, hold your tongue, hold your tongue, I pleaded with myself, but I wasn't going to last.

I wanted to send my fork clattering loudly onto my plate. I wanted to strike Lili across the face, scream at Morgan to stop staring at me, and conjure an elephant to come out of Mallory's throat—all simultaneously. But those would all result in a big scene where *I* would be made out to be the villain, and *they* would win. It wasn't right. It wasn't *just.* I was here to make a good impression, ease the Casters' worries, not prove them all right.

"The prophecy—" Mallory started, but I interrupted with a small cough, and the witch lost her words.

Producing the most innocent smile I could manage, I said, "You know, *Mallory,*" not bothering to mention her title, "there's so much talk of this prophecy, and I have yet to hear it. Where exactly could I find it?"

She gritted her teeth at me before sneering. The whole room had gone quiet now, so she leaned in to whisper. "'Tis not for ears such as yours," she told me. Each word radiated with her concrete disdain for me.

"And why not?" I countered, tilting my head to the side and scrunching my facial features as though I were truly confused. "Is it because of what I am, or because I'm not part of the royal family?"

"Both," she spat out bitterly.

"Well, then," I snapped, "I'll have you know that I'm just as much of a witch as you are, so that clears up issue number one." Although the crowd around me had quieted, my voice ached to break into a louder volume. I folded my hands neatly into my lap and whispered so that only our party could hear me. "And if all we're left with is issue number two, then it sounds as though I'd be free to hear said prophecy if I were to marry your nephew. Is that what you want?" I asked, batting my lashes at her. "Or do you want to hand it over willingly so we can hold off on that whole charade?"

Mallory and Morgan's tempers flared past the point of ferocity and straight to the point that steam was practically spouting from their ears. Lili choked out a sharp gasp, and the two men on either side of me, as well as my sister, unintentionally let out short, airy laughs, all hardly able to believe the words that I had just let slip from my lips.

Chad and I hadn't fully fleshed out the prospect of marriage ourselves, other than in relation to the ever-looming prophecy, but the old crones had to hear it. And clearly, it was the ticket to shutting them up. That was all I wanted. Hearing the stupid prophecy didn't seem nearly as important now that silence blessed my ears. They could shove the prophecy up their arses for all I cared.

I focused on my breathing as the heat from the silence began to boil. Everyone's chests heaved up and down at different paces, all struggling to steal the air from the others.

Lili stood abruptly from the table, catching the rest of us off guard. I watched as she lifted a clean fork to her glass and clinked against it a few times. Every eye flew over to the witch as a small, embarrassed laugh left her lips. "Well then," she let out as pink flushed her cheeks. "I think now is the perfect time to thank our lovely hosts for this splendid evening." She paused gracefully, a perfect image of a hostess as the crowd clapped politely. She gave Chad a small smile before looking back up at the crowd. "But I assure you, the night isn't over yet. There will be dancing in the ballroom, and we'd love for you all to stay and socialise."

She threw a hand into the air, and fireworks burst from her fingertips. The crowd oohed and aahed as the witch gave out the false pretence that she owned the damn place. My eyes flew over to Chad to see him staring at her apprehensively. His brow was raised ever so slightly as though wondering what the hell she was doing, but when she looked at him, he quickly glanced away. His nostrils flared with irritation that placed a bandage over my own bruised ego. At least he didn't condone her actions.

Mallory tossed her napkin onto her plate and smiled approvingly up at Lili before red smoke cleared all the tables.

Shaking his head, Chad pushed back his chair and offered me his hand. I took it, pushing back my own chair, but it scraped against the floor loudly. Mallory's face shone with disapproval, and I resolved not to look at either her or her sister for the rest of the night.

I squeezed Chad's hand and he bent down to lay a kiss on the back of mine. Blood rushed up to my cheeks as he straightened back up and stared at me.

His eyes shifted in warning towards his aunts. "Tonight's all about networking," he reminded them firmly. "Very few have agreed to work with us, even though they've been in allegiance with us for centuries," he said, widening his eyes at the audacity of it all. "Let's not muck it all up by bickering with one another."

I gritted my teeth, wanting to do far more than bicker with Lili and his aunts, but as Chad's firm hand pressed against the small of my back and he led us across the dining hall, I knew he was right. Tonight was bigger than the grudge I'd forever hold against those women. There would be plenty of time to argue with them in private once Florence was eradicated.

A wave of silence and deep bows to the new king followed us out of the room. Chad nodded gracefully as he passed all his guests, and I took in the way each of them fought to tear their eyes off of me and onto their king to return his greeting. Once we were out the door and into a tall corridor lined with guards, I caught Chad's eye as he smiled at me.

"What?" I asked, a sly smile across my face as we entered the grand ballroom. "Working up the courage to apologise for your lovely aunts?"

Chad let out a low laugh. "Oh, I think my aunts' behaviour is past a simple apology—more onto a full grovel. Shall I get down on my knees here?" he asked, pointing to the slick, black dance floor. He raised his brows in a special way I couldn't resist, and I bit my lip. "I could kiss your foot, even drool a bit to really prove my sincerity," he suggested.

Even though the thought of his aunts and his prophesied future wife made me want to throttle them all, my jaw strained against the smile that wanted to peek through. "I suppose that would be a start," I quipped. "A very small start."

I could hear Hydie, Connor, and the rest of them close behind, but the thought of the handsome king grovelling at my feet made me wish they'd all go away. Chad's thumb rubbed against my lower back, and warmth washed over me.

Pulling to a stop, he leaned into my ear. "Oh, I have the feeling I'm going to have to spend the rest of my life making it up to you," he whispered, and thoughts of me threatening to marry him only moments before made my body swelter. He placed his hands on my hips and slowly turned me round to face him. Chills crept up my back, cooling me off as he moved his hand to my cheek, caressing it. "Before I go around to talk to all my guests, I'm going to place a kiss right here," he said softly. "Think you can handle such a strong display of my love, or should I set the guards on you?"

"I dunno," I replied, peering up through my lashes. "I'll do my best to control my natural urges to toss you across the room, but I'll make no promises."

I allowed his lips to brush lightly against my skin, tempting my arms to react, but they stayed put. Ignoring the whispers in the room, I closed my eyes, but the kiss was too quick.

"Now," he said, leaning back from me, and I opened my eyes. "I'll distract my dear aunts, but I think I'll leave you to deal with Lili on your own. Clearly, you can handle her," he said, amused. "Just try not to completely scare her off. We can't afford to lose anyone else," he let out with a weary breath.

"I have no idea what you're referring to," I lied, raising my chin up at him.

The sound of her irritating voice filled my ears, and I cringed. Chad's eyes darkened in a friendly warning.

"Keep your head clear," he instructed. "Who knows, maybe one day the two of you will learn to be friends."

I let out a short laugh, and he tilted his head down at me as the distance between us grew. When his skin left mine, he gave me a wink, and then drifted away to save the world. He went to collect his aunts and led them over to a group of warlocks who had to break their glare towards me to bow to Chad and his aunts.

I let my ears lead me over to Hydie and Connor, cursing myself for taking my eyes off my sister once again. Taking in the way Lili hovered next to them at the edge of the ballroom, I fought to smile at them.

The room was dead. The orchestral instruments played on their own, but no one danced to the music. Other than the sound of Chad's small talk as he made his way around the ballroom, the chatter was scarce. Perhaps the other Casters didn't want to be caught off guard in the event that Connor or I decided to attack. I half wished Lili was frightened of us enough to leave us alone, but the bitter part of me knew it was better she stayed by our sides, staring awkwardly into the crowd. There was a chance it would show the others we were to be trusted if she could stand next to us unscathed. And at the very least, it ensured I'd be able to keep an eye on her in case she did have a secret agenda of her own.

"Very odd decision to hold the crowning here," Lili pondered aloud, sipping gingerly from a glass of champagne. "The Castelo de Lisboa is beautiful, but Lisbon, Portugal? I've heard it's a tradition thousands of years in the making to hold it at Castwell Castle. Curious that wasn't the case this time. Don't you agree?"

I shrugged, trying to assess what she was hinting at. What game was she playing and why couldn't she ask her question outright?

"Change isn't always bad," I told her, giving her only the slightest of glances before continuing to look around the room. "Sometimes it's necessary," I added, evading her question, but curiosity sparked me as well. Perhaps Chad was holding true to his promise that Lili would never enter the home we shared.

"Hmm…" she said with an unconvincing shrug. "Just wondering, that's all."

Half an hour of bitter silence filled our little bubble, only interrupted by the sounds of Connor's constant fidgeting, Hydie's soft sighs of boredom, and Lili's occasional sip of her drink—silent to most of the others in the room, but just pestering enough for me to hear. The thought of at least appearing cordial or interested in Lili crossed my mind for the thousandth time, as well as the idea of attempting to mingle with the guests to show them how harmless I was, but the urge to return home kept my mouth shut each time. Just as I was about to call it a night at long last, Chad appeared before me.

"Mind if I steal Azalea away for a dance?" he asked as though he had caught us in the middle of some riveting conversation.

My eyes shot over to Hydie, remembering the promise I had made to myself, and I opened my mouth to decline. Perhaps Lili wouldn't do anything, but his aunts surely would now that they weren't tied to Chad. I glanced around the room to locate them, but Hydie's soothing voice made its way into my mind.

I'll be fine, she told me bravely through our connection. *We'll still be in the same room.*

"Only if my *queen* approves," Connor chipped in, staring straight at me, and I nearly elbowed him in the ribs.

Did he have to joke about my fake title in front of Mrs Prophecy? Calling me "princess" in private was fine, but apparently, my upgraded "title" couldn't remain between us.

Lili let a small laugh fall from her lips before taking another sip from her glass. "Don't worry," she offered ignorantly. "I'll help keep her company."

I gave her a smile which turned out to be more of a wince.

That's precisely what I was afraid of, I responded silently.

Chad wrapped an arm around my waist and pulled me onto the otherwise empty dance floor. I fought a frown from my face for fear the extra security of the night would take it as a threat.

"Chadwick," I whispered firmly, "I don't think it's a good idea to leave Hydie alone."

"They don't bite, my love," he told me as he twirled me around. "Unlike *someone* I know," he teased.

I glared at him before glancing anxiously around the room. Everyone eyed us suspiciously, but as a new piece of music began to play, a few other couples joined in. My muscles relaxed to let Chad lead me around the dancefloor. Hydie gave me a brave look, and Connor looked back and forth between the two women as though readying to ask a question. I gritted my teeth, hoping he could sense the wrath I'd unleash on him if he asked either of them to dance.

Trying to relax, I looked back at Chad as he pulled us off to a new direction. "Any luck with your guests?" I asked, wishing we could go back to how kind some of them had been when I met them last February. Now in October, they were all so cold towards me.

He bit his cheek. "Not yet, but the night is young. There is someone I'd like you to meet, though."

My heart skipped a beat in time to the music. So much for leaving. I swallowed down my fear and gave a firm nod. "If you think it will help," I told him, but sweat began to chill my body. "Who?"

"Her name's Eyeara. She's the elven princess of Antarctica," Chad threw out before pursing his lips in thought. My eyes flew over to a crowd of elves with fair blue skin and dark blue lips before I gave a shudder. "We have a personal history together, so I believe she'll be more willing to hear us out than the other elves."

Goose pimples pricked my skin. "Define, 'personal'," I tested through the unpleasant feeling that coated my throat like acid.

"We may or may not have been an item at one point," he told me in a sheepish whisper. His chin, however, remained high for appearances.

"You two used to date?" I asked as all the breath left my lungs.

In reality, I should not have been taken aback. He was gorgeous. Of course he'd been with other people before I came along, different species or not.

"Yes," he replied softly, waiting for my reaction with worried eyes.

I wanted to rub my face, to wake myself up from this dastardly situation, but I couldn't. Chad would never have to feel this way about me—this strange feeling of knowing I was once in love or destined for another. Not realistically, at least. Florence may have created me with the intent for me to marry him, but he and I would never be.

"All right," I decided with a heavy exhale. "A flirty librarian, a past girlfriend, a future wife according to the stars… Anyone else I should be aware of?"

"Oh, just everyone else here, now that they know what you are," he replied lightly.

A smile broke across my lips at the obnoxious man before me. "My next boyfriend is going to be a virgin," I declared.

Chad tilted his head back to give a hearty laugh, and I knew I could never give him up, regardless of all the other women who were after him.

He repositioned himself so that my arm was linked through his, and he led me across the room to a group of five elven women. Light blue fabrics draped over them like frozen waterfalls, nearly camouflaged against their skin. Their slender necks stretched out a touch longer than a human's, and elegantly pointed ears peeked out of their long, flowing blue hair.

Before anyone spoke, I took the opportunity to cast one last look at Lili and Connor as they stood next to my sister. I bit my cheek, wondering which of them I trusted *less* to watch over her.

"Princess Eyeara, might I have a word?" Chad asked diplomatically.

"Of course," a beautiful blue elf replied.

Her lips curled upwards to form a kind smile, and I realised I had seen her before. She had been at the Saint Valentine's Ball, sporting a sly grin—perhaps a hint she knew Chad more closely than it would have appeared. Too closely, it would seem. Her smile had no doubt marked her knowledge of what Chad and I had been on the verge of becoming.

The start of my steps faltered as she took her place next to me, not even bothering to station Chad between us. Her heart was calm and steady as she looked at me with curiosity rather than fear, and Chad gently pulled me along to lead us towards the outskirts of the ballroom.

"You remember Azalea, don't you?" Chad asked, leaning forwards a bit to direct his question to the brave elf.

"Yes, and it's a pleasure to officially meet you," she said kindly, her eyes focused on me. "I've heard so much about you."

Of course you have, I thought to myself, remembering Lili had said something similar the first time I had met her. What strange woman hadn't heard all about me at this point? Regardless, I decided to dislike the elf less than I disliked Lili. There was a clear distinction between a past lover and a supposed future wife. But perhaps I wouldn't make things entirely easy on her. I would test the waters a bit.

"It's a pleasure to meet you too," I told her pleasantly. "It's almost as though Chadwick didn't want us to formally meet at the last ball. How curious," I taunted, giving Chad a glance out of the corner of my eye. Now she knew I was aware of their previous relationship and wouldn't feel the need to keep it a secret. "Perhaps he didn't want you to share all his imperfections before he truly swiped me up," I added to help keep things light.

"Oh yes," Eyeara replied, joining in on my banter. "He has quite the way of keeping things to himself until the most inopportune moments. Doesn't he?"

"Most definitely," I agreed. "Perhaps you could give me pointers on how to cope with such a deceiving counterpart?"

"'Deceiving' is a bit harsh, don't you think?" Chadwick interjected, but with a wave of Eyeara's hand, his input was dismissed.

"'Deceiving' is precisely the word I would use, Azalea," she decided firmly. "Tell me, were you aware the guests of this lovely coronation knew what you were before you arrived?" she asked to prove her point.

"If only I were so lucky!" I exclaimed playfully. "Although, he did give the option to leave early, so we shouldn't be too stern with him. I should've seen it as a warning."

"Reminds me of a certain Valentine's Ball I was invited to last winter," the blue elf said, tilting her head at Chad, "where a beautiful woman was on his arm, claiming his heart."

"Now tell me if I'm wrong, Eyeara," Chadwick cut in curtly, "but I believe I'm allowed to bring whoever I want to my own ball."

"Of course, Your Highness, but a vampire?" she asked, tutting her teeth at him to feign her disapproval. "You certainly have a way with secrets, don't you?"

My eyes examined the floor, wondering if there was more Chad was keeping from me. My mental list of things to interrogate him about was getting out of hand. Either way, I liked getting to know Eyeara. She was blunt. She didn't keep her mouth shut as the others did—didn't leave the truth of what I was drifting through the air like a word too taboo to speak aloud. I gave her a quick glance to take in the smile she was giving me before casting my gaze around the room, a slight red hue added to my cheeks.

"I believe having a substantial amount on my plate and *intentionally* keeping secrets are two entirely different things entirely," Chadwick responded, trying desperately to sound justified in his personal choices.

"He *did* tell me about the prophecy about this almighty sorceress he's destined to be with," I admitted. "At least partially. Not that he let me get away once I was informed, but perhaps he's learning. Slowly, if not quite surely yet."

"I must say, Chadwick, I'm deeply impressed with you," she teased. Then she turned to me. "More warning than I was given, but either way, I'm glad to be rid of him. You're much more suited for him, if I do say myself. Especially more than any dimwit his wretched aunts approve of," she added, her eyes flickering over to a certain blonde in the room, and I fought to keep in a surprised laugh.

Yes. I quite liked her. More than the witch she referred to at least.

"Speaking of his aunts," Eyeara went on, "that was truly dreadful how they treated you that night. I don't know how you didn't **MURDER** them after that stunt with the toad. I would've been livid!" she exclaimed.

I winced, remembering the slime as the creature had clawed its way up my throat. I had nearly forgotten that a good handful of the people here had witnessed that scene play out.

"Trust me," I told her through a grimace, "that's *precisely* what was on my mind."

My eyes widened as soon as the words blasted out of my mouth, and my cheeks grew warm. I felt Chad's body tighten against mine, and the deep need to slap myself in the face ensued. That was *not* what I should be admitting to a Caster right now, especially one who was taught from birth to believe vampires were nothing more than vile creatures.

A small sound, not too different from the croak of a toad, left my lips as I hurried to retract my statement. Eyeara merely let out a laugh and quickly waved the comment away with her hand.

"You are not the only one to have felt that way about those two witches," she said, leaning into me as she released the secret, and Chad cleared his throat, causing her to stand upright again.

"Are we still on these dreadful formalities, or would it be all right to move onto business?" Chad asked with such a mixture of unease and wit that I couldn't help but laugh.

"Always ruining the fun," Eyeara sighed, shaking her head playfully. "Now, Azalea, tell me about life as a vampire-witch. What new take do you have to offer with everything that's been going on?"

"Well," I began, not knowing what she knew or didn't, "I was turned into a vampire by the leader of the rogue beings who started all of this, so naturally I'm against him."

"Curious," she said, truly pondering how such a thing could be. "A vampire against her own creator... You know, it's rumoured that vampires are morally bound to their sires."

"Perhaps 'involuntarily bound' is a more appropriate term," I suggested, "but I assure you, any connection he and I share is a dreaded one. One I hope to sever by means of his death." I didn't bother keeping in my hatred. I wanted her to know the extent of things, where my loyalties lay.

"Connection..." she said thoughtfully. "And pardon my intrusion, but I must know. Was there ever a romantic connection between you and Florence?"

I cringed at his name. It took me off guard to hear her say it aloud. I looked at Chad, and sensing my hesitation, he nodded, signalling for me to continue.

"No," I told the elven princess, selecting my words carefully to avoid an unintentional lie. "No genuine romantic history, although Florence would like very much for there to be one. I would never become involved with him that way. Not by choice anyway," I added with a shudder.

"How then?" she asked boldly. There was no hesitation or fear in her eyes, just a thirst for truth.

"Well, there was a stolen love potion that served as a small interruption, but that's behind us now," Chad answered for me. His tone suggested he was bored with the topic, but I knew boredom was not the right word for how he felt.

"Fascinating!" she exclaimed, her eyes wide with interest.

"Anyhow," I continued, just as eager as Chad to steer away from that part of the conversation, "my coven and I have the same beliefs, and we're fully pledged to fight against Florence."

I looked at Eyeara, holding my breath as I waited for her response. She studied me carefully, pursing her lips off to the side before opening her mouth.

"You see," she started, tilting her head towards me, "I'm much more progressive than the elven council, yet I hold significantly less power. You have my approval, Azalea, but I'm afraid it means little in the grand scheme of things."

The height of my shoulders declined rapidly at her words.

"Surely you can convince them otherwise?" Chad insisted, but the blue woman shook her head slowly before opening her dark lips once more.

"No, I'm afraid not," was her only reply. Her eyes held more information behind them, but her throat interfered in voicing it.

"Well," I decided before tilting my head back up at her and giving her a friendly smile. "Perhaps throw in a good word for me every now and again," I offered, and she smiled in return.

"Of course. Besides," she replied, the mysterious gleam returning to her eye, "I have a feeling fate will prove the council wrong."

I stared back at her, lost for words, but a grin formed on her face, just as sly and all-knowing as the first time I had laid eyes on her, and she bent into a curtsy.

"It was a pleasure talking to you," she said to me, before repeating another curtsy towards Chad.

I gave a pathetic excuse of a curtsy back as my arm was still linked with Chad's, and her smile grew.

"It was a pleasure speaking with you too," Chad replied, his voice a bit detached as he said it.

With one last smile at me, Eyeara turned and glided back to the other elves whose suspicious stares were still trained on us.

"That went well," I told Chadwick, turning to him now that it was just the two of us. "Or as well as it could've gone," I added, knowing full well one conversation was insufficient to change the minds of an entire race, but Chad's tongue clucked disapprovingly.

"Fancy another dance?" he asked, tearing his eyes away from the blue figures who stood with taut stances across the room. "I feel I need a distraction from the pit forming in my stomach."

My hand travelled to his arm to comfort him. "I suppose. But you'll be telling me more of these secrets you keep while we dance."

His eyes flew to mine, suddenly forgetful of our failed attempt at a solid ally, and I pulled him back out to the dance floor, ready to berate him for any information I was missing out on.

"Well?" I encouraged as I placed my arms in position to dance with him, but I was taken back by the expression he wore. It was far more defensive than it ought to have been.

"If I hide things," he said clearly, furrowing his brows to magnify his sincerity, "it's not to be cruel. It's to protect you. You have a lot on your plate. I don't want to create more stress for you."

"All right," I said slowly, trying to see his side. "I can understand that, but it seems as though doing so is only adding to your list of worries, and fooling mine. We're partners. We need to help each other out. Besides, if you withhold information, how can I trust you? I'll always wonder if there's something unsaid or worry there's something important you're keeping from me."

Chad let out an understanding breath. "You're right," he said, and my heart clenched from the possibilities that pricked at me. "I understand. I'll work harder at communicating better."

"Regardless of how busy we both are?" I clarified.

"Regardless of how busy we are," he confirmed with a nod, and he placed a gentle kiss on my forehead.

A small part of me relaxed. I could get used to this show of affection. He wasn't afraid to show he loved me. *That* I could trust.

"So tell me everything," I teased, resting my head on his shoulder as he drifted from side to side to the sweet melody that played through the air. I willed it to soothe me. There was nothing he could keep from me about Florence that could surprise me. I knew he was cruel. I knew what vampires like him were capable of. I just needed to know what was going on out there.

Chad opened his mouth, but the moment was abruptly cut off as several guards came crashing onto the dance floor.

My heart quickened, closely followed by the loud pounding of every other heart in the room, and the music skidded to a halt. Bewildered looks flashed across everyone's faces, and at least twenty more guards appeared in their own clouds of smoke. I swivelled around, craning my neck and focusing my ears until I found my sister. She and Connor were weaving through the crowd to reach us, and I let out a breath, thankful for their proximity.

"Your Highness," a guard said, urgency ringing through his voice. His breath wheezed in a struggle to release the words from his mouth. Chad turned towards the man, one hand tightening protectively around me as he waited for the news. "There's been another attack—a vampire coven in Chippenham, England."

"And you're certain it's him?" Chad asked, his whole body rigid against mine.

"We're certain, Your Highness," another guard confirmed.

A sick game of waiting to make his move. His stillness, his sudden attacks were carefully placed to ensure his true location remained hidden.

Chad gave a firm nod before catapulting instructions. "You two stay here," he told the guards who had spoken before turning to the rest of them. His voice was calm yet authoritative. "Go back to the coven. We'll join you shortly. As for the rest of you," he said, turning to his guests. Horror was stricken across their faces. "I know many of you haven't pledged your allegiance, but if you wish to see firsthand the dangers that await if we don't put an end to Florence now, then by all means, come fight."

Hydie's arm brushed mine as she and Connor reached my side, and I thanked the heavens for keeping them close. The danger wasn't at this castle, but it still felt too near.

Figures blurred around us in a surge of rushed movements. The Casters began to back away from the invitation, shaking their heads as they disappeared, swirls of magic hiding their cowardly faces. My eyes met with Eyeara, but she gave me a regretful look before she turned to follow her clan out of the hall, no witch magic to transport them away. My lips parted in disbelief when so few remained in the room. How could they leave when the war was staring them right in the face? How could they so readily turn down their king?

Chad's hand found its way to my chin as he gently turned my face to focus on his. His eyes poured into mine as his shoulders lifted with his breath. "You and Connor go with Nigel to get a head start on Florence," he instructed, jerking his head towards a nearby guard. "I'll make arrangements with Abigail to keep Hydie safe, and then we'll transport as many as I can back to Chippenham to help," he informed me, indicating the other guard.

"I can take Hydie," I insisted, knowing his role was to be at the forefront of it all, not hiding my inexperienced sister from the battle that was ensuing.

"Save your energy for kicking Florence's arse when you see him," he told me, and a smile lit up his face, all the way to his green eyes as he stared at me.

He turned towards Lili as she appeared by his shoulder. He gave her a firm nod in some unspoken language, but then his lips met my forehead, and Connor was carting me off to the guard who was to take us back to England.

I turned back to see Chad disappearing behind his green smoke, Hydie safely in tow, and then met Lili's eyes.

"Good luck, Sunshine," she said, her tone earnest and sincere, but my body froze at her words.

Connor tugged me along harder, but the arm he pulled went numb. Ice swelled up my heart to the point it might break—might completely shatter—from the simple word.

I had been called that name before. A woman had uttered those words on a night I'd never forget. Not after the war, not when Florence was dead, and most definitely not now that she had said it again. For that had been the most dreadful night of them all. The night Florence and some mysterious woman had swept in and changed my life forever.

Are you taking me to Hell? I had asked, the view of her face obstructed by my tired eyelids.

No, Sunshine. We're taking you somewhere far worse.

Yet as people crossed back and forth in front of Lili, the smile she wore bore no signs of foul play. And as she disappeared without a trace, Nigel grabbed hold of Connor, and we were lifted away by a burnt-orange cloud of smoke.

Jade Austin

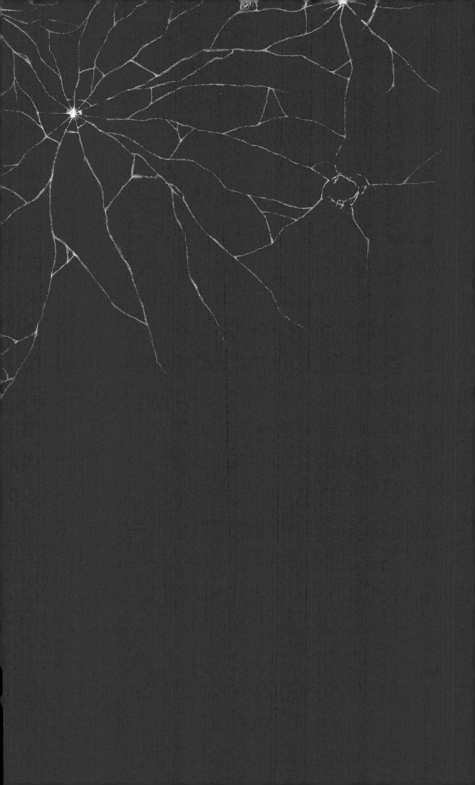

Chapter 23: A Hovel in the Ground

S mall white lights obscured my vision, distorting my hearing with it. If anyone else had muttered a farewell, it was completely drowned out by the splitting headache that slammed into me.
Sunshine.

Pure chaos ensued around me. I was brought back to the present by screams and the smell of poisonous blood that could only mean one thing. Death.

The lair of Chippenham wasn't located in a graveyard as they were at Downy and Loxley Lairs. This one was hidden in the woods. A forest, thick with trees, surrounded us. The trunks reached high in the air, and the coverage of the leaves hid the entire night sky.

Screams and the rush of running bodies worsened the ache in my head. I scanned the crowd, searching for a place to start, someone to help. My eyes met Connor's, but he looked just as lost and helpless as I did. It wasn't until Nigel ran off that something seemed to awaken both of us. Connor and I separated, each being called to another cry. I flew off to a spot far in front of me, which was plagued by screams that came from young lungs.

Weaving through the trees, I encountered a hole I hadn't seen before, dug deep into the ground. Within a single second, I was sliding into it, somewhere underground, and into a new set of chaos. And though I knew what I had heard, I was vastly unprepared for the sight before me.

Hundreds of children, anywhere from newborn to ten years of age, were being thrown into large cages, with only the soft flesh of the other children to break their fall. Cages meant for feral animals. Dirt and tears streaked their faces. Fear pierced their eyes as their small fingers gripped the metal bars that held them.

Dried mud formed the walls, ceiling, and floor of the underground fortress—a home more suitable for giant beasts rather than people. Brightly coloured fungi, as large as my hand, lay scattered among the wreckage as if someone had dropped them in a hurry. Everything that had once made the hovel a home was strewn across the dirt floor. Creatures ran around the massive, dark room, identifying themselves as vampires with their bared pointed fangs as blood trickled down their chins, but I felt no pull towards any of them. Florence was nowhere in sight.

A vampire thrust his lower half against a young woman as he tried to force her into one of the cages. Enraged by his disgusting gesture, I flicked my fingers towards him, aiming to strike, but nothing happened. No reaction from him, no jet of purple, not even a sputter. I stared down at my useless hands. Of all the times to not work, why weren't my emotions letting their pent-up anger out at him?

Throwing that strategy out, I sped towards him and tore the woman out of his grasp, sending him straight into the cavern's wall with a crunch. Gravel showered down from the ceiling. I looked back at the woman, fear shaking her whole body as I noticed her stomach for the first time: protruded, rounded, full. She was pregnant. Before I could take it all in, a fierce yell left my lips as I urged her to go and hide. Her eyes widened but she did as I said. She pushed another man out of her way so that he, too, crashed up against the wall, and then she scurried down a long, dark tunnel.

I stared after her for just a second. A pregnant vampire. I couldn't unsee it.

A familiar swooshing sounded off in the distance, and after a few moments of me grabbing vampire after vampire and forcing them away from the children, Chad appeared down the tunnelled entrance. He was closely followed by Abigail, Cristin, and a few other members from the Loxley Coven, each of whom held a jug containing at least three gallons of clear liquid.

Holy water. They had gotten it.

Ten more people came sliding into the room, all of whose frightened faces I had seen at the coronation. My breath caught as I realised how grateful I was that at least some of them had come to help.

Chad's eyes met mine and he quickly ran to me, kneeling down to help pull the children out of the last cage. He took in their tiny faces and then threw me a terrified look.

"I can't use my magic," he whispered, and my panic truly began to set in.

"But—" I stammered before the realisation of it all slapped into my face.

My eyes flew to the fungi I had so quickly dismissed as though they were of no importance. *Mushrooms*. Mushrooms I recognised from a trip to France I had once taken with Charity and Abigail. Mushrooms Abigail had used to counteract the security cameras powered by witch magic.

I grabbed at the now empty cage. Despite its bulk, I lifted it as though it weighed no more than an envelope, and began collecting all the mushrooms in it as quickly as my body would allow. When my trained eyes were certain I had collected them all, I shut the cage door. Hauling the cage up the steep slant of the tunnel, I ran out into the woods, far past the point we had magicked ourselves in at, and abandoned the cage to run back the way I had come.

Prickles poked at the palms of my hands as I drew further and further from the fungi that had halted my powers—something I hadn't always been able to detect until it was gone. I ran until the entrance came back into view, past the cluttered trees, and then dove right back into the vampire lair.

Chad and the others must have felt their powers returning as I had. Blasts and shocks of magic jetted out towards the horrid vampires who had come to steal the children. Several vampires tried to flee, but I refused to let a single one of Florence's cronies get away without paying for their sins. My power fled from my palms, casting an electric purple shield over the entrance, zapping each one who tried to escape their doom.

I watched as hundreds of beings ran through the large room, and I scrambled to discern who to send sparks of magic towards and who to spare. Screams of torture came from vampires I had never seen before as the holy water showered upon them. Their skin melted like plastic as a dark grey smoke consumed them, feeding off them like the scum they were until all that was left was a smouldering puddle of mud on the floor. In a matter of minutes, the teeth-bared vampires who had attacked the coven were left to soak into the ground.

I took in precisely four breaths before I let my magical barrier flicker into nothing. Chad and his guards fled out into the night, and more screams and sizzles of those who had tried to flee before I had cast my shield followed. My body stood paralysed except for my gasping lungs, but after a few minutes, Chad returned, Connor following closely behind.

I rushed over to Chad and wrapped my arms around him, engulfing him in a hug so tight I was afraid he'd stop breathing. I pulled back, but he placed a hand on the back of my head, drawing it into him so he could place several kisses on my face. His eyes roved over me, checking for marks and injuries, but any wounds began to heal themselves until all that was left was the blood that stained my dress.

My eyes flew to Connor, searching him for signs of injury, then to Abigail, Cristin, and everyone else I knew, checking to see if they were all right as well. Apart from a few scratches and a limp in Connor's walk, everyone seemed fine. But my brow furrowed as I realised that we were the only beings left in the room. The babies, the children, the pregnant woman, and the rest of the coven had run from the havoc to hide elsewhere.

A clatter gathered everyone's attention and drew my eyes towards the tunnel I had seen the pregnant vampire disappear down. It bounced off of the dirt walls and into our ears. An infant's cry followed, and with a brave breath, Chad took my hand, and we led the way down the dark corridor, wondering what we were going to find next.

The place was dark and damp. I closed my eyes, and all the sounds within the lair rushed to my ears. But the only sounds—the infant's cry and the panicked hushes of others—took us to a single door.

With an effortless flick of Chad's wrist, the door blasted off of its hinges to reveal a small room crammed with at least fifty stragglers. From youthful, plump faces to wrinkled ones, they stared back at us, the chatter of their teeth and the baby's cry breaking their fearful silence. But this wasn't all of them. There had been far more during the attack. These were merely the coven members who had decided to stay and hide rather than flee.

Blood matted their clothes and hair, decorating their dirty skin like carelessly placed accessories. Yet there was something eerie that seemed to connect them all.

They all had blue eyes.

"I've heard of this coven," Abigail's voice came from behind me. "This coven feeds on their young if they're born as mortals." The eyes of the cowering vampires darkened as she took a step forwards, then she looked back at me, sorrow flooding her eyes. She breathed out in a whisper, "They're evil."

Chapter 24: Only If They Choose to Be

Abigail's words sparked a memory. She had told me about this coven during one of my first nights at Loxley Lair. They had mastered the art of impregnating themselves—a technique that was rare for vampires—then fed on their young if they were born as mortals, and raised the ones who turned out like themselves. The information crept its way up my neck and into my mind. I cringed at the feel of it, the idea that someone could drink the blood of their own child.

The Casters behind us murmured angrily, their heat rising in the form of hatred. A male elf stuck his chin up higher, eyeing me carefully, waiting for me to prove I was just as cruel as the vampires who trembled on the dirt floor.

Swallowing down an anxious gulp, I turned around to face the vampires. The holy water had destroyed several of their attackers, but had it managed to melt any of the vampires who lived here? Were these merely the ones who had hidden in time? I didn't know how to distinguish myself from them, but I would *never* sink as low as **MURDERING** a child.

An older vampire sneered at us as though we hadn't just saved their lives. "We are *not* evil," he hissed out from his place on the floor.

I turned my head towards him, cocking it to the side before I replied, "*That* is yet to be determined."

Chad shifted his weight from foot to foot, staring at what remained of the coven in front of us. "Are you all accounted for?" Chad asked them, and a younger looking woman shook her head at him.

Abigail gently took my arm in her hand. "Florence isn't here," she whispered, her eyes grazing over the children with a hopeless expression. "We're going to check on our lair," she added.

Chills coated my skin as I realised what Florence's absence might mean. What if this was all a diversion? A way to steal my sister from right under my nose?

I twisted to face Abigail, to tell her I was coming with her, but she squeezed my arm reassuringly. "Everything will be fine," she told me gently. Her soft eyes peered anxiously around her, probably wondering how much to say in present company. "I'm sure the guards and the wards kept everyone safe. Besides," she said, inching closer and giving me a very elderly sister type of look, "helping here may prove beneficial."

I looked back at the few witches, wizards, and elves from the coronation, mixed in with the crowd of Loxley members by the doorway. Abigail wasn't wrong. Staying may sway the Casters to trust me. Those who had come didn't fight to save these vampires, that much was certain. No, they stayed to observe—to see the fight firsthand and make their decision from there. If I stayed, perhaps I could figure out a way to convince them I was as good as Chad claimed.

Nodding back at Abigail, I decided she was right. It was possible Florence knew about my sister, but with the wards and my friends keeping Hydie safe, it bought me time.

"All right," I told her. "Just keep her away from anyone with red eyes," I begged, not wanting to mention Hydie's name around people I was sure I couldn't trust.

Abigail turned to weave her way past the Casters with the dark image of mistrust carved into their expressions, but a woman from the floor lurched forwards, grasping onto Abigail's arm.

"Please!" the woman begged on her knees, desperation coating her scratchy voice. Her hands moved frantically up and down Abigail's arm, coaxing her to listen to her plea. "He'll send them back. He won't rest until we're all dead. That's what he told us if we didn't fight for him. But they're too young," she said, pointing back to the children. "They can't fight, and we can't desert them to join his cause. His issues are not ours."

One arm flung towards the rest of her coven. "Use it," she insisted, her eyes darting to the jug of holy water as red tears began to stream down her cheeks. "Use it on us and it'll prove we're not evil. We feed on the blood of our young for survival—to shield them from the vicious life they would have—not to be cruel. We breed for companionship. Test us!" she screamed out hysterically. "Test us, and then help us. Please!"

We all looked down at the jugs of water the Loxley members had been taking with them. The vampires on the floor wore mixed expressions, having seen the effects it had on those who weren't worthy of redemption.

Chad's eyes scanned over the blue-eyed children, and then over to the Casters who observed him closely, awaiting his decision as though it were a test.

"One bottle would not be a complete waste," Chad decided, though guilt clouded his eyes.

There was a slight pause before I heard Cristin swallow and hand over a jug, half-full of the liquid that could bring even more death into the already morbid night. It sloshed around, threatening to spill, and nearly every soul in the room leaned away from it—Caster and Night Crawler alike.

"Perhaps we could just stick their hands in to test them," Chad suggested.

As he took the holy water, the sight of the container sparked my memory.

"Abigail," I whispered, grabbing hold of her arm before she could leave. My eyes intercepted paths with the blue elf, and I lowered my voice in the hope that he couldn't hear. "There's a cage filled with large, colourful mushrooms about three hundred metres north of here," I told her. "Can you collect it on your way back?"

A shadow of confusion washed over her face before she must have realised the significance of the mushrooms. "Of course," she said quietly, and then with one last look at the blue-eyed children, she left.

As the Loxley Coven parted ways, Connor gave a nod in farewell and limped out with them, Cristin supporting his weight as they went. I was left in the room with the vampires who lived there and Chad while his guards and the other Casters, including the blue elf, watched carefully from the doorway.

I looked away from the tall blue man, feeling the doubt and fatigue in my heart. Part of me was glad the Casters would stay, hear the full story, and watch as we used the holy water on the vampires, but part of me was afraid it would be counterproductive. If every single vampire from the coven were to dissolve, it could incriminate the rest of us.

I cleared my throat, hoping my voice could conceal my fear. "Let's start with the children and then take them to another room in case the others aren't as pure of heart," I announced. They didn't need to see more torture than they already had, and the look in their pure eyes told me the water would do them no harm.

Chad nodded in agreement before holding the jug out to the children one at a time, missing the disgruntled looks one of his guards gave me. I averted my eyes, refusing to give in to the guilt he was trying to splash onto me—guilt of what I was. What I couldn't help but be.

After the kids were all cleared, some of the guards took them back to the main room, and the temperature started to spike. Several vampires began to struggle, and my keen eyes tracked their rash movements as the fifteen or so of them who were left tried to flee. Chad shoved the jug towards them, and they shrank back against the wall, hissing at him. I bared my teeth at them in warning.

But still, there was chaos. Some screamed out, refusing to partake in the test, and my heart was torn between mercy and not falling for their tricks. My eyes flew from person to person, but Chad squeezed my hand tight, steadying me for what we both knew had to be done.

"You heard the king's orders," another guard barked, and Chad flinched at the title.

The guard sent a stream of grey magic to twist around the hand of a particularly defiant man, and yanked it into water. Steam erupted from the top of the bottle as the water bubbled, and the grey magic released his hand. Screeching at the top of his lungs, the man jerked his arm from the container, but there was no hand left on the end, just a smouldering nub.

His screams echoed violently against the dirt walls. He crashed down to the floor, grasping at his injured arm, rocking back and forth to soothe his pains as he screamed a slew of curses at us. I closed my eyes tight to try and block it all out, but it didn't help. The guard stumbled back from shock, his throat bobbing before his eyes flew to Chad, waiting for his command. Chad approached the vampire as he continued writhing on the floor. Avoiding the man's flailing limbs, he grabbed the man's forearm and used his other hand to cast green waves of smoke around the blistering nub. Slowly, the stump grew upward, elongating until it sprouted fingers and nails once more. Emerald vines wrapped their way around the man's wrists and ankles to constrain him, but the man was too exhausted to fight them off. Shivers wracked his body as he curled up into a ball and accepted the floor as his resting place.

A vision of my father rotting in a jail cell next to this man was enough to soothe my worries. There was a place for people like them, and it wasn't roaming around this earth freely.

"Please, madam," a frail voice whispered from behind me, and I turned to see the same young woman from before, her stomach stretching out before her. She had to be around eight months along. As she sat in a heap on the floor, her eyes darted nervously to the water as it sloshed around its clear container, drawing in closer to us like a snake.

"I was turned into this only a few short months ago," she pleaded, "and I need a doctor. I need to make sure my baby is safe. I've done terrible things. I've—I've drank blood from innocent people, lost in the woods before this coven found me and took me in. I don't want my baby to suffer for my sins."

I bit my lip until it bled, weighing the options. Deciding whether it was moral or not to cast her hand into the water, to make her unborn child feel her pain as her hand melted away to nothing. It was too cruel.

Chad's warmth radiated towards me as he neared and bent down to the woman. "How did you feel in your heart after you took those lives?" he asked her softly.

She blinked at him a few times, searching him over, taking in his dirtied formal wear, his hands, and then lingering just a second too long on his neck. My muscles clenched, ready to react faster than she could if she tried anything. But then I took in the way she relaxed, and the slow breaths she took to contain herself, and she breathed out a single word. "Terrible." Her voice caught on the word as though she meant every syllable.

Another scream shook the underground lair, but Chad's guards quickly repeated the process their king had just performed to replace the severed arm.

Chad stirred uncomfortably but pressed on. "If that's true, you'll be just fine," he explained to the woman sweetly. "But if it's not," he added, his voice turning vastly more stern, "then I'll heal your hand as quickly as I can, and we'll discuss what comes next."

Chad stood up straight before reaching to grab the water from his guard, and I knelt down to her in his place. As he carried the water over to us, his eyes squinted with hesitation, as though asking me if this were the right thing to do, and I gave him a firm nod.

The woman threw one more haunted look at me, but I took her hand in mine, placing a finger between each of hers. "Let's do it together," I told her, bravery reaching my voice but not my heart. Her trembling hand masked my own fears as we plunged our hands into the water.

I think it's really important to understand someone is only evil if they choose to be evil, Abigail had once told me. *Is that who you want to be?*

The water sizzled before the woman flung her hand from it, and a bit of water splashed onto her dress. My stomach lurched its way into my throat, but the water hadn't hurt us. We were both unscathed.

Relief flushed both our faces. I looked over to the blue elf to see if he wore any sign of a revelation on his face, but he merely studied me with blank features.

The pregnant woman looked up at me, trying eagerly to catch her breath. "And my baby?" she asked, an aching tone coming back to her. "I want to know it's okay. I want to make sure my transformation didn't harm it."

"Here," Chad offered, handing the jug back to a guard and kneeling down on the floor once more. He looked back to the woman and took her wet hand in his. "Lay back a bit and I'll take a look." Helping her to lean back, he conjured a thick cushion for her to lay on. It looked dirty and ragged as though it had come from somewhere in the underground lair.

For the time being, no more screams of pain informed us of unworthy souls as Chad's hands hovered over the woman's face. The dark circles around her eyes cleared before his floating hands travelled down to her stomach. For a moment, he stared down, his brows creased and his eyes focused beyond her dress, until a smile crept onto his face.

"Your babies are just fine," he told her, and both of us jerked our heads back as we took in his words.

"Babies?" she asked, emphasising the plural form he had used.

He nodded as his smile continued to grow. "There are two of them," he replied before shifting his hands to her side to get a better view. "Do you want to know more? Perhaps the sex?"

She nodded eagerly back at him, her sorrow finally fading away.

"Well," he began again, "this one's a boy, and..." His fingers delicately curved their way to the lower side of her abdomen. "I think this one's a girl."

Her smile brightened until I could see the beauty she possessed, not just the frightened vampire she had become. It was brief while it lasted before her face darkened once more. "And—and are the babies going to be like me? The... *thing* I've become?" Her voice was raw and her arms wrapped around her stomach like a warm embrace.

Chad's shoulders fell a bit. "That I'm not sure," he said carefully, "but the fact that they survived the pain you must've gone through for your transformation, well..." He sighed a breath full of uncertainty and sadness. "The odds aren't very good they're still mortals."

A single red tear dripped down her face, but through her quivering breath, she gave a nod. "I thought as much," she told him. "But at least they're alive."

Another scream filled the room, and I quickly shifted to block her view. "You're very brave," I let out, eager to distract her—ease her mind a bit. If not for her, then for her babies. I let out an airy, awkward laugh. "You know, I think I'd want it to be a surprise, the sex of the baby. See them for the first time and see what I've got."

To my relief, she let out a small laugh of her own. "No," she said, continuing to run her hands along her stomach lovingly. "I'm glad I know. I'll have time to pick out their names now."

A guard behind us cleared his throat to gather our attention. "Your Highness," he started, "that's all of them."

Three vampires lay on the ground with ropes of magic binding their appendages together. Three people who'd make a lovely addition to the Loxley prison. The rest of them clung anxiously onto the ragged wall, eyeing us as though we were ghosts they didn't know whether or not they should fear.

"The man who sent his followers to attack your lair," Chad began to ask the Night Crawlers, "do you know his name?"

They nodded but stayed silent, afraid to speak it.

"Join us," Chad offered them. "We know you can't fight, but if you pledge allegiance to our side, we will offer all the protection we have to offer. You were right," he directed towards the lady who had pleaded for the use of the holy water. "Florence will stop at nothing to harm you when he finds out his cronies failed to capture your children. He'll try to lure you in with promises of freedom, but a world where creatures like us are brought out into the open will not bring freedom, it'll bring chaos. He'll use vile means to defeat those of us who wish to remain hidden."

"We will not join you," grumbled the man whose hand had been the first to melt off. Dirt scattered out from in front of him as his breath blew out in a rage. "You're a Caster. Your kind has done nothing for us for thousands of years."

"Apparently, saving your arses tonight means nothing to you," I snapped at him. "Besides, *you*, unlike some of the others, don't have a choice as to what your fate is," I told him, looking down at the ropes that bound him.

But as I looked around at the others expectantly, every one of them held their tongues. The same thoughts, it seemed, fogged their decision.

"What are you?" another woman asked quietly, her eyes squinted at me. "I saw you in the other room. You had your hands out in front of you like you were trying to do magic, but you have our speed, our eyes, and our teeth," she noted.

I blinked a few times before furrowing my brows. "Well," I started apprehensively, "I'm both." I let that sink in a bit before continuing. "I was born a Caster, although I didn't truly know it. I was forced to hide my powers for much of my childhood. Then I was bitten by Florence just over a year ago, and turned into a vampire."

A few of them shuddered, but I wasn't sure if it was from his name or the memory of their own transformations.

"Why have you chosen the Caster's side?"

I shook my head. It wasn't that simple.

"It's not about Casters versus Night Crawlers," I told him, my nostrils flaring as I tried to force the irritation out of my tone. I wished I could mentally summon Chad's coronation speech or have him recite the whole thing over, but I knew they wouldn't listen to him. "Look," I said, scanning my eyes over all of them. "I know you're all frightened, and I know it's probably the last thing on your minds right now to join Florence, but he's cunning. He'll force you to do things against your will, and we want you to know that you don't have to choose his side just because he's a vampire. There are Casters working with him, and as you've seen tonight, Night Crawlers are working with the king of Casters," I said, gesturing to Chad. "Only, we're trying to *save* the souls who are good, worth saving, while Florence is taking innocent lives to fight his sadistic cause."

"You must be desperate if you're asking us," one of them rang out, a woman who looked to be the same age as me, but her fierce tone informed me she was years wiser. "A last resort. Even other vampires have shunned our coven, all because of our desire to have children. Our hunger for blood is no different from your own. We've been forced to hide out here. Holy water or not, we know what you think of us, and we will not go where we are not wanted."

Chad's jaw was tight as he tried to keep patient.

"We won't ask you to choose tonight," he informed them, letting out a deep sigh as he ran his hand through his hair. "We'll provide you with protection and shelter until you can find some for yourselves, and a chance at peace, but the rest is up to you." There was a stern look in his eyes as he stared around at them. "But remember," he warned, "war can change people. If you join his side, it could turn your soul dark, and if that happens, we won't hesitate to coat you in this liquid," he said, gesturing over to the holy water.

There were a few hesitant nods.

"Let's move out," Chad told his guards.

"But there's more of us," one of the vampires said. "They could be out there still. We can't leave without them."

Chad let in another slow breath to steady himself. "Then we'll go with you to find the other members of your clan," he told them, and even though he didn't utter the words aloud, there was the big question of *if* they were still alive.

The light in Chad's eyes was snuffed out with exhaustion, and I felt my muscles growing heavier from my own fatigue.

Chad's hand made its way to my cheek, running his thumb along it softly before giving me a soothing smile. "Go to the lair. We'll take care of this coven, and then I'll meet you there shortly to discuss the rest," he instructed, but a haunting memory fluttered before my eyes.

"Lili," I said quickly, trying to block out the image of her face, the sound of the word she had muttered. "There's something I need to tell you about her," I added as I scanned his guards. I lowered my voice, moving closer to his chest as I held onto him and whispered. "Please, just—stay away from her. Wait for our discussion."

Chad's heart rate increased from the suspense I hadn't meant to cause, yet he gave a confirming nod, and green smoke swallowed him up whole.

As soon as my feet met the shiny floors of Loxley Lair, and my own purple smoke cleared, Hydie ran into my arms and grasped me tightly.

"I'm so glad you're all right," she breathed out, her voice a rush of worry. "Abigail was just telling me everything that happened."

My eyes ascended towards Abigail as she approached us, the same worry taxing her face.

"Were all the children all right?" she asked softly. "Did all of them survive?"

I let out a heavy breath. "Yes, all the children are fine."

Her eyes fell to the floor, more questions lingering on the edge of her lips. "And are they all to be cared for? Do they all have a home?" Abigail asked.

My answering sigh was full of regret, knowing just how much she and Cristin yearned for a child to call their own. Giving her a small nod, I said, "They'll be taken care of."

She shrugged with an almost convincing smile. "Thought I'd ask."

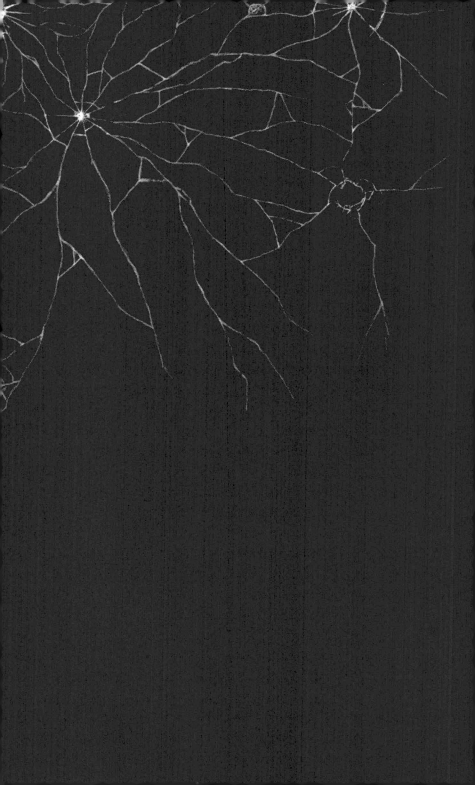

Chapter 25: Sunshine

I spent nearly an hour pacing back and forth in Abigail's room, she and Hydie trying to ease me out of panicked breaths and a tightened chest. I had been calm. I had gotten through the entire attack in Chippenham, but now I was in ruins.

Florence had outsmarted us once again. He had pulled his tricks out of his sleeves, and we had all been so blind, so utterly useless, dancing and bickering over nonsense. He had wormed his way through the country, infiltrated a lair, and had nearly dominated them, and for what? To tear mothers and fathers from their strange blue-eyed vampire children? To keep babies as trophies? To grow an army against those who wished to remain hidden? It was barbaric. Why not just come out and announce what we were to the world? What the hell was he waiting for?

My heart hammered out of my chest. My feet carved a path into the carpeted floors while echoes of Abigail and Hydie's voices attempted to barge their way into focus, but Lili's voice screamed above it all.

Sunshine.

The word she had thrown out so carelessly scraped against my ears, like a match striking flint, igniting an infinite legion of fear in its wake.

She was working for him. She was working for Florence and had been the whole time. All while I had left Chad to play detective with her. All right under my nose.

A light puff of wind sounded from above, marking Chad's arrival to Loxley Lair, and I pulled my hands away from the clawed position they had taken against my scalp. My eyes flitted over to Abigail, and she gave me a nod before I disappeared, reappearing on the floor above to run into Chad's arms.

My chest met his and he grasped the back of my head, his other arm wrapped around my waist, and I breathed in the scent of him. His clothes reeked of sweat and dirt from the hovel in the ground, but underneath it was the smell of his soap, his breath, and his blood as it pounded through his enraptured heart.

"Everything's all right, my love," he whispered, breathing warm air against my hair. "It'll all be taken care of."

A single puff of magic resonated behind him, and he let his grip on me release as he turned to his guard, Nigel. Chad's fingers lingered on mine, twirling around them until they interlaced gently together. The patter of footsteps preceded the sight of Abigail and Hydie as they came up the stairs, closely followed by Charity, Leo, and a hoard of other Night Crawlers. O'Brien and a werewolf stood by Connor, who now looked to be healed from his cuts. Most of the coven had come home after news of the attack spread like wildfire, and the room filled with anxious bodies, all waiting to discern the latest update.

Nigel's heart beat loudly as small beads of sweat gathered above his brow. His eyes took in the severed halves of the manananggals, the pale blue eyes of the vampires, and the hunched-over backs of the werewolves, whose bodies had slowly morphed from years of shifting to crawl on all fours. His shoulders relaxed ever so slightly as he met the familiar faces of Connor, my sister, and me.

"This is Nigel," Chad introduced to us all, tilting his head up. "He's the head of my guard and my most trusted soldier."

"Your Highness," Nigel addressed his king, bowing his head at Chad. "Permission to relay the events of the night?"

"Permission granted," Chad replied through strong, steady lungs. If not for the red lines that garnished his eyes, and the diminutive cracks within his lips, a being with inferior eyesight would be ignorant to the drowsiness that weighed heavily against him.

"We're uncertain how he did it," Nigel began, his eyes focused on the mystery, ignoring the creatures he was raised to fear, "but none of the facial recognition software went off."

A rumble of confusion filled the room. I watched as several people exchanged looks, fear and surprise laced through their expressions.

"How is that possible?" Chad asked, squinting to pinpoint the reason within his mind. "We have every camera on earth searching for him."

"That's just it," Nigel continued, his voice wavering away from a formal tone. His brow furrowed as he tried to comprehend the events. "The software method would've worked, but there was a string of blackouts." He looked up at Chad, remembering who he was. "Your Highness," he rectified, bowing his head once more. "All the technology within a kilometre went out like dominoes. The blackouts led their way in a trail, right to the edge of that forest. When we arrived, we could hear the screams."

"Have you retraced the steps back to where the blackouts started?" Charity asked.

"We have some guards on it as we speak," Nigel replied.

Chad added, "When I'm done here, I'm going to go help investigate myself."

I frowned, trying to piece it all together. How had the night twisted into some horrible nightmare?

I turned back to Nigel. "At the coronation, a guard said you were all certain it was Florence," I started. "How were you so sure it was him if his face didn't appear on the cameras?"

"I saw him, milady," Nigel said with an exasperated truth that rang through the air. His eyes roved over everyone else in the room. "I ordered my men to go help, but just as I was about to come and report the attack, I saw him." Nigel's eyes grew unfocused at the memory. "His eyes were red, and he smiled at me like he knew who I was—like he knew exactly who I was going to report to—but instead of stopping me, he ran away. He was so fast. I couldn't even track his movements."

Red brushed his cheeks as he looked around the room, embarrassed by his admission. We all knew how fast vampires could move. Fast enough that mortals, Casters, and even some Night Crawlers couldn't see. But for Florence to run, and let Nigel come warn us?

Chills crept up my back. What was Florence playing at? The questions that swarmed my head kept forming.

"My guards have all been informed of what Florence looks like," Chad explained. "These blackouts though..." he added, his voice trailing off into oblivion as he frowned. "I mean, I understand he's working with Casters to create a trail of blackouts. What I don't understand is how they could produce a blackout so thoroughly as to block every bit of magic within a kilometre radius."

"That had to have been the effect of the mushrooms," I uttered.

Abigail, Cristin, and a few others nodded, but Chad and Nigel looked at me curiously.

"The mushrooms," I began, "the ones littering the floor of the underground hovel?" But they both stared at me blankly, still not understanding their significance. I turned back to Chad. "When I got there, I couldn't use my magic. At first, I thought it was just me, but when you told me you couldn't use yours either, I figured out that the mushrooms were blocking it. That must be why Nigel couldn't transport us closer to the lair."

"They're magic mushrooms that gnomes farm to deactivate witch magic," Leo explained further. "They harvest them as protection, and the gnomes who live here are kind enough to supply us with them if we ever need them."

"I've used them to get past security cameras before," Abigail mentioned. "It turns them off long enough for us to get by unnoticed. That has to be how Florence is getting around undetected."

"And Azalea collected so many," Cristin added, "perhaps the more you have, the larger the blackout."

"'Nd have there been any other blackouts before this one?" O'Brien asked.

"Not that we've noticed," Nigel reported, "but it's highly possible we could've missed it, especially if he wasn't travelling very far."

"We'll have to do something about the mushrooms, won't we?" Chad asked rhetorically.

"Perhaps something, but not entirely if it creates a trail," I thought aloud.

I studied the floor as the others continued to speak. A trail straight to Florence was daunting, but necessary nonetheless. What we needed to do was control the amount of gnome magic he had, and use it to capture him.

"Azalea," a voice squeaked from off in the distance. "Azalea, I have an idea."

Fendel, I realised with excitement. I had only heard his voice once before, but I'd never forget it.

"I'll be back," I whispered to Chad as everyone discussed possible next moves. "I'm going to go have a word with Fendel."

He gave me a nod, and then I slipped out of the entrance hall and down the long corridor. The light from the moon shone through the long windows of the greenhouse, illuminating half the walkway. Ornate wall sconces helped brighten the rest of the corridor as I made my way down to the gnome's quarters, following the sound of Fendel's tiny heartbeat. It pattered with the same excitement he contained in his high-pitched voice.

The door creaked open as I approached it, and after walking into the room, I shut the door behind me. The tiny gnome stood before me with his pointed hat and long beard. The otherwise gnome-less room was quite a change compared to the last time I was in there, but Fendel's face brightened the same way it had that night.

"Good evening, milady," he greeted with a chipper hop.

"Good evening, Fendel," I replied, kneeling on the floor next to him. A smile curved my lips as I took in his full flesh form, unabashedly shown, rather than his usual mask of porcelain. "Might I ask why you're eclipsing yourself in the shadows?" I asked, looking around the dimly lit, lonely room. "You have my word that Chad won't harm you, or any other gnome," I told him softly. "He's not like his aunts. You can show yourself in front of him if you wish."

"I'll consider it, Miss Azalea," he told me with a sceptical look. "It's hard to rewire the fear witches have caused gnomes for centuries."

"I understand," I said, still hoping he'd come around. Either way, I was beyond delighted that he was on speaking terms with me.

"Anyway, milady," he squealed, "the other gnomes and I have been working very hard to catch Mr Florence. We're trying to be very good spies for you. We didn't know mushrooms were missing until Miss Abigail gave us the ones you found. We inspected them quite thoroughly, and think these ones may have been missing for a very long time indeed. Years even."

"Do you think Florence could've stolen them from here then?" I asked.

"Oh no, milady," he said quickly. "Gnomes don't grow this type in Europe. These ones are grown in the Americas, in the especially cold and rainy parts. We're going to alert the gnomes overseas so they can protect the rest of their supply."

"That would be wonderful, Fendel," I told him, a lead weight lifted from my shoulders. As much as I liked the method of tracking Florence, giving him an endless supply would weaken our forces. If he only had a few remaining mushrooms, that would be ideal. "That'll be so very helpful. What would I do without you?" I asked earnestly, and a rosy hue brushed his cheeks.

"Of course, milady," he piped. "Your spies are hard at work."

The sound of murmurs and footsteps from down the corridor indicated a dissolving crowd, and after my eyes glanced towards the door, I looked back at Fendel with the brightest smile that my tired cheeks could manage.

"Cheers, Fendel," I told him.

"'Tis our pleasure!" he replied happily, and then he turned to hobble off further into the room, shouting, "We'll keep you updated!" as he rounded a corner.

I stepped back into the corridor, closing the door behind me as mushrooms, Florence, and Lili crowded my mind. When I looked up at the owner of some approaching footsteps, O'Brien's kind eyes met mine.

"All right there, Azalea?" he asked, stopping his stride as the friendly smile I had seen so many times sprouted on his face.

"Yeah, of course," slipped from my lips, but it was such an automatic lie. I sighed, shaking away the false pretences with my head. "I mean, no, but I suppose I will be soon enough, you know?"

He nodded back at me, and I took in the way his eyes flitted away from mine for just a second before they landed back on me. "We'll catch 'im, Azalea," he told me firmly. "We'll catch 'im if it's the last thing I do, all righ'?"

"O'Brien," I let out, tilting my head at him sternly as I put a hand on his shoulder, grounding him to this moment. "Don't say such depressing nonsense. You'll go on to do many great things," I added firmly, "far after we capture the arsehole." Despite the ache in my heart, I forced myself to give him an encouraging smile.

His smile shined a bit brighter, and I let my hand fall from his shoulder.

"Thanks, Azalea," he said. "Anyhow, I was jus' checkin' in with ya before I go out. We've got ourselves stationed all over to help. I'm in charge of the Downy Lair in case Florence goes pokin' 'round there again."

"Be careful out there," I told him softly.

"O' course," O'Brien agreed.

I bid him farewell and made my way back out to the entrance hall where Hydie, Connor, and Chad stood waiting for me. Abigail must have dispersed with the rest of the coven.

I walked up to Chad, wondering if I should include Hydie and Connor in on our talk about Lili, but as he cupped my cheek into his hand, I decided a private conversation might be best—at least to start off with.

He ran his thumb gingerly along my cheek, studying my face with worried eyes. "Do you have the energy to take Hydie home?" he asked. "I need to take Connor to his flat above the pub, and then tie up all the loose ends from the night."

My heart skipped a beat, and my hand overlapped his as it held my cheek. "No," I said quickly. I shifted my eyes over to my sister and the werewolf before returning them to Chad. In a hushed tone, I told him, "I mean, I can take Hydie home, but I *need* to talk to you before you go back."

I watched as Chad nodded, his head saying one thing, and his face portraying another. His jaw clenched and he dropped his hand, causing mine to fall with it.

"I'll meet you at home then," he said before turning towards Connor.

"Ladies," Connor said in farewell, and he and Chad disappeared in a cloud of green smoke.

Hydie's eyes wallowed in sadness as she took me in. As I held her hand and we disappeared behind my lavender cloud, I finally understood the look to be pity.

"Oh, don't look at me that way," I told her as our feet landed on her bedroom floor.

"He's too tired," Hydie tried, her voice soft, yet just as decisive as my own. "He's under more stress now than he was before the coronation and the attack. He won't have the mental capacity to hear you out about Lili tonight."

I gave her a severe elderly sister look, hoping it would cause her to retreat. I hadn't said a word to her about Mrs Prophecy and my newly found accusations, yet she hadn't been able to keep her nose out of my mind long enough for me to consider filling her in myself.

"He's fine," I said firmly, succeeding in proving my stubbornness more than my actual point. "He'll hear me out, and he'll confront her, and all will be well."

"Azalea," she pressed, frowning at me for being so blind. "He doesn't have the ability to push her away, especially not tonight. He thinks he needs her help."

"And how would you know?" I countered, stepping in towards her fiercely. "Did he confide all this in you?"

"I can hear parts of his thoughts," she said simply, refusing to back down. "They're scattered and overwhelmed, but that much is clear. He does a fair job of blocking me out of most of it, but what I can tell is that he's desperate for help. And as much as we'd all like to be rid of Lili, Chad needs her."

"He does not *need* her," I objected. "Our side will be better without her. She's evil," I added, completely unable to control my temper.

"Listen to him yourself then," she said, crossing her arms in front of her. "Just focus on his mind."

I turned abruptly on my heel to face the door of her bedroom. Grasping the knob, I glanced back at her to say, "I, unlike you, have the ability to stay out of peoples' minds and let them tell me things on their own."

Hydie glared back at me in a way that felt so familiar, so much like home even though it infuriated me to no end.

"The woman who was there when Florence changed you," she pressed, clearly unable to mind her own thoughts. "You obviously don't remember her voice if you didn't recognise it the first time you met Lili. It's just a word, Azalea. You have no more proof than you did before."

"It doesn't matter. I remember *how* she said it," I snapped.

Hydie put her arms back down to her sides, apparently giving up on me and my hot temper. "Well, when you're blabbering on to Chad about all this, I wouldn't lead with that as your main evidence," she growled.

I couldn't even think, I was so furious. "Goodnight," I called out as my only reply.

Only a smidge of remorse clawed at me as I shut her door loudly and trekked to my room. Tonight was too much. Too much intensity, too much death, too much uncertainty. I didn't notice that I was pacing back and forth once more, nor that my hands were tugging manically at my curls, all while a chorus of Lili's voice went pounding through my head saying, *Sunshine, Sunshine, Sunshine,* as though the word itself held the burning flames of the sun—the very flames that would turn me to stone if I let them lap freely onto my skin.

The sound of Chad's arrival made me turn on my heel and head towards where he stood next to our bed. The fierceness of my pivot made him flinch, but as the exhaustion reappeared on his face, and Hydie's warning played through my mind, words flew out of my mouth to try and counteract it all.

"She's a liar!" I exclaimed, with far too much volume and exertion than I thought possible for the way my very bones ached to crawl into bed.

"Who?" Chad asked, deep creases on his forehead marking his confusion.

I gawked at him as though he had gone mad. "Lili!" I shouted. She was the entire reason I needed him to come back here—our entire discussion revolved around her.

"Oh," Chad breathed out, all the air leaving his lungs with the single syllable, and apparently his intuition as well if he couldn't sense the evil that oozed from her. "Look," he tried, taking a slow step towards me. "I know it's awkward—"

"Awkward?" I gasped, not believing my ears. "Awkward is so far off the chart of relevance that I can't even think right now."

"Then what is it?" he asked calmly.

I rolled my eyes at his insolence, only my sister's words clouded my better judgement to lead with Lili's comment.

"All the clues are stacking up against her, Chadwick," I fumbled, having lost it completely as exhaustion forced out all my inner thoughts.

"Azalea," he warned sounding knackered, but I promptly ignored him.

"For starters," I went on, not bothering to slow down, "where was she during the attack?"

"She was with my aunts," he countered easily.

I scoffed. Such an easy alibi. "We know for a fact there's a Caster helping Florence, delivering letters and whatever other drivel he has her doing," I claimed, no longer entirely sure my reflection had been telling the truth. It was more likely that the pink-haired woman was a decoy. "We know the woman is blonde, and now she's far too close to the information thanks to you—"

"But I don't think Lili's the one—" he cut off.

"—and her magic," I tried eagerly, his blindness gritting my teeth. "There's something off, something strange, something—" I tried desperately to grasp at straws, to figure out just what it was that bothered me. When Lili had rotated that magical map at his aunts' house, the fireworks she had shown off at the coronation dinner, and when she had disappeared without a trace… It lingered on the tip of my tongue until it finally rolled off. "Her magic is *invisible*!" I exclaimed.

"What?" Chadwick asked. His eyes scrunched so hard I wondered if his brain was completely deprived of sleep by now. "'Invisible?'" he questioned, sounding more dumbfounded than necessary.

I rolled my eyes at him. "Yes. Her smoke?" I asked as though it were obvious. "Little puffs of magic," I nearly screamed, flinging my hands around wildly. "I can't see it. It's invisible. It's not there or she's—I don't know, *masking* it somehow."

"Wait," he said, squeezing his eyes shut all the way and then pinching the bridge of his nose before looking at me once more. His hand waved slowly in front of him as though it would untangle his bafflement. "You mean to say, you can *see* people's magic? As in, more than just your own?"

Now I was being dragged into the pool of confusion. My heart faltered for a moment before nodding my head at him. "Of course," I said, the bite behind my voice now vanquished. "Can't—can't you?" I asked for no reason at all but to try and buy time before finding out I was the odd one, different in yet another way, but it didn't help when Chadwick let out an astonished laugh.

"No," he said with far too much amusement for my liking, and he jerked his head forwards to start what felt like more of an interrogation than intrigue. "What's my colour then? My magic?"

I frowned at him, scolding him with my expression. "It's green," I told him flatly, hoping that would be the end of it, but of course it wasn't.

"Hydie's?"

"Gold," I replied with a shrug.

"What about Aunt Mallory?"

"Red."

"And Aunt Morgan? What of hers?"

"Also red," I spat out, getting increasingly more annoyed with each question.

"Blimey," he nearly whispered, his brows poised high in disbelief. "That's truly fascinating."

I stared at him, my emotions spent with worry. "How is it fascinating?" I asked. Exhaustion was taking hold of my tongue too. Any attempt at holding back my cheeky attitude went to waste.

"Well," Chad went on to explain, rubbing the back of his neck wearily, "witches and wizards can only see their own magic, can't they?"

I glared at him for asking a question I clearly didn't know. "Well, why wouldn't you mention that?" It was completely exasperating. How could I see others' magic when the colour was only meant for them?

"How would I know you could see something I couldn't, unless you told me?" he responded, his voice slightly calmer, but his interest pursued. "It would be a bit hard to hide our magic from mortals if they saw a big cloud of smoke around us every time, don't you think?" he asked, and I looked away from him, realising for the first time that it made sense. "Can Abigail see our magic?" he pressed. "The colour of it? Perhaps it's your vampire eyes."

But I shook my head, not entirely sure. "I don't know," I let out with a heavy breath, "only, that hardly makes sense either." Something tugged at me, something Hydie had said. "Hydie mentioned she couldn't see our father's magic. She asked me if his red magic was stirring, so I must've been able to see it when we were younger, when she knew me properly—before I was turned into a vampire."

"It's curious," Chad said, grinning at me madly. His fingers reached towards me to play with the front of my dress. "You keep revealing qualities of a powerful sorceress. It's almost as if you're part of some important prophecy."

I scoffed loudly as though it would prove my point or blow away the ridiculous timing of his comment. My hands flew to my temples, blocking any other distractions from bludgeoning their way past my mental shield.

"Chadwick, all of this is completely beside the point!" I called out in pure disbelief of how quickly the conversation had flown away from its original purpose—how quickly I had let it. His hand dropped from my dress, but then a sense of understanding dawned on his face. "The witch," I pressed on.

"All right, can I just state my viewpoint—" he began, holding his hand out in front of him, but I swatted it away.

"She's a traitor," I interrupted, already having heard his apparent viewpoint from Hydie. "When I'm talking to her, I can *feel* it. She's hiding something."

He looked taken aback. His next words crept out slowly and carefully, but I knew he wasn't going to understand. "Now, Azalea, you think every—"

"I know, but this time I'm right." I paused for a second, almost correcting my statement to reflect that I was most likely right about the entirety of my list of suspects, but that wasn't the point. "All right, but I have this feeling—"

"Oh, codswallop," he said, harsher than normal.

His shoulders fell in a slump as though the conversation itself were producing more wear on him than the events of the night had. I shut my mouth from the mere impact of his words. Quiet as they were, I could tell he simply wouldn't have it. His eyes flew up at the ceiling, lingering there as though he could hardly look at me. Sleep collected in his eyes like wishes tossed into a well, but rest was not important when the woman he spent so much time with had been there the night I was bitten—egging Florence on like they knew they were going to tear my life to shreds.

"Lili's doing her *job*," he enunciated fiercely, "and if you haven't noticed, Azalea, I'm busting my arse doing mine." As firm as it was, his voice was nearly a whisper. "You don't understand how much pressure I have on me every single day. I understand your worry, I do, but I cannot lose an ally right now, all because you have a 'feeling'."

But I couldn't rein in my volume as he had. I lost that battle before my shaking body could even try. Screw allies.

"I know you're busting your arse," I screamed out. I began pacing back and forth for the third time that night, praying my feet would take some of the aggression from my tone, yet they didn't. "She is *one* person," I insisted, "and it's more than a feeling, it's a *memory* of her. I heard her the night Florence changed me. There was another woman there with him—I asked her if they were taking me to Hell, and she muttered something eerie like, 'Oh, I'm taking you somewhere far worse than Hell, *Sunshine*,' and do you want to know who else called me that same fucking name? Lili!"

Chad squinted his eyes as though it were difficult to see the direct connection. "It's a *pet* name," he shrugged off.

"An *ironic* pet name for someone who goes around befriending dark vampires," I tossed back irritably.

"Or a rather *fitting* one for someone who detests vampires like my family and every other Caster out there," he said, waving his hand about again.

"Oh, really? *Every* other Caster feels that way?" I tested, but my sarcasm was briskly ignored with a wave of his hand.

"'Sunshine' is endearing," he continued, with hardly any regard for my feelings. "It's like warding off bad spirits when she says it."

I gawked at him with immense frustration coursing through me. "Do you hear yourself?" I asked in an airy tone. Did he really just say that to me of all people?

At that, he let out an elongated grunt, rubbing his hands roughly over his spent face. I stared at him, my heart tugging at itself as if it were going to implode, but he uncovered his face, and I could see the entire war raging behind his sunken eyes.

"That's not what I meant," he tried. "You're not a bad spirit."

But it was too late. The damage had been done and he knew it.

"Tell me about the prophecy," I demanded, my voice finally low from the immense blow to my heart. "The whole bloody thing, because apparently, it's so important to keep her around in case you have to go off and marry her. Perhaps being privy to that information would help me wrap my head around your insistence to have her near."

His glance rose to the ceiling before landing on me again. "Aunt Mallory was being ridiculous—as always. The prophecy is talking about you—"

"Does it say my name?" I barked back.

"Well, no," he began, "but—"

"Then what does it say?"

His nostrils flared as he let a long, deep breath into his lungs and then back out. "It's heavy," he told me, scrunching up his face with discomfort.

"Then, by all means, share the load," I countered, aggressively waving my hand at him. I wanted to let the bed hold my weight, but my stubborn knees locked in place, refusing to give my body rest.

Chad let out a hard breath as I breathed in. "It's a prophecy of the stars," he said softly, allowing his temper to simmer back down. "There's no exact translation, but it tells of a flower in the form of the most powerful witch. She's the key to it all. The leader of the Casters is supposed to take the flower for life, and together, they'll defeat the darker power. It's said that if the king doesn't marry this powerful flower, then the timeline that includes a successful win will unravel." He glanced at me with a shimmer of something like hope in his eyes. "It all seemed like sheer balderdash until I met you."

Words scurried out of my brain like traitorous rats. My lips parted, perhaps to ask questions, but there were none that I could voice. It all made sense, yet at the same time, it didn't. I had heard bits of the prophecy, pieces Chad had told me, parts Mallory and Morgan had let slip out, but this was my first time hearing about the flower.

Azaleas and lilies swirled in my head, battling one another. The image of his aunts' tarnished gardens, the way Mallory had mentioned the removal of the azaleas to replace them with lilies.

The prophecy could go either way—Lili or me. It was clear which way his aunts swung in the argument, but I couldn't pretend that Chadwick hadn't consistently made it clear that he was pulled in the opposite direction—to me.

"When I met you, there was ardour stirring within me, whispering how important you'd be to me one day. You let your name slip from your lips—a flower—but then you showed me your ID, which held an entirely different name on it. At first, I thought you were a spy or a ploy sent by my aunts, but something told me you were special."

I stared back at him, remembering my fake ID with a false name. I recalled the first time we had run into one another in the library, and the surprise I felt when he remembered my name. My lips locked up tight as I mulled over it all, but Chad thought better than to leave me alone with my thoughts much longer.

"Now, let me be entirely transparent about something," he said firmly, the edge of frustration coming back into his voice. "I do not keep Lili around because of the prophecy. If anything, it makes me want to push her away, and at first, I did. I pushed and pushed, but my aunts pushed harder. And now she's become extremely valuable. Where my connections are weak, hers are strong. She's on the verge of getting more people to join ranks with me, and if I sever ties with her, everything I've been working to build will crumble. So please hear me when I say that I wish I could do something to make you happy, but right now, this is bigger than us. You've got to understand that."

I looked down to the floor. I didn't know what to say. My brain was too worn down to understand any of it fully. But my silence was taken as defiance rather than space for thought.

Chad let out a tired sigh, and I knew he wouldn't make it if the argument continued on. "Azalea," he let out, forced patience on his tongue, "I have a thousand things to go fix, and zero energy to do it, so could you please just—hold these suspicions in your head until you have some cold, hard proof?"

Something cracked inside of me. I hadn't seen him so upset with me, not for a while at least. It's not as though I wanted to talk about her. But the way it all made me feel inside…

The chills wracking my body kept me frozen in place. I couldn't move, or turn away, or do anything, much less look at him.

Examining each thread of the carpeted floor by my aching feet, I told him, "I think I'll head to bed."

Hydie was right. Chad and I were far too knackered for this conversation. I needed to let him finish up his duties so we could both think clearly, though the adrenaline that rushed through my aching heart pleaded otherwise. There was no sleepiness left. Not one single drop.

The nod he gave me as I forced my eyes back to him was curt, a king dismissing his subject. "And I should head back to help the guards—make arrangements for whatever's coming next."

As soon as he said it, I knew I didn't want him to leave, not truly. I wanted to hold him, convince him to be careful, fight for him to believe me, but there'd be no more listening going on tonight. At least not about *her*.

I mirrored his cold, emotionless nod before trotting off to the bathroom and shutting the door behind me as calmly as I could. I leaned against the door and closed my eyes, longing to hear a knock, a regretful breath, but the only sound that came from the other side of the door was a whoosh of his magic, tearing him away.

A rogue tear fell from my eyes, and the tormented breath I let out unleashed the rest of the crimson flood. Grabbing at the fabrics on my body, I stripped them off quickly and took in all the dirt, blood, sweat, and God knows what else that covered them. I clambered into the shower to wash away the grime of the day. My lungs begged for air as I let out all of my worries, aches, and pains into the stream of water that cascaded down my skin. Emotions I had been holding in for far too long relinquished themselves down the drain and far away.

A shower couldn't soothe me, a book wouldn't distract me, so I did the one thing that never failed me: I transported from room to room to wear myself out. I made it further than usual, magicking myself into ten different rooms before my eyelids were weighed down enough for sleep. At least one good thing would come of tonight. I was getting better at appearing in different places. I was getting stronger.

On my walk back up to my bedroom, I checked on Hydie. Her body lay in her bed, fast asleep with rhythmic breaths flowing through her lungs. Her heart beat steadily, and I wondered if she ever had to endure nightmares as I did. I desperately hoped not. The thought of my own nightmares caused an internal panic to rise, and I wished I had Chad's soothing hands to remedy it. When I reached our bedroom, I decided that perhaps sending a letter was the next best thing. I hadn't meant to layer onto his stress, and at the very least, he should know that.

When I pulled the door open to my bedroom and stalked over to where my purse was hung up, I could hear the hum of its magic, its glow signalling that there was already a letter waiting for me.

A rush of both fear and joy crashed into me as I wondered what his note would say. Without letting my mind fall too deeply into the wintry abyss of assuming the worst, I unfolded the letter and ran my fingers along his neat writing.

That was very harsh and unfair of me to snap at you like that, and I truly apologise. These are dangerous times. I should watch everything I say as though it was my last, and after I retrieved my head out of my arse and remembered that, I felt horrid leaving you like that. I'm sorry.

As much as I'd like to put all your worries to rest, to prove to you that Lili is not the imposter you say she is, I can't. There will always be the possibility that I'm wrong, and I own up to that, but for right now, it's not feasible to completely cut her off. I do, however, promise to be more careful because nine times out of ten your wit seems to prove me wrong.

I love you, Azalea. And even when I'm being a complete wanker and you have every right to hate me, I still hope you love me too.

-Chadwick

Staring down at his letter, I considered lightening the mood, and thanking him for not chopping my head off like kings of the past have done when their significant others disagreed with them. Instead, smoke clouded my mind, not as fog, but as various colours with rich, vibrant hues, and I settled for something much less confrontational.

Why haven't you ever asked about my colour?

I asked, unsure whether or not to feel insulted. His reply took only seconds to appear in my purse after I had sent my own, almost as though he were eager to hear my response.

It's not very polite to ask someone's colour. A lot of things are very sacred to witches. There's so much that's meant to be private. To a mortal, it would be like asking someone the colour of their underwear.

Ah. I was wondering why you never asked me that either. I wear a fresh pair every day in the hopes that you'll ask.

The light teasing snuck its way in. I couldn't help it. I didn't want to go to bed angry with him.

> You're more than welcome to divulge the information on your own...

A phantom grin tempted my lips but the exhaustion within me whipped it away.

> Perhaps a riddle best left for you to solve yourself, if my body ever allows you to get that close.

> Your magic then. What colour is it?

I bit my cheek, hesitant to say for a moment. If he hadn't just told me it was meant to be private, it would have been easier, but I didn't have anything to hide from him really.

> Purple.

> Of course it is. That suits you. What shade?

My chest grew warm at his response.

> Lavender. It's a mix of soft and vibrant, but it turns violet and bolder when I feel strongly about something.

A few moments crept past before his next response, and I knew it was wrong to keep him occupied for much longer. He had so much to do to attempt to rectify the night.

> Yes, I think that fits you perfectly.

> And green fits you perfectly as well.

I stared back down at the page, not wanting to let him go, but knowing he must.

> I'll let you go. I know you have lots to do, Your Highness. I love you.

I hoped the quip would bring a smile to his face even though my own lips were too stubborn to do so.

Even when I've been a right arse?

I pressed the pen to my cheek, pondering over everything we had each said. Perhaps he and Hydie were right. Perhaps the war did need Lili. I wondered if my hate for her was merely jealousy.

I placed the pen to the paper once more before scrawling out one last line.

Even when we've both been arses.

But I still wasn't quite sure if my accusations were unjustified.

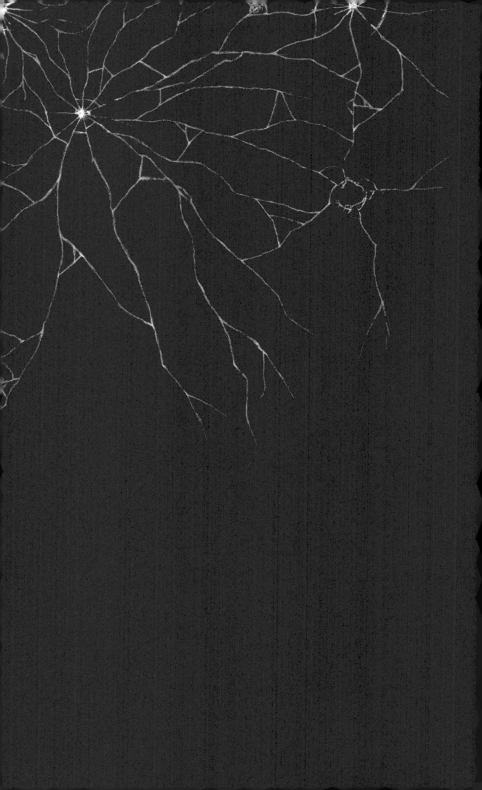

Chapter 26: Generous Offers

A fortnight had passed since Chad's coronation, and he was exactly right; being a king did mean more time away from home. But he brought me along nearly every time the sun was down. It was the only time we spent together, constantly surrounded by his guards, attempting to solve puzzles even though too many pieces were missing.

Chad only experienced brief stints of sleep throughout the day, never a full night's rest, but through all the tracking, conversations of war, and absolutely no privacy, Chad stole soft glances at me. His green eyes shone brightly with a happiness that was meant just for me. His fingers often found their way to mine, running along my palm, entwining my fingers with his—silent apologies that slowly seemed to heal the crack in my heart. Small touches that left me warm, tiny embraces that made me feel safe.

Retracing the trail of blackouts resulted in no remarkable outcome, and even when Chad brought me along with him to scope out the beginning of the trail, there was nothing that led me towards Florence. His scent ran cold. There was no pull, no draw towards the man who created me, just a plague of memories as his hands forced me against my bed, or down to the crisp forest floor. Those memories, and his red eyes came eagerly to haunt my dreams.

Between Florence and Lili's voices invading my nightmares, sleep was a battle. There was a constant war between exhaustion and not wanting to face the scene that played on the inside of my eyelids. Dreams of the small boy and girl came less frequently, causing me more worry than relief. With the fewer dreams came no more clues as to where they were, or *when* they were from. Guilt began to settle in my stomach as I pondered Chad's belief that they may be lost to the past.

I sat in a study within Castwell Castle, watching a large screen display face after face, none of which were Florence's. There were no black screens, no missing pieces, and no sign of him anywhere. Long green curtains shielded the daylight from seeping in, and as much as my body yearned for sleep, my eyes stayed glued to the screen.

A whoosh of air sounded from somewhere in the castle, and after only a few minutes, Chadwick found me in my latest hiding spot.

"I thought you might be here," he said plopping down into a seat next to mine. "I have half an hour before Nigel and the others will be expecting me back. I just needed to get away for a moment, kiss my girlfriend, take a shower, and grab a quick bite to eat," he listed off.

Heat rose to my cheeks, but I pressed on to business. "Speaking of eating, do you think you can teach me how to brew the blood duplication potion?" I asked, tearing my eyes from the screen to take him in. "We're running a bit low, and I think it's about time I learned to make a decent batch."

"Yes," he said through an enormous yawn. His arms stretched above his head before draping over the armrests of his chair. "Of course. We can do that tonight when I get back. I need to brew more of my energising potion as well. The effects are clearly wearing off," he said, referring to his yawn. "We can make them at the same time. Two birds, one stone."

I winced at the thought of trying to concentrate on two different potions when I was already so ruddy crap at making one.

"Don't worry, my love," he said, already fighting through a second yawn, "you'll get better at it. It takes years of practice to master."

A small snort escaped from my nostrils as I took him in. Gravity weighed heavily on him as he sat slumped in the chair. His dark hair was all over the place, swirling around in a way that made me want to run my fingers through it to muck it up even more.

"Do you think we could just use your previous idea of framing someone for the **MURDER** of the prime minister's daughter?" Chad asked aloud, staring off into the distance, his mind back to his duties when he was meant to be taking a well-deserved break. "Perhaps we could convince your father—"

"No," I said firmly. Even the idea of my father being alive wasn't one I was positive I wanted. "That man is not going to have anything else to hang over me. He'd use it as a tool against me, I know it."

Chad nodded, his eyes falling back to mine. "That's fair," he told me, letting out an airy breath. "Well, I'm going to go take a shower. Care to join me?" he asked, a dark grin painting its way onto his face.

"Now, you know the ceilings in the bathroom are too low," I said, smiling at him from the corner of my eye. I had thrown him into the ceiling far too many times to consider risking it now when he was in a hurry. "Besides," I added as the heat returned to my cheeks and spread through to the rest of me, "even if breaking your bones wasn't the most likely scenario, which it is, I think I'd need far more than half an hour with you after these past few months of being denied full access."

The grin across his stubbled face grew evermore mischievous. "Perhaps Nigel could cover for me, if only for a bit longer," Chad countered. His fingers circled along the end of the wooden armrest, and he arched his brow, becoming all the more enticing.

"Perhaps we can try while the potions are left to simmer tonight," I suggested, glancing back at the screens as I bit my lip to contain my smile. There was nothing more I'd like to try.

"All right," he said in a low voice, but as he got up from the chair and bent down over me, I immediately regretted my decision to wait. His smooth hand traced the centre of my neck, all the way up to my chin, before angling it towards him so I would stare into his green eyes. "But your absence in the shower will be greatly noted," he finished.

The sound of his pulsating wrist played in my ears. The bumps on my tongue tingled, and my teeth ached to take the smallest of bites into the soft flesh that lingered right below his thumb. His fingers left my chin, but his smile stayed as though he knew just how much he tempted me—just how delicious he truly was.

"You know where to find me if you change your mind," he teased, and then he left the room, walking slowly towards the door as my eyes lingered on his body.

I stared after him and into the corridor, even after he was gone from view.

I should go up to the bedroom, I thought. If not to join him, then at least to get a small peek before diving under the covers and falling asleep. Perhaps the sight of him would combat the nightmares away.

My body rose from the chair on its own to follow after his path. It placed one foot in front of the other, but just as I went through the doorway, abandoning the screen behind me, a strange feeling punched me in the gut.

Cold sweat gathered on my skin just as sorrow and fear slammed into me, drowning my lungs. I tried to gasp for air. Emotions that were not mine morphed with my own until they were all I could feel. The walls before me disappeared, and flashes of my teeth sinking into Chad's neck filled my eyes, before the panicked cries of *"You're going to **KILL** him,"* circled within my head like a swarm of bees. Morgan's voice snapped away from me, and the walls reappeared just as easily as they had vanished, but the sound of her sister's voice replaced it.

"How kind of you to answer," Mallory said dully in greeting.

My entire body froze. Her voice was far away, somewhere within the castle to the point my ears had to strain to focus on it, yet it was her nonetheless. It sounded as though she were here, but she couldn't be. Chad had placed wards on the castle to keep her and her sister out.

Chad let out a heavy sigh before a soft chime of his magic ensued, and he drawled out, "You have two minutes. What do you need?"

"Only two minutes to spare for your aunt?" she asked sourly. "I thought we raised you better than that."

"Less now that you've wasted precious seconds," he grumbled.

I lingered in the corridor, no longer wanting to travel up to the bedroom, but itching to hear what the witch had to say after her sister had sent such a powerful vision—whether on purpose or on accident, I wasn't sure. My fingers traced along the coarse texture of the stone wall, my ears focused on their voices, and my mind tried to brace itself for whatever would come next.

"Well, I'm afraid two minutes simply won't do," Mallory snarled. "Is the *beast* there with you? Or is she out, leaving children as orphans?"

Wicked old hag, I thought mirroring her bitterness in my own mind.

I prayed I was right about her not truly being in the castle so I didn't risk wringing her neck.

No, I corrected, taking a deep breath to soothe the borderline hatred I felt for the witch. She was unpleasant because she had lost her sister to a vampire, leaving her only nephew as an orphan. She was a woman whose heart needed healing.

Chad, however, didn't take kindly to her words. "Is there a point to this call, or are you solely here to aggravate me?" he asked. I could hear his teeth scraping together. There was no patience in his tone.

"There's some unpleasant news I've been tasked with sharing, and I'd rather not waste my breath on it twice. Summon her," she demanded, her voice dull with feigned boredom regarding me.

My heart pounded as I leaned my shoulder against the corridor wall. The cool feel of the stone bricks met my arm, but the shiver that overtook me was not merely from the cold. Unpleasant news was not what I needed, nor did I require either of his aunts' company if I wanted any chance at restful sleep.

"I don't think she'd like to talk with you, Aunt Mallory," he tested boldly. "Tell me your news and I'll relay the information to Azalea myself."

"No," she drawled back. "I'm afraid she has to be present, Chadwick, and believe me, I wish so dearly that wasn't the case."

"What's the news," he tried again.

"Summon her and find out," she enunciated, her foul attitude coating her tone.

I wished desperately I had gone to bed, but it was far too late for that.

"Azalea," Chad said regretfully, his volume unrisen as though he knew I was hidden in the eaves. "Could you join me in our bedroom?"

Our bedroom. Why in the name of all things holy was Mallory's voice coming from our bedroom?

The childish urge to pretend I hadn't heard the request fluttered past like a beautiful butterfly, coasting ignorantly through spring winds. Oh, how I longed to follow it through a meadow—to forget Mallory's audacious request to speak to me and frolic freely instead.

My foot slid reluctantly along the smooth floor, yearning to stay glued to the spot, not wanting to leave such an enchanting safe house, but some ill-tempered part of me forced my feet to travel up to the bedroom.

As I walked in, I realised Mallory wasn't here in her true form. Her face played in the mirror above our vanity, sucking in her cheeks and glowering over at me as if she hadn't just requested my presence.

I mimicked Lili's polite curtsy as I took in the scowl of the woman who was determined to hate me.

"To what do I owe the pleasure?" I asked, masking my sarcasm with an amicable smile.

She glared back at me through the enchanted portal I had grown to hate. As if pulled by a string of arrogance, she tilted her chin to the sky, casting her eyes down at a creature so far beneath her. "The elves have come to the decision that they wish to speak to you," she spilt bitterly. It was as though her hands were tied and her tongue was forced to have the dishonour of speaking to me.

My body went taut. I could hear Chad's body shifting uncomfortably as he drew in closer to me, but I was too busy losing my mind to tell if it was from his own worry or in an attempt to comfort me. The edges of the room began to blur as I stared so intensely back at her, half praying it was some cruel joke. Forcing down the immediate shock like a slimy toad I had to swallow, I blinked to regain my sight.

The witch's cheeks were still sucked in, holding all other information under lock and key as she carefully observed me. I watched as her eyes took in the fear on my face, and as her ears noted the vacancy of my voice. Even Chad's hesitance put me further on edge as he cleared his throat beside me to ask the question that filled my mind as well.

"Why?" he asked simply, just as dumbfounded as I was.

Why would the elves wish to speak to me? I was an enemy and a nobody, all wrapped in one. Eyeara had said herself that nothing would come from her speaking on my behalf.

"Beats me..." Mallory's voice lingered unpleasantly in the air—disgusted at such a seemingly impossible notion.

"When?" was my next response, as short as the breaths I fought to take in while my lungs collapsed on themselves.

The wicked witch was in no hurry to ease my worries. "Now," she contended, and I couldn't help but despise how she mirrored my own shortness with her response. Although her mouth did not lift, her eyes brightened as she raised a brow at me, relishing in my fear that seemed to coax the rage I had felt from her only moments ago. Her arrogance had conquered miles of terrain and whittled its way past the wards to thrash me.

Chad's hand wrapped around mine as he spoke to his aunt with fire in his throat. "Are they in town, or are we expected to fly across the seas for such an impertinent meeting?" Chad snapped.

"They will not speak to her in person, and heavens, who could blame them," she said, dramatically raising her volume in time with the roll of her eyes. "If I were King Eyeron, I wouldn't want to speak with her at all. Either way, they've settled on speaking to her through the mirror."

"But you *aren't* him, so your words are pointless," I said, with more stature and calmness than I thought possible when speaking to the snake.

She hissed back at me, and I couldn't help but grin smugly at such an appropriate response.

"Well, if you were wise, which I suspect you're not," she quipped, "I wouldn't keep them waiting. You are free, aren't you? Or does this impede on your feeding schedule?"

"Now is perfect," I told her before Chad could interject. I was thankful she couldn't hear the pounding of my anxious heart as it screamed out that "now" was, in fact, the opposite of perfect.

I looked at Chad to see him studying me. His chest lifted and fell at a pace slightly faster than normal, and his expression conveyed intrigue at the thought of what the elves wanted with me—intrigue, but also a touch of hope I didn't think was warranted. My heart contorted with conflict as I looked back to his aunt in the mirror.

"Will I be allowed more information before I'm thrown into the deep end, or are you going to let me sink?"

"Sink or swim, vampire, I don't care," she spat out, and I was lucky we were miles apart so I couldn't feel her venom spraying over me.

"We're on the same side," Chad cut in sternly. "Sabotage and rudeness will do no good, Aunt Mallory."

"Anyway," she dismissed, "I've arranged for a conversation through the mirror. They'll talk through one that hasn't been dipped in a potion, so there's no way that the vampire will come through to attack them."

"I didn't attack them at the coronation," I pointed out.

"There's a grand difference between meeting you under the watchful eyes of an entire union and meeting you face to face privately—with no witnesses to see you attack," she replied.

Chad's body moved forwards as he went further into defence mode, but I squeezed his hand tightly to ease his anger.

Without further ado, Mallory gave me a cruel smile, and waved her hand in front of her. Red smoke clouded the view of the mirror before her. The room she stood in disappeared and was replaced with an icy backdrop, and the bodies of three pale blue elves.

Their skin, long arctic-blue hair, and lavish robes blended into the ice behind them. The elf on the left was the one who had ventured with us to the new lair. The same flat look held his features as he took me in again. The elf on the right moved his eyes up my body, assessing the threat I held, but I was unsure by his emotionless expression if he detected any. In the centre was another tall elf who wore a large crown adorned with frosted silver and topaz stones. It rested behind his pointed ears and just above his quizzical brow. The hue of his blue eyes and the shape of his thin face mirrored Eyeara's, but there was a fierceness that soaked his features, whereas his daughter's face radiated kindness and warmth.

He and the two male elves beside him bowed their heads in greeting.

"King Chadwick," said the elf in the centre.

As Chad bent his head down in response, it jerked me into the world of formality and royalty, and I gave an awkward curtsy to the men in the mirror.

"King Eyeron," Chad greeted back. "To what do we owe this honour?"

"We were hoping to have a word with your *comrade* here," he told us, emphasising the word "comrade" as though the conversation was meant to be with me alone.

Chad lifted the hand that was wrapped around mine and tilted his head to welcome more information. "We're all ears," he invited, making it clear that he wouldn't be leaving my side.

The elven king nodded, even though a shadow of disapproval danced across his face. The angle of his long neck moved his head in a better position to observe me.

"King Chadwick has told us of your... unique lineage," King Eyeron said calmly, "and after *much* consideration, we attended his coronation. Princess Eyeara has spoken very highly of you in the time since, and after the course of events that took place that night in Chippenham, my brother, Eyetronus, witnessed what many of us thought impossible: a Night Crawler with what appears to be a soul…" His voice tapered off at the insult as though he wanted to savour the taste of it on his tongue.

I discreetly gnawed on my own tongue. The action succeeded in holding back the cheeky response that flowed so easily from the soul he was surprised I had. I made no effort to smile at the elf. Chad's focused breathing suggested he was battling an identical struggle, so I squeezed his hand gently to comfort him. The small movement gathered the attention of the three elves, and as their eyes flitted down to our hands, the elves did nothing to hide their distaste.

Guilt caused my grip to loosen. Rubbing our relationship in their faces was not the best method of winning them over, yet Chad's firm grip held tightly around my fingers, speaking volumes about what he thought of their opinion. A tiny part of me relaxed at his solidarity.

As the elven king's eyes meandered back to mine, I immediately wanted to crumble. They pierced into me like a knife, turning its hilt without remorse. Instead, I stared straight back into his eyes, not allowing him to see me as weak.

"And has this sudden discovery of my soul increased the chances of you working with us?" I asked, thinking back to Eyeara's words. She had been so certain that the other elves would be resistant, even after meeting me, but perhaps the attack on the vampire coven had altered their feelings.

"Slightly," King Eyeron replied. "We've been discussing the matter at great lengths, and have decided upon a bargain. If you allow Icaron," he suggested, gesturing a hand to the elf on the right, "to accompany you wherever you go, we'll consider joining your cause."

"Wherever I go?" I asked, glancing over to the elf, who remained mute. "Like a spy I willingly allow to stalk me?"

"Whatever way you choose to think of it is irrelevant to me," the king deflected, careful to keep his sturdy stare into me.

"I don't fancy that idea," Chad said firmly. "How would you feel if I sent my guards to investigate every move of Queen Aria?"

"Well, that would be vastly different, considering she's a queen and already in good graces with the Casters, seeing as she is one."

"I'm a Caster too," I interrupted, ignoring the fact that he was a king. Hopefully Chad's title granted me some protection. "I'll remind you it wasn't my choice that a vampire sought me out in the middle of the night to quench his thirst."

"Even if the same vampire who changed you is now leading a war against my kind?" he asked, freezing the waters he tested with his frigid words.

"I'm afraid we'll have to decline your *generous* offer," Chad told the elf king. He glanced down to the floor before looking back up at the mirror, but his tone remained powerful. "That's an incredulous breach of privacy that no one should be subjected to."

"I'm sure it wouldn't be *everywhere* she went," Eyeron continued, checking his nails from boredom. "Her whereabouts couldn't possibly be that interesting."

"No thank you," Chad replied curtly.

King Eyeron shrugged his shoulders. "Suit yourself," he drawled out calmly. "Then the deal is null and void."

But it felt like an opportunity was slipping away.

"Wait," I let out before I could help it. It was unreasonable, most definitely, but perhaps a compromise would make the invasion worthwhile.

I looked up at Chad and he stared back at me with patient eyes— eyes that lingered within the range of hope once more. Glancing back at the three elves, their pointed ears ready to listen, I said, "If our king will allow it, I believe we can arrange a fairer quid pro quo." I felt as Chad's hand lifted and he ran the back of his fingers along my bare arm, encouraging me onwards. I swallowed before letting my eyes crash back into the pale blue colours that blended together on the other side of the mirror. "Icaron," I continued, looking at the elf on the right, "is more than welcome to join us on any ventures we take *outside* of this castle. We'll inform him of any movements I plan to make, but he's not welcome to enter these walls. If nothing noteworthy or incriminating happens after one month, then an accord will be made ensuring that you'll come to our aid when we need it."

The blue king pursed his lips in thought, his eyes glued to mine, then took a deep, resounding breath.

"Two months," he bargained through a hiss, watching me carefully to see my reaction.

"In two months' time, Florence could **MURDER** hundreds more," I pointed out, not allowing the urgency to slip out with my words. No. I wanted him to see how calm I could remain under his pressure.

"I'm afraid that's a chance I'll have to take," Eyeron replied with an airy presence.

"'Afraid' is exactly how you should feel in the face of your hesitance to assist," Chad countered, commanding the elf's attention with his fiery tone.

Heat lashed its way around me, breaking through the chill the elves gave off.

Eyeron's lips curved into a sly smile as he took in Chad's words. "There's one more stipulation to add if we're to have a deal," he exhibited, his comment directed straight at me. "You are to wear an elven bracelet decorated with jewels that hold the power to track your location. If you move, we will know. If you take it off, we will know, and if you refuse, then no deal."

Chad's eyes squinted with immense irritation. He opened his mouth, and began with, "You can go and shove that idea right up your—" but I promptly cut him off, placing a hand on his chest in warning.

"I accept," I interrupted.

When Eyeron clicked his tongue, his smug grin widening as his brows rose at Chad, I realised that interrupting a king was the wrong move to make, regardless of whether or not the king in question was my boyfriend.

Eyeron's expression towards Chad oozed with a disrespect that made me cringe, so I stepped closer to the mirror, dropping Chad's hand so the elf could direct his nasty looks at me instead.

"But your *king* is correct on where you can shove any more of your schemes," I snapped, reminding him that he was lesser than Chad. "So don't waste your breath creating more amendments."

Shock clashed into his smugness and then was promptly replaced with a twinkle in his eye that I loathed even more. "Of course," he told me. "The bracelet will be delivered later today, and we look forward to any communication about your whereabouts."

I smiled back at the elf, hoping to conceal the slight tremor of rage that shook Chad's body. "Pleasure doing business with you, gentlemen," I remarked with a tone of satisfaction.

The glint in King Eyeron's eyes shimmered again, but he made no claim as to whether the deal was satisfying to him. Instead, he looked back and forth between Chad and me with malice clouding his features. "We'll be observing you closely," he warned us both, "for wiser men have been fooled, and prettier witches have deceived."

I blinked at the words that I knew were meant as an insult, but raised my chin as Mallory had to give the appearance that I was stronger than I was. The elf's words lingered in my mind, and I wondered if it was good or bad that he referred to me as a witch rather than a vampire for the first time.

"King Eyeron," Chad said, bowing his head to the elf in farewell.

"King Chadwick," he returned.

Chad flicked his wrist, leaving a web of cracks along the mirror, and only our faces in the reflection.

Jade Austin

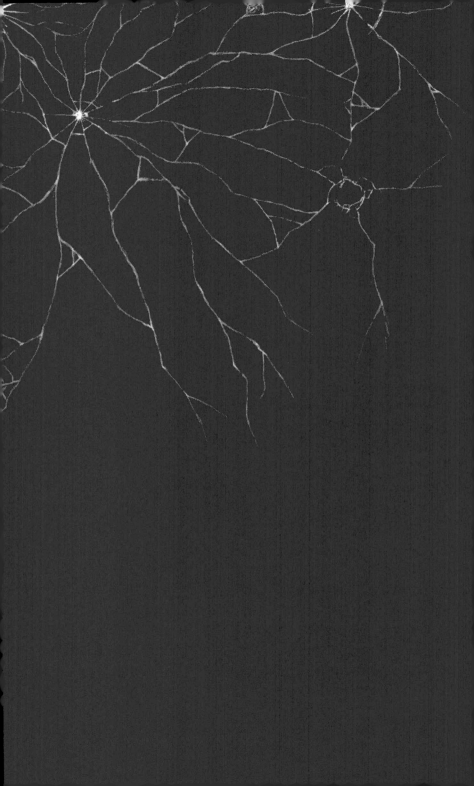

Chapter 27: Chains

I stared past the cracks in the mirror and into Chad's eyes as they glowed with fury.

"If we were not recruiting for a war, I would've pulverised him for his actions," Chad snarled. "To even request placing a chain around you is an outrage, and then to speak to you like that!" he said, scrunching up his face in disbelief. "What a pompous bastard."

Oh, the irony of a king calling anyone pompous.

Chad pointed his index finger upwards, wagging it in between us to mark that he had just realised something. "Eyeron is taking advantage of my lack of experience and our need for them to fight, all so he can spew out his own prejudices against vampires," he went on, before absentmindedly flicking his wrist again to repair the mirror. "That's what he's doing. Either that or the elves are the Casters feeding information to Florence."

The words burst through his clenched teeth as he started to pace back and forth across the carpet, tracing the same trail I had tracked only a few weeks earlier. His heart pummelled against his rib cage like a rampant animal fighting its way out. Infuriated hands roved through his hair, ruffling it the way he always did as though it would force his brain to come up with a reasonable solution. I looked at his hands, wishing they were my hands running through his soft, dark hair, magic flowing freely through them so I could erase all his worries. Only, I didn't trust my hands. My emotions were too strong to channel my purple rays into anything positive.

"We'll be careful," I said gently, feeling in my heart that the traitor was not King Eyeron, but Lili. Truth be told, however, I was too far lost in my own thoughts to understand the ramifications if I was wrong.

As I thought about all the elven king had said, fear wrapped its impenetrable rope around me until I forced it deep down, detaching myself completely from the present, the future, and the things that weighed me down.

Fantasies of our past ventured freely into my mind as I blocked out all the rest. Back to a time when Florence was a single person, not in control of an army. A night when Chad truly became mine to hold.

"You once told me we could run away from all this," I murmured, lost in the memory I would cherish forever. "You said you would abandon the war and leave everyone behind with it if I asked you to. So tell me," I said, making my way slowly to where he stood. A suggestive smile tempted my lips, one that only my dissociation from reality could produce. "Is that offer still on the table?"

For a moment, his eyes nearly glazed over as he stared right through me, and my breath caught as I realised part of him was considering my ridiculous request. How small or large a part, I didn't want to know. But then his eyes refocused to travel down the slope of my neck, and heat radiated off him so vibrantly that all my blood flushed its way to my cheeks.

"I'm only joking," I told him, tilting my head to the side, and his eyes flashed back to the present.

An airy laugh left his lips. "Of course," he told me sweetly, cupping my face into his hand, "but to run away with you would be more than I could ever hope for."

His thumb ran its way gently over my cheek, and I melted against it. It was my favourite way for him to touch me these days.

"Perhaps more good will come from the elf's presence than harm," I suggested, trying to place hope back into his eyes, or at least a touch of humour. "Besides, it might be fun to give him something to watch," I teased, flicking my brows up at him.

"Yes," he said, mirroring my own mischievous grin. I watched as the light grew in his eyes before a sense of darkness and pleasure swept into its place. I glanced down at his lips as he added, "I quite like that idea."

My powers prickled along my palms, ready to react if his lips met mine the way I wanted them to. Thoughts of latching onto him took over completely, and I had to throw my irrational hands behind me in order to protect him. I wrung my fingers, wishing my stupid magic would leave me alone, if only for a night, or a day, or an hour—

"Five minutes," he said abruptly, and the smallest of jumps escaped me. His green eyes brightened at my reaction. "I'm going to take a shower. Go down to the potions room to drink the last of your blood duplication potion, and then meet me down in the armoury."

"The armoury?" I asked, not understanding the sudden change in plans. "It has to have been at least twenty minutes. Nigel will be expecting you back soon," I noted.

"You and I haven't trained together in weeks," he said with a shrug, "and now might be the only chance we get for a while."

I looked longingly over to the bed I was meant to be fast asleep in, and then down to my clothes as I gave in. Time with Chad was vastly more important than sleep tormented by nightmares.

My eyes drifted back over to Chad. "I'll have to change—"

"No," he cut off, his eyes trailing down my dress. "That won't be necessary. We don't have much time, and you won't always have the opportunity to change into proper fighting gear." Leaning in closer, his warm breath caressed my neck, and I closed my eyes to memorise the feel. All sense of time, space, and direction was lost as he whispered, "And don't be late," into my ear.

A gust of air brushed against me, taking Chad along with it. Sounds of him undressing behind our bathroom door met my ears, and my eyes flew to the clock on our bedside table.

6:55 in the evening.

I kicked off the ridiculous heels I had been wearing and carried them over to the wardrobe to swap them for a more sensible pair of shoes. I'd be needing them if I was going to have any chance at kicking his arse. I settled for a pair of long, black boots, hoping he wouldn't notice the slight wardrobe change, and then grabbed a hair tie before leaving the room.

Using my vampiric speed, I ran down to the potions room to drink the last of the blood. I waited just a moment to make sure it was enough to satisfy my hunger, then ran most of the way to the armoury before slowing to pass a few of the guards. I nodded at them in greeting, not wanting to alert them by moving too quickly.

The clock in the entrance hall bounced along the stone walls as its first stroke of seven chimed. My heart raced. Chad specifically told me not to be late.

A sixth and seventh chime rang through the castle as I rushed past two more guards and then burst through the armoury door. It swung back and forth on its hinges as Chad took me in from where he leaned casually against a shelf of freshly sharpened swords and daggers.

"What?" I asked innocently. I grasped all my curls and positioned them at the top of my head to draw them away from my face. "*Technically*, I'm not late."

He sent a blast of magic just past my shoulder, causing me to drop my handful of hair. The squeak from the door immediately halted, replaced by the *click* of the lock.

After gawking back at his true target, I glared at him. "Was that truly necessary?" I asked, lucky his stream of magic hadn't brushed my shoulder before I was even ready to defend myself.

"Sorry," he replied, not sounding apologetic in the slightest. His devilishly handsome grin sprouted on his face. "*Technically*, I don't have much time."

My tongue pressed to the roof of my mouth to suppress my own grin, but it was of little use.

I walked slowly over to Chad, taking my time to get back at him. "And remind me, when exactly did you decide to do this training, especially when you knew you had so little time? I was unaware we had a session today."

"I think it was right around the time you completely bypassed your own privacy in order to gain aid in the war," he said, scrunching up his face as he pretended to think hard. "Either that or when you told the king of elves to shove something up his arse."

A laugh left my lips. "And that made you feel *how*, exactly?" I asked, genuinely intrigued as to what the possible connection was between the elf's arse and training.

"Quite impressed," was Chad's response.

I smiled at him as I finally managed to tie my hair up out of the way. With a suspicious glance over his shoulder to all the weapons he stood next to, I stepped closer to him. Letting out a breath to prepare myself for the training, I asked, "Did you have swordplay in mind for today?" My eyes roved over the long, silver blades. They seemed too long, clumsy, and slow to be of any use against a vampire. What could a sword's purpose be besides attacking a mortal or pulling it out of a rock to declare the next king?

I moved my hand over the hilt of one of the daggers, as long as two of my hands, but short enough to conduct with some speed. My fingers trailed over an amethyst stone, but Chad's hand cradled mine, halting its movement. His warm breath ran its way along my exposed neck as he stood behind me. I turned my head to look at him, but his eyes remained focused on my hand as he ran his fingers gently over it.

"In the past few months, there have been so many times that these hands have stopped me from doing the things I want to do to you," he whispered, and my head leaned back into him as my eyes closed to imagine exactly what he had intended each of those times.

"So what's your intention now, Chadwick?" I challenged, leaning into him so I could feel him against me. "Have you dragged me down here to cut off my disobedient hands?"

He let out a short laugh, refusing to blink as he stared at my hand. "Something like that," he quipped in a hushed tone, and just as my knees were about to give way and buckle from beneath me, his grip tightened on my hand, and he spun me around, off to the side. His eyes finally met mine, and without taking them off of me, he grabbed the dagger off the shelf and gave me his characteristic grin, the one that never failed to make my heart race.

He placed deliberate steps towards me, and I trekked back at the same timing, like a dance, until my back pressed up against the far wall. Grabbing both of my hands, he shoved them high above my head. I could feel his magic shooting from his palms and wrapping their way around my wrists, linking them together in a chain. Then he reached his arm back before driving the cold metal of the dagger into the centre of the chain, pinning my hands to the wall. A hot breath escaped my lips as a warmth grew over me, and I realised that training had never been on his mind. No, he was up to something entirely more pleasurable.

"Tell me, my love," he said softly as his hands trailed down my arms and along my sides, tickling my skin as they went. "If your magic would allow it, what would you want me to do to you?"

Chills slithered down my spine at his touch, and as his hands gripped the front of my dress, I knew exactly what I'd want him to do to me.

"Take this fucking dress off of me," I commanded, and fire licked across his features as he gladly obliged.

He yanked firmly at the corset that wrapped my chest, and the hooks broke free. Leaning closer to me, he slipped his hands underneath the dress so he could pull the rest of the fabrics up in one long, swift motion. The bunched-up fabrics rose until they hovered over my head, around my arms, and with the flick of his wrist, green magic created a frost along them, freezing them in place above me.

Bumps covered my skin from the cold air and his eager gaze as he took in my nearly bare body and all of its curves. Then he moved his warm body against mine, both hands holding tightly onto my hips before he let a hand trail down to my thigh and snatched it up so that my boot dangled by his side.

I watched as his eyes drew closer. Letting his lips brush gently against mine, he murmured, "I distinctly remember telling you not to change before our training session."

I smiled wickedly, slightly vexed he had even noticed. "And what are you going to do to punish me for it?" I asked slyly. My magic sparked at my fingertips at the same time desire sparked in his eyes.

"How about I show you?" he dared, and his teeth bit onto my bottom lip before he sucked it into his mouth.

I gripped tightly onto his green ropes that held my hands upwards as my tongue explored his mouth. The feel of him, the taste of him, it was perfect. A hand found its way up to mine as his other one gripped tighter onto my thigh, pulling my entire hip into him over and over again. I closed my eyes and tried to memorise the feel of his lips as they travelled down to my chest. His hand let go of mine to fiercely pull down my bra so his mouth could rove over my breast freely. I wanted to grab onto his hair as he did it, but purple sparks shot out of my hands, raining down on us like snow as his tongue swirled around its target, and I was thankful for the magical handcuffs that succeeded in keeping him safe. He switched his tongue to the other breast, latching on and sucking hard before his lips retraced their path back up my neck, and then to my lips once more. His fingers slid right over the wetness that had gathered in my knickers.

I gasped against his lips as his fingers tugged the moist fabrics to the side, and I fought to keep up with my laboured breaths as his fingers danced along my slits. My head fell against his neck, nodding into it as I breathed out a cry of, "Yes," begging for more. My tongue slithered carefully up his neck, and it took everything in me not to bite into his flesh as he thrust two fingers in, moving them in and out as his hardness stayed trapped inside his trousers, but pressed eagerly against me.

He used his hand that gripped my thigh, dragging his trimmed nails against it as his neck rolled around, immensely satisfied with the work my lips were doing to it. His thumb moved in circles around my front to thank me. Pressure began to build in my core as I moved my lips back to his, and I let out a gasp as it grew and grew. His circles worked their magic and my stomach tightened.

The start of a moan escaped my lips as I let out a beg of, "Untie me." I needed to touch him, to pleasure him at the same time as my release.

He let a satisfied laugh tickle my skin as he shook his head against me, but the mere thought of grasping onto him sent me over the edge. A loud moan came out of me this time as his fingers continued their diligent work, and my body felt as though it was floating so high above the ground, for so long, until finally, my body shook and I could breathe once more.

"Fuck," he breathed into my neck, and my entire body convulsed again from his warm breath. "You make what I'm about to do *very* hard."

My stomach seemed to twist itself into a knot as I looked at him, my lungs eagerly trying to catch my breath, but as he slid his fingers out of me, another gasp left my lips, and I pressed my forehead into his shoulder to try and gather myself.

"And what exactly is it that you're about to do?" I managed to ask between our panting breaths, and he leaned into me once again.

Grasping both of my wrists, he murmured into my ear, "I have to leave."

My chest fell with disappointment. He couldn't go. Not after all that.

"But don't think I've forgotten the most important part of your training," he added slyly.

I tilted my head as far back as I could to get a better look at him, trying to understand what the hell he was on about. I didn't want him to go. I didn't want to do any training for the war. I just wanted to reach into his bloody trousers and work to make him feel as good as he just made me feel. But he laughed, and I had to ask as curiosity bit into me.

"And what, pray tell, would that be?"

A gleam of mischief shined brightly in his eyes. "You must learn how to get out of magical handcuffs," he said, and a snarl instinctively left my mouth as I looked up at the green magic that still had me strapped to the wall. The dagger with amethyst stone remained stabbed firmly into it.

My eyes went back down to his, not bothering to lift my fallen jaw. "You've got to be joking," I tried, but he shook his head, and his smile remained on his face.

He took one more good look at me as he drew away, *fully clothed*, while I stood there in boots and undergarments that weren't covering me properly, my dress frozen in place over my head.

As though it helped, he flicked his wrist and the frost covering my dress vanished. Gravity pulled at it so it fell over my face a bit, obstructing my view as the clicking of his footsteps echoed farther and farther away from me.

"It'll be good practice," I heard him call out as he must have neared the door to the armoury.

"In case of what?" I asked, blowing at my dress to free my vision once more, but it didn't work. "In case my boyfriend leaves me locked up again?"

He laughed as though I were being ridiculous. "In case you're ever tied up in the middle of a war." I heard his footsteps stop and my heart quickened as I knew he had reached the door. The same bloody door two of his guards were posted outside of, and they might get a real good look if Chadwick didn't block the sight of my mostly naked body.

"Wait," I tried one last time, urgency seeping out of my voice as I yelled to him. "What if someone finds me like this? What if Hydie comes looking for me—or—or Connor," I let out, but the bloody bastard just chuckled.

"You'll be fine, Azalea," he told me calmly. The sound of soft skin brushing against a metal handle. "Don't worry. I already told Poppy. She has strict orders to come set you free if you're still down here in an hour."

What does he mean, he already told her? I thought furiously, and the realisation struck me in the face. *Five minutes*, he had said. He knew exactly what he was going to do to me after those five minutes. And he had not only showered and dressed, but he had apparently run to the fairy and told her I'd be here, stripped down to my knickers.

But before I could hurtle any harsh names in his direction, he shouted that he loved me and I heard the click of the door behind him.

I shook violently at the chains until the dress fell mostly back into place over me. After thirty minutes of frustrated grunts and frantic attempts to force my magic against the chains, I finally broke free from his stupid green trap. With arms made of jelly, I stormed up to our bedroom and struggled to write Chadwick a very heated letter about how lucky he was that he was off trying to fight a war at that particular moment, rather than facing my wrath, which was drastically more dangerous.

෴

A package arrived that night. Poppy knocked on the bedroom door, waking me from my fear-induced sleep, and as I fought to stay in my dream of the two small children, eager to discover their location, the flutter of Poppy's wings brought me back to the present.

Blood flushed my cheeks as I remembered Chad's words, promising that the small fairy knew exactly where to find me if I didn't free myself from the green chains. The innocence that draped over her face as she looked at me, however, helped reassure me that she didn't know the condition she would have found me in if she *had* gone to collect me.

Poppy gave a huge heave as she dropped a box made of ice onto the sheets next to me, and wiped off the sweat that had congregated on her green brow as she worked to catch her breath.

"Here you go, Azalea," she told me in her usual cheery voice. "This just came for you."

"Cheers, Poppy," I replied, sitting up and wiping the sleep from my eyes. "Is Hydie still awake?"

"Yes," she said with a vigorous nod. "She's just eaten supper. Would you like me to tell her you're awake?"

"Yes, please."

The green fairy nodded excitedly before zooming back out of the room, a spark of her magic closing the door behind her.

I looked down at the frozen box, reaching for a small paper that was attached to it. The words upon it were written in a formal scrawl, decorated with extra flourishes along each letter, giving it the false appearance of being a foreign language.

The note read, "*To Azalea, the girl with a taste for blood and the thirst to prove herself. Sincerely, King Eyeron.*"

I rolled my eyes, wishing to only speak to his daughter in future instances where communicating with the elves was necessary.

The ice bit at my fingertips as I pulled the box open, the frozen hinges gently scraping together as they turned. Inside the box sat a beautiful silver bracelet with light blue topaz stones, and frost swirled around it. Its style was nearly identical to the crowns that both Eyeron and Eyeara wore.

At least it's a pretty chain, I thought to myself, and as I dressed for the day, I intentionally put on a light blue dress to match it—proof the arrogant elven king couldn't tear me down.

As soon as I followed the sounds of Hydie's breath and found her curled into a chair in the library, she peered over her book to look at the bracelet.

I rolled my eyes as I plopped myself into the chair next to her. "Don't even get me started," I told her, and she smiled back at me.

"What's on the agenda for today?" she asked, marking her spot with a bookmark before closing the book and placing it on her lap.

I shrugged. "I think we should do some more training, but then later I was thinking of going down to the pub to keep Connor company. It's the night before the full moon," I told her.

"I thought you said he no longer transforms when there's a full moon?" Hydie asked curiously.

"He doesn't," I said with a sigh, staring off into the distance, "but the potion doesn't take away the itch that comes with it, and though he tries to put on a brave face, he's still just a scared little pup on the inside."

My eyes flew up to Hydie, hoping that my words weren't a reason for her to fall for the charm he tried to place on her, but she shook her head and let out a laugh.

"Relax," she insisted. "I'm not interested in him."

I sighed with relief as my heart slowed back down a bit. "I know, but he can be so insistent," I muttered. "Besides, he's too old for you anyway."

"He's a year younger than you," she commented.

I glared at her for causing a spike in my blood pressure as she defended the age gap. "But *four* years older than you," I pointed out.

"I am eighteen now, so it's not completely out of the question," she replied casually.

I gawked at her. "You are *not* relieving any of my stress by saying that."

"Oh, I'm only having a laugh, Azalea," she teased, leaning into me. "Calm yourself."

I'll calm myself when I've placed a chastity belt around the werewolf, I thought, but Hydie flicked her brows at me tauntingly.

"I heard Poppy's thoughts earlier," she brought up, changing the subject. "Did you know that when fairies blush, the green in their cheeks shifts to an odd yellowish colour?"

I narrowed my eyes at her, waiting for her point. "And what thoughts did you eavesdrop on this time?" I asked.

"Just her suspicions that you and Chad were engaging in 'sexual intercourse' in the armoury," she tested lightly, turning away from me to look at me from the corner of her eye.

I choked on my own spit. *So the little fairy* did *know what we were up to.*

"Oh, gross!" my sister exclaimed, sitting up straighter in her chair so she could lean away from me properly. Clearly she had heard my private thoughts. "I was hoping Poppy was mistaken. I have to train in the armoury too, you know? Where else have you two done the nasty?" she asked as her nostrils flared with disgust.

"Well..." I said, glancing down at the chair she sat in.

She stood up so quickly that the book fell from her lap and flopped open on the floor. "That's disgusting!" she cried, carefully stepping over the book to flee the room.

"Where are you going?" I called after her, just as she neared the door to go out into the corridor.

"I'm going to change into my training gear, and then we're going into the *maze* to practise," she enunciated, only pausing to glare at me. "Far away from any of the spots you two have fondled each other in."

I sucked in my lips to keep my smile in.

Going to the maze isn't going to help with that, I told her through my thoughts, and with a cry of disgust, she turned to exit the room for good.

ભ

After a few hours of training in the maze, Hydie and I both retired to the house for cool showers, and then I headed over to the pub. I didn't know how to inform the elven king of my motive to leave the castle, but relied on the chain around my wrist to notify him instead.

The cold night air was fierce against my cheeks. My ears remained perked as I walked to the bar at a mortal's pace. No pull forced me in Florence's direction, no red eyes peered at me from around corners, but fear of an attack wasn't in only my mind. It lingered in the minds of the few people brave enough to walk the streets.

I crossed under a streetlight, eyeing the gaggle of four women wrapped tightly in winter jackets as they made their way towards me. They didn't even get within a hundred metres of me before they crossed the street to walk on the other pavement. Not five minutes passed before a man walking alone did the very same thing.

I looked back at the man as he continued his way away from me, and thought about the latest report on the mortals' news. The whole country was being warned to stay indoors as soon as the sun set, and although the quiet streets seemed to prove that most people were taking heed of the wise advice, it still felt eerie to be walking alone in the streets of London when they should have been bustling at this hour.

When I neared the pub, a slow heartbeat and laboured breathing came from the alleyway, and I was immediately pulled into a horrid memory. Florence's face, dripping with an innocent woman's blood, fogged my mind. It was the first hunt I had ever taken part in, the night I had helped bury the woman's dead body. The vision cleared, but when I opened my eyes to peer into the dark alleyway, Florence wasn't there. Instead, an older man with grey peppered along his blond hair sat on the dirty ground, mucking up his fine suit. His knees were bent as he leaned against the grimy bricks, hopelessly staring off at the wall across from him. As I passed by, his eyes met mine, and even though I glanced away quickly, my heart fell.

I recognised him. He was the prime minister, the woman's father.

I entered the pub and took a seat on the stool across from where Connor was standing behind the bar.

"The prime minister is out in the alleyway," I told him quietly, although the low volume was hardly necessary. There were only a few other people in the pub, and they were seated at a table away from the bar.

Connor nodded, pushing his lips off to the side so one of his cheeks puffed out. "I know," he said solemnly. "The poor guy comes here at least three times a week. It's the last place anyone saw her, and unfortunately for us, the security footage is proof that Florence led her out into *that* alleyway."

I nodded, remembering the photograph from the paper. "Perhaps it makes him feel closer to his daughter," I suggested as guilt ate away at my insides. The prime minister didn't know she was truly gone, but based on the look I had seen in his eyes, hope of her survival had started to dwindle away.

The voice of a belligerent man rose above the quiet noises of the bar. The pungency of the alcohol on his breath blasted into my nostrils. As he swayed to the side, his arm wrapped around the woman next to him, and I noted that the woman did not look very happy about the gesture. He was precisely the type of man Abigail would take as her victim.

"I was just talking to a chap the other night who's convinced it's vampires," he said angrily, slurring his words together. "And you know what? The more I drink, the more it makes sense."

One of his friends from across the table laughed at him. "Oh, belt up," he said lightly. "You don't really believe that."

"I do!" the first man exclaimed, frustration blasting out of him. After a long swig of his beer, he slammed his cup back down onto the table and let out a loud belch. "And the government believes it too," he insisted. "They're keeping it all hushed, but I was out walking the night all those bodies showed up at the cemetery. All the bodies were pale, and I heard a detective say they'd been drained of their blood."

I stirred in my chair, exchanging anxious glances with Connor before peering back over.

They still haunted me. All two hundred and thirty-two bodies.

The woman next to him scoffed, pushing his arm off her. "Knowing you, you were probably sloshed like you are now," she said.

"I was not!" he claimed fiercely, but the way he immediately calmed down and took another swig convinced me otherwise. "No. They're advising that we all stay in at night because vampires are imprisoned by the sun. They can only come out at night, can't they?"

"You're a bloody idiot," another woman suggested, but the man didn't back down.

"You think it's a coincidence there are fewer attacks now that most people retire to their beds earlier?" He laughed loudly before downing the rest of his drink. "When you turn up dead, we'll all know why."

They grew silent, and then as though they could feel our eyes on them, they looked over at Connor and me, and we quickly turned away. My eyes widened at Connor in the embarrassment of being caught staring, and he returned the sentiment with a weary expression.

"But I'm not afraid," I heard the man bolster from behind me, and I tried very hard not to turn back around to look at him. "I reckon I could handle one of them."

I stared down at the bracelet on my wrist. There were chains on all of us these days, mortals, Casters, and Night Crawlers alike—restrictions holding us back from living freely as we once had. Perhaps one day soon the drunk man with little regard for Florence's cruelty would be proven wrong—would be put in his place—but for now, it didn't matter. Even someone as hubristic as this drunk deserved to live out his last days without fear, though it was possible there weren't many of those days left.

"He's not wrong about more people staying indoors," Connor whispered, resting his forearms down on the bar to talk to me. "If it gets any worse, I'll have to shut down the pub 'til things ease over."

I bit my cheek, nodding even though it all felt so surreal. "Hydie said all the schools are pushing back their in-person start dates again, as an extra precaution," I said. "She's been doing her studies online, but even if they were going in person, I don't think it'd be wise for her to go in. Not until Florence and his forces are brought down."

Connor nodded in agreement, his eyes flickering over to the group of patrons before landing back on me. "Any update from the gnomes?" he asked hopefully.

I let out a tired breath. It was almost as if consistently interrupted sleep wasn't enough to re-energise me.

"Yes," I told him. "The gnomes in the Americas have all hidden their supply of mushrooms, but apparently some creature native to the United States is giving them trouble. Fendel said it's more of a hindrance than anything to truly worry about though. Nearly all the gnomes in the world know by now not to trust anyone with the mushrooms until this all settles down." I didn't have the moxie to add the word "if" in there. "Abigail and Cristin were just in Vatican City getting more holy water from the pope, so that's good at least."

"Rome, eh?" Connor asked, his cheeks pulling up into his usual smile. "No one ever takes me on adventures anymore. I'm just stuck here in an empty bar," he complained.

"Was our trip to Germany earlier this year not enough to keep you satisfied?" I quipped.

Connor gave me his brightest smile yet before saying, "Not until I get to sink my teeth into Florence," and I completely understood.

◌

By the time we closed up the pub and I transported myself home, Hydie was fast asleep. Taking to the study, I situated myself in my usual spot to study potions and spells. When that grew unbearably dull, I pulled a map of the world onto my lap. I studied it, running my hands along the seven continents, hoping to feel an inkling of a pull. Occasionally, I'd look up at the large screen as it scanned over face after face to no avail.

A few hours after sunrise, my eyes started to close, my head began to curve into my chest, and sleep nearly took me, when all of a sudden, an invisible force jerked me awake. My heart pounded against my ribs as I looked around the still room, but after a few short seconds my eyes were drawn back to the screen, and there he was: his devilish charm, his slick blond hair, and his dangerous red eyes.

Every sound deafened as the sight of him drew me in. I didn't realise I was on my feet. I didn't know my hand had reached out to his sharp features until I touched the screen and a bit of magic zapped my fingertips. Without thought, I threw my arm behind me and the map flew into my hands. I tore my eyes away from the man on the screen and buried my face into the map, my fingers shaking from both fear and excitement. My eyes zoomed all over until they landed on a spot in the western hemisphere, and the parchment began to burn. A small stream of smoke lifted off the map as an orange spark lit it up. I blew on the spot, and a scorch mark appeared, marking my target. A jolt of excitement ameliorated the pit that usually occupied my stomach, and as I read the words next to the small black dot, the dark hole vanished from my core entirely.

Seattle, Washington, it said.

As I ran through the castle and up the stairs, clutching the map tightly with eager hands, all the sounds crashed down into my ears and became chaos. I pushed open our bedroom door, ready to write to Chad about my findings, but when I entered the room, he was already there.

Items of all shapes and forms flew around him, landing neatly into a trunk that sat open on the floor, but I steadied my stance and prepared myself for the challenge.

He would *not* be going without me.

"Where are we going?" I asked firmly, deliberately not questioning whether or not I was invited.

To my surprise, however, his face ignited and formed a pleasant smile. "I was hoping you'd ask," he said, and my heart filled with excitement.

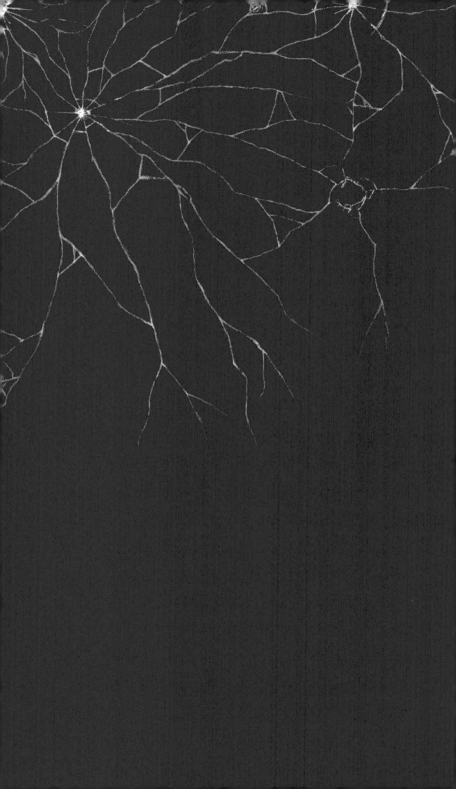

Chapter 28: Witch

A s soon the alert sounded, I ordered Nigel to write to that elven arsehole king and tell them where we were off to," Chad told me as he continued bustling around the room, packing for two. "For the time being, it appears that Icaron is wrapped up in something, so lucky for us, it means he's unable to join us."

"Good thing I have this trusty bracelet for them to track me by," I said sarcastically, dangling the chain from my wrist, "in case they feel the need to check in."

"Such a lovely thought," Chad replied with a lack of enthusiasm. He still wasn't very optimistic about the bargain we had made with the elves.

Chad's hand ran through his hair, mucking it up, and his eyes darted around the room, searching for anything he had forgotten to pack. I jumped in to help, grabbing a few items for myself and shoving them into the second trunk.

"What's the use of packing?" I asked, wondering how far Florence could get in the mere seconds we wasted. "Can't you conjure whatever we need?"

"I can conjure things within a range," he explained, disappearing into the bathroom to get more, "but we're going to be on the other side of the world, aren't we?" he asked, his voice echoing off of the bathroom walls. "It's too far."

I nodded as he came back out, then moved aside to change out of my dress and into proper fighting clothes.

"We should bring Connor too," I suggested.

Chad's hands paused their swift movements, and his mouth stood ajar for a moment before he closed it.

"What? He'd want to come," I insisted, yanking a tunic over my head before fastening a belt around it. "He was just telling me how he wants to go off on another adventure." My tone was determined, but regardless of whether or not Connor wanted to come, I knew I'd be dragging the werewolf along with us. There was absolutely no way I'd leave him alone with Hydie for God knows how long.

Chad nodded, apparently deciding it wouldn't take too long to go fetch Connor. He resumed his speed as he said, "Okay. We'll stop by the pub on our way out."

After throwing on some flexible pants and sensible boots, I reached for my trunk, but fate had something else in store.

Thunderous quakes shook the castle. Clinks of every object rattling against its surface filled my ears, and I clutched a bed post to steady myself. Chad whipped his head up to look at me so quickly that his neck threatened to snap off. As his wide eyes bored into me, my heart raced. The earth stilled as abruptly as it had awoken, but chills still covered my body.

"There's been a breach," Chad said briskly.

No sooner had the words left his mouth than he was grasping my arm and transporting us out to the front gardens to inspect the attempted break in.

Winter winds lashed against my skin as a million scenarios stampeded through my mind. Darkness was swallowed as Chad conjured a bright orb within his hand, and as I focused my eyes beyond that of a mortal's ability, I confirmed that the faint shimmer of the domed ward still held strong. Fear, however, swirled around as I searched the grounds for the perpetrator. Whoever it was couldn't have succeeded in getting in. It had to be a misfire—a failed attempt. Yet breaths separate from ours sounded in my ears, and an eerie feeling told me if they were willing to try once, a second attempt at breaking in was soon to follow.

The fabrics of Chad's shirt crinkled where I gripped them tightly against his chest. His pounding heart synchronised with mine. He kept a firm hold around my waist, his other hand poised in front of him, ready to fortify his land, but a small figure sat up from the ground where he had apparently been stricken, and quickly toddled forwards.

Chad lowered his hand as a small gnome came running towards us, this time wise enough to halt before he reached the nearly invisible barrier. A sigh of relief left my lips as I realised who the attempted intrusion was made by. Poor Fendel had tried to get through the wards and failed. At least we knew they were working.

"Milady! Milady! We have news!" he squealed urgently, forgetting his bluff of a porcelain disguise amongst all the excitement. "There's been a sighting of Florence in North America, milady," he said urgently.

My shoulders fell at the news that was not actually new. Half the world must know where Florence was by now if Chadwick, Fendel, and

I all knew about it on entirely separate accounts. And if that was the case, then it was nearly certain Florence would be onto us.

The bloody bastard was going to flee the country before we even got there.

"Thank you, Fendel," I told him quickly, forcing a smile. "We're off to pick up Connor, and then we'll be headed straight to America to scope it out."

"Let me come with you!" he squeaked madly, standing eagerly on the balls of his small feet. "I have friends there. And I can be your messenger if anything goes awry."

I exchanged glances with Chad and he gave a slight shrug, implying that the choice was mine.

Looking back at the gnome through the thin shimmer of the ward, I nodded. "Although I hope all goes well," I began, thinking of the daunting implications behind the gnome's request, "we'd love for you to join us, Fendel. Could you do me a favour first?" I watched as he nodded eagerly in reply. "My sister's asleep in the castle," I told him, glancing back at the stone exterior. "Go to Loxley Lair. Make sure Abigail knows we're going to America, and have her watch after Hydie for me. Then when you've finished, meet us at the Castle on the Rocks pub."

"The attic," Chad corrected, and my eyes flew over to him as he suggested it. The one place in the castle I wanted to venture to the least. He gave me a small nod in confirmation before looking back at the gnome. "My magic has its limits, as I'm sure does yours. A trip that far would completely wipe me out. We need to use a portal."

The mirrors, I thought to myself, fear creeping up my spine, but even through the hollowness that began to grow within me, I forced a brave smile and nodded at the gnome.

Chad's hand extended, dissolving through the ward, turning it a faint golden hue. Fendel's eyes widened as though he had made a grave mistake showing himself to a wizard, but as Chad wrapped his fingers around the gnome's hand, the tension in the gnome's shoulders eased. Green magic shone around the gnome for a fraction of a second before Chad gave the small creature a warm smile.

"You'll be free to come and go from this castle now," he informed Fendel. "The wards won't blast you back anymore."

A shiver shook Fendel's body as his defences instinctually went up. A veil of shine leaked across his face and down his arm, like he was torn whether or not to freeze himself into place. Deciding that it was a bit too late to fool the wizard into thinking he was already frozen, Fendel let out a trembling breath and nodded up at the Caster before him.

"Yes, Your Highness," he breathed out, and with a puff of colourful smoke, he disappeared.

Chad pointed a hand at the castle and closed his eyes as a jet of green flew towards the tall structure. "There. Our trunks will be waiting for us in the attic," he said. Then he faced me, gripping my hands in his, and whirled us off to the flat above Castle on the Rocks.

∽

Connor's face scrunched up as though we had just offered him a rotten egg to eat. "Um…" he let out hesitantly. "I think I'll just stay safe in London. I'll take care of Hydie—keep her company."

"No," I dished out firmly. "You're coming with us." My fierce eyes must have been just the encouragement he needed because he stood up from his bed and clumsily set to work, stuffing random articles of clothing that lay in heaps around the room into a sack. Only, that didn't stop his mouth from resisting.

"But someone should stay to make sure she's—" he tried.

"It's already been handled," I told him, furrowing my brows at him. I didn't understand. He had just told me he wanted to go on an adventure, and all of a sudden he was hiding with his tail between his legs?

"What? Is she going to man Castwell Castle on her own?" the werewolf asked, walking over to his bathroom and stuffing his toothbrush straight into the bag without any thought of covering it first. "That doesn't seem like you, Azalea. She's barely had time to train. I should stick around to protect her. I think I'd be a good fit for the job." He came out of the bathroom to give me a stern look as though I were being daft.

His pause perturbed me. How did he have so much time to waste when we had finally spotted Florence for the first time in months?

My jaw clenched and my hands flew to my hips as I stared him down, my toes tapping impatiently against the ground. Chad's hands immediately found their way to my shoulders, rubbing them gently to ease my frustration. It didn't, however, stop me from glaring at his friend from across the room.

"Abigail's looking after her," I replied through gritted teeth, shutting down his request.

He let out a small laugh as he went back into the bathroom, grabbing more items to fill the bag. "You can't expect a vampire to be more protective than a werewolf," he insisted, but I failed to see the humour in it all. "It's in my animal instinct—my genetic code!"

"I'll take my chances," I growled back, picking up a stick of deodorant that sat on the dresser beside me, and handing it to him as he walked back over to us.

270

He winced before zipping his bag shut and flinging it over his shoulder. "Fine," he snapped back, all hints of happiness void in his eyes. "Suit yourself."

Chad shifted awkwardly, then grasped onto both of us. There was a swish in the air, and as soon as our feet touched the attic floor, we heard a loud *pop,* and Fendel landed next to us.

"Milady, that sister of yours was not very happy when I showed up with Miss Abigail," Fendel told me, his eyes shifting to the corner as he took in Chad with suspicion. "Says she doesn't like being babysat when she's gone through the trouble of all that training."

I gave a polite smile. "I'll be sure to tell her when we get back that 'all that training' she has done is for an emergency, not so we can throw her straight into the lion's pit," I said before adding as an afternote, "and Fendel. Call me Azalea, will you?"

"As you wish, milady—Azalea," he piped up, and I smiled at his error.

I realised with a shudder that I was once again surrounded by the countless mirrors. The chest of information was back in its rightful place, but the key was missing.

Fendel and Connor shifted their weight from side to side as their eyes examined the room for what I assumed to be the first time. A sinister feeling crawled across my skin. As they took in their reflections across the hundreds of mirrors, a sense of relief washed over me as my eyes braved the glass, and my own purple hair was displayed, rather than pink.

I reached down to grab my trunk, but Fendel quickly placed a hand to block me from touching it.

"Allow me to carry the luggage," he said, and after Connor took his bag off his shoulder, Fendel placed a hand on the bags one at a time, and they shrunk down to the size of a coin. Picking them up from the ground, he slid them into his pocket and waited.

Chad gave me an encouraging smile before he turned to one of the mirrors. "Victoria Sallows in Seattle, Washington," he instructed, and my heart caught as his reflection nodded back at him on its own accord.

My hand instinctively clutched onto his shirt. As he took a deep breath, he gently removed my hand from his chest and held it in his. Then he bravely stepped through the magical portal. It shimmered like a vertical body of water, and as I scrunched my eyes to brace myself, he pulled me through after him.

The chill from the liquidised glass reminded me of ghosts floating through me—cold and terrifying, with the sense of being unable to touch the ground.

We stepped out onto aged wooden floorboards, splintered and coated in a thick layer of dust. The angled ceiling made the room feel like it was caving in on us, and I noted we were in an attic. The shelves that filled the room, cluttered with cracked crystal balls, bent tarot cards, and other witchy items, gave it even more of a claustrophobic feel. Pale, ghostly fabrics covered some of the items in the room, and the only source of light was a tiny slit in the window. Small as the window was, the slit was even smaller, and hardly any light from the street peeked through. We were surrounded by darkness.

Chad lifted our hands and placed a gentle kiss on the back of mine. His eyes twinkled as he stared at me, reminding me that everything was going to be all right. A faint shimmer came from behind me, and I looked to see Connor's face melt through the glass, the edges swooshing out like molten metal. Fendel's tiny frame melted through after him, but a wave of porcelain shimmered across his features before being replaced by an eruption of goose pimples across his skin.

"This place belongs to a witch," Fendel whispered. "A witch with the stolen souls of my brethren. I can feel it," he breathed out, and my chest tightened once more.

Chad pulled me towards the window, his other hand positioned carefully in front of him to make sure he wouldn't knock into anything, since his non-vampire eyesight wouldn't help him navigate in the dark. When he reached the window, he bent down to the slit that allowed in the small trail of light, and I took in the slats of wood that were obstructing the view to the outdoors.

Turning back to me, Chad whispered, "Perhaps it's best if you take Fendel outside before I talk to Victoria. Just to be safe," he added.

I gave a firm nod, wanting to escape the witch myself, and I hadn't even met her. "Gladly," I told him.

"Sunrise isn't for hours," Chad noted. "I'll have to wake Victoria up to see what she knows, but it's possible she won't know anything yet." His eyes strained to truly see my face in the dark. "Do you feel anything?" he asked gently.

He knew the shame I felt about my connection to Florence—the connection I wanted so eagerly to sever. But I shook my head. I didn't feel a pull. I couldn't tell how far the vampire had managed to run in such a short time. I didn't know how close he had to be for me to feel his presence.

Chad shifted uncomfortably before swallowing hard. "Connor," he said, turning to his mate. "You should stay with them in case Florence is lurking nearby or plans on returning."

Connor nodded, just as silent as I was, but when I looked at him, his face didn't read fear. It read a mixture of wear, boredom, and unease. I hadn't expected him to feel so disconnected from it all when he voiced his initial unwillingness to come along. On the other hand, he was used to sleeping in after closing the pub so late. He had been snuggled in under his sheets when we arrived to whisk him away. And now that we were all the way across the world, in a vastly different time zone, I didn't know when any of us would be getting rest.

"Will the witch be alerted that we're here?" Fendel asked with a tremble in his voice.

"No," Chad replied quietly. "These portals are one of the perks I get as king of the Casters. It gives me free rein to pop in when official business is in order. Now let's find the door and take you lot outside," he added decidedly.

Since I could see the location of the door clearly, I guided Chad over to it and pulled it open, cringing at the squeak it made. I didn't want to think how the witch would react if she caught a vampire, a werewolf, and a gnome lurking in the dead of the night.

Connor trailed behind us as Chad held onto one of my hands, and Fendel stood on my other side, clutching tightly onto the hems of my tunic. I brushed a hand along the top of the gnome's hat to help ease his worried mind.

We went down a flight of stairs, and I could hear the deep breathing of the witch as she slept soundly. When we walked down another flight of steps, we entered a part of her house that was set up as a shop. It reminded me of how Connor's flat sat above the pub, except this shop did nothing to conceal her true identity as a witch.

One look around made it very clear that she was hiding her powers from the mortals in plain sight. There was a sign for palm reading, and shelves selling rings, crystals, and rocks of all sizes and varieties. There were posters of star charts and lunar calendars displayed on the walls, mirrors of every sort lining the room, and beads hanging from a doorway that led farther into the shop. As we neared the shop's exit, we passed a stand with books on astrological signs and mind reading.

"Victoria is a member of the American Council of Witches," Chad explained in a hushed voice. "She and the rest of the council are in charge of approving or denying the magic that's shown to mortals. They give them a small taste, just enough for them to yearn for it, but not quite fear it. It's a small step towards being accepted amongst normal humans."

Green magic shimmered from Chad's hands, surrounding the door, and it gave a slow click before it creaked open. Cold air and the light chorus of windchimes greeted us as the four of us stepped out into the night.

As we tiptoed into the street lined with shops and pubs, I decided we must be in downtown Seattle. Yet the city was all quiet. Wooden boards were nailed across the windows of every building. The glint of moonlight as it reflected off a shiny surface caught my attention, and as my eyes drifted down, I jumped. Shivers covered my skin as I took in the tiny faces of at least ten frozen gnomes, horror across their faces.

Magic began to swirl in the pit of my stomach, ready to free the poor souls, but Chad's body went rigid against mine. He winced as my heated eyes met his, but his expression pleaded with me to keep my magic in.

"We'll need information from the witch—and trust," Chad began, and he leaned forwards to speak to Fendel. "After that, I'll come back in a few weeks, when she's less likely to suspect it was me, and I'll free them all. All right?" he promised firmly, and the gnome gave a timid nod in response.

Allowing Chad to lead me forwards, I craned my neck around to look back at the witch's shop. "Victoria's Best Kept Secret" was posted above the door. The windows had wooden boards across them as well, but these boards were decorated with graffiti that bled onto the stone of the building. Hateful words assaulted my eyes, but of all of them, the largest one that popped out was the word "witch."

My mind fumbled over the sight, my eyes flickering back and forth between the first letter and the last, trying desperately to comprehend why anyone in the mortal world would believe that this Victoria was truly a witch. Perhaps being on the council hadn't been enough for the witch to remain safe. I glanced over to Chad, but he looked more saddened than confused.

"I'll be back soon," he said, squeezing my hand one last time before he turned to walk back into the building.

Connor stalked across the street without a word and stopped when his feet mounted the other pavement. My eyes roved over the unfortunate gnomes in the garden, imprisoned for merely being in the wrong place at the wrong time—for being born a gnome.

Fendel's hand patted the back of mine, and I looked down as he gave me a sad smile. "One battle at a time, milady," he told me as sorrow drowned out his last word. I didn't have the heart to remind him to call me Azalea. His sentiment was brave, but his heart clearly ached for his enslaved comrades.

I nodded back, Chad's promise to come back and free them playing in harmony with my own promise to free all the gnomes from the witches' clutches.

I crossed the road and listened as Connor let out a long sigh. He slumped down to the ground, leaning against the brick exterior of one of the buildings. He stared blankly up at the dark sky, his shoulders slouched. A sign above him marked the building as a dance studio, and I wished I could look into the past, before boards were a necessity. I longed to marvel at the merry couples who danced over the slick wooden floors, but alas, I could not. The studio was as dead as the streets in these early hours, and there was a whisper of fear in the air, the sense that this whole trip would be for not, as searching for Florence so often was.

I let my body fall gently against the wall before it slid down the rough siding. As I settled into a woebegone stance beside Connor, I let out a defeated sigh. A cold breeze blew past, carrying the scent of rain, and I scooched in closer to Connor to steal some of his heat. As Fendel took a seat beside me, we all waited for whatever news would come next.

"This blows," Connor groaned, staring off into oblivion, and I nodded silently.

I didn't know what I expected coming here—to have a run-in with Florence as soon as our feet touched down in the states? Perhaps a quick conversation with him later after a mid-day tea?

After half an hour or so, Chad came back out of the house and ran across the street to join us.

"It turns out the riots in America are worse than I feared," he said, standing in front of where we sat. "There was a report a few weeks ago about a vampire sucking someone's blood out in the open, and people are outraged."

"A 'few weeks ago' as in you've heard of this report before?" I scolded, thinking back to the night of his coronation. Fury started to bubble up within me. I had explicitly told him not to keep things from me, yet here he was, telling me about the attack far too late.

Chad quickly shook his head but then stopped mid-shake to furrow his brows. "I mean, yes, but I had completely forgotten," he tried, the surprise in his voice expressing his truth. "The American Witch Council handled it all themselves, modifying the memories of the witnesses, erasing the footage. I didn't think much of it to be honest. That sort of thing has happened loads of times, even in Britain. It's usually with new vampires. Every once in a while a vampire will turn a mortal and leave them to fend for themselves without a coven. The thirst will get to them and they'll attack in the open. The AWC knew this attacker wasn't Florence, or else our system would've picked it up. Victoria just informed me, however, that the video was leaked. She and the rest of the AWC believe Florence is behind *that* part at the very least. Now anyone who appears remotely connected to the mythical world is getting backlash for it."

"Hence the 'witch' graffiti," Connor said bitterly, gesturing his hand back at the shop.

Chad nodded. "Businesses are temporarily closing and locking up tight until the storm blows over," he continued.

"Do you think that'll happen in Europe?" I asked. My muscles tensed at the notion, and Fendel moved closer to me.

"I dunno," Chad replied with a shrug. "If Florence and his people start attacking out in the open more frequently, then yes. But we need to figure out how the footage was leaked when all the cameras are under our control."

"Three guesses who," I taunted, feeling that it was Lili all the way down to my bones.

"Then why are we here?" Connor drawled out, his eyes still glued to the witch's house. "What does all that have to do with tonight?"

"Victoria and I contacted the rest of the AWC, and as far as they can tell, there wasn't another attack tonight, but Florence was close to here. There was a native tribe that spotted him again about thirty-five miles south of here."

"A native tribe?" I asked. "Are they witches?"

Chad nodded as he looked down at the three of us, his eyes scanning over us in turn. "They have magic, but Victoria says they think of magic as sacred. They don't use it nearly as often as we do."

"So it's less likely they'll turn me to stone?" Fendel asked timidly.

"No one's going to turn you into stone, Fendel," Chad said kindly. "We won't let them."

Fendel nodded but his small body remained tense against me. I rested my hand on his shoulder to comfort him, and let out a soft breath.

"What's the plan?" I asked, feeling the exhaustion weigh down on me.

"Well," Chad began, letting out his own heavy breath, "the natives live on a reservation. The leaders may have more information for us. I haven't been there before and there's no open mirror on their end, but I can take us close. We'll have to go on foot the rest of the way if you two don't mind taking Fendel and me along for the ride."

Connor and I nodded. It was starting to feel exactly like our trip in Germany. No pull to lead me to Florence's whereabouts, Connor transforming under the cover of night with Chad atop his back, and me running beside them. Only this time we had the company of a gnome.

ᔆ

Thirty minutes later, the dirt floor came back into focus as we pulled to a stop. Under the cover of the trees we had travelled through, Chad and Fendel slid off Connor's back so the werewolf could morph into his human form.

"It should be just past that ridge," Chad told us, gesturing in front of him. "It's best if we walk the rest of the way. We wouldn't want to rub it in that you're a vampire and you're a werewolf," he added, pointing to each of us in turn.

We walked over the ridge, and a modest wooden house came into view, tucked into the forest, away from the city lights. The wind blew against the sweat I had acquired from the run, sending a chill across me, but with the cold sensation came the eerie sense that someone was watching us. My eyes flew to the others. Shivers wracked their bodies from the breeze, but none of them seemed to feel what I had. Fendel's eyes darted about, as though a witch would pop out at any second to freeze him. His small legs worked hard to keep up with the pace we took. Connor kept his eyes on the ground, his face concentrated into a frown, and Chad, who was leading our way with hurried steps, glanced back at me with the expression of boyish hope as though the answers we sought were just beyond the door we neared.

I focused my senses on the world around us, on every creak and rustle, on every forest creature's sounds as our fast footsteps woke them from their slumber. But more footsteps met my ears, leading me not to the forest around us, but to the house itself.

"We may have to wake up every magical being within the state before we find our answers," Chad joked, turning his head back to us again as he ascended the few steps to the front porch.

"Something tells me that waking them won't be necessary this time," I replied, halting at the bottom of the stairs so Fendel could remain a safer distance away.

Just as Chad's face twisted into confusion, the door to the house opened abruptly, stopping the rest of our group from taking another step.

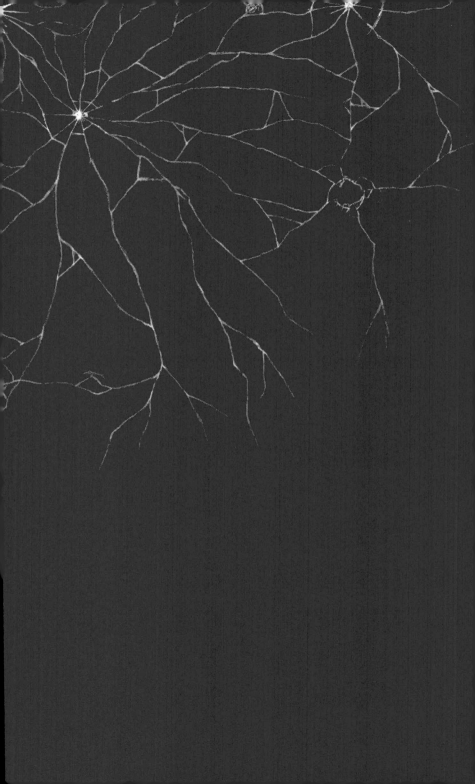

Chapter 29: Country of Origin

Chad's body jerked back from the sudden introduction as a man with long black hair and aged, medium-brown skin took him in. The man folded his arms, standing as a blockade in the doorway. Darkness shadowed over him. Not even the moon was at an angle to share his features, and I was thankful for the sight that being a vampire had given me. I watched anxiously as his eyes assessed Chad first, and then me, Connor who stood breathlessly by my side at the bottom of the steps, and the tiny gnome who clutched onto my shirt as if his life depended on it.

"Hello," Chad forced out through lungs that sounded as though there was very little air left in them. "My name is—"

"I know who you are," the man said with a deep, fierce voice.

Fendel instantly turned to his statue form, the folds of my tunic trapped in his strong grip as a shield.

"Then perhaps you know why we're here," Chad tested gently, taking a step back onto the stairs to give the man more space.

The man continued to inspect us with heated eyes, and I wondered whether he'd find trustworthy features amongst our faces. As the quiet in the air stretched, his eyes bored into mine, and the urge for me to speak prickled my throat. My lips parted to explain the purpose of showing up on his doorstep in the early hours of the morning, but the crisp winds switched directions, and a foul stench filled my nostrils.

I saw Connor's body tense in my peripheral vision, and when his head jerked around to the woods to locate the source, I knew he had sensed it this time. A twig snapped far off in the distance, and I pivoted my head back to Chad to warn him since he hadn't so much as flinched. But the man in the doorway tilted his head at me, and I lost all my words.

"You hear it, don't you?" he asked quietly, keeping more information on the tip of his tongue.

Another crack sounded, this time closer, and I nodded, aching to inch closer to my mates. The smell lingered in my nose: filth, rot, and poisoned blood.

"I can smell it," I told him warily.

My body cringed at the thought of what could be lurking out there. The lack of a pull informed me that it wasn't Florence.

I closed my eyes and let the sounds of the entire forest rush into me. Moist, heavy breathing entered my ears. It was strange—different from the ones I had come across in this life. Something dark and deep within me whispered that the foreign stench was a different creature entirely, one I had never encountered before.

"The wind carries its stench," the man said, and I fought off the flinch from the sudden sound of his voice.

He took his eyes off of me to gaze out into the wood, drawing mine up to the leaves of the trees. Chad's heart pounded with confusion. Twigs snapped underneath his boots as he looked around, but there was no way he could sense the threat the way the rest of us had. My hand levitated to my face and attempted to block the stench.

"What is it?" Connor asked, his eyes shifting ever so slightly into their wolf form so he could try and spot the creature.

"It is known by many names," the man said, his voice foggy, but his stance was still strong. "They've haunted the woods here for hundreds of winters. They begin as humans, but are turned into creatures, feasting on humans with a hunger much like bloodsuckers and moon howlers," he said, looking down at Connor and me with knowing eyes. "They lose all sense of their own identity, and live off human flesh just like their brethren."

"Should we attack it?" Chad asked, fear seeping into his voice now. His Adam's apple bobbed under the weight of the information.

"This one has just eaten," the man declared, and I wondered if the blood I smelled was his proof, yet I didn't understand how anyone with a normal nose could identify it. "Wendigos, as some call them, usually haunt the tops of the forest, climbing from tree to tree unless tempted by someone they wish to feed on or turn into a beast such as themselves. That's when they creep down to the ground."

"And what types of people tempt them?" I asked. My heart pumped faster as a horrid feeling slithered against my mind.

"Most of the time they only turn people who are selfish by nature," he informed us, but his word choice led me to believe there was something else I was missing.

"And the other part of the time?" I pressed, and his eyes left the trees to return my gaze.

Taking a step into the moonlight, he studied my face once more. I took a step closer to him, needing to know more, but Fendel's frozen hold on my clothes only allowed me one step. Faint whispers filled my ears as I waited for the man's answer, but I couldn't sort through them fast enough to untangle them.

I took a deep breath. "You said 'most' of the time," I explained. "What of the other part? Why else would they attack? When?"

"In nightmares," he breathed out, and my stomach lurched.

Nightmares, my thoughts echoed. So many horrible dreams had come to me. There was little doubt that my mind would welcome the wendigo in.

"If a wendigo visits you in your sleep, then it'll visit you in flesh," he said. "And not even a vampire is fast enough to evade them."

I felt as though I would freeze like Fendel from all the sharp pins of ice that pricked my skin as the man looked at me. He knew I was a vampire. But how?

Chad came down the stairs and placed a caring arm around my waist, shielding me from more than just the cold. The sun would come peeking through the trees soon, and we'd all need rest. But if rest tempted the wendigo to come nearer, I wouldn't let sleep take me. It was too far to travel home without a portal, but I'd wait.

Another twig snapped, and I looked up towards the night sky to see a set of glowing white eyes. A dark creature hid amongst the treetops, moving so quickly that not even my eyes could take in its full shape except for its long antler-like horns that peeked out, camouflaging themselves with the branches of the pine trees. Then the trees rustled one by one as the wendigo trailed away from us and deeper into the forest.

"That creature is why the other bloodsucker was on our lands," the man told us, and I cringed before looking back at him. "We believe he was trying to get them to join his side."

My eyes dropped to the ground. The feeling of despair and hopelessness punched into my gut before I looked back up at the man. "Do you think it worked?" I asked.

"No," he said mystically, staring off into the wood again. "Wendigos only act of their own accord. Not by that of a man, or your kind," he said, gazing deep into my eyes. "But a whisper on the winds tells us that the one you seek is headed toward the southeastern coast."

A look of sudden realisation flashed across Chad's face in a panic before it disappeared behind composed features. He angled his face towards me and his green eyes glinted with confidence. "Then that's where we'll go next," he said, holding me tighter.

The man took a step out into the night, closing the door behind him before he descended the steps and made for the side of the house. I watched him curiously as he walked away.

"Not tonight you won't, Your Majesty," he said in a gravelly voice, without glancing back at us. "The sun will rise soon."

He turned the corner and Fendel unfroze, pulling at my clothing to lead me over to where the man had disappeared. When the four of us reached the end of the house and looked at the man, he was unlocking a shed.

"You'll sleep here for now," he instructed, apparently finding trust in our features after all. "We won't invite you into our home, but you may sleep on our property."

He pulled the doors to the shed open and grabbed out two large, orange parcels. One of them he tossed to Chad, and the other he tossed to Connor, both of whom caught them with a heave.

"These tents will shield you from the sun, and then you can continue your journey when the night falls again." It was almost a command rather than a suggestion. He tilted his head to take us in again, much more gravely this time. "But if the wendigos decide to attack," he added in a dark tone, "you're on your own."

The four of us stared at the man, not quite sure what to say until he began to walk back towards the house, and Chad broke the silence.

"Your generosity is very much appreciated," Chad said as the man climbed the steps back up to his home. "May I ask what your name is?"

The man placed his hand around the doorknob, pausing to stretch his fingers, like he was battling some internal ache. As his eyes stayed pasted to the silvery knob, he said, "I am Koda of the Puyallup tribe. And though your enemy is ours, there's nothing else I can do to help you in this war. My people have agreed to stay out of it."

Koda's eyes flew back to us, and though Chad tilted his head down with disappointment, he nodded back to the man. Without another word, Koda opened the door and disappeared inside.

I stared at the closed door, examining every grain of the wood as Koda's words replayed in my head. He wouldn't join the war. No one with a good heart seemed readily available to fight, other than the few who already had. All the while, Florence was building an army. It didn't make sense. How could good people allow him to win so easily?

Connor began to tug open the bag in his hand, and Chad threw his bag down to the ground with a soft thump. Before he could bend down to begin setting up camp, my anxious hands grasped onto his shirt and turned him towards me.

"I don't want to sleep," I told him, fear of the wendigo brewing in my eyes. "I'll stay up and keep watch."

Metal posts clanged together, and Fendel waved his hands around, a stream of iridescent colours flowing out of his palm, as colourful as a rainbow. The materials from both bags flew out, rearranging themselves in the air until they formed fully assembled tents.

Chad placed a caring hand on my cheek, drawing my attention back to him as his warm magic pulsed out, sending waves of serenity to soothe my boiling blood. "I'll protect you from your nightmares tonight."

I nodded my head slowly, not knowing how he intended to do so, but trusting him nonetheless. He placed a soft kiss on my lips, too quick for my tired mind to register it until it was gone. Then Fendel conjured up a pile of blankets and tossed one to each of us.

"But the idea of keeping watch is a good one," Chad added.

I heard Connor scowl and when I looked over at him, his eyes were squinted with irritation.

"Great," he said, lacking the enthusiasm that his word suggested. "*You* get to sleep with a pretty girl, and I get to sleep with a gnome." I let out an awkward laugh, and he glared at me before he vigorously unzipped his tent and climbed inside. "This whole trip is bullshit," he muttered under his breath.

I stared at the tent as Connor zipped up the entrance behind him, regretting my laugh, but not having an inkling as to why he was acting this way. I knew he wasn't the most mature twenty-two-year-old, nor did he have the most trauma-free past, but it was unlike him to act so bitterly. Usually, he was an insatiable flirt mixed with fluff.

My eyes shifted over to Chad to check his reaction, but he only gave me a close-mouthed smile before unzipping our tent and tossing his blanket in.

Fendel coughed, breaking the strange silence that had loomed. "I'll take first watch tonight," he squeaked before venturing off a few metres and propping himself onto a cushion he conjured.

Feeling a tad guilty for whatever unknown reason, I glanced back over to the tent Connor had just burrowed himself into and then turned to Chad. "I'm going to talk to him," I decided, handing him my blanket. "I'll see if he's all right. He's been a bit touchy since we left London."

Chad replied with the slightest nod before going into our tent, and I went to unzip the other.

I clambered in, ignoring Connor's body language that clearly stated I wasn't invited.

"Are you all right?" I asked, crossing my legs as I sat down next to him. "You've been a bit testy since we left."

"I'm just dandy," he let out, not bothering to mask the fact that he wasn't. His face fell flat as he fidgeted with his backpack, tossing it back and forth as though he were hesitant to let go of it—almost as though he was prepared to leave at a moment's notice.

Then it hit me. Guilt swelled in the pit of my stomach as I truly took him in for the first time since we had left London.

He hadn't wanted to come here. Regardless of how he yearned for an adventure, he had insisted upon excluding himself from this one.

And the dance studio.

I closed my eyes, shaking my head. It had to remind him of his parents. They had been the inspiration for salsa dancing nights at the pub. They had taught him the steps when he was young. Of course he didn't want to go to America, not with all the horrible memories from his childhood—memories of a time he wished so dearly to escape to. It was the country he had been bitten in, changed forever into a werewolf, and then tricked into **KILLING** his own parents.

"Oh, Connor, I'm so sorry," I whispered, ashamed by my own oversight. "I didn't even stop to think about what this country meant to you." How could I have been so oblivious?

"It's okay," he said, waving his hand in the air as if it hardly mattered, but it felt more like a ruse to hide his emotions. "It's about time I manned up and came back here."

He placed his hands behind him as he sat, leaning back in a casual sort of stance, but the sorrow and guilt within me took over completely.

Ignoring the sexist comment that would normally have earned him a whack in the stomach, I wrapped my arms tightly around his torso, wishing to make some of his pain disappear. For a moment, as we sat with my head pressed against his chest, he froze. He probably expected my usual response to his chauvinistic comments. But then I felt his breath catch, and he hugged me back. He patted my back awkwardly, likely not knowing what else to do, but he let me hug him.

After a moment, I pulled back, realising I shouldn't hug him so tightly. "How are your injuries from the other night?" I asked, assessing his face for any remaining scars, and then down at the leg he had been limping on, but I found no visible, long-lasting effects.

"Oh, I'm better now," he said, breathing out an air of excessive arrogance. "It only takes me a little longer to heal than you with your freakish vampire speed," Connor jested, his big, brown puppy-dog eyes shining brightly at his own joke.

"That's an awfully brave thing to say in front of only one vampire," I quipped. "Perhaps you should try saying that the next time you're at Loxley Lair. I wonder if a werewolf could survive a vampire bite."

"It can't be hard if a witch could do it," Connor replied with an arched brow.

I nudged him in his side for such a personal attack, and he nudged me back harder, causing me to fall over onto my forearm.

"Bastard," I called him through my laughs, but he smiled his usual bright smile, and it gave me hope that he'd be all right.

"Now go get some sleep before it's your turn for the night watch," he commanded firmly. "If I get eaten, or mauled, or attacked by a wendigo, all because you fell asleep during your turn, then I'm going to come back to haunt you."

I gave him a motherly sort of smile. "Are you sure you'll be all right?" I asked.

"Of course," he said back, but I couldn't help but notice the way his eyes avoided mine. "Besides, in a few hours I'll have my very own lifelike doll to snuggle up with," he jested, more traces of his usual humour returning.

I gave a laugh, rolling my eyes at him. "I'm sure Fendel will love being referred to as such," I replied, and then after wishing him a good rest, I crawled my way out of the tent and snuck right back into the one next to it, before I could let the fear of the wendigo overtake me.

Chad was lying on his back, staring up at the tent's interior peak when I came in. After nestling myself into the blankets next to him, my eyes followed his gaze. With a flick of his wrist, a map of the stars floated above us, twinkling as they told a story of what was yet to come.

"Mars is the brightest it's been since the second world war," he said, pointing to a red orb that stood out starkly. "There's going to be so much blood, so many lives lost, and I can't figure out a way around it."

He turned his body to me and gently ran a soothing hand along my cheek. I closed my eyes, soaking in the feel of his warm skin against mine. How could we figure out a way around it when we didn't know how it would come about? What would Florence do? When would it come? Where?

Chad let out a deep sigh. "Are you ready for me to take away your dreams for the night?" he asked, but sleep felt so out of place amongst all these worries.

I shook my head, not ready for sleep just yet. A thought wandered across the path my mind travelled, and I opened my eyes. "Why haven't you done this before?" I asked. "Eased my troubles so I wouldn't have nightmares?"

He shrugged in response, a bit of hurt written into the curves of his face. "My mum used to have dreams," he told me, continuing to stroke my face. "You're a lot like her. Your dreams have a purpose, even the bad ones."

I lay there for a moment before letting out a heavy breath. I didn't want to think about my nightmares, or his mum, anymore. I wanted to mentally prepare for what would come when I awoke.

"So what exactly is on the southeast border?" I asked, sleep beginning to tempt my eyes. They threatened to close under the weight that pulled them down. "What's this thing that Florence is after?"

"Well, if it's what I think it is, it's just *off* the border," Chad noted thoughtfully. "Or *who* to be precise. And then we have even more reason for concern." He shifted beneath the blankets. "That's where most of the mermaids reside."

I thought on it for a moment, taken back by the idea of mermaids, but I wasn't entirely sure why Chad was so concerned. Were mermaids wicked in this world? Abigail had told me a long time ago that mermaids were part of the Caster side. Why would Florence seek an alliance with an entire race he knew was against him? Either way, the possibility of spotting a mermaid sparked something pleasant inside of me.

"I think it'd be rather exciting to meet a mermaid," I told Chad nostalgically. "As long as they don't fall for Florence's trickery, of course. Something in my useless memory tells me I loved them as a child. Or the idea of them at least."

"Well, trust me," Chad said, tilting his head forwards a bit, "they're not as pleasant as one would think."

"How so?" I asked, wearing my disappointment plainly on my face. I turned to my side and propped my head on my hand to give him a good look.

"First of all," Chad began, exasperated as he mirrored my position, "getting to them is a bloody nightmare. Then the mermaids themselves are quite difficult to bargain with, but I'm hopeful it'll all turn out how it's meant to be. They've been on our side—the Casters' side—for centuries. I don't expect that to change now. They want to stay unknown to mortals as much as the witches and wizards do. Florence is making a right arse out of the whole lot of us, waving the truth about, but it'll be hell if we don't all remain hidden. And even if he does announce the existence solely of vampires, it won't be long until the mortals begin to suspect more of us, especially if they're already marking Victoria's house with spray paint."

Chad let out a long breath. I knew he was tired and worn down, but part of me sensed a separate burden that weighed down on him. His free hand traced a line on the blanket, considering how to put it into words. I let my fingers run along the back of his, trying to ease his worries, and he laced his fingers between mine.

"There's something else you should know about Lili and the mermaids, but I can't tell you until after it's too late."

I furrowed my brow, trying to comprehend what he meant. Whatever it was made my skin crawl with anxiety. "Why can't you tell me now?" I asked curiously. It didn't make sense for him to bring it up if he wasn't going to release the information.

"I'm trying really hard to fill you in on everything," he told me earnestly. "I don't want you to feel blindsided, but this is something I can't tell you. You being unaware will help them find trust in you."

The puzzle pieces swirled around until they became utter chaos. I could no longer tell where the edges were, or what side was up. I bit my lip, not liking the idea of being in the dark, but not seeing a way around it if I didn't even know what it was.

"At least I'm telling you," he stressed endearingly. "Well, more or less."

I let out a laugh. "Less," I clarified. "So much 'less' that it hardly even counts."

"But at least now, you can't say that you didn't know there was something you didn't know," he said.

I took a moment, absorbing it all in, accepting it as my own knowledge—the lack of it. There was, however, still one question that he could answer. "How are we going to get to the mermaids exactly?" I asked with a jaded breath. I envisioned sparkly mermaids swimming their way to the coastline to talk to us, but clearly, that couldn't be the case if they wished to remain unseen by mortals.

"Certain magical realms," Chad answered, "require certain magical avenues of transportation to get to them. If one doesn't take that method, then it informs the mermaids that said person is untrustworthy. If one *does* take that method, well then…" He stopped, his gaze going right through me.

"Yes?" I ushered.

"Well, then it's *less* likely they'll be attacked," he said, still not meeting my eyes.

I swallowed hard as I took in the terrifying answer I hadn't been looking for. Then I opened my mouth, ready to ask the sequential question in what I hoped was a brave tone. "And what is the method of transportation we must take to visit them?"

Chadwick's eyes finally met mine, the stars from the map shining brightly within them. "We're going to need a ship," he whispered.

"A ship?" I asked, dumbfounded.

"A ship," he confirmed with a flirty smile.

I let that smile coax me into a reassuring, dreamless sleep.

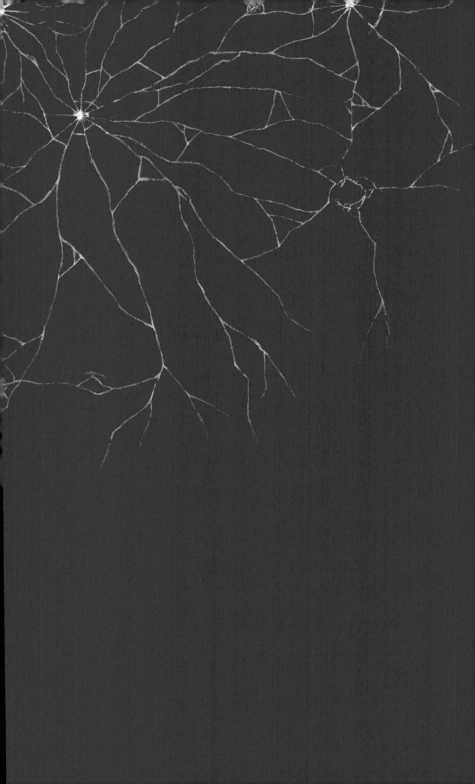

Chapter 30: Bright Lights

Rustling sounds and a foul scent of meat woke me. I sat up straight, the memory of wendigos and Florence playing across my mind. It took a second to ground myself—to remember why orange fabrics peaked above my head, and why blankets that weren't mine were wrapped around my lower half. I threw the cover off myself, hastily unzipped the tent's opening, and jerked my head out to see what had made those noises, and who was being eaten alive.

Chad and Connor stared back at me, surprised by my urgency. Their hands paused their journeys of carrying sandwiches to their mouths. As my brain worked hard to accept that the smell had come from the sandwiches and not the torn remains of the men I stared at, my mouth flew open as I tried to understand how it was already nightfall once more.

"We're just eating a quick bite before we leave," Chad said, gesturing his head towards the house. "Koda and his wife were very kind and brought us some food, but we should pack quickly. There's a ship waiting for us in Florida. Nigel and some of the other guards are meeting us there for the journey."

"But the wendigo," I started. "We were supposed to take turns for lookout. You should've woken me," I insisted as a bit of guilt brushed against me. "It's not fair for you all to keep watch while I lay here useless."

"*This* one wanted to let you sleep," Connor replied, tilting his head towards Chad, who gave a culpable grin as he busied himself with a hearty bite of food. "Mentioned something about you needing beauty rest."

Chad suppressed the smile that sparkled in his eyes before nudging his friend in the ribs. "I *mentioned* that you should stay out of the sunlight," he corrected. "Although you did look rather beautiful as you slept. I've never seen you so peaceful. I figured you needed the rest," he said softly.

My cheeks heated. Of course it was a stupid idea for me to do watch. I *was* useless in the daylight.

I clambered out of the tent, holding my breath as they finished their food, wondering if I'd rather take in the stench of the wendigo one more time than have to endure the scent of human food. When Fendel came skipping merrily out of the woods with a dead bird in his hand, squeaking about his intentions to cook it, I decided to busy myself with magically packing up the tents. Anything to distract me from the innocent animals who had died to fill their bellies. I second-guessed my urge to **KILL** Florence for just a second before reminding myself that he was anything but innocent. Then I contemplated whether it'd be better to watch his skin melt off from holy water, or his blood to drain out after the effects of my bare hands.

After the boys were done eating, we returned the tents, and Koda and his wife bid us farewell. Since the journey to the southeastern tip of the country was far, we went back to Victoria's shop, and she begrudgingly allowed us to use her mirror for transport. We pulled through to another witch's house in southern Florida, Fendel grasping tightly to my fresh tunic the entire time. When we stepped back out into the moonlight, Connor thought it wise to make a joke about the witches chasing after us to claim Fendel as payment for our transportation. I whacked him in the stomach for being such an insensitive tosser, but despite the scowl I gave him for the rest of our journey to the waterfront, I was secretly happy. At least Connor was back to his usual chipper self.

The smell of the ocean teased us as we walked in its direction, and the salt from the water was a pleasant contrast to the smell of the burning flesh from breakfast. I was thankful that the air here wasn't as crisp and frigid as the winter air in London and Seattle.

When we arrived at the port, several men who I recognised to be Chad's guards were waiting for us, but I hardly had time to acknowledge them in as I gawked at the ship behind them.

The breath left my lungs as I took in the enormous structure. At least twelve billowing white sails shook against the wind, all connected to three masts that towered high above us. The ship had multiple levels carved from a dark wood. Ropes sprouted from all over the ship, connecting in what seemed to be random spots, and a sage green flag displayed a silhouette of three witches. It was identical to the statue in front of Castwell Castle. The ship swayed in the ocean waves like a mother rocking her child to sleep. As I stared up at it, I became entranced by its beauty. I had never seen such a ship in real life, at least not that I remembered, but either way, it seemed like the ship, with its old-timey grandeur, had sailed to us from a fairy-tale land. It shouldn't be allowed in the dark world I lived in.

A tugging at my sleeve gathered my attention down to Fendel as he pulled at me anxiously. His eyes fixated on the guards as they prepared to sail, shimmers of porcelain flickering across his skin.

"This is where I leave you, milady," he said, too frightened to remember to call me by my name. "I wish to go check in with the other gnomes in America to see how things are going with the mushrooms. Then I can return to London. I'll update the Loxley Coven of your whereabouts and help keep an eye on your sister."

I smiled and nodded down at the poor gnome. He'd had enough close encounters with witches in the past twenty-four hours. I didn't blame him for his resistance to throw wizard guards and mermaids into the mix as well.

"Thank you, Fendel," I told him, reaching down and squeezing his tiny hand in mine. "You're an incredibly big help."

He beamed up at me, and extracted our luggage from his pocket, placing them on the ground to allow them to grow to their full size once more. Then after one more uneasy look towards the guards, he bid Chad, Connor, and me farewell. With a *pop*, he was gone.

"I'm glad to see he's coming around to me at least," Chad noted as he picked up our trunks and began to walk towards the dock to greet his men.

"No thanks to *someone*," I emphasised, not letting Connor get away with the cruel joke he had made moments ago.

The werewolf merely gave me his typical goofy smile before both of us followed Chad.

Some of the guards were already atop the ship, prepping it for sail. The rest were on land, waiting to greet us. Nigel bowed as we approached, but a certain blue elf drew my attention.

"Ah," Chad whispered into my ear. "Looks as though Icaron's here to babysit."

Icaron bowed down to Chad, his light blue skin ghostly in the moonlight. His lips stayed poised in a closed-mouth smile after Chad greeted him properly, not a word slipping through, and I wondered if the elves outside of the direct royal family were allowed to speak.

Two guards collected our luggage and carried them up the ramp to the ship. As we followed them up, my stomach immediately became queasy from the rocky movements. I bit my lip, fighting down the sense that I should have asked the gnome to bring me along with him.

My eyes followed Chad as he walked forwards, immediately pulling at different ropes, and looking completely at home on the large ship.

"Tell me," I pressed Chad as Connor and I approached him, "why would one already have a ship to visit the mermaids?" I wondered what sort of business he had needed to conduct with them in the past, and I couldn't help teasing him a bit to lighten the mood. "Any mermaid ex-girlfriends I should be aware of before we get there?"

"Of course not," Chad replied, still busied by the ropes. "It was more of a…" He hesitated before landing on the word "fling."

His eyes finally met mine, a smile sprouting within, but I was going to hit him. I was definitely going to hit him.

"What?" he asked as he took a large step back to avoid the possibility of such a blow. Oh, how well he knew me. "I was a bit choked up after Eyeara dumped me."

My face scrunched up in disgust as my mind immediately jumped to different reenactments and possible contortions on how intercourse with a mermaid would even work, but Connor cut off my thought process with a crude demonstration. I snarled at both of them.

"No need to be jealous," Chad insisted, taking in my furious expression. "It didn't last long, and it meant nothing," he added, rubbing my arm.

I quickly swatted his hand off of me. I wasn't sure what to reprimand first—the fact that the poor mermaid meant nothing to him, or that he thought I was jealous. I went with the latter. "I'm not jealous," I spat out, but it may have been a lie. One he instantly caught onto.

"Careful, my love," he said in warning. "You won't be able to hide that envy once we get to the centre of the Bermuda Triangle."

My jaw fell open. "They're located in the Bermuda Triangle?" I blundered, hardly able to control myself. All thoughts of sexy mermaids momentarily fled my brain.

"What?" Connor exclaimed, equally as put off.

"So you've heard of it?" Chad asked, feigning innocence as he leaned back against the side of the ship.

A ridiculous sputter escaped from my lips before I shouted out, with an immense amount of cheek, "Yes, I've *heard* of it! It's only the most feared place in the Atlantic."

"Who knows how many ships have crashed, and then completely disappeared there?" Connor joined in, waving his hands about to stress the severity of the mortal peril we were about to face. "This is suicide—a completely impossible quest."

"Well, that's where they hide," Chad replied with a shrug as if there was nothing more to it.

Lost for words, I glanced over to Connor, and his gaping mouth informed me that he was just as lost as I was. I had the urge to tease him about his dropped jaw as he always did to us, but I no longer possessed the energy. Turning back to Chad, I asked, "Why can't you just transport the ship there by magic?"

"Certain magical realms can only be entered in certain ways," he said, repeating the same phrase he had told me before. "Besides, it would take far too much power, and Demriam will take care of us when we get there... hypothetically," he added. The way his cheeks brightened, I didn't have to ask him if Demriam was the gorgeous mermaid he'd had floppy fish sex with.

"Only, that's not quite the worst of it," Chad teased with a sly grin.

Connor found the will to join in again. "What?" he asked hotly. "Is a kraken going to pop out and swallow us whole?"

"Not, exactly," Chad countered, fighting off his own laugh. "We're going to need to tie you two up."

I gawked at him for about the hundredth time, too shocked to be bothered with whatever Connor's reaction was.

"To the mast of the ship," Chad clarified, and I rolled my eyes at him.

"Cheers for the superfluous detail," I spat out between clenched teeth. "Now can we get to the bit where you explain why that's necessary?"

Chad's amused tone only served to stoke my irritation. "Some refer to the mermaids as sirens, and you're a vampire, and you're a werewolf," he said, gesturing to each of us in turn. "Both of you have hearing too exquisite to withstand the mermaids' calls. Normal ear plugs would be ineffective, and perhaps magical ones as well. Their songs can bewitch even the best of us."

"Is that how this 'Demriam' lady hooked you?" Connor jested.

"Er, no, but that's beside the point," Chad said, shaking his head as though he were finally ready to have a serious conversation. "Their songs are mesmerising. If even one of us can hear them, they'll make us steer the ship into a rock, and we'll end up shipwrecked."

"And since *we're* so keen on hearing, we have to get strapped down, while the rest of you flounce about?" I asked, eyeing the elf with pointed ears, wondering why *he* wasn't getting strapped down with us.

"While the rest of us sail the ship," Chad corrected gently.

My eyes flew to the main mast, and my shoulders fell as I took in my fate. The water rocked around us, leaving a queasy feeling in my stomach before we had even officially set sail. I looked back at Chadwick and gave a brave nod before shoving my wrists out in front of me.

"Shall we get it over with then?" I suggested, misery resonating in my throat.

He gave me a wink. Connor began to grumble under his breath, accepting his fate as well. The guards readied the ship and we set off into whatever misfortune lay ahead. Whether it was Florence, a shipwreck, or a storm of another form, I simply didn't know.

There was an unwavering smugness upon Chad's face as he stood before me, adjusting his electric green ropes, tying us to the mast, and ensuring we couldn't escape. I was glad Connor wasn't looking as Chad's green eyes brought a heat only he could produce to my cheeks, tempting me to break free and latch onto his lips as he raised a brow and pulled tighter. When he leaned in closer, my knees nearly gave out at the feel of his warm breath caressing my neck.

"Reminds me of a time not too long ago when I tied you up," Chad whispered in my ear.

Words only for me.

The memory I had already been thinking about focused brightly in my mind.

But Connor, who stirred uncomfortably against my arm, gave a ridiculous cough. "Yes!" he exclaimed dramatically. "It reminds me of the time you tied me up too, Chad. Fond memories," he added, shaking his head dreamily before giving up his act, and scolding the two of us. "Now can we get a move on?"

"No one asked your opinion," Chad quipped, pulling the ropes tighter around Connor, and I winced as the ropes tightened around me with it.

Connor let out a laugh. "But now that we *all* know how kinky the two of you get in the bedroom," he spat out much too loudly, rolling his head around in a circle to point at the entire crew, "maybe we should discuss—"

But I didn't find out the rest of what he was saying, because at that moment, Chad's fingers shimmered with green smoke, and a cold, plug-like substance filled my ears, blocking out all sounds. As I craned my neck to look at Connor, I noticed that the green smoke not only created blocks in the werewolf's ears but also in his mouth.

Chad gave his mate a provoking smile, raising his brows to intensify the challenge, and I felt Connor struggle against the ropes threateningly, but they held tight. I couldn't help but laugh at the two of them.

ભ

We were tied up for hours, waiting for some mysterious trigger to alert the mermaids. My muscles ached with exhaustion. The boat rocked around tauntingly as though it were merely doing it for laughs, knowing my stomach couldn't handle it. I stood, planning which way to crane my neck to avoid getting vomit down the front of my outfit, and brainstorming methods of how one could projectile vomit instead. From the corner of my eye, I watched as Connor's head drooped lazily around, and I gritted my teeth, envying his ability to sleep through all this commotion. Chad must have decided Connor was sufficiently subdued, because he'd removed the gag from his mouth at some point.

The ocean gave a particularly violent lurch, and just as I was ready to shout for Chad, and demand he untie me so I could lay in a foetal position, I saw a bright light crack across the sky.

It rumbled the entire sea, shaking me down to my core, and Connor jerked his head up with a start. His lips moved quickly, forming the word "what" a few times, but no sound came to my ears. The light cracked again, illuminating the night sky, shifting it to a striking shade of violet for just half a second before the sky returned to black once more. Wind blew icy chills across us, making the hair on my skin stand on edge. I looked down past the ropes, focusing my eyes on the bumps that played across my skin. I tried to ground myself in the moment—focus on slow inhales up and steady exhales down—anything to distract me from the motions that made my stomach weak. But as I watched the small curves along my skin, large droplets of water began to crash onto their surface.

Another flash of lightning accompanied a sudden downpour of rain. The men stared in awe as a dark cloud that had come from nowhere unleashed torrents of water upon us. Within seconds we were all soaked. Water crashed across the wooden planks at our feet, flooding the deck, and my heart pounded as the icy ocean chilled me to the bone.

Splashes of water played at the men's feet as the crew intertwined paths, all running to some unbeknownst station, either tightening or loosening sails, I hardly knew. A wave grew beside us, leaping violently onto the deck, drawing the ship lower into the ocean before allowing it to bob back up, not yet taking the boat as its prisoner.

The silence was eerie. My panicked hands clawed at the ropes, but my mind was torn between staying tight to the mast and being thrown around the deck like a fish out of water. I could feel Connor against me, his elbow knocking into me as he tried to loosen the ropes, but it was no use. The magical chains were impenetrable. Of all the times for Chad to produce his strongest rope, I couldn't believe it was now.

The bright lightning in the sky came in shorter and shorter intervals until the whole sky was a maze of jetting white lines. It was alive, working in cahoots with the sea to trap us—to shipwreck us like all the others who dared to enter the forbidden triangle.

Amongst all the chaos, my eyes darted from side to side, searching for Chad but failing to find him. A brash movement haunted the corner of my vision, stealing my attention—a dark thief in the night. My neck followed the movement as fast as it had come, but the wooden mast I was tied to blocked my view. I pivoted my head all the way to the other direction to see if Connor had seen it too, but a quick movement in front of me stole my attention yet again. This time the culprit stayed in my view just long enough for me to take it in, just long enough for me to see its long, seafoam-green hair, and skin that shimmered with brown and gold and green as it morphed into a long scaly tail. The creature grasped onto one of the guards and took him overboard. As a formidable splash of water revealed their landing, my hands froze against the ropes, no longer trying to gain freedom—no longer wishing to become an easy prey for the mermaids to take straight into the dark depths of the ocean.

I looked over at the other guards, fiddling uselessly on the ropes, plugs in their ears, and the focus in their eyes told me that none of them had seen the mermaid or the guard disappear. Fear pulsed through me, resuming the struggle I forced against the ropes, yet they held tight, refusing to release me. A third mermaid tossed herself through the air, taking another guard captive over the opposite edge of the boat, and a scream left my mouth—a scream no one could hear. I twisted my body around, trying anything to get their attention, but the only one who seemed to pay me any mind was Connor. I felt his hand grasp onto mine. His once sleepy eyes were now wide as he used them to ask if I was all right. I widened mine back at him, shaking my head vigorously, and directing them back to where the guards had disappeared into the icy waters.

Connor's hand tensed as Nigel's body was taken, and then another guard, and another, but even with his voice added, our cries for their attention disappeared into the void of sound.

Finally, Chad came into view, and his eyes met mine before they fell down to the way my hand was clutching Connor's, and then back up. He sent a stream of green magic, and the ropes unravelled from around us. My body flung forwards, and I struggled to balance as the ship lurched once more.

Drawing on my vampire reflexes and combining them with the purple magic that flowed through my veins, I began to run towards another mermaid, but something grabbed me around the waist. We flew through the air until my body crashed into the cold ocean, a thousand needles marking my skin as we sank.

A bubble formed in my mouth as I held tightly onto the air that still lingered in my lungs. All I could think about was the pain the cold caused. My arms and legs were held out in front of me, paralyzed from the ice, as the creature pulled me deeper. A splash at the surface revealed Chad's body, his cheeks puffed with air, his arms and legs making wide strides as he swam down towards me, but the entity clutching my waist was too fast. Lower and lower we sank, until my chest couldn't take it anymore. Bubbles escaped my mouth, and water filled my raw lungs.

I watched as Chad's green eyes darkened with fear.

I watched as his hand reached out for mine.

I watched as he realised he was too far away.

Suddenly, a bright light burst out in front of me. Every part of me yearned to follow it, but I couldn't. I just kept going down, away from the light, until everything turned black.

Hopelessly black.

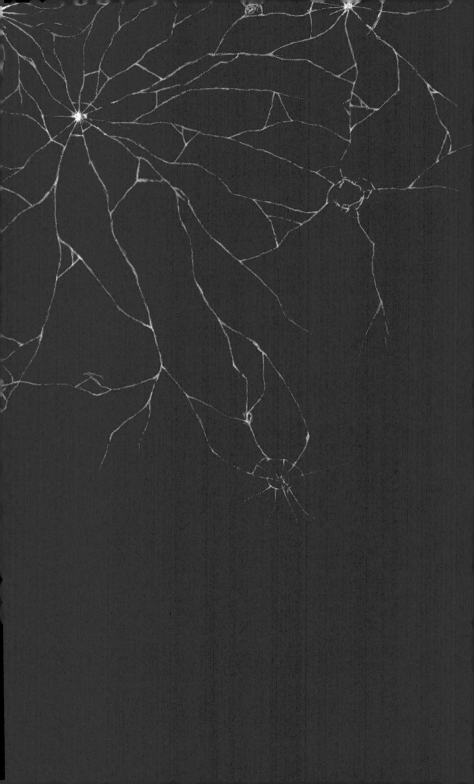

Chapter 31: Enchantresses

A song.
Familiar.
A woman.
Those eyes.
Bright green eyes.
But with a flash of white light, they turned into her son's.

I woke up to Chad's hands running over my hair, frantically gathering the long, curled strands as the contents of the entire sea seemed to make their way up my throat. My knees sank into the ground and my hands attempted to grasp the surface, to steady myself in any way, but it simply crumbled into tiny pieces until very little of its grainy texture clung to my hands.

"I'm sorry," Chad's voice whispered into my ear. "I'm so very sorry. They were attacking and took down the entire ship before they realised who I was." But even through his soothing touch and soft coos, my whole body arched and released the water over and over again, until all of it was displayed before me, sinking slowly into what I realised was sand.

A mixture of saltwater and sweat soaked my body. As soon as the retching was over, and had taken all of my energy with it, I closed my eyes. Chad pulled me in close to him, scooping me up onto his lap and holding me against his chest. His hand clenched tightly onto my hair. The salty scent mixed in with Chad's, and I clutched his shirt, refusing to let him go as I breathed him in. The burn in my throat was nothing compared to the fire in my lungs. They were raw as though barnacles had scrubbed the insides of them while I was out, but the air eagerly clawed in and out of them, making up for the lost time.

Strange breaths and heartbeats overshadowed the waves as they all crashed into my ears. Sounds reverberated through lungs I had never heard before, and my body went rigid. All sense of time and whereabouts deserted me, and the energy to lift my head stayed abroad.

Chad's breaths instantly turned from quickened relief to a heated anger. The muscles in his arms and chest tightened against me as he turned his head to address the strangers, forcing out words through a clenched jaw. "Tell them to stand down." Immovable, like a mountain, the command rang out, the waves of his sound bouncing off several others.

Fear tightened my grip on his shirt. His demeanour held more vigour and disgust than I had seen from him in a long time. As my mind raced to catch up, to remember where we were or what had happened, piercing red eyes pressed into my memory. We were chasing after Florence.

My gaze flew up, but his cold eyes were not in sight. My heart pounded as though it, too, were trying to force its way up my throat as I hastily turned my head, searching for him, dissecting the crowd, expecting to find him. Yet no red eyes met mine. Not his eyes, not his pull, not Florence. Instead, creatures with shimmering green-gold skin shrivelled away from Chad's soaked guards, cringing from the pure force the king had spoken with. Each of them had long, green hair, and completely naked bodies, which they made no effort to conceal.

I burrowed my face back into Chad's chest, but the image was ingrained into my eyelids. Their scaly, youthful skin, their glowing, sea foam green eyes, the curves of their perfect bodies, and the way the guards had slowly reached out for them as the women drew away, hoping they'd come back. But as the image of their lustful bodies refused to leave, one detail suddenly flopped out like a fish. These women did not have tails. They all had legs.

Chad suppressed a grunt as he pulled both of our weights up from the ground, cradling me close as my legs draped over one of his forearms.

"My apologies, Your Highness," the strong voice of a woman replied. "It's been many moons since some of us have seen a man. Our urges are quite hard to ignore."

I opened my eyes and forced my aching neck to turn towards the strangers. A wall of rocks curved around us, leaving a small window for the waves to crash onto the shore, hiding the beach from the rest of the world. Large boulders sat in the water, completing the circle created by the rock walls. Atop the jagged surfaces were mermaids with incomparable beauty. The ends of their tails were dipped into the water, but the rest of the women had feet planted on the dry land. Each seemed to be partnered with at least one guard, and at the centre stood the most radiant one of all.

The tall, slender woman stood before us, selectively ignoring Chad's command to leave the men alone, as none other than Connor stood before her. She towered nearly a head taller than him, making him appear trivial by comparison. Her beautiful dark brown skin transitioned smoothly into gold and green scales further down her bare body. Moonlight shone on the scaly hand she used to clutch Connor's chin. Her eyes were filled with a strong desire as she studied his tan skin with the intensity of the sea. Long, curled dreads of sea foam green hair entwined their way around a golden spiked crown before flowing over her shoulders and past her shapely hips. As she used Connor's chin to guide him off to her side, her naked body became completely unshielded, and I averted my eyes again.

Chad gently placed me into a sitting position on a large rock, then turned to the resplendent woman. "Queen Leira," he greeted her firmly. He had met her before.

"And I hear it's *King* Chadwick now," she reciprocated. "My humble apologies for not making it to your coronation. We've been marooned here from all the muck you land creatures have been stirring up."

Her hand trailed down the front of Connor's shirt as he gawked at her, mesmerised. She led him forwards easily as though she had him on a leash. But Connor's pathetic fascination with the woman was outweighed by the sheer curiosity I felt towards the queen as I watched her long legs bring her closer.

What the hell were they if not mermaids?

"Mermaids," Queen Leira said fiercely. My eyes were forced back to hers, and as she met my gaze with great magnitude, I could sense her in my mind, reading my thoughts. "Sirens. Water spirits. Enchantresses. We're known by many names. When we step foot onto land, we grow legs and," she hesitated, her eyes glancing down at herself before smiling up at me, "*other* parts, so we can mate. You see, there are no mermen in the waters. We must seek human men from the land."

At the mention of the word "men", her head jerked back to Connor. His posture immediately perked, having eyes for only her. Slow movements and the sound of the shifting sand under bare feet drew my attention to the other mermaids. As they inched closer to the guards, the men eyed each of them lustfully, drawn in by their spell. They no longer wore their protective ear plugs to block out the charm. The mermaids played with the men, twirling the guards' hair around their golden-green fingers or grasping at the fabrics of their shirts. Nigel was on land, wrapped up in one of them. The mermaids must have brought all the prisoners they had taken overboard to this cove, only stopping when they realised just whose boat they were attacking. Icaron, who seemed immune to their charm, stood tensely as he glowered at the mermaids. His blue arms were folded in front of him. But this left one single mermaid without a man to claim.

The lone mermaid with dark skin and glowing green eyes kissed with golden light stayed a few metres away from anyone, sitting on a boulder like the one I sat atop. She inched towards no man, and her eyes were not filled with lust. They were filled with fury as they darted back and forth between Chad and me.

The slightest nasally laugh left the queen's nose, a sound so low it was unlikely anyone else heard it. As I looked back at her, a sudden joy flared in her eyes. Then they flickered over to Chad as she raised her chin arrogantly.

"I'm sure you remember my daughter, Demriam," she said, referring to the mermaid who looked to be the same age as her. In fact, each mermaid looked to be as youthful as the next. "From what I remember, the two of you had a lot of fun during your previous visits," she continued, drawing out her words as though she couldn't wait for me to piece it all together.

My heart nearly capsized as I looked back over to the lone mermaid, but the scaled woman did not take kindly to my attention. Demriam jerked her head forwards and hissed at me so violently, I swear I felt venom burn my cheeks, but it was nothing compared to the grotesque images she blinded me with.

Everything tangible vanished from sight and was replaced by a heavy scene of her and Chad ready to engage in the throws of passion. His mouth conquered her neck as she closed her eyes, running her hands over his bare back, and his dragon tattoo whipped its tail around excitedly.

I had no eyes to shut, no ears to cover, and no legs to run. I was trapped in my own head. The moment lasted an eternity as I was forced to watch their bodies grinding against one another. The rapturous mermaid arched her back and opened her eyes. She stared straight into me as her hips undulated against Chad's.

"Stop!" Chad's voice yelled from far away, and a violent rope pulled at my navel, jerking me roughly back to the present.

I quickly stared down at the sand below me, hoping the granular pieces would scrub the image clear from my head until it was as raw as my lungs.

Chad cast his eyes to the ground as they burned with fury. He breathed through his teeth, spit flying out as though it would extinguish the anger he felt. "That was *not* necessary," he snapped at the both of them as my body seemed to fold in on itself, crumbling pathetically.

"You know why we're here. You've heard of our war. Have you seen the man with red eyes or not?"

His voice boomed over all else and I was glad for it—glad for a distraction from the enchantress's hateful gaze, from the image she had sent me, from the way Queen Leira ran her finger absentmindedly around Connor's neck, and from all guards who had lost every single sense at the sight of the women's tantalizing breasts.

The queen pursed her lips. "Rings a bell," she cooed, thinking with seemingly great difficulty as she searched the sea for answers she knew readily. "There was someone in our oceans, sailing around not long before you, searching for us. We sent a storm that wiped him and his crew out, but his skeleton doesn't litter the ocean floor like so many others before him. Somehow, he got away."

Caster magic, no doubt. Caster magic from an insufferable blonde who seemed to have her hooks in Chad as well.

The look of accusation must have been clear on my face, and Chad tilted his head as he threw me a look of caution. The queen could hear my thoughts. I wondered if the rest of mermaids could hear them too.

"We want you to join our side," Chad blatantly told Queen Leira. "Fight against him. Florence wishes to tell the world about us and—"

"I know what he wishes to do," she interjected with a hiss, and for the first time, anger clouded her eyes and coated her voice. "I've heard whispers of it in the wind. But it is not we who need to fear knowledge of existence. It's land creatures like you. We've ruled these waters for thousands of years, seeking out ships and sailors. We breed with those who crash from the storms we create. We do not need to leave these waters for hundreds of years if we do not wish to. Our population will survive. Thus, we will stay hidden," she added firmly. Her anger abruptly washed from her face, and was replaced by a bitter determination to let the rest of the world burn while they remained protected by the water. "You are on your own."

She angled her head back to me in one swift motion, a speed halfway between mortal and vampire. My stomach cringed from the sharp impact.

"You, on the other hand, are having a hard time surviving, aren't you?" she asserted, drawing nearer still, and it took everything in me not to cower from her tall form or from the truths she spoke. "I can see into your soul, see your pains, your sorrow, your past. *You* are cursed."

My lips parted, but only a single word came up as I fumbled over what to say. "Cursed?" I decided on. My nails scraped against the boulder as I attempted to keep my balance at the news.

"Yes," she said with an eerie calm. Her word spilled out like a peaceful river, but I knew the deep plunge of a waterfall was nearby—jagged rocks waiting patiently at the bottom.

This time it was the queen who sent images to my mind.

The boy and girl from my dreams.

Asleep.

Their screams.

My hands along Chad's back.

His lips on mine.

Purple magic propelling him backwards.

The crack of his spine.

Stone segments of the ceiling raining down on us.

With another pull at my stomach, the queen dropped me back onto the beach. All the air was sucked out of me. My eyes blinked away the images she had sent me. Heat brushed across my face as I thought of all the moments she had seen—*my* moments that were not meant for her.

Her stare was as intense as ever as she said, "Yes, a witch's curse has been placed upon you."

Every nerve in my body stood at attention. A witch's curse? But was it a curse that kept me from finding the children, or prevented me from being intimate with Chad? I couldn't see the correlation. Either way, there was my usual list of suspects. Lili, Chad's aunts, or even his mum. His mum had visions of children like I did, so perhaps I was cursed to focus on the children rather than on her son, but the idea of a ghost casting a spell seemed unlikely.

I looked back up at Queen Leira, wondering why she was giving me such vague information and doing absolutely nothing to help me along further. "And is that something I can undo?" I asked through gritted teeth.

My eyes flew to Chad, searching his face for some insight, if he thought he could undo the curse, but his face was scrunched in confusion.

Queen Leira said nothing to deny my ability to break the curse. She merely stared at me, continuing to tilt her head before saying, "Save the children."

Apparently, her idea sounded grand even to her own ears because she nodded slowly, her eyes never leaving mine.

What a simple task, I thought furiously as my nostrils widened at her words. *Let me just go and find them. Why didn't I think of that myself? And by all means, don't bother answering my direct question.*

Her lips slithered into her sickening smile. It was cold, and cruel, and unhelpful to say the least. I opened my mouth to snap back at her as her smug grin filled my heart with rage, but she deflected it by turning to Chad. "The man you seek is not here," she said dismissively.

Her fingers danced along Connor's cheekbone, toying with him before she pushed him away and brushed off her hands. Her long, toned arms fell down to her sides before her eyes tore into Chad. "We will not help with your war," she said firmly, "and if you leave without another word, we may very well provide you with a safe journey out of here." It was a fierce demand disguised as a request.

Her glare pierced into me as she tilted her head down, egging me on to utter one more word.

Connor let out a whimper from the absence of her touch before foolishly opening his mouth to stammer, "Bu—"

A shot of thin, green binding flew from Chad's palm, promptly blocking the plea from leaving his friend's lips. Then turning on his heels, Chad grabbed my hand and led me to the sea—past the other boulders, past Demriam and her fury. His gaze didn't return to the sea-witches as though doing so would turn him into a pillar of salt. He trudged into the water, pulling me in after him towards an empty ocean. Our ship was gone.

When the water reached past my knees, Chad let go of my hand to free his own. A scowl covered his face as he stared into the ocean, and then emerald-green magic flowed from his hands. The earth below the water quaked with the same hostility Chad poured into it. Waves pushed against me, reaching up to my chest. Suddenly, a wooden mast rose out of the waters, followed by two more. Splashes from the guards announced they were joining us. I turned to see them blinking hard, shaking off the enchanting hold the mermaids had over them, and they, too, raised their hands to help Chad restore our method of travelling back to the mainland.

Piece by tattered piece, the ship rose out of the ocean, the front end completely torn from its rear, leaving it in shambles. The sails were battered and shredded. The deck was a splintered wreckage. As more of the mangled ship resurfaced, the men worked, mending every crack and bend of the ship's body with their magic.

I looked back at the women as they dove into the waters, headed away from us. Their golden-green tails flipped out of the ocean to give them more speed.

I could no longer hold my tongue.

Forcing the words out of my throat, through the pain that still lingered from my vomiting, I turned to Chad and asked, "Why didn't you fight? Why didn't you persuade them to join our side?"

He let out a troubled breath. "You heard her. They wouldn't have let us leave if we argued," he explained, not turning to face me. He was still focused on his magic. His voice strained as he spoke, but it did nothing to stop me from continuing.

"What if they join Florence?" I asked, folding my arms, but I quickly put them back out to help counteract the weight of the crashing waves.

"They won't," he answered, sounding completely sure of it. "Florence won't rest until every magical being is found out. He wants to stir panic, but when word *does* spread of the mermaids' existence, we'll be there waiting for them. There are no *ifs* about it, only *when*." His voice bit with a mixture of bitterness and pride as the situation dug into him.

I pressed my tongue to the roof of my mouth, not satisfied at all, but I had other things to get out, other fish to fry, and I would not let them sit. "And this hot-tempered mermaid of yours—the one you had a 'fling' with. Her mother said they interact with humans to breed." I let that settle in for a moment before asking my question. "Is it possible you have a child out there? A young mermaid with your green eyes? Is that why Demriam was so furious at me?"

Chad dropped his hands and the ship crashed down into the water. His guards quickly picked up the slack and lifted it back into the air to finish mending it. He turned back to me and trudged through the water to hold onto my hands. Staring deep into me, he shook his head.

"A 'fling' is a strong word that I should not have used, for it's not something I let go all the way—ever," he stressed, squeezing my hands, intensity in his eyes. "I stopped myself before it took that fate. I grew up hearing of the spells mermaids put on men, and after a temporary lapse in judgement, I came to my senses," he told me. His feelings of how ridiculous the whole scenario was rang out through his voice. "I knew I'd find my soulmate someday, and my soulmate does not belong at the bottom of the sea."

Placing a soft kiss on my forehead, he gave me a look to ask if I was all right. I nodded my head, releasing him to help his men once more.

I thought about a million things as they finished rebuilding the ship and sat it gently back into the water. Waves sloshed towards us even higher, but one by one, colourful clouds of magic swallowed the men, transporting them back to the ship.

Glancing back, I noticed Connor, only ankle deep in the ocean and staring helplessly back towards the cove. He was completely lost in his own world. Chad took my hand, and we splashed towards Connor. As soon as Chad placed a hand on his mate's shoulder, green smoke surrounded us and transported us back to the ship.

The guards were bustling back and forth, readying the ship for sail, but there was a war in Chad's eyes. They flittered across the deck as though a scene was replaying in his mind. As furious as I was by this fruitless journey to America, the tension that gripped Chad's entire body revealed he was even less satisfied with the outcome than I was. A sudden stir from Connor's direction, however, stole my attention.

"We should go back," the werewolf declared loudly, and I pivoted my head to see his gaze still glued to the forbidden cove. "I forgot something there," he lied, and I rolled my eyes at how easily he had fallen for their charms.

"Forgot your brain, is more like it," I quipped, but then I looked back at Chad, finally realising something.

Chills wracked through me, all the way from my sopping clothes to my spine. "They read minds," I told him, and he winced as he looked back at me. "Is that what you couldn't tell me until it was too late—the thing you kept hidden so they could see if I was trustworthy?"

Chad's eyes squinted fearfully as he forced a nod. He knew I was upset. "If you knew they could," he said gently, "your mind would've been instinctively closed off. They needed to read at least one of us without interference—see what we've been through—see our true character."

"And Connor couldn't have been the guinea pig?" I parried. "He's a Night Crawler too."

"Nope," Connor said happily, finally prying his eyes away from the mermaids' cove and over to me. "I already knew they could read minds. I've learned all about the mermaids. I mean—did you *see* how sexy they are?" he asked, gesturing behind him. "How could I not? I had to find out all about them if I wanted to catch up to Chadwick over here. And Demriam was pretty and all, but did you see her mom?"

I lost control of my temper so fast that I didn't have time to suppress my powers, nor point them elsewhere before they came shooting out of me like lightning. They crashed straight into the bloody werewolf.

Fear flashed across his features, and I could see the whites of his eyes as my magic propelled him backwards, his arms and legs pointed straight at me as he was blasted over the side of the ship. The howl he emitted filled the crisp night air just before he plummeted into the sea below. Chad and every single guard ran over to the side, just in time for Connor's giant splash to strike their faces. Icaron merely stared at me, watching to see what I'd do next, probably gauging if he should report me to the elven king.

Chad cast a bewildered look back at me, his jaw nearly reaching the deck as droplets of water trailed down his face, but my stubbornness rang true.

I shrugged my shoulders, feigning innocence, but my pounding heart would have given me away if he could hear it. "What?" I snapped, but the viciousness I was trying to portray was betrayed by my own airy laugh. "If he can yell, it means he's still alive," I pointed out.

That's when another detail shot out at me, and the smile was wiped clear off my face.

I took a step back from Chad, my eyes growing wide. "Chadwick," I started threateningly. I couldn't even process it clearly, I was so furious. "You said the secret had to do with the mermaids *and* Lili." I blinked at him a few times, hoping he'd shake his head, or deny my thought process, but the bastard retreated closer to the railing. "Chadwick," I warned again, coiling my fingers into tight fists as the magic brimmed along my palms once more. "Tell me Lili can't read my mind."

His hesitation gave away the answer. "She has connections," he tried quickly, probably hoping that the speed of his voice would counteract the shock I felt. "She had to trust you in order to trust *us*."

Purple electricity cracked at my fingertips, and though the guards couldn't see my magic, it was likely they could sense it. Every guard edged towards me, their bodies tensed, completely forgetting about Connor in the freezing waters below. Chad held out his hand, urging them to stand down, but it infuriated me even more. I didn't need him to call off his dogs. I'd knock them all overboard if any of them tried to come near me. The rage that boiled within me was immense as I thought of every little snide comment or jealous remark I'd thought in Lili's presence, and it horrified me.

"Look," Chad started again, "I don't know how strong her mind-reading powers are, or if she can hear every word, but I needed her to hear *something* to prove you were innocent."

"Then let her read your mind!" I yelled back.

"It's not that simple," he insisted. "If you know someone can read your mind, it's nearly impossible to think only truths or to try not to block them out. The gift of reading minds varies greatly from person to person. It's possible she only heard scattered thoughts or a few words, and you've only ever met her twice—"

"That's an insane invasion of privacy!" I countered.

"But *you* agreed to it!" he exclaimed, his eyes wide as he begged me to listen to him.

I shut my mouth and blinked at him, wondering what the hell he was on about. The guards' stances seemed to loosen up a bit from the lull in our shouting match. I heard small splashes in the ocean, and Connor's growls demanding for help back up, but I closed my eyes to block it all out.

"What do you mean, I 'agreed' to it?" I asked Chad fiercely, opening my eyes. He should know to be careful with his response, or he'd be thrown off the ship next. I cared very little if Demriam decided to pull him down into the dark sea.

Very cautiously, he walked towards me, slowly lifting his hand to flick his wrist, and a letter appeared in his hand.

"I packed this in my suitcase," he told me, explaining how he had conjured it. "I take it everywhere just in case you remember or figure it out."

I eyed him maliciously as he came near enough, and ruefully, I swiped the letter from him. My hands shook as I unfolded it, and I immediately recognised my own handwriting. In a hurried scrawl, I had written that Chad had told me Lili could read my mind, and I had allowed him to use a time bubble on me to remove the information from my mind—all so I could help with the war. The letter was proof I had agreed to it, and although neither of us had suspected that I'd be meeting her the night we went to Chad's aunts' castle in Lancaster, he and I had made the pact in time.

I looked back up at Chad, heat scorching him from my gaze as I crumpled the letter in my hand. I couldn't believe he was right, but unfortunately, it did sound like something I would do if it meant helping him. Either way, I didn't like it.

The letter burst into flames in my palm, and one of the guards, thinking it was the right time to do so, sent a stream of colour over the side of the ship. Connor crashed onto the deck, completely soaked through and smelling faintly of wet dog. His shoes squeaked as he pulled himself upright, but my glare was still trained onto Chad. His breath rose up and down as he stared back at me, waiting for me to decide whether or not I was still mad at him.

"Was that necessary?" Connor shouted at me, but I didn't have time for him to whine about my spur-of-the-moment reaction of throwing him overboard.

So I turned on my heel, making my way towards the staircase that led to the lower levels of the ship. I was going to find a bed and try to take a nap. It was the best way of avoiding all the anger that was pent up inside of me, and the vomit that was starting to reaccumulate in my stomach now that we were back on this bloody rocking ship. Besides, what was I going to do? Argue with myself for allowing thirty seconds of my memory to be erased? Try to think of every thought I'd had in Mrs Prophecy's presence—how much I despised her—how much I didn't trust her?

I found my way down to where our trunks sat neatly next to a small bed. Right as the boat gave a large sway from an oncoming wave, I plopped myself down onto the bed with a sigh. Calming my nerves with long breaths, I focused my powers on the fabrics of my outfit, drying away the cold saltwater that soaked them.

Queen Leira had said I was cursed, and if anyone had the most to lose by me dating Chad, it was Mrs Prophecy. She must've come up with the clever idea when she realised that I was the one stealing Chad away from what was presumed to be her fated birthright. It would have been before she ever had the chance to hear what I thought of her since my nightmares of the children, and my sexual aversion to Chad preceded meeting her. Not that she would ever in a million years admit it. No, I'd have to break the curse myself.

I lay back on the bed, and after what felt like an hour of tossing and turning, swearing to myself that I'd never board a ship ever again, my mind finally relaxed enough to let the nightmares in. Only this time, I welcomed them willingly.

I dreamt of the children, asleep in their beds, just as I had seen them in Queen Leira's vision. After a few moments, their mother appeared in the darkness of their doorway. Hatefulness and plotting brewed behind her sunken eyes, and though I didn't know what she had in store for the children, it was more than just the motion of the sea that made me feel sick to my stomach with fright.

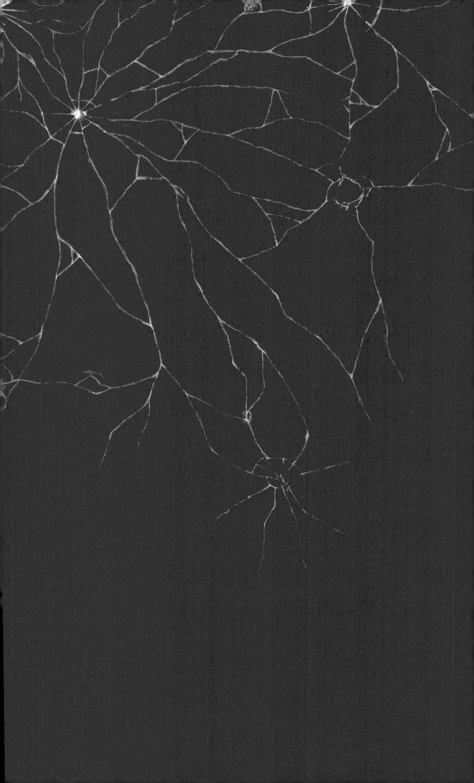

Chapter 32: Shutdown

*T*he sound of footsteps clicking against the floor woke me. A moment later, Chad entered the berth of the ship, worry pasted on his face as he took me in.

"We'll be arriving at the port soon," he announced, cautiously inching closer to the tiny bed in case I was still cross with him. "Are you all right?"

I nodded through a yawn and gestured for him to sit down next to where I lay. The cot bent from his weight, and his soothing hand began working its way along my scalp, massaging it through my curls, relaxing the troubles that were captured in my mind.

I was all right. I was cursed, presumably by the woman I was growing to hate more and more each day, the man I loathed most in the world was still out there stirring up mayhem, but something told me everything would be all right in the end.

I let out a long sigh. "Perhaps I can set up the facial recognition software to search for the children from my dreams," I suggested. "A few months ago I heard the little girl say she attended school. I don't know her name, but I know every part of her face by heart. I don't know why I didn't think of it earlier."

Chad nodded, placing his head against my forehead. "I think that's a brilliant idea."

I opened my mouth to reply, but an annoying song cut into the air like an alarm. My heart froze as my eyes flew down to Chad's pocket.

His hand dove down to retrieve the source of the song, and he pulled out his phone. I watched his eyes scan over the caller ID. Guilt immediately coated his features, and he looked at me like a buck in headlights. The grimace remained on his face, and he tried to hide the expression by standing up. He pressed the button to receive the call, and put his phone to his ear. Quick beeps coursed through the air as he frantically tried to decrease the speaker's volume—to shield the voice from my ears—but it was no use. Her voice rammed into me like a train going full speed.

"My King," Lili started—the wicked witch herself. I pressed my tongue tightly to the roof of my mouth as she referred to him as hers. "I know you told me to only call if there was an emergency, but I promise you'll want to hear this."

All the other sounds—our anxiously beating hearts, the ocean, and the crew above—died in my ears as I focused on what she had to say.

"What is it?" he asked. Confidence rang through his voice as though he could tackle whatever obstacle arose, but the creak of wood as he fidgeted his feet against the boards of the ship suggested his self-doubt.

"There's been another attack in London—on mortals," she told him. "The Queen of England has initiated a countrywide shutdown. Everyone's going completely mad over here. You must come back."

I focused on my deep inhales and exhales to soothe the jitters that convulsed through me. Chad let out a breath that swirled with fear and defeat. He turned back to me, and I watched as his throat bobbed.

"How many dead?" he asked her quietly.

"Over a thousand," she replied, the cold, aloof answer of a soldier relaying data.

Shock overtook me as I sat up from the bed, the covers falling off my shoulder. Lili compared it to the attack where the bodies of over two hundred mortals were dumped above Loxley Lair. The same attack that the mortal police were made aware of, the attack we couldn't hide from them. Florence was getting worse—much worse. Chad, Connor, and I were of no use, floating across the Atlantic chasing after him, all the while, his ship had capsized, and he had run back to Britain to take out his rage.

A million thoughts darted through Chad's eyes. His mouth hung ajar as though he couldn't believe his ears. He shut his lips to gather himself before opening them again. "We'll be there soon," he told her, his eyes still on me. Then he hung up the phone without another word, as there truly were none.

I couldn't focus with all the panic that flowed through me—surreal, terrifying, and haunting all at once. I flipped the covers off myself and grabbed his hand, ready to report the news to the people up above.

The ship rocked and the acid in my stomach returned with a vengeance, halting my stride towards the stairs.

"What's wrong?" Chad asked, gripping my arm to steady me.

"Just seasick," I told him. It didn't matter in light of what had happened on the other side of the world.

Regardless, he placed his hands on my stomach and magic flowed from his fingers, easing the storm within. "Better?" he asked softly.

"Immensely," I replied gratefully.

"Perhaps flying is more your forte," he suggested, allowing his lips to curve up slightly, but the smile didn't meet his eyes.

My face mirrored his. "I think I'll stay on the ground from now on, thank you very much."

When we got up to the main deck, the port was in view as the ship approached it, but off to the east, a faint light met the surface of the ocean. Chad summoned Connor and the rest of the crew to tell them the news. Connor glared at me as he approached, but apologising for throwing him into the ocean was the last thing on my mind.

As soon as the news left Chad's lips, the strong pounding of hearts filled my ears, all beating quickly, clashing at different rhythms as they took everything in. Even Connor's glare morphed into shock and sorrow. Chad told the guards which ones he'd be taking with us, but the light on the horizon only increased, and I knew I shouldn't go with them. The sun was already up in England. It wasn't realistic for Chad to place a protection spell on me. Holding his hand the entire time we investigated the **MURDER** scene would be problematic. I could use a potion to ease the burn from the sun, yet the idea of seeing Lili and knowing she could read my mind was too much for me to handle.

My eyes met Connor's, and I widened them at him, slightly tilting my head to beg him to go with Chad. He widened them back, not wanting to go, so I tried again, more urgently this time. To my relief, he nodded grudgingly. I'd be damned if I let Lili around Chad without either Connor or me there, not after everything that had happened.

We retraced our journey back to Castwell Castle. Shortly after we arrived, Chad and Connor left to assess the damage. I made my way through the castle, following the sounds of the telly to where I found Abigail and Hydie on the sofa, staring at the screen with their lips parted, disbelief in their eyes.

I sat down next to them and Hydie patted my arm in greeting, but her eyes stayed focused on the massacre. The news broadcaster repeated the same report that Lili had, but the mortal's version of it. The enhanced lockdown would take place to eradicate the kidnappings and **MURDERS** done by deranged humans—humans sadistic enough to "pose as mythical creatures" by piercing the necks of innocent people and draining their blood. The entire United Kingdom would be subjected to a sunset curfew. Recordings of the British militia lining the streets preceded information on all the schools that would be delaying their in-person start dates again to help keep the younger generation safe. Everything was pure chaos as the world began to tip upside down.

Hydie's eyes were glued to the screen as though she was in a trance. "It seems it doesn't matter that I deferred from uni," she commented.

"I need to get back to Loxley Lair so I can report the news to the rest of the coven," Abigail breathed out, her voice hardly a whisper, and after I nodded my farewell, she left.

Hydie and I kept our position on the sofa, even an hour later when Chad and Connor returned.

"Back so soon?" I asked. Perhaps I should send Connor with Chad more often if it cut the work down by so much.

As they walked over to us, I motioned for Hydie to scoot over so the blokes could both squeeze in next to me. They plopped onto the sofa with heavy sighs, and Chad put an arm around my shoulders.

"There's a fortnight that'll serve as a buffer before the shutdown truly commences, and then at least a month of everyone being boarded up after sunset," Chad mentioned, but we had gathered as much from watching the news. "It felt silly to stay and meddle when the mortals were taking charge, and everything had already been decided. I have my guards and the rest of the Casters taking precautions. They're diligently setting wards on as many places as they can, but it's not safe to do much magic out in the open right now, not if we don't want to expose ourselves to society. We wouldn't want to make Florence's life easier by outing ourselves. Now all there's left to do is wait it out."

I settled into Chad, glad he and Connor were back.

"Won't it all just create more hysteria, having a lockdown?" Hydie asked, and I couldn't help but agree.

The thought of Florence going down rows of houses, one by one, to attack those without wards made chills crawl across my skin. Sitting burrowed in your own house would do nothing to keep him out. It would be days before the bodies were reported if he **KILLED** them within their own homes, just as it would have been with Detective Harrison if Hydie and I hadn't found him.

"Well isn't that what the queen wants—more hysteria?" Connor asked dully. He wore the same far off look as Chad and Hydie as we all sat trying to envision the consequences of a nationwide panic. "If people are having their liberties taken away, they'll start giving a shit. The queen probably thinks it'll help bring whoever's in charge of the **KILLINGS** to come to light."

"We *do* give a shit," I piped in, "but Florence is all over the place and nowhere at the same time. If we could catch him, we'd turn him in."

"Which we *will* do," Chad insisted, "only, the bloody vampire is too clever."

"Conniving," I corrected, and Chad nodded in agreement.

Our breaths all seemed to sync into one collective sigh of doubt—doubt Florence would ever pay for his sins. He was too skilled at hiding, and he was always one step ahead.

"I'll have to shut down the pub," Connor let out solemnly, and Chad nodded back at him no doubt feeling as glum about it as Connor did.

An idea sparked in my head as I placed my hand around Hydie's and turned to the boys. A warmth spread through my chest as fond memories of the pub flowed in, and although it felt silly to do in light of the current situation, it was still something we all needed in order to cope.

"One last Salsa Night?" I suggested, a hesitant smile sprouting on my face.

Connor and Chad gave me toothy smiles in response.

Chad pulled me in closer to him so I could rest my head on his chest. "I think that's a brilliant idea," he said.

He placed a kiss on the top of my head, and we spent the next hour twirling Hydie around the sitting room, teaching her the basics of salsa dancing. After much discussion, we all convinced Connor to move into Castwell Castle with us, at least until things settled down. It would be safer for him to stay here with us, regardless of my suspicions that he was after my sister.

For a small while, we erased thoughts of death and the end of the world from our minds.

We cast away the gloom that surrounded us.

For just one moment.

Even if it would all turn to shreds.

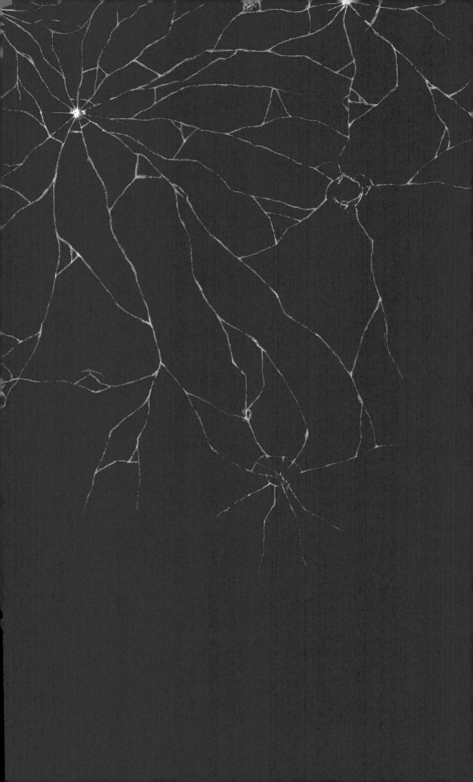

Chapter 33: I Know of Him

"Welp," Connor announced, flinging the fridge door open and instantly making himself at home. "I think that's all my stuff from the flat—everything I'll need for the next month at least."

I propped myself on the kitchen counter, crossing my legs underneath me as I took another sip of blood through a straw. It was probably the last scene Chad's family ever expected to play out in their grand Caster castle. Hydie leaned against the counter next to me, wearing a cute dress fit for salsa dancing, and eating a mince pie before we left. I was happy I had finally learned how to create the blood duplication potion and to have it in front of me, overpowering the disgusting stench of Hydie's food. Chad stalked in closely behind his mate, giving me a devilish smile as he placed himself before me and put his hands on my hips.

"I don't smell a lick of sweat on either of you," I observed. "When I moved in, Chad had me running all around my bedroom at the lair. I was busting my arse to gather everything when he could've done it with the snap of his fingers," I said sourly before biting my lip to suppress my smile.

The fridge clanged shut to reveal a ravenous Connor carrying about ten different sandwich ingredients in his arms and half a slice of bread jammed into his mouth. Yet it didn't stop him from responding.

"Naw," he mumbled, showing off the disintegrating remnants of bread in his mouth and waving the other half of the slice around. "Chad just did his little wristy thing, and it all went into my new bedroom."

A head of lettuce slipped out one of the sacks he was holding, but Chad flicked his wrist and levitated it safely to the table, all while keeping his shining eyes on mine. Butterflies swirled around my stomach as his lips twitched, fighting back his own smile. I could tell he was ready for our night out. And I could not fucking wait to get my hands on him on the dance floor.

Poppy came fluttering into the room so urgently that it caused my heart to flip over. She flew straight up to Connor and whispered in his ear at a magical decibel nobody but the recipient could hear.

"No, no, no," Connor insisted, bits of moist bread flying out towards Hydie, who promptly lifted her elbows from the counter and stood back to glare at him. "I've got it, Poppy. Don't mind me. I'm totally capable of making my own sandwich."

The look in the poor fairy's eyes as she silently pleaded with Chad to control his friend suggested it wasn't the sandwich that bothered her, but the mess Connor was bound to make—nothing out of the norm from his typical visits.

Chad winked at the green fairy. "Don't worry, Poppy. Since he's going to be here a bit more often, I'll be sure to house train him," Chad quipped, and Connor squinted his eyes at him as he shoved the other half of the bread into his mouth.

"Ha, ha," he exaggerated. "Very funny."

Chad nuzzled his face into my neck and then eyed me, begging to steal me away for a moment before we headed out to the pub. I gave Connor an anxious look before glancing over at my sister.

Hydie tilted her head down a bit, letting her smile play out slyly. *I can handle him,* she assured me.

I gave her a smile before tossing back the last of the blood and setting the cup on the counter. I hopped off, but Chad quickly swept me into his arms. There was hardly time to tell Connor and Hydie that we'd be ready soon before Chad's green magic wrapped around us, and we landed in our potions room.

In one swift motion, he plopped me onto the floor, immediately reached for three different phials, and emptied their contents into a lit cauldron. The liquids hissed and steamed a violet mist as they swirled together. He added a petal from an azalea flower as a final touch before ladling it into a potion bottle. It flowed magically into the thin opening, not wasting a single drop.

"All right," Chad said excitedly, "so the counter curse we tried last night didn't work, but I'll bet you anything this potion does just the trick. I once saw it take a curse off of an imp who had been sentenced to thirty years of slumber, and it once cured a cross-eyed curse I accidentally placed on my dragon when I was younger," he rattled on, so nonchalant about the whole ordeal.

He handed it over to me, and I could hardly contain my chipper mood as I swigged back the glass. An overly sweet goo coated my mouth, and I swallowed it down, eager to get it off my tongue. I looked up at him, shrugging as I waited for the potion to take its effect, but there was a lustful look in Chad's expression as he stared back at me.

With one fluid motion, he used a single arm to grab me around my waist and lift me onto the counter so my lips were level with his.

"I quite like you up here," he purred. His arched brow made me want to attack his face with my tongue. "Thankfully, this potion is supposed to take effect immediately."

Uncertainty of whether the potion had worked clawed at the back of my mind, yet my sexual urges began to outweigh my patience as he kept his green eyes on mine. There was a hunger in them that I wouldn't be able to resist for long.

I moved to close my legs, pressing my thighs together to hide the wetness, but he took no hesitation in yanking them apart. Wedging himself between my legs, he grabbed the back of my head and attached his lips to mine.

A heated kiss like one I could only dream of whisked my mind away from the room to somewhere immensely more magical as his tongue slithered against mine. His lips left mine for only a moment as he took an arm and cleared all the potion ingredients from behind me. Glass shattered, new mixtures sizzled, but none of it mattered as he leaned into me, driving me back with his lips.

I felt the weight of him as he climbed on top of me, gripping onto my wrists and shoving them up over my head, but as his lips moved down to my neck, I couldn't take it anymore. I freed my hands from his grip, running them through his hair. I had longed for this. Needed this. Craved it.

He bit gently on my neck, and my back arched in pleasure. My eager hands left his hair, tugging his shirt over his head. They travelled over his strong chest, then lower and lower, until something pulled violently at my stomach, and I was sitting upright on the counter again.

Chad stared at me from a metre away. Everything was back to the way it had been. Magical items crowded the counter behind me once more rather than lying sizzling and shattered on the floor. I grabbed at my head. My mind was competing fervently with my lungs to catch up to the present as they gasped for the air Chad had taken out of them.

"What—what happened?" I asked, but as soon as the words left my lips, my chest fell with disappointment.

I knew exactly what had happened. The bloody potion hadn't worked. A time bubble had been necessary to undo the damage the curse had caused.

Chad frowned at the ground, deep in thought. "It should've worked," he said, more to himself than to me. "Well, it worked, but only for a moment."

Too short of one at that.

He looked back up at me. "There seems to be a process about the whole thing. Queen Leira told us to save the children first," he said, moving his lips to the side as he thought of possible strategies. "I'll try to free up some time next week to take you to the library. I have an idea of something that could help."

The thought of saving the children lifted my dispirited soul. We had added their faces to the facial recognition hunt, but there hadn't been any bites. I wondered what good the mortal library would do, but suspected it had something to do with the witch librarian who worked there.

I smiled, thankful for Chad's attempts to help, and hoped that whatever his plan was would work. "If we go to the library," I started, holding back a laugh, "will you stay with me the whole time?"

He lifted a brow curiously, waiting for me to continue.

"I don't think I can endure the librarian's heated stares on my own," I explained, and he laughed. Between her, fish lips, and Mrs Prophecy, I couldn't take the women clawing at my flesh to get to him. At least Eyeara had the decency to turn it into a joke rather than hatred or harsh stings like Lili did.

Chadwick placed a hand against my cheek and brushed his thumb across my lips before nodding, and thoughts of our previous kiss rushed back to me.

I tilted my head down, my long, purple curls falling down around me like a willow tree, and I couldn't help but to pout. "Thanks for leaving me a glimpse this time," I said, remembering an instance not too long ago where his time bubble had erased my entire memory of the kiss and every touch. At least this time, I still had the taste of his lips on mine.

A devious smile spread across his lips and a laugh rumbled from deep in his chest. "Don't worry," he chuckled, running his hands up my arms and over my shoulders. "I'll let you have another taste tonight while we dance."

I was going to **KILL** whoever put this bloody curse on me.

An obnoxious howl sounded through the castle, interrupting my thoughts of what I'd like to do to Chad. It bounced its way off the stone walls and all the way to us. Our eyes travelled up, following the sound, and another laugh left Chad's lips, this time lighter.

"I think that's wolf-talk for 'hurry the hell up'," he interpreted before looking down at me and taking my hand.

I let him pull me off the counter, and he wrapped his arms around me. Staring into his dazzling emerald eyes, I prayed no one would take him away from me tonight. Just for this night. No phone calls, no attacks, no visions, or jealous women trying to get in between. Just one more night of freedom from the stresses brought on by Florence and all things malicious.

Chad's fingers lightly pushed their way through my hair and he placed a kiss on my forehead—a safe kiss. His lips stayed on my skin, brushing against me as he spoke. "Are you ready?"

I nodded into him and green smoke surrounded us, transporting us to the entryway.

Footsteps drew nearer as Connor and Hydie walked towards us from down the corridor. I winced at the idea of having left them alone together.

Connor's arms spread wide like an impatient bird as he called out, "About time! What took you so long?"

"Just failing at potion-making," Chad offered, and I gave him an encouraging smile.

"Is that lovely elf going to be joining us again to babysit?" Connor asked.

"No," I replied, thinking of the cold way Icaron always stared at me. "Dancing didn't seem to intrigue him."

"I hope we get a small crowd at least," Connor said as we left the entrance hall and made our way out into the cold night. "We made a sign and everything. It's huge. We posted it right outside the pub door. It says, 'Come to my fucking bar or the vampires will get you'," he said, using his hands to enunciate every syllable. "You know, I think it might work. Little do they know, I actually have a vampire as a friend, so I could be true to my word."

Hydie let out a laugh before gasping as she took in Chad's bright green car for the first time. "Are we taking this?" she asked in disbelief.

Chad nodded to her as he lifted a door towards the sky and held his hand out to help us in. "Ladies," he offered, and I couldn't help but notice Connor's face fall as he realised he wouldn't be sitting in the backseat next to my little sister. Chad gave me a wink as he helped me in and then closed the door behind us.

When we reached the pub, we were delighted to see a nearly full car park. A sign was posted above the entrance to Castle on the Rocks, but it read, "Last Salsa Night Before We're Locked Up," and today's date on it. Connor's eyes marvelled at the crowd inside as he made his way over to the bar to help out. Apparently, threatening adults with a lockdown increases a pub's revenue. That and a well-placed sign.

Chad, Hydie, and I set out for the dance floor, laughing as we attempted to dance as a trio. Chad and I would try to lead simultaneously, resulting mild injuries from the crashes we made. Hydie would step with the wrong foot and squish our toes. We'd twirl her one way, she'd go another. It reminded me of how much I'd grown in my dancing skills.

After a while, Chad looked up at the bar and watched as Connor and the other barmen bustled back and forth, serving the multitude of guests that hadn't been here in ages. "I'm going to go relieve Connor for a while," Chad said. "He deserves to have a bit of fun tonight too." He gave my hand a squeeze before going to switch places with his mate.

Connor quickly joined us on the dance floor and looked straight at Hydie. "Do you want to dance with me?" he asked her, twiddling his eyebrows up and down at her.

"No," she replied simply, and his brows froze from the shock.

He only took a second to recover though. "Then let me make you a drink," Connor suggested, but I was the one who declined this time.

"How about *I* make her a nice drink?" I offered, tilting my head down to eye him threateningly.

"I'll do it, *Mom*," he exaggerated as he grabbed Hydie's hand, and they wove their way through the crowd to get to the counter. He whispered in her ear, "Trust me. You do *not* want her to make it."

My laugh escaped at his childish energy—energy he managed to possess at only a year younger than me. I made to head in their direction, but a firm hand grasped onto mine, and my heart stopped. A memory so similar to this flashed before me. The same location, the same feel against my hand as a stranger held onto it, but this time there was no note and no blonde woman trailing away. This time, the stranger stared back at me.

"Azalea," the man breathed out, disbelief washing over his face as his hazel eyes searched mine. "Is it really you?"

I stared back at him, studying him as though it would help me remember, but his curly brown hair and skin tone that was just a touch darker than mine rang no bells.

My shoulders rose with my inhale as my face fought to decide what expression it wanted to take. Surprise? Confusion? Happiness? I hardly knew.

"It's me, Wyatt," he tried again. "Your eyes," he noted, staring deeply into them, examining them carefully like he had never seen them before. "Wicked contacts. I nearly didn't recognize you. You look wonderful! I—" His voice broke off as he took me in, his persistent eyes travelling over the length of me.

I stirred uncomfortably, slipping my hand slowly out of his. He looked as though he were seeing a ghost. To him, I was someone, but to me, he wasn't even a memory.

My mind was in disarray. What could I even say? "Oh, I don't exactly know who you are. I've been too busy getting the memories sucked out of me from a magical potion. Don't mind me." Arg. No. Of course not. But there was nothing I could say, so I stood there, squirming like a dying rat.

My eyes flew over to the rest of my group, who had suddenly quieted across the crowded bar. I was only vaguely surprised to see they were already staring back at me. Connor had paused whatever drink he was making for Hydie. Chad's forearms rested against the bar as he leaned forwards, his eyes straining to discern what was going on between me and the mystery man, and Hydie was seated on a stool in front of them, worry stricken across her face.

Do you know this man? I asked her. She would remember better than me.

No, she said, her eyes squinted as she examined the man before me. *But I know of him.*

My hairs stood on edge as I looked back at him. Her tone had suggested her hesitation, but I wasn't sure if it was because of my history with him or because she knew so little to decipher more of his identity.

"This is going to sound mad," I told him softly, lowering my voice as though it would help lessen the shock, "but I was in a really bad accident." I looked down at the ground before looking into his curious hazel eyes. "A *nasty* car accident about a year ago, and I suffered a hit to my head. I don't remember anything."

Wyatt's breath caught and his eyes fell to the ground, shattered by my words. I stole a quick glance up at the bar. One of the other barmen tried to get Connor's attention, but he merely held up his pointer finger, his gaze never leaving us. He didn't like this situation any more than Chad, it seemed.

The lines on Wyatt's face deepened with confusion. "You—you don't remember anything?" he let out, but Connor's faint voice caught my attention before I could answer.

I watched as the werewolf's lips moved, straining my ears to hear what he was saying, and heard my own words coming from his mouth. Connor, with his extraordinary werewolf hearing, was using his talent for evil to pry into my private conversation and relay the details of it to his mate.

Heat crept up my neck to my cheeks. Suddenly I wished Wyatt and I were alone—away from Chad, Connor, and Hydie, and their inquisitive stares, away from the music, the bustling crowd. I wanted a moment where I could ask him everything I've longed to know about my past now that I knew he was a part of it.

I looked back at Wyatt, feeling like I was in some alternate universe where the pieces of my past were flying at me like shards of glass. I watched as the sharpened bits drew closer to my eyes, and attempted to blink my tongue-tied state away. Wyatt, Chad's mom, my father, and my sister, all in a few months? After nearly a year of hardly knowing anything?

"No," I told Wyatt, "I really don't remember anything, although bits and pieces of my childhood have come back to me in my dreams."

"So, you know—" He glanced awkwardly around at the crowd as though he, too, were wishing them all away. He moved in towards me until his face was only a few centimetres away from mine. I could feel his breath running over me. His tone was hushed, secretive. "You know what you *are* then, right?"

A spidery chill crept up my back as I stared into his wide eyes, disbelief drenching every part of me. He knew I was a witch. How could he possibly know? How close had we been for me to tell him my deepest secret?

"H—how—" I stuttered.

"You told me," he whispered, drawing in even closer. Between my own pounding heart and Chad's from across the way, it was hard to concentrate—to focus over the noise as the man before me whispered secrets of the past. "We were so close and then—you were just gone," Wyatt continued, stumbling on his words as he forced them out. "I waited for you every night, Azalea, praying you'd come back to me, but you never did. I was so scared for you." He reached out to grab my hand but stopped abruptly. His heartbeat jumped into the mix, pumping fresh blood quickly through his body as he slowly lowered his hand.

I fought back the urge to bite into him, drain him of all his blood as though it would bring back my memories. I shook away the temptation and looked into his eyes once more. Sadness seemed to haunt his features, and a soft choke escaped his lips as they fell open. He staggered back a step. His chest rose up and down a bit quicker than it had before, and realisation seemed to cloud his thoughts like the storm looming over his head. Whatever past we really did have together had been washed away with the rain that night, over an entire year ago.

Unjustifiable guilt weighed down on me. I knew above all else that not remembering him wasn't my fault. I remembered Hydie, hardly, but not him. I didn't want anyone to feel in their heart that they were forgettable.

I grabbed onto Wyatt's hand and immediately heard Chad stirring against the countertop, and Connor as he finished retelling the last part of my conversation. The heat that their movements brought to my cheeks forced me to let go of Wyatt's hand, but I whispered to him regardless.

"I don't remember you, but I'd very much like to get to know you again," I told him softly. Not only that, but part of me *needed* to know.

Wyatt's eyes shifted, lighting back up, and his lips followed, curving into a smile that showed his teeth. "We used to be chem partners at uni," he said happily, and I was thankful he didn't ask me more about the "accident" or where I had been, although it was inevitable that those questions would arise. "That's how we met."

Based on the sound of Chad's gritting teeth, I knew I had to end the conversation, or least pause it for now.

"Look," I said to Wyatt before exchanging glances with Hydie one more time, but she offered me no more insight. "I have to get back to my mates, but we should catch up some time," I told him.

Fear contorted his features and he studied me, taking me in as though he might never see me again. But I wanted so desperately for that to not be the case.

"You probably still don't have a phone, do you?" he asked, and my breath caught at his words. He really had known me, hadn't he?

"No," I replied, and my heart lifted when I remembered that I had access to one. "But my—" *Shit*, this was awkward. "But Chad has a phone. I'll get it from him so you can put your number in it."

Before I could convince myself otherwise, I left Wyatt standing there and manoeuvred my way through the crowd to Chad.

"Chad," I breathed out, not bothering to explain things when Connor had already filled him in on every word. I held out my hand and gave him a hopeful look, pleading with him to understand how important this was to me.

He stood up straight, slowly taking his eyes off Wyatt to look at me, and his serious expression struck me. "We should go," he said simply.

I blinked at him, my head falling back a bit to study him. Was he really not going to give me his phone?

Anxiety started to rise within me, and I couldn't think clearly enough to form a full sentence as a clock somewhere ticked angrily. "Stop," I begged him quietly.

For a second, the feeling of hurt flashed across his features, exactly the way it had when I had been fed a love potion, but this was no love potion. This was not Florence. This was an opportunity to find out who I was. Something Florence had taken away from me.

But Chad's only response was a soft, "Let's leave. Now."

I looked over to Connor and Hydie, hoping they'd tell Chad he was being ridiculous, but Connor wouldn't even look at me. His gaze shifted away from mine, refusing to be of any help, and Hydie lifted her shoulders, gazing back at me cautiously. She didn't know what to do.

I felt a twinge of betrayal. Anger stirred in my chest at the lot of them, and I willed my magic to simmer down inside me. I would *not* let it slip from my fingertips, revealing to the entire pub-full of mortals that witches truly existed.

Air sucked its way in through my nostrils, but it did nothing to calm the rising fire within me. "Do not act like this," I warned them, gritting out every syllable. "All of you. You don't know the battle I face every day trying to remember who I am, and you will not guilt me out of wanting to find out," I demanded. I held out my had, urging Chad to give me his stupid phone and stop acting so childish. After pursing his lips, he reluctantly reached into his pocket and handed it to me.

I was too pissed off to say thank you as I snatched it out of his hands, mirroring his childish behaviour, and then stalked back over to Wyatt. When I reached him, I unlocked the phone and handed it to him. As he typed in his number, he let out a short, airy laugh. Handing the phone back to me, his attention flickered over to where I had gone, over to Chad and the rest of them.

"Well, this is bloody awkward, isn't it?" He stroked his hand through his curly hair, giving another sideways glance at Chad, and my eyes followed suit.

My stomach churned as I watched Chad give Wyatt a smile that was nothing short of rude. To be honest, it was more a cross between a grimace and a glare than a smile. The urge to send a lavender zap across the room at him to remind him of his "kingly" etiquette crossed my mind, but I locked Chad's phone and clasped my hands around it instead.

Giving Wyatt a *genuine* smile, I said, "Well, thank you for your number." The words flew out of me so quickly as the idea of leaving suddenly became something I yearned to do. "I'll reach out to you."

He nodded back at me, but I didn't wait for his reply.

I bit my tongue as I walked out of the pub, not bothering to wait for the rest of them. I urged my magic to unlock the car door, and willed my muscles to close it carefully, not wishing to repeat the time I had completely shattered his car window. Only Chad and Hydie followed me out into the car park. Connor was no doubt eager to stay behind to help at the pub rather than face my temper. My jaw stayed clenched the entire silent ride home as I endured the sound of Chad's grinding teeth and Hydie's fingers fiddling helplessly with the folds of her dress. When we returned home, I gave Hydie an apologetic hug goodnight in the entryway, and told her I loved her. As Hydie hiked her way up the grand staircase, Chad took my hand, a swirl of guilt and sorrow coating his features, and without even looking at me, he transported us to our bedroom.

I won't fight with him, I resolved, focusing on my breaths as I rushed to ready myself for bed, regardless of whether or not I was tired. *He works so hard. It's his stress talking, not him. I'll sleep on it and we'll talk when I have a clear head—not when I won't be able to bite back my harsh words.*

Yet it was either fate or stubbornness that wouldn't allow me hold up my end of the bargain.

"There's something wrong with him," Chad said abruptly, and I sucked in my cheeks, knowing myself too well to believe I could hold back my words now.

"Don't," I warned again. I would *not* be guilted.

His shoulders rose with the building pressure that he, too, seemed to be facing. "You can't be sure you know him. This could be a trick. Florence could've picked up any random bloke off the side of the street to get into the pub and talk to you. It's probably part of some grand scheme to kidnap you," he said angrily, his voice raised as though it would help prove his point.

"No," I said, shaking my head. Disbelief cushioned the anger I had felt only seconds before, and it shone through my tone. "Wyatt knew things about me. He knows I'm a—"

"*Florence* knows you're a witch," he cut off, but I couldn't accept his warning, not even as a possibility.

"Hydie has heard of him," I told him, searching frantically for more evidence in my head. "She told me. She knows his name," I insisted.

"So Florence could've easily found that out," Chad insisted, and he began pacing back and forth, sending my nerves into a more crazed frenzy than they had already been. "Florence knows you don't have a memory. He's the one who bloody took it. He knows where the pub is. He knows he can't get in, and he knows your mind is so fragile that you'd believe a trick so easily."

I gawked at Chad as he halted in front of me, ready to slap him across the face for insinuating I was a gullible idiot. "Is it so hard to believe I could have other relationships before you?" I spat out, the anger returning to my veins. "That *I* had a life before all this, *Mr Casanova*." He had bloody ex-girlfriends literally coming out the ocean, but he felt the need to blow up over Wyatt?

"Of course not," he spat back, fury equal to my own shining through his eyes, "but you don't see me holding hands with any of my exes."

"No," I snapped out, my arms flying around to make a big show of things. "Just flouncing around with your future wife."

He huffed out a sarcastic laugh. "You blow everything out of proportion when it comes to Lili, when really, you just need to rein in your jealousy, and then everything would be fine," he accused, turning the tables back around.

"My jealousy?" I shouted back, completely dumbfounded that he had forgotten that his own unwarranted envy was the reason this whole row had started in the first place.

"You know what?" he asked, switching tones from an angry one to one that sounded slightly crazed. "We're going to the library tomorrow to break this curse," he decided firmly, and I laughed.

"Oh, so *King* Chadwick can suddenly clear up his entire schedule for his girlfriend?" I yelled out, throwing my hands up at his ridiculousness. "How convenient that you can drop Mrs Prophecy on her arse when I finally have someone else to coo over me the way she does to you."

"'Finally'?" he asked, dissecting a single word and ignoring the rest of my accusation.

I scoffed, knowing I had chosen the wrong words, but still flabbergasted at his madness. "Is that truly the only part of my speech that you heard?" I asked, staring at him blankly.

"It's the only part that isn't complete horse shit," he sneered back, and my magic sparked threateningly at my palms. Then he opened his mouth again and said, "Half an hour before curfew starts tomorrow, we're going to the library. Be ready."

My nostrils flared at his command. I glanced over to the clock, but when I went to look back at him, a green cloud was left in his wake. Purple sparks built in my hands as the anger boiled within me and then ignited into a full-fledged fire. The flame flung itself towards the place he had just stood. It flew out past the cloud, dispersing it with the wind it created until there was nothing left of his magic. Instead, the fire crashed into our bedroom mirror and spread across the room.

I stood there for what felt like an eternity, watching as it melted the bed hangings, broke down the wood, and disintegrated the carpets, before a powerful bubble swelled in my core, and I watched the fire move in reverse, all the way back into the palms of my hands.

Every lick of fire vanished, along with the damage it had created. Not a char, not an odour, not even a smoulder was left as evidence of my rage. I yanked off my clothes, replacing them with a t-shirt, and climbed bitterly onto our bed. My palms itched for another release, a less drastic method to get out my temper, but one didn't come. So I sat in my frustrations until they waned on their own, wishing Chad would come back so I could give him another piece of my mind.

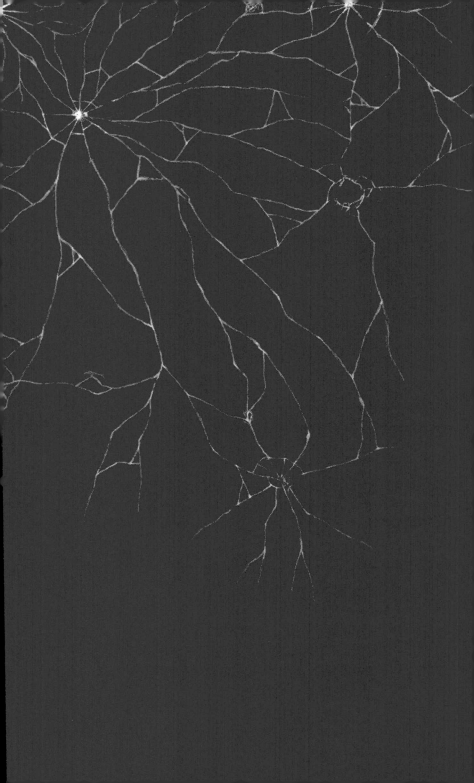

Chapter 34:
Past, Present, or Future

T he girl.
Her brother.
Morgan's echoed screams.
You're going to *KILL* him. You're going to **KILL** him. You're going to **KILL** him.
Florence's glowering red eyes.
My devious reflection as it dropped the candle in the attic, whispering that the fire in Castle on the Rocks had been entirely my fault.
The pain in Wyatt's eyes as I told him I didn't remember him.
And the look Chadwick had given me, as though I had shattered any hopes of the two of us being together.

I twisted in bed, clutching damp sheets in my clammy hands as Chad's real eyes met mine. My chest rose and fell too quickly, but as green irises transformed from shock to a soft worry, a song played from far away.

His heart skipped a beat and his nostrils flared as though he had heard it to, but then interest trickled out of him until there was no trace of whether he had heard the song, only worry for my panting breaths as they rallied on.

"Nightmare?" he asked lightly, and I nodded back at him.

The guilt I promised I wouldn't let consume me seized my heart. I watched as Chad stood in front of the mirror, looking back at me, his hands frozen in position as though his mind had forgotten to continue buttoning his shirt. His feet tottered ever so slightly between the pads of his feet and his heels, as though itching to draw closer, but a war that forged in his head must have told him not to.

My eyes fell away from him as they fought back crimson tears, and my grip finally loosened its hold on the sheets to grab my legs and pull them up to my chest. I didn't want him to see me cry, or rock myself back and forth like a cradle, so I held it all in, hoping he'd leave and stay all at once—hoping our fight had been a nightmare too.

"It's probably my fault," he said quietly, snuffing out my hope like a flame.

No. Not a nightmare, I decided.

He flicked his wrist and the light in the room sharpened, casting a shadow of him across the floor. I watched the dark figure as its host continued to fasten his shirt, his brash words from hours before echoing in my mind.

"Hydie wants to come with us to the library," Chad told me, and I closed my eyes, noting the way his voice portrayed no mentions of bitterness from our row, but no happiness either. It was almost hollow, like the battle had taken all his emotions with it.

"All right," I said, glancing over to the clock. It was nearly time to go. How had I managed to sleep for so long?

Dragging myself across the moist sheets, I tugged at the corner to begin changing them to fresh ones, but a puff of air travelled up underneath them, and the green comforter landed neatly into place with a swirl of matching smoke. My eyes flew to Chadwick and he smiled back at me, small and hesitant like a secret. It wasn't quite an apology but a temporary treaty. Yet I wasn't ready to forgive him for the way he had acted.

The rest of the time we readied ourselves for the trip in silence, the sounds of the house keeping my ears company instead. We met Hydie in the entryway, worry etched across her face. The worry only lifted to return the smile I pasted on my own face to try and ease her troubles.

"For time's sake, we'll transport there," Chad told us. "Curfew starts in half an hour. Somehow I think a bright green car so near to sunset would stick out a bit. Don't you think?"

Before we could answer, Chad placed a protection spell on me and took our hands in either of his. As soon as we had transported to the alleyway beside the library, he freed Hydie's hand but kept my protection from the sun intact by keeping my hand in his. Once we were through the rotating doors and walking down the centre of the library, away from the windows and the sun's violent rays, Chad dropped my hand as well.

My eyes journeyed away from the books and danced along the computer screens, taking them in as the three of us formed a line, side by side. A thought sparked in my mind, and my eyes widened with it. A spectacular thought—a truth, a revelation, a—

Memory, Hydie finished, and I turned to see her watching me closely.

I swallowed, not wanting her in my head at the moment, but I was too overwhelmed to try and push her out as a bit of the numbness I had felt washed away. Instead, I nodded.

A memory.

I looked to my other side to see Chadwick, his eyes trained straight ahead, aimed towards wherever our destination was. His jaw moved around, and I listened carefully as his tongue explored the roof of his mouth, all signs he was mulling over something in his head. He was distracted—too busy to pay us any mind.

I looked back to my sister, and the password I had used so many times to log into those computers flashed before my eyes. It was a silly password, one I had deemed as complete codswallop, yet it finally made sense: chemwizwy448.

Hydie raised her brows at me, waiting. *What does it mean?* she asked.

I forced a bit of embarrassment down my throat, and resolved to hold my head high. I would not feel guilty for wanting to learn about my past.

It's about Wyatt, I told her. *He was always better than me at chemistry even though I was a witch. He thought it was funny so he called himself 'Chem Wiz Wy.' The number refers to something about the course or the room we met in,* I thought towards her, straining to remember more, but it hardly mattered. How ironic. There were so many times I had sat in this massive room, pouring over books about amnesia, and cursing them for telling me how bits of my memory would come back to me when I least expected it.

We reached a counter in the back, the one right under the large clock the sneaky witch-librarian was usually posted at, but for now it sat empty.

Chad craned his neck around, searching for the woman, but my eyes fell back on Hydie. I chewed my cheek, gathering the courage to ask before letting it blunder its way out.

What colour was Wyatt's aura? I asked her, darting my gaze cautiously back and forth between her and Chad, guilt creeping up my spine for pondering such a thing. Incorrigible guilt that flat out refused to stay down.

Her eyes flickered over to Chad, who met hers before looking away, and then she met my stare once more. *It was brown,* she let out, and I wondered if she felt culpable for divulging the information. *I think it means he's struggling internally right now.*

I gave her another nod and instantly hated the feel of it. My bloody head was going to fall off from all the nodding and silent communication.

I just wanted to talk normally again—to not have this cloud of doom and gloom hanging over me like a damn storm.

The librarian stumbled out from behind a bookshelf, and she made her way to the desk in a hurry. I flinched at her sudden appearance. Seeing Chadwick, she did an awkward curtsy and then quickly straightened herself up, her eyes darting around beadily as she realised her odd reaction for the centre of a library.

"Your Highness," she greeted in a whisper, attempting to retract her previous bow with a singular nod instead. "Your coronation was beautiful. I was so *honoured* to be there."

I rolled my eyes at the dim-witted witch, and Hydie stifled a laugh at the ditzy behaviour. Chadwick, however, put on his usual charming grin that had been known to win the librarian over since the first time I had been here, and I watched as her knees nearly buckled with joy. "Dim-witted" was an understatement.

"Kristy," he said, leaning across the counter towards her, putting on a friendly voice. "I know you're probably busy getting ready for close," he said, glancing up at the clock way above her, "but do you think you could take us to that back room of yours? These two Casters and I have some important business to attend to, and I think you might be the only one fit to help us."

Her eyes widened in delight, but fell when she took in Hydie and me for what appeared to be the first time that evening. A darkness swept over her features, and I heard her fingernails scraping anxiously against her arm as she stared at us. My eyes flew back to Chad, hoping hers would follow, and between that and the charming smile he attached to his face, her shoulders relaxed as she was caught in his gaze. A bit of pink came back to her otherwise pasty face.

She broke into a hoppy, brisk walk, leaving her desk behind, but her gleeful gestures gave no suggestion as to whether or not we should follow her. It was as though her mind was too distracted by the presence of her king to focus on such seemingly superfluous manners.

Chadwick fought so hard to keep the smile from his face as he turned on his heel and looked at me. "You were right," he whispered, leaning in my ear. A bit of warmth I hadn't known was missing returned to me. "This smile could charm her into doing anything, even if there's a cheeky vampire thrown into the equation."

The start of a laugh slipped through the cracks, and I had to hold my breath to keep the rest in. He was ridiculous. How dare he make me laugh when I wanted to hate him?

We followed her to a staircase I had never noticed before, tucked behind a bookshelf. Advancing up the stairs, I wondered where she was taking us until we happened upon a bookshelf, hidden in a far corner.

Glancing around carefully to ensure no mortals had followed, she let out a breath. Her hand waved over the bookshelf, and a gaping black hole appeared. I gasped quietly, my mouth slightly ajar. Hydie's expression mirrored mine, but I could tell by the relaxed expression on Chad's face that he had been here before.

The hole was large enough for us to walk through, and as soon as the four of us went in, a swarm of colours swirled around us, shining blues, violets, and greens upon our skin. The colourful smoke replaced the need for walls as it twisted its way around and formed a long corridor, moving freely as though it were alive. The floor was as black the night that was slowly overtaking the sky outside. Had the librarian not stepped on it first, I wouldn't have believed there was a floor there at all. Down the corridor we travelled until we reached the end, where a single, arched door waited for us. No knob presented itself, but it didn't matter. The woman boldly walked through it, and it dissolved into a brown smoke before solidifying itself once more behind her.

"It's a door only Casters can walk through," Chad explained before gently wrapping his hand around mine to show me it was all right.

Hydie followed suit, taking my other hand into hers to form a train, and with one more exchange of hesitant glances, Chad walked through the deceiving door, trailing my sister and me behind.

The librarian's eyes instantly met mine when we reached the other side, bitterness smeared across her face as though she was hoping the enchanted door would cast me down to Hell. Her eyes stayed glued to mine, not glancing at Hydie, who she must have sensed was only a Caster and not an abominable cross with a vampire as I was.

Desperate to avoid her eyes, I gazed around the small, dark room. The black walls were solid, not swirling with magic as they had in the corridor, and they weighed down on us like they were caving in. Our bodies cluttered the space, struggling to fit around the tiny tables that stood at the centre. They formed a triangle, and atop each was a dim orb that conquered most of the space on their surfaces.

The librarian gestured for Chad to step into the middle, but he shook his head, tilting it a bit as he gave her his bright smile.

"This time it's going to be Azalea," he said with a sweet, luring voice. "She has the same gift that the queen had—visions of small witches and wizards who need saving, only it's quite possible her visions are from the past. I need you to help narrow down their timeline."

Her eyes lit at his words, the thought that he needed her, and she returned his smile before her eyes flickered darkly over to me. She pursed her lips and lifted her head perhaps a centimetre to insinuate that I should walk into the triangular formation, and with much hesitation as to what would happen next, I followed her instructions.

The three of them stood watching me, as though I was expected to do something, but I didn't know what.

I lifted my shoulders helplessly. "What exactly—" I started.

"Think of them," the librarian told me, and after both Chad and Hydie gave me encouraging smiles, I did as the witch told me.

I squeezed my eyes shut and thought of them. I thought of the little girl, the nightmares she had to face in this life, the screams, the tears as she clutched onto her tiny brother. I focused on her eyes, the curves of her face, the purple in the fire, every clue that might lead me to them, and I heard a sharp breath catch from somewhere in the room, throwing off my focus. I opened my eyes to follow the sound, but was blinded by a sudden light.

All three orbs were lit with shimmery white lights. Within them were clouds. They shifted around like water as though it had been disrupted by a gentle hand moving along its surface. I looked up at Chad, watching as the glow of the fog cast a reflection in his eyes. He took a peculiar interest in one of them, searching for any sign, just as Hydie's eyes met a different glass ball and her head tilted up, her mouth opening at a discovery.

"Each crystal ball," the librarian began, startling me, "represents a time. One for the past, one for the present, and one for the future." Her voice trailed off, leaving crumbs that cluttered my mind with thought as I travelled deeper and deeper into the fog.

My eyes followed Hydie's to the ball she was gazing into, but I could only see the white swirls and nothing else. I stepped closer to it and bent down to my knees, focusing my vampire sight until each wisp turned into millions of particles. I willed them to part like drapery, and they bent to my command. The image of a small room shifted into view, with a girl sitting cross-legged in a dining chair, frozen in the moment.

I clenched my jaw as air entered through my nose. When I let it escape through my lips, a purple mist left with it, sinking past the glass, blowing the scene into motion, and taking away the last of the fog with it.

My excited heart pounded as I watched the girl's fingers trace the age lines in the wooden table before her. I didn't dare look away for fear she would disappear. She looked the same as she always did, and I prayed I wasn't too late to help her.

The clank of pots and pans and boiling water sounded from nearby as she absentmindedly played with the table, but then her fingers stopped. Slowly her eyes drifted from the surface to stare at a place outside of my view. Her chest began to rise and fall quickly as she stared ahead, but her eyes suddenly moved to study a new location. She focused on the very air around her until she whispered out a single name: "Azalea."

She could sense me.

"Which timeline is this?" I asked the witch from somewhere else in the room. "Past, present, or future?"

The librarian didn't answer me, but I didn't risk taking my eyes off of the little girl. "Which one? Past, present, or future?" I tried again, more urgently this time, and I could hear her flinch at the rise in my voice. Good. Maybe the fear that I'd attack her would prompt a response from her.

Please don't be too late, I pleaded one last time before the answer slipped from her lips.

"It's the present," she whispered, and my lungs inhaled a breath of satisfaction—a breath of hope.

Chad cleared his throat from outside the triangle, and he directed another question towards the woman. "Can you tell us where she is?"

I heard the sound of her hair brushing against her shirt as she said, "No."

I shifted uncomfortably, dread and relief mixing in my chest, and leaned closer to the image of the girl. "Can you hear me?" I asked through the crystal ball. "Can you tell me who you are, or how to find you?"

The girl gave no response. After a few more attempts to speak through the orb, Hydie's voice filled my head.

Keep talking to the little girl, she instructed, *but not out loud. Talk to her like we do.*

My knees inched closer, and I furrowed my brow to concentrate, but right at that moment, hell seemed to break loose behind the glass.

"Mum! Don't hurt him!" the girl screamed. Her chair rocked dangerously against the floor as she scrambled to get out of it, but a splash sounded, and another child screamed at the top of his lungs.

The girl ducked down to the ground, just in time to dodge a pot that was crashing through the air. Her brother's cries mixed with the mother's as more kitchen items flew through the room, crashing into the walls and then back again. The girl crawled under the table, clutching onto one of its legs as pots and spoons and water swirled around the room like a hurricane, but no colour accompanied the magic that spun them all around.

"Noel!" the mother screamed out, still out of view, "tell him to stop! Make him stop using it!"

As though it was a responsibility she had taken on several times before, the girl began sobbing out, "Leon, stop!"

I watched clear tears stream from her eyes. She begged her brother to calm down, but the way she stared hopelessly away from him made it seem like she knew he wouldn't.

I didn't know what was happening, or what the mother had done to start his wizarding tantrum, but something in the girl's features told me it wasn't Leon's fault. Placing both of my hands on the orb, I took Hydie's advice.

Tell me where you are, I tried to tell Noel. *I'll come get you. I can take you and your brother somewhere safe.*

The thoughts she threw back at me were chaotic. They swirled rampantly before her, overpowering her words until they were all a blur. Then her eyes turned stark white and I could feel her. She was a part of me. I was being pulled towards her. My body shook. I took my hands off of the crystal ball and everything turned white.

∞

Suddenly I was on my bum, and the white light snapped out of sight, quicker than it had come. All the light in the room had vanished without a trace, and the orbs were dark once more. Chad and Hydie came into view. Their faces were stricken with worry, just as they had been after I had fainted at my father's house. Chad's arms pulled me into his warm chest, and a breath of relief left him in a hurry. His hand clenched tightly onto my hair.

"You can't keep worrying us like that, Azalea," he breathed out before grasping the sides of my face and pulling me back to get a good look at me. His brow creased as his eyes scanned over my face. "Are you all right? What happened?" he asked urgently.

Hydie's soft touch met my skin as she, too, wrapped her arms around me. Her face was pressed against my chest as I nodded, letting out a heavy breath of my own. Chad's fingers fell from my face, and my gaze lingered over his shoulder to where I could feel the librarian's eyes burrowing into me. Her face was hard with distaste, but her eyes squinted in wonder.

I swallowed before placing my arms around Hydie, and she sat up to look at me with a much friendlier version of curiosity than the librarian. Between Hydie and Chad, I couldn't tell who looked more stressed out by my slight fainting spell.

With a massive inhale, I shook my head at them reassuringly. "I'm fine," I insisted before my eyes squinted at the floor to focus on what had just happened. "I'm more than fine actually."

"Did you find out where they were?" Hydie asked.

My lips curled with excitement as I took the both of them in. "Even better," I said before biting my lip to contain my optimism. "She's going to take me there herself."

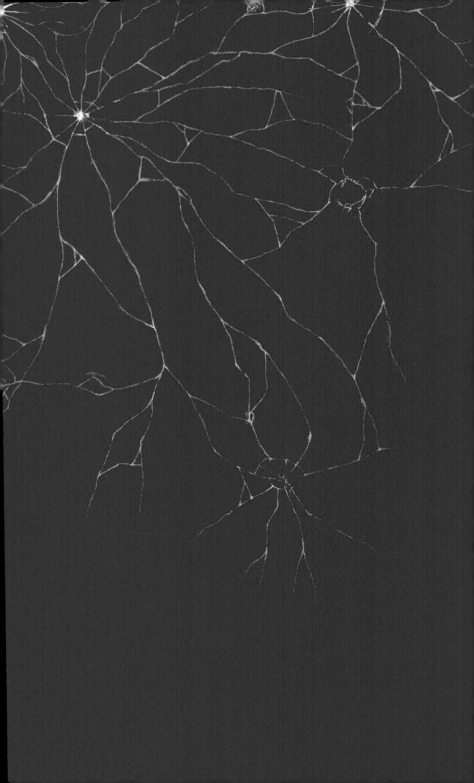

Chapter 35: Save the Children

*T*ake you there herself?" Abigail echoed.

Her feet nervously trekked back and forth, etching lines along the carpet. The lounge of Loxley Lair felt cold and empty as I pondered why stress was consuming my dear friend's features—why she wrangled her fingers in one hand, and why she chewed her lip as she became lost in her own thoughts.

Chad had delivered us straight to Loxley Lair before heading off to Greece for an important meeting—one he had no doubt postponed to distract me from Wyatt and send me on my old course towards the children. Not that I'd admit it to him, but it had worked.

Hydie let me rest my head on her lap as I lay across the sofa, my face buried in my hands from the disbelief of the whole scene—the whole feeling coursing through my very blood, pulling me towards the small witch and wizard. My sister's hand stroked my hair to try and soothe me, but every nerve in my body was anxious, jumping with the urge to go after the children.

"Yes," I said into my palms before removing them to stare up at the ceiling. "She's trying to take me there as we speak. I can literally feel her pulling me in their direction. It's as if I can transport straight there, but Chad said it would be too risky. We can't transport somewhere we've never been. Greater witches and wizards have been torn to shreds trying, but I know the children are in England. I know the children are in Bath. I can transport us close to there, and we can go on foot the rest of the way."

Abigail's face creased with more worry as she shook her head, unsure of the course of action. "We could wait until Cristin gets back from his hunt, or get Chad to come with us," Abigail suggested. "And what about the elf that follows you? Perhaps he could come help."

She bit her lip, but I couldn't understand her hesitation. Of course, she had never seen my dreams of them. She hadn't seen the fear the children had for their own mother. The little boy had created a magical storm of pots and pans, and after the display of forbidden magic, there was no telling how the woman would react.

"No, we have to hurry," I told Abigail, fiddling with the frosted chain around my wrist. "King Eyeron didn't seem inclined to send Icaron when we messaged him. Apparently, saving children is beneath him. Besides, it could be hours before Cristin's back, and Chad's at some important meeting with some Casters in Greece. He swapped his whole schedule around to take us to the library."

I didn't bother mentioning it was for selfish reasons, even though voicing the truth tempted my tongue. It was unimportant at this moment. So my bitter grumble stayed suppressed as I thought about how poorly Chad had reacted after our run-in with Wyatt. His decision making was starting to seem less about how exhausted he was and more due to him being a huge prick.

"So we're going to follow this pull of yours, and just prance into their house?" Abigail asked as she pinched the bridge of her nose. "Then what? Kidnap them?"

"No, of course not," I insisted firmly, but honestly I had no idea what our next step would be.

"How do you know it's the mother we have to take them from?" Abigail asked. "Have you seen her hurting them in your dreams?"

I blinked at her a few times as I thought of all the dreams I'd had of the children.

"I've seen them hiding from her. I've seen their bruises, the fear in their eyes, and their mother refusing to let them use anything that might relate to magic," I let out desperately. "And the queen mermaid confirmed they needed saving. Who else would it be from? Besides, we can find out when we get there."

"What if the pull is Florence tricking you?" she asked with wide eyes.

"It's not," I told her. "It's different. It's more—" I paused to try and figure out the right words for what was coursing through me. "It's innocent, pure, yet terrified—nothing like the pull I feel from Florence."

"And we have to follow it," Hydie added. "If their mother is anything like our father, we have to take them away from her. It'll save them years of trauma."

346

"But what if their mum *is* like your father?" Abigail asked fervently. "What if she's a Caster who's suppressed her powers? We could go there and she could attack us. Wouldn't it be better to wait for Chad?"

I wanted to say I could handle the mum without Chadwick, but blasting a woman to shreds in front of her small children didn't seem like the grandest idea. I had never seen her use magic, but Abigail was right; it didn't prove that their mum didn't possess it.

I fought away a calming breath, too terrified it would soothe the pull I felt. If it vanished, I might never get it back. Instead, I let my nerves continue to shake. It had taken too long to discover their location. Nothing would stop me from going to them.

"Abigail," I told her firmly, "I can handle it, I promise. If you don't want to go, just say—"

"It's not that," she said quickly, falling to the floor in a heap in front of Hydie and me. She pushed the billows of air from underneath her long dress to buy time for her jumbled thoughts. "It's not, I just—" Sadness filled her eyes as she stared at me and then up at Hydie. "It's just terrifying, you know?" she asked, and we nodded back at her. "What if we take them away from her and they miss her? What if they're scared of us?"

I focused on Abigail to understand, and her voice played through my head.

What if I want to keep them as my own?

I didn't understand how I had entered her mind so easily, but I knew I didn't like the feeling. Guilt flashed across my face—guilt for listening to her inner thoughts, guilt for not understanding her hesitations earlier. Abigail and Cristin had been trying for their own children for so long—something that was rare amongst vampires, but came so readily to the coven in Chippenham. And now we were about to face another who didn't deserve the hearts of the children given to her.

"Perhaps we can split up," Hydie suggested, soothing Abigail's worry with her words and my guilt with her hand as it ran through my hair once more. "One of us can talk to the kids, and the other two can deal with the mum."

Abigail gave a tentative nod, her lips remaining shut.

"Then we'll see if there's somewhere safe they could go," I suggested, "like a granny or a distant cousin, or elsewhere."

I didn't want to give Abigail hope when I didn't know the outcome, but I could see the yearning in her eyes, and it made me wish for a happy ending—for the children, for Abigail, and for Cristin.

Stubbornly, she shook her own hopes out of her head to focus on the mission. "Let's go figure it out then," she breathed out.

"There is another small problem though," Hydie let out, and I could feel her hand tense against my head. "It's after curfew. We're not supposed to be roaming the streets now that the shutdown is in place."

I sat up and looked at both of them. It wouldn't do us any good for the mortal police to slow us down. "Then we'll have to work hard not to get caught," I said bravely, and they nodded back, mentally readying themselves for the journey.

∞

Purple smoke disappeared from around us as we touched down on a forest floor. Through the trees, we could see to the city road where every fifty metres stood an officer with a shiny badge, wilfully enforcing the country's new rule.

We stayed within the forest, quietly travelling in the direction that the young girl pulled me. Eventually there was a break in officers, just a bit wider than the rest.

Turning towards Hydie, I scrunched my face up at her before whispering, "I have an idea, but it's one you might not like."

"I'm listening," she replied, only a small ounce of hesitation flowing out.

"I think I could carry you and run the rest of the way, and Abigail," I said, glancing over to her, "you could follow. We would be too fast for the police to see or hear."

Hydie gave an indifferent shrug. "It's worth a shot."

We ran the rest of the way, not a single police officer shouting after us, or even realising we were more than just a sudden gust of wind. The streets were otherwise empty, and the rope that pulled me by my stomach delivered us to our location only minutes later. As my feet gradually came to a halt, Abigail pulled up beside me. I placed Hydie down and took in a large building with several doors.

The flat was three stories tall and wide enough to house at least a hundred people. Lights flickered behind shut drapery. Everyone was keen to keep hidden from the mysterious **MURDERERS** of the night.

Hydie staggered beside me from the sudden stop, but even before my hand flew out to keep her body steady, a whiff of air entered my nostrils, and chills swept across my skin.

Blood, I thought fearfully. *So much blood.*

Hydie's body tensed from my thoughts, and the way Abigail's heart pounded informed me that she could smell it too. Our eyes met for a brief second before I was dashing up the stairs, ready to break the door down before my fear brought me to my senses. I paused, only long enough to use my purple magic to unlock the door rather than alert the whole building, and turned the knob.

The door creaked open to an empty room. My eyes darted around the darkness, taking everything in with the utmost focus. My ears tuned out Abigail and Hydie's footsteps behind me to listen to the intense beating of two small hearts. A third beating came slowly—too slow— struggling to pump the remaining blood through to the rest of its body.

I froze as Abigail and Hydie joined me, equally fearful to investigate what had happened within these walls. The pull, however, tugged harder than ever, and I allowed it to lead me the rest of the way, past the dining room still littered with pots and pans, through the small corridor, and past the closed door that did little to hide the stench of blood. It led me to a door I had seen in my dreams, a door belonging to the small girl and boy, a door that now shielded them from whatever fate their mother had taken.

I glanced back as Hydie slipped her warm hand into mine. Abigail's eyes lingered on the door that hid what must be the mother before she edged closer to me, our plan to deal with the mum adjourned until we found out what state the children were in. Sinister thoughts raced through my mind, assuming the worst, wondering what had happened in between the magical tantrum of kitchen items and this very moment. The memory of my own father's blood splattering across my face gave me fear that the children may have accidentally caused something gruesome.

Hydie gave my hand an encouraging squeeze before I opened the door, and the three of us forced our feet towards the twin bed, where there sat a lump the size of two small children hiding under the covers. We watched as it trembled and listened as the rattled breaths morphed into intensified horror.

Before I could utter a single soothing word to tell them we weren't foes, I heard the girl's breath catch, and she flung the cover off to reveal her and her brother for the first time.

"You came," Noel said, bits of her hair lifted from static as she sat up and stared back at me. Fresh tears streaked her face, yet through them, she gave a smile of elated shock. "I knew you would come," she added before shaking her little brother excitedly. "I told you she'd save us, didn't I, Leon?"

Leon urgently grasped onto his older sister with one arm, his face peeking out to scowl at the strangers before him, distrust radiating as he took each of us in. He pulled his other arm into his chest, drawing his knees up to cradle it, but sharp breaths left our lungs as we took it in.

Boils the size of tea bags littered his arm, and in places where the pus-filled lesions were vacant, darkened skin peeled off in sheets to reveal raw, red flesh. Air refused to enter my lungs as I stared at it— excruciating, brutal, and dangerous.

"What happened?" Abigail asked, rushing to kneel beside the bed and reach for the boy, but Leon retracted his arm with an agonising cry. She forced her own hand to retreat, a mix of sorrow and fury flashing across her face. Her hand fell down to the bed, twitching as it yearned to reach out and examine the injury, but the boy burrowed his face into his sister, her stomach muffling his scream.

"Shh, shh," Noel said, rocking her brother gently to soothe his terrors. "You're going to scare them away." She looked back up, fierce bravery masking her fear as she studied Abigail. "He used—the 'm' word—even though he knows he's not allowed. Mum saw him, and put his hand in boiling water as punishment."

I closed my eyes and swallowed hard as the scene replayed before me. I had heard his scream from the crystal ball, I had seen the aftermath of the shock the boiling water had caused—the hurricane of emotions swirling around the room as Noel hid under the table and called out to me, begging for aid.

Hydie sniffled as I slowly placed one foot in front of the other, careful not to spook the children, then knelt down beside Abigail, and spoke as softly as my panicked voice would allow.

"I'm Azalea," I whispered, hoping the boy would relax enough for me to try and heal him. I looked into Noel's bright eyes as she stared back at me with such hope only a child could have—hope that a fairy tale lingered around the corner—ready to whisk them off to some magical place. But it was vastly more complicated than that. "This is my best friend Abigail, and my sister Hydie. We've come to help you two. You see, Hydie and I are special like you are, and we want to help get you somewhere safe, where no one will ever hurt you."

Noel nodded, taking us all in with curious eyes before they lingered a moment longer on Abigail. "I know," she said, her gaze landing back on me. "But Leon doesn't like strangers. He doesn't like anyone except for me."

Swallowing hard, I tried, "Leon," in my most gentle voice. "Can I see your arm so I can try and make it feel better?"

The boy jerked his arm away, and the whole room shook around us. The bed rattled against the floor and a lamp fell with a clatter, but Noel soothed her brother with her calming voice.

Abigail shifted her weight, still aching to reach out to the boy, but I furrowed my eyebrows, no longer able to ignore the stench of the blood from the other room. The faint heartbeat slowed even more, quickening the pace of my own.

"Noel," I began softly, "can you tell me what happened to your mum? Did she get hurt somehow, like from the magic?" I knew firsthand how easy it was to harm another when you were hurting, physically or mentally.

She flinched from the word she was forbidden to say. The hope waned from her eyes as they darted over to the dark corridor then down to Leon's arm. "That's not what did it," she said, her voice quivering from sadness. "She's tried before, but I think she's really done it this time."

I heard Hydie shift behind me, and I exchanged glances with her and Abigail before looking back at the frightened children. "Done what?" I asked, but I had the dark feeling I already knew.

"Left us for the devil," she breathed out, and I closed my eyes against all the sorrow they had faced at such a young age.

The children hadn't hurt their mum, she had hurt herself, severely by the smell of it. But she was still alive.

I took in a deep breath to steady my nerves and forge the bravery I felt the children may need in that moment. "Hydie," I said kindly, turning to face her as I stood back up. "Why don't you stay here with Noel and Leon while Abigail and I go check on their mum?"

Abigail's body tensed from the floor—her qualms about leaving their side readily displayed on her face—but I gave her a meaningful look. She could smell the blood. She knew it was something she and I could handle far better than Hydie could, so begrudgingly she came with me.

Even without the smell, it would have been easy to find our way there in the small flat. When I turned the handle and pushed the door open, a puddle of reddened water sullied the bathroom floor. Our eyes trailed up to the bath to see the mother soaked in a pool of water and blood. Deep gashes covered her wrists, and as my eyes flew behind me to make sure that the children couldn't take in the sight, I pulled Abigail into the puddle and shut the door behind us.

The water splashed at my feet and absorbed into my dress as I knelt beside the woman and cradled her head against my shoulder. My heart pounded out of its chest, too loud for my brain to capture thoughts of what to do, but my hands acted on their own.

Purple swirled out of my palms, raising the water into the air, casting it from side to side, trying to separate the molecules once more, to extract the blood from the water. But whether from my panicked, irrational movements, or from lack of practice, the blood remained bonded to the water, and I couldn't put it back into her pale body.

I stood up, wiping my hands on my dress, rocking on my heels to mentally prepare myself. I could undo this. I could create a time bubble around the woman and make it so that this insanity had never happened.

Taking a deep breath, I tried to summon whatever power had taken over me to reverse time. Magic pulsed at my fingertips, slowly building to their climax. A lavender bubble began to grow as I pulled my hands apart, stretching it out, and right before it was about to explode, I aimed them at the woman in the bath.

But the bubble popped, taking a mass proportion of my energy with it.

Sweat dripped down my brow and I wiped it off, readying my worn body to try again. I shook out my hands, rocking forwards again to pump myself up, but nothing short of a tiny zap came from my fingers as I flicked them towards her.

Doubt scraped its way across my mind, scooping out the confidence I had and replacing it with insecurities. I couldn't do it. I couldn't undo the pain. But why? Why couldn't I reverse time when I was actually trying?

A rip sounded from behind me, and I looked to see Abigail holding up a letter, bits of it torn and still taped onto the mirror.

"It's a suicide note," Abigail told me, her eyes scanning over it in disbelief. "The vile woman truly believed the children belonged to the devil, and that this was her only way out."

"Well, she's about to earn a ticket straight to Hell if we don't get blood for her right now," I proclaimed, using my magic to seal the woman's wounds. At least then she could keep in whatever blood she had left. I lifted her from the bath, and shuddered as the warm water drained down from her clothes and onto my own. "Not that she wouldn't bloody well deserve it for abandoning her own children, but we need her alive if we're going to find a place for the children to go. They must have some family—someone who loves them and would yearn to know where they are."

Abigail folded the letter before holding it down to her side. The hem of her grey dress grew darker as the blood-water seeped higher onto her skirt. Her typically kind face hardened as she took in the dying woman, but softened once more when her eyes met mine.

"Transport her to Loxley Lair so the children don't see her like this," she said softly. "Get someone to set her up in the hospital wing and begin a blood transfusion. We can figure out what to do with her when we have more answers."

I gave a firm nod before disappearing in a cloud of vibrant violet smoke.

The hospital wing glowed orange as the candlelight danced across the walls, identical to the night I had arrived at Loxley Lair. Only this time, it wasn't my blood that dripped onto the floor, it was this woman's.

I laid her onto the hospital bed, her body nearly lifeless and frail, before I dashed out of the room, past the greenhouse, and to the closest breath that I recognised.

My hands grasped onto O'Brien's shirt, and the vampire stared back at me with wide eyes as I panted heavily.

"O'Brien," I forced out between staggering breaths. "Are Charity and Leo here? I need help in the hospital wing."

"The hospital wing?" he asked, puzzled, but his urgency echoed mine.

"Yes," I let out, "it's a long story, but I brought a woman with me. It's possible she's a witch, but if she is, she's in denial of it. She tried to **KILL** herself to escape her children, but we found her, and she needs a lot of blood."

O'Brien took my arm and ran us back to the hospital wing, immediately grabbing bags of blood and intravenous tubes to get started.

He powered on a machine, his hands moving quickly to make up for lost time. "Charity and Leo aren't here, bu' I know how ta set this all up." He looked up from the woman's body to frown at me for a split second and asked, "Her children—where are they?"

"They're safe with Abigail and Hydie for now," I told him, moving out of his way as he worked. "Once she's awake, we'll find out where to take them."

"Just don' bring 'em here," he said as the red liquid swirled its way down a tube and straight into the woman's arm. "We have two new werewolves here, and Malia jus' had a slip with a mortal." He shook his head at the whole ordeal as he went to grab some gauze and other materials to tend to the woman on the bed. "It's dangerous enough keeping *her* here," he said nodding at the woman on the table, "bu' I'll do my best ta keep those with weaker wills away from her."

"They might just get a chance to drain her blood when we're done with her," I noted, unable to look at him when I said it. "If she doesn't want to live in the first place, perhaps we can make a win-win scenario out of it."

I looked back at O'Brien in time to see him give a weak smile. "That is *if* we can get her back," he commented, glancing towards the machine that beeped slowly, in rhythm to her heart rate. "I've got things here, pet," he added softly. "I'll do my best and send word ta keep ya updated."

"Cheers," I told him, giving him a smile before disappearing in purple and returning back to the empty bathroom.

I sat on the edge of the bath, eager to catch my breath and rest, if only for just a moment. My hand gripped the wet porcelain surface as breath after breath rushed into my lungs. I looked down at the blood-water, disappointed I couldn't reverse time. I should have practised the time bubble—made sure I could do it on command in case I needed it again.

Soft whispers travelled to my ears, soothing me ever so slightly, before I looked around at the mess in the bathroom. Standing up slowly, I waved a hand, clearing away any evidence of the blood or water from the bath and floors, off my dress, and off my skin. Then I retraced my steps back to the tiny bedroom.

Noel was clutching tightly onto Abigail, who stood with the small girl in her arms. Hydie was seated in front of the bed where Leon sat shivering. His knees were bent in towards his chest, and his brutally injured arm was cradled in such a scared, timid way that must have made the blistering hurt worse.

I cringed as I took in the sight of his arm again, but looked at Noel as she spoke. "Your sister's trying to talk to him the way I do, in our heads," she said in her high voice. "He's never said a word out loud. Mum called him mean names for it, but she's wrong. He knows how to talk, he just doesn't want to."

"I told them that's how we talk to each other," Hydie said before glancing back at the boy, "but I think it's going to be a while before he trusts us. He still hasn't said a word, even mentally."

I nodded at her before turning to Noel. "We're going to try to make sure your mummy's all right, but while we wait, we're going to take you somewhere safe," I told her firmly. I didn't want my tone to give her reason to question her own fate. "Noel," I began, shifting uncomfortably. "Have you ever made yourself disappear and turn up somewhere else?"

The small girl shook her head. "No, but Leon did once when he was even littler. We searched all over the place for him, but then I found him hiding under my bed," she said. She gave a yawn and rested her head on Abigail's shoulder.

I watched as Abigail's lips pouted happily at the small gesture.

"Well, I live in this really cool castle," I told Noel, "and we're going to take you there for a little bit until your mummy comes round. But first, I need to heal up your brother's arm."

I tried to reach slowly, but Leon hurriedly scooted away from me on the bed as though I were a monster rather than someone who was trying to help.

"He thinks you're the devil mum told us about—the ones who she said would come get us," Noel whispered.

So I edged in even slower, kneeling down beside the bed once more.

If you let me heal it, I tried softly, hoping he could hear me, *it won't hurt anymore. It'll take all the pain away. Wouldn't that be nice? You have to let me see it though.*

He looked over at his sister before slowly stretching out his arm. I fought back another cringe as I took in the peeling skin and blisters. Hovering just over the top of it, I let my practice of healing Chad flow through me, and purple magic wrapped around Leon's arm. The peeled skin laid itself back in place, and the boils simmered down until his arm matched his other—smooth and unharmed as it should be.

"What your mummy did to you was very wrong," I told him firmly yet kindly, "and we'll never let her do that to you again. All right?"

He nodded hesitantly, still not inching towards me, but he let me pick him up slowly. I let out a breath of relief. *Progress*, I thought, and Hydie nodded before holding onto my other arm. As Abigail took hold of Hydie's other hand, I thought of how exhausting it was going to be to hoist them all to Castwell Castle. Either way, I tightened my grip, and away we went.

Leon grasped onto me firmly and then we touched down in the entrance hall. He instantly tried to wiggle free from my grasp, and I had to use my reflexes as a vampire to set him down gently before he could fall. I heard a gasp and turned to see Noel glancing around with pure awe and amazement.

"Are you a princess?" Noel asked.

"Not quite," I told her, thankful Connor wasn't in the hall to suggest otherwise. It wasn't wise to get into the politics of it all with her, especially when Chadwick and I were on rocky terms at the moment. "But I know a king," I said with a smile.

"Then I think one day you'll be a queen," she replied excitedly, her eyes soaking in every inch of the grand room.

All thoughts of sleep disappeared from her features, but as I read the late hour on the clock, I knew it'd be best to get them down for a good night's rest.

"You can both stay here until we find your granny or someone to look after you," I told them as Noel slipped down from Abigail's arms to hold on to her brother's hand.

"We don't have a granny," she said nonchalantly. "We don't have anyone besides mum, unless you count my last teacher. Mum tries to keep us inside so no one will find out what Leon and I are."

I exchanged glances with Hydie and Abigail, realising that this was much closer to a kidnapping situation than I had originally thought.

"Let's get you two down for bed," Abigail told them, "and we'll figure it all out in the morning."

The three of us took the children up to a bedroom close to Hydie's and my own, readied them for bed, and tucked them in. Leon clutched onto his sister, refusing to give us eye contact, and my heart broke for the poor boy. To only ever be shown kindness by one person in the three or so years he had been on this earth. To have your hand cast into boiling water for having magic you couldn't control. And to be freed only to be trapped in a world that was on the brink of a war. It simply wasn't right.

As I looked down at both of them, turning off the light and wishing them a good night, I decided we had to do everything in our power to do right by them.

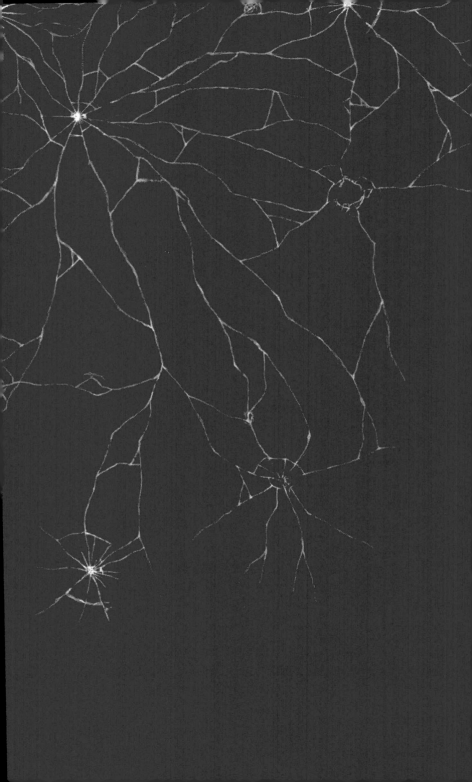

Chapter 36: Ypovrýchio Kástro

I wrote to Chadwick, and although he wrote back instantly to make sure we were all okay, it would be a while until he was due back from Greece. Hydie and I took a restless nap, worried the children would wake in the middle of the night and wander aimlessly around the castle looking for us. Abigail returned to Loxley Lair, but she came back to Castwell Castle a few hours later with Cristin in tow. Eventually Connor stumbled across the lot of us on his way for a midnight snack, and at the crack of dawn, Chadwick returned home to catch up on what he had missed.

"O'Brien was able to nurse their mum back to health," Abigail informed us, rigid against the chair she had chosen in one of our sitting rooms. "And even though she's still loopy, she's just as wretched as I knew she'd be."

Cristin nodded in agreement, apparently having had the pleasure of meeting the women who so readily gave up her own children to the demons she believed were after them. He intertwined his fingers with Abigail's, comforting her nerves the best he could. His dark fingers against her pale ones formed the perfect yin and yang.

I shivered at the thought of speaking to the mother. I couldn't even bring myself to visit the prison. I couldn't force myself to confront my own father, let alone this woman. And knowing what I was capable of doing to people like her, perhaps it was best that I stay far away.

"She isn't safe at the lair," Cristin told us. "A manananggal has already tried to eat her organs. We could toss her into the prison, but it's a prison for men."

"Perhaps we can send her to a mental institution," Connor suggested grimly. "She could blabber on about her witch children there and no one will believe her."

"More and more people are starting to believe in vampires," Chad declared, shutting down the idea. "It's only a matter of time before they start believing her tales of witches too."

"Then perhaps we should let the manananggal have her and be rid of her," Connor suggested fiercely, his gaze on me for approval.

I bit my lip, not wanting the decision to rest on my shoulders, and shifted the conversation. Pivoting to face Abigail, I asked, "Were you able to find out more about their extended family?" I asked.

"There really isn't anyone to take them in," she said, masking the hope from her voice. "It was hard to understand everything the woman was saying through her fatigue and fits, but we're pretty sure she's not a witch."

"She said their father was the one who had powers," Cristin informed us. "Either way, we'll ask the gnomes to be sure. They figured it out with Azalea easily enough. But the mom mentioned she didn't find out that their father had powers until she was pregnant with Leon."

"Then he mysteriously died shortly after," Abigail continued.

Connor let out a harsh laugh before adding, "'Mysterious' my ass."

"There's no doubt she had something to do with such an untimely death," Hydie said.

I couldn't help but nod. The woman must have **KILLED** him like my father **KILLED** my mum.

"She said she thought her 'normal' blood could wash out their magic, but when it was clear that wasn't the case, she resorted to more violent treatments," Abigail said sadly, and we all sighed and shuddered, feeling the same exact way.

"She doesn't deserve to be a parent," Chad commented, catching my eye, but I quickly glanced away from him. I wasn't particularly in the mood to hear his opinion, not when he was so quick to brush off my opinions on Wyatt.

"She kept ranting over and over about how she wouldn't be this way if they weren't the devil's spawn," Abigail huffed out, rolling her eyes at the memory of the woman's audacity. "She was screaming at us that putting Leon's arm in the boiling water was meant to squash the magic out of him."

The words tugged at my heartstrings, and it was hard to swallow as I wondered how many more children were out there facing parents who thought their magic was evil.

Hydie's sad eyes told me she was wondering the very thing I was. "There's no squashing of magic," she avouched softly. "We would know."

"Well if the lair isn't safe, and they have no family, could they stay here?" Cristin asked. "Abigail and I could come help."

"I know of a place that's even safer," Chad said, his voice travelling straight towards me, but I looked down to the folds of my dress and fidgeted with them. I could feel his eyes burning into me, wishing I'd return his gaze, but when I didn't, he continued. "In Greece, I have a safe house. I was just visiting it when I was there. I placed protection spells from the sun on all the windows, and added even more wards than there were before. Depending on how bad things get here, we may all need to relocate there. Perhaps instead of moving the children twice, we can set the four of you up," he suggested to Abigail and Cristin. "If you're willing to watch over them, of course."

My heart settled at Chad's words, how in tune he was with Abigail and Cristin's desires, his attentiveness to keep the children safe. I rewarded him with a genuine smile, and the tiniest glimmer of relief shone in his eyes.

"Most definitely," Abigail replied quickly, her back straightening from her excitement, and Cristin nodded, equally as accepting of the offer.

"It'll keep them away from the war as long as possible," Chad added.

"We could pack our things and be ready today," Cristin told us.

"That will be perfect," Chad accepted. "There's one more preparation that Azalea and I will have to do first though," he added, and I couldn't help but look at him with curiosity. His green eyes were already on me, and as he leaned forwards to speak to everyone, his eyes never strayed from mine. His body was a mix of composure and hesitancy as he asked his next question with his eyes as much as with his lips. "There is a trick to getting there, and if it's okay with you, Azalea, I'd like to take you there before we bring everyone else."

Words left me as I stared back at him. I wasn't ready to be alone with him just yet, let alone accept an apology if he had one, but there was little time to fully form that conclusion when the gentle patter of footsteps stole my concentration.

The light sound from far in the castle perked most of our ears, and Chad and Hydie, having caught on to the presence of something their ears couldn't hear, waited for the Night Crawlers in the room to make a move.

"It's Noel," Abigail said, immediately rising to her feet. "She's awake. I'll bring her down and tell her we're all in here so she isn't frightened."

Cristin gave his wife an encouraging smile and squeezed her fingers, and then Abigail was off to collect Noel. A moment later, the two of them entered the sitting room, a perky hop in Noel's step as she held Abigail's hand.

"Good morning, Noel," I said softly, sitting up in my chair to better greet her. "This is Cristin, Abigail's husband, our dear friend Connor, and this is Chad," I told her, adding impressively, "the *king* I told you about."

But Noel's face didn't light up as it had when she first arrived at the castle. Instead, it scrunched with disgust as she took Chad in.

"I've seen you before—in my dreams," she said, tilting her head away but keeping her eyes on him. "You were kissing Azalea, and it was gross. So I used the 'm' word to stop you two. After that, you were pretty good about keeping your lips off of each other," she said, recoiling a bit as she gestured to Chad, and I cringed right along with her.

Blood rushed to my cheeks as I stared at the child, over to Chad, and then back in pure disbelief. "You mean to say that you're the one who put a curse on me?" I asked.

"I suppose," she said with a shrug. "But don't be sad," she said quickly to Chad, "after that, I started to like you more."

Chad's facial features mirrored my shock. His usual composed expression was now that of a normal human, not a Caster king. His jaw was ajar, and when he closed it, I watched him swallow down the truth we had wondered for months.

I can't believe it, I thought as I looked back at the little girl. Of all the possible sources of the curse, or solutions that popped in my head after the mermaid queen had told me to "save the children", this was not what I had expected. I had expected to feel less stress after saving the children, and in turn, be able to focus on taking down Lili—wringing her neck and fighting off her bizarre, invisible magic until she relinquished her dark curse over me—but no. No such pleasure would befall me it would seem.

Standing from my chair, I walked over and knelt before Noel. She kept her small hand cupped around Abigail's. I took her free hand carefully and blocked out the eerie silence of the others as they stood watching us.

"Er—" I started, glancing over at Chadwick before I looked back into her eyes. "Do you think you could... take *back* the spell?"

Noel's forehead creased. "You mean—I'm allowed to use it? The 'm' word?"

"Of course," I told her, completely forgetting for a second that she was probably terrified to use her powers with how her mum had always reacted. I let my thumb run along the back of her hand to ease her troubled mind. "The people here in this room are all special in their own way. We'll never try to make you into someone you're not."

A look of excitement flashed across her eyes before she scrunched up her nose and gave it a wiggle. Without turning her head, her eyes landed back on Chad as though the mere thought of letting him kiss me again wasn't worth being allowed to freely use her powers. "You want me to use it so you can kiss him again?" she asked.

Embarrassment coursed through my veins, leaving my body warmer than normal. I was tempted to take Noel to another room so the two of us could continue this conversation on our own. I couldn't look at everyone else. I wanted them to disappear so I didn't have to bear the ridicule. My focus dropped long enough to hear Connor let out a short, airy laugh, and although I instantly tried to block it out once more, it made my blood both boil and freeze simultaneously. But it wasn't embarrassment only for them, or the situation. It was the embarrassment of being wrong. This little girl had cursed me, not Lili. She hadn't done it to be malicious. No, she merely did it so she wouldn't have to dream about it.

A strain of guilt tried to poke at me for accusing Lili—for insisting it to Chad—but the most stubborn part of me kept my eyes focused on the small girl in front of me as I stared down at her with hopeful eyes.

"I don't think you'll have dreams of me anymore, not now that we've found each other," I reasoned, hoping to persuade her to free me.

"I suppose I can undo it..." she whispered, glancing around at the faces I was too humiliated to look at. "Just don't tell Mum I did it."

"Of course not," I told her, furrowing my brows to show my sincerity.

As my face turned into an encouraging smile, a jet of purple flew from her small palm and eclipsed itself into my chest before it exited my body, a larger and darker violet orb this time. It was a minuscule sun rotating in her hand before she tightened her grasp, and it was gone.

I marvelled at her small hand, and the warmth within me grew.

"Purple," I whispered to her, and her smile grew as she nodded back to me.

"You can see it?" she asked joyously. "It's the same colour as your hair."

"I can," I told her unashamedly. "It also happens to be the same colour as my magic, you know?"

Her heart beat faster. "Maybe that's why you came to my dreams," she remarked brightly. "Our colour is the same."

My brows rose as I thought about it. Perhaps she was right.

"Are—are we demons?" she dared, sadness filling her eyes.

"No," I blurted out. The wicked idea her mother had forced into her precious mind sent a familiar pang to my heart. "My father used to say the same thing to me. He used to tell me I'd go to Hell, but they're both wrong. We're not demons or the devil. You're a witch—a good witch, with a kind, caring heart. They're just afraid because they can't understand it."

She nodded tentatively before looking around at the others. "Are you all witches then?" she asked curiously, tilting her head as she studied us with wise eyes.

"Not exactly," I said, avoiding her eye contact for a moment to ask the room for help. I didn't want to scare the poor girl by teaching her about werewolves and vampires. Not so soon at least. Eventually she'd have to know, but not just yet. So for now, I left it at that. "Are you sure you don't have any family that's worried about you right now?" I asked instead.

"I'm sure," she said plainly. "Mum never let us meet any family in case they found out what we were. She made me change schools three times this year, but for the past few weeks, she's kept us hidden at home."

"That explains why there weren't any hits on the facial recognition screens," Chad said.

Noel's stomach gave a sudden grumble, and all our faces turned to worry. I stood back up, and my gaze fell on Abigail.

"Are you hungry?" Abigail asked, and Noel quickly confirmed the notion with a nod.

"How about you take everyone to the kitchens," I suggested to Hydie and Connor before turning to Chad and accepting my next quest. "Chad and I will go scope out this Greek place and meet you back here once we've finished."

"Of course," Hydie replied, standing from her chair, and the others followed suit.

"I'll show you the way," Connor said, smiling down at Noel. His tone was light and playful as he wiggled his ears at her. "I'm a professional when it comes to food. I eat it all the time."

"Only, he makes a right mess that upsets the fairies," Hydie jested lightly, and Noel's face lit up.

"Fairies?" she squealed. "Can I meet them?"

They continued down towards the kitchen, all of them basking in the girl's felicity. I turned to Chad, a smile on my face. "I quite like her," I decided as they rounded the corner.

Chad nodded in response, smiling back, but the soft look in his eye told me he was trying to read me—gauge whether or not he had safely landed back on my good side. I looked away quickly to communicate that he had not.

"Let's get this over with," I said stubbornly, and I let him take my hand so he could deliver us to the mysterious safe house.

Out of the corner of my eye, I watched as emerald smoke surrounded his hand, and he placed a small bottle within my palm, using his warm fingers to wrap mine around it.

"It's already daylight in Greece," he said, his gentle touch leaving mine so I could drink the potion. "I'll hold your hand to enact the full protection spell, but at a certain point, I'll have to let go to take you to the castle."

I uncorked the phial, glaring at the idea of holding his hand when I was still so cross. I couldn't decide if it was truly necessary for us to be travelling there alone, but I went along with it either way.

As soon as the purple liquid vanished down my throat and I felt my skin harden in response, Chad made the empty phial disappear. He smoothed his hands along my waist, pulling me into him with a mischievous gleam in his eye that read he was going to try and tempt my anger away with his touch. I raised my brow at him in warning, and reconsidered having Noel take the curse off of me, but he held me close so he could no longer see my face. His head tilted against my hair, and he pushed back my curls so he could place two fingers against my temple. Slowly, his fingers traced down my cheek, along my neck, and down my arm, creating tingles across my skin as the protection spell activated. Without letting his skin leave mine, he intertwined our fingers together.

"Hold on tight," he whispered into my ear, and although I resented his charm, I obeyed, and green smoke whisked us away.

Sunlight glistened upon my skin, so strange, so foreign, so pleasant. A taste of the world I had forgotten. One Wyatt could help me remember, but no.

I removed myself from Chad's arms, but internally growled when he kept a tight hold on my hand. Part of me wanted to reach out to Wyatt, regardless of Chad's reservations. Another part of me cowered at the idea of finding out more about the life my mind had so readily forgotten. Potion or not, most of the things I had come to find out about my past were grim and better left forgotten. Yet all of me wallowed in misery from my indecisiveness.

Chad's eyes took me in, as hesitant as ever to speak his mind, but my lips tightened and I gestured for him to lead the way. Thankfully, he dropped the matter and led me along the peaceful streets of Greece.

It was still early and few people were out, so we were left with a calming environment to explore. The city sat upon a hill where cylinder-shaped buildings with smooth white walls and blue domed roofs climbed up the side, intercepting the paths that swirled up like a maze. Cool winds carried the sounds of animals and people beginning their morning routines, and the swishes of the ocean played nearby. As the sound of the waves grew closer, I fought off the chills that coated my skin and took in the beautiful sight of the city.

Strings of lights connected the trees as we walked along them, hand in hand. I was mesmerised by the magical feel, the way the sun cast shadows so clear across parts of the town, and highlighted the rest, the salty taste of the ocean on my tongue. As I looked around, I decided I didn't want to come back to reality.

Chad opened his mouth but I intercepted his thoughts, too afraid he'd bring up the things I'd rather not think about.

"So what do we have to do?" I asked quickly, and he shut his mouth. "What's this mysterious trick that will allow us all to enter?"

A smile played in his eyes so I looked forwards, keeping focused on the pleasant feel of the city before us.

"Transporting them all will be the best way to get them in and out of the castle, but as of right now, I'm the only one who can let others in. After I let you in for the first time in a special way, you'll become what's known as a holder. You'll be able to transport them in and out whenever they need, whether to feed, or replenish supplies, or even if they need some fresh air."

I thought it odd he added the last one. Would they not be allowed to open the windows, even at night? Would it weaken the protections laid onto the building?

We neared the docks, and as I took in the sight of the ocean, its beauty vanquished. There was something about being pulled to its deepest depths by a mermaid and vomiting up the entire sea that took away its appeal.

"All the mirrors within the castle are perfectly ordinary," Chad said, taking in the view of the ocean. "I made sure they weren't portals as an extra precaution."

A grin lit up my face and I looked down at the wooden planks we walked on. "I like this place already," I said. What a treat to be surrounded by mirrors I could trust.

He led me out to the edge of the dock, and my brow creased. Why had he taken me here when we should be going to this castle of his?

Chad turned into me, still holding my hand, and protecting me from the sun's rays, but a gleam sprouted in his green eyes, and I knew he was up to something. "So about that whole curse thing…" Chad began. "Do you think we'll be able to—"

"Is that why we're out here instead of going up to wherever your bloody Greek castle is?" I asked, unapologetically cutting him off. I rolled my eyes at the sheer bollocks he had. "So you could discuss the potential of getting under my skirts again?"

Chad let out a taken aback laugh. "Of course not, but I didn't realise we were going to completely ignore the curse now that it's been broken," he let out. "At least we know it wasn't my aunts or anyone else—"

I broke off his jumbled nonsense with a threatening glare. "Don't you dare," I huffed angrily. "This conversation is completely out of the question. I'm still furious at you for shutting down the idea of me talking to Wyatt, and for your stupid mermaid ex-girlfriend, and not telling me that Lili could read my bloody mind, and probably about fifty other things I've forgotten, or otherwise been brainwashed to forget."

"I have *not* brainwashed you to forget anything—else," he added after I gave him another vile look. His brows rose to feign innocence and he pointed his finger at me as though it would help me recall the next bit. "Besides, you agreed to the whole mind-reading business with Lili," he reminded me.

"That doesn't mean I can't be mad about it," I spat back.

"Yes it does," he countered, his face reading genuine shock over my stubbornness.

"Oh yeah? Watch me," I declared, resisting the urge to drop his hand.

Chad sighed, but his features still softened as he took me in. "Look," he started, pulling me in towards him a bit. "I'm sorry I acted like a right wanker, but you of all people should understand the bad feeling I have about that guy."

Wyatt. I knew why he'd say that. I was always on about my bad feelings about Lili without any hard evidence that she was evil, other than her compulsive behaviour to act like a bitch whenever I was around. Regardless, she hadn't cursed me, and my stupid blonde reflection was the mysterious woman who had given me Florence's letter, not her.

But to avoid admitting that just yet, I stuck my nose up in the air and sourly avoided the discussion.

"Chadwick," I said, enjoying the way he flinched at his name, "I don't want to talk about your suspicions, so if you could lead me to this safe house of yours, without steering me in the wrong direction, that would be lovely."

"Steer you wrong?" he asked, cocking his brow in a way that normally would have made me attempt to break the curse with my mouth on his. "Now when have I ever done that?"

I gestured around the castle-less city and the open water as though it was obvious, but his smile merely brightened.

"This is the part where I let go," he whispered, and I watched my own curiosity ignite in the reflection of his eyes. "It'll burn slightly, but only until we get inside, so be quick to follow my every move."

He took a few steps back, and I felt the friction against our fingers as he drew so far apart that I could no longer reach him. My skin began to singe ever so lightly, but I hardly noticed. Continuing to back up, he placed his hands in his pockets until his feet neared the edge of the dock.

"Be quick to follow," he echoed softly.

And then with a sly, daring grin, he leaned back and fell flat against the glittering surface of the ocean.

I blinked a few times, my arm still stretched out towards where he had disappeared, only putting it down when I reached the edge and peered over. He was gone—not a sign of his body or a ripple in the water to remember him by.

His words echoed once more in my mind, but I was no more ready to plunge into the frigid waters than to accept his apology. After a second's hesitation, I knew better than to think he'd let me freeze or drown, not after all the times he had kept me safe and warm while swimming in our lake. So after turning around and ensuring that no one was watching, I closed my eyes and took a leap of faith.

I hardly felt the water hit my back. I hardly flinched when the water—warm and buzzing with magic—surrounded me. And I nearly let go of the bubble in my mouth as my eyes parted and took in the sight before me.

A beautiful Greek structure glistened under the water. Tall white cylinders rose from the ocean floor, shining in a light green-blue hue. Massive domes topped the towers, more grand and extravagant than the buildings above, capturing the culture in a way I never thought possible. A castle lost at sea.

Chad swam ahead of me, appearing small in the distance as his arms and legs made wide strokes towards the castle. He looked back at me, his eyes smiling since his lips couldn't. Yet he was only halfway there.

I held in a laugh, remembering how dreadfully slow non-vampires were at swimming, and as my long curls floated into view, I pushed against the water behind me and sped towards him.

My hand grasped onto Chad's as I reached him, and he jumped as though a fish had slithered against it. His face brightened as I took him along for the ride. Long strands of seaweed and clumps of rocks and coral sat below us, littered by curious sea creatures that wove their way between. They played amongst the bubbles we made on our trail.

We reached a soft green door, and it towered over us, as grand as the rest of the castle. Glints of gold carved their way along it, slithering up like the ocean plants we had just hovered over, and an ornate, golden knob sat at waist height, perfectly in the centre of the left and right sides of the frame.

Our feet touched down by the entrance, a tingle of magic keeping us from floating back towards the surface. As Chad took the lead, he twirled me around in one fluid motion so that my back was towards his chest. My lungs began to ache for air, but his touch gave me strength. One of his arms wrapped around me while the other travelled along my arm, lifting it towards the golden knob like a dance. His fingers lay delicately over mine, shadowing them as they led mine to the knob and curved their way around it. His face nestled against my neck for just a second before our hands turned, and with a blinding flash of light, our bodies reappeared inside without ever having opened the door.

Our feet set down on white marble floors, tinted by the greens of the ocean. Not a single part of me was wet as we stood in the foyer, just as dry and warm as we had been at home.

The whole interior glistened from the ocean, light filtering in through the tall windows that stood three times my height. The sea surrounded the exterior of the castle only, yet it felt as though we were still a part of it. I looked around as a school of fish swam by outside, casting shadows across us. I took in the large, iron stair rail that curved up to the higher levels, the ceiling above it towering enough to reveal at least five landings above us. Although the water swirled around us, my stomach was thankful that the castle was stationary on the ocean floor.

"Welcome to Ypovrýchio Kástro," Chad whispered into my neck.

I jumped away from him, having completely forgotten he was caressing me in a way that felt so natural. Inwardly, I cursed his name—his comforting touch in a time I didn't want to be comforted—and he gave me an apologetic smile.

"Epo what?" I asked flustered, pretending to take in more of the castle.

"Ee-poh-VREE-chee-oh KAHST-roh," he enunciated, still carrying through the traditional accent. "It means 'underwater castle' in Greek."

"Ah. Makes sense," I replied simply. "The children are going to love it here."

He nodded sombrely. "And now you can bring them freely," he commented, and I nodded back. "There's a part where you can climb up over nearly invisible steps, and you can enter a room with a clear floor. If I was lucky, my mum would take me here when she had council meetings in Greece, and I'd lay there for hours watching all the ocean life."

A grin played across my face as I thought of little Chad ogling at sharks swimming by, and I imagined Noel and Leon doing the same. I thought of all the things they'd be allowed to do if we kept them away from their mother.

"Chad," I asked suddenly, letting my eyes focus on him with curiosity. He looked at me with patience written across his face as he waited. I cleared my throat as though there was a bit of courage lodged in it that I needed to summon up. "Their mum said something about hoping her 'normal blood' would wash out their magic, and I was wondering… Do you think part of my magic was washed out since my mother wasn't a witch?"

Chad stared back, blinking a few times. He glanced at the floor and then back to me, uncertainty in his gaze. "It varies," he said as a very real answer.

Grey clouds of the looming prophecy hovered over my head. How could I be expected to be the most powerful sorceress in the world if I was only half-witch?

"Depends on what?" I pressed, disappointment sinking in my heart. I watched as his eyes studied the ocean's reflection as it danced across the floor.

"Genetics," he said quietly, his mind thousands of miles away, but then he looked up at me with his piercing green eyes. "My dad was a mortal," he told me blatantly, and I raised my brows in surprise. He never talked about his father. "He was mortal, yet not a witch or wizard alive could say it made me weaker, although I'm sure King Eyeron would beg to differ."

"Good thing we don't care what the elf king has to say then," I dismissed, hoping to ease Chad's mind on the matter, and he smiled back, informing me I had succeeded.

"Speaking of Eyeron," I continued, holding up the icy chain around my wrist, "I'm surprised Icaron didn't follow us here."

"Perhaps you've proven your loyalty enough times," Chad said with a shrug.

With those questions off my chest, I let out a deep breath. "Shall we go collect the rest of them now that I'm officially a 'holder' of Ypovrýchio Kástro?" I tried.

He nodded firmly, but his eyes fell back to the ground before returning to match my gaze. "Yes, but before we go, I just wanted to tell you that I'm sorry, Azalea," he told me softly. "I'm sorry for all those reasons you mentioned up on the dock, and more. I love you, and I never meant to start a row."

Now it was my turn to cast my eyes on the floor. "I know," I replied, forming a smile that didn't quite reach my eyes, and I truly did know. Yet I still didn't want to discuss it.

ભ

A few hours later, we returned to the underwater castle, Abigail and Cristin bringing their belongings in tow, along with suitcases full of children's items that Poppy and the other fairies had collected for Noel and Leon. As soon as we transported them all there, Noel gasped excitedly.

"It's like I'm a mermaid!" she shrieked, immediately taking off to investigate.

Leon ran after her to join in, but I grimaced at her off-putting comment.

"You know, mermaids aren't as spectacular as they're made out to be," I called after her, but I couldn't tell if she could hear me through the fit of laughter she let out as she pressed her nose up against the large window to take in the blue fish swimming by. Thus, I grumbled to myself, making a mental note to teach the children a very valuable lesson on never trusting a mermaid.

Chad stared down at the ground, sucking in his lips. Naturally, I glared in response. How dare he feel the urge to laugh at me after his fishy ex-girlfriend throttled my entire mind?

"Leon still hasn't said a word to us," Abigail uttered from beside me, watching as Noel listed off all the things she could see in the ocean.

"He's probably never experienced kindness from an adult," I assured her, hoping she wouldn't blame herself. "Noel said their mum kept them away from others. She had teachers to show her kindness. Leon's too young to attend school."

"Relax," Cristin told her, placing his hands on her shoulders and massaging them as he drove her towards the children. "Leon will fall in love with you just as quickly as I did."

"Hopefully I don't have to be crying over the body of the innocent mortal I **KILLED** for him to develop loving feelings for me," she sulked out grimly.

I let out a small laugh. Cristin, the saint-like vampire, *would* fall for a beautiful vampiress who was so torn up about **KILLING** a mortal. It was no wonder they got along so well.

They left our side to join the children, and after a moment, I caught Chad's eye, watching me with a small smile as I had been watching Noel and Leon.

"What?" I asked, itching to sneak into his mind.

"Nothing," he said with a shrug, "just thinking about Valentine's Day."

I reciprocated by staring at him blankly.

"You know, our anniversary?" he added on, and I glared at him.

"I know when our anniversary is," I drawled, annoyed. "I just don't understand its relevance at this exact moment."

He gave another shrug that only succeeded in irritating me more. "Well," he resumed, shuffling his feet anxiously across the marble floors, "it's right around the corner. The annual ball has been cancelled due to all the chaos with the shutdown and the attacks, so I was thinking we could do something special, just the two of us."

I studied him carefully, deciding how long I should stay mad at him before it was considered childish. Part of me cringed at the thought it might already be past that point, but the rest of me remembered the past he was keeping me ignorant to through Wyatt, and through forgetting Lili could read my mind. Not to mention the way the mermaids had so easily scavenged through my head. All of which he could have prevented but chose not to, leading me to believe I was allowed to be cross. Either way, an evening with just the two of us might be just what we needed to ease the tension—especially now that the blasted curse was broken.

"I've made it very clear to everyone that I'm not to be interrupted that day, unless half the world's on fire, no less," he said, a gleam in his eye. "If you'll have me, of course…" he finished, his voice trailing off with a fear he let only a few see.

I nodded slowly, watching as a bit of hope returned to his eyes. "I'd like that," I declared firmly. "I'd like that very much."

"So it's a date," Chad said with a smile, one I returned. "Nearly a year ago now I told you I'd choose you above all else. I'd run away with you, cherish you for the rest of my life, and I still mean it, Azalea. You mean the world to me, and I know I haven't been doing a very good job at showing it, but I still mean every word."

"I know," I told him, and I rolled my eyes at such a touching moment that tempted tears from my eyes. "I know, and I love you."

∽

The next few weeks flew by. When I wasn't attempting to help with the war, I spent my time at Ypovrýchio Kástro, failing to produce a time bubble but succeeding at teaching the children small magic tricks. I worked to align my sleep schedule with theirs, but it was a feat that was easier said than done. And although I wouldn't admit it aloud, I was excited for my anniversary with Chad.

He was off, busy as usual, but it was a pleasant sort of break that would make Valentine's Day worth the wait. The night before, I laid out a few outfits in our bedroom, trying to decide which one I liked the best. And as I lay in bed alone, thinking of all the possibilities tomorrow would bring, I fell into a slumber, one I hoped Chad would wake me up from as soon as he got home.

We were surrounded by a dark castle, black paint chipping off its aged walls. Cobwebs coated the chandeliers, and black candles flickered all around. A crowd with red eyes gathered in the front of a large hall, all facing me, yet no fear coursed through my veins. I was not afraid. I was home.

Florence was seated at the front of the crowd, lounging across his chair lazily, but his eyes lit up when a shuffling sound drew everyone's attention. A man I knew dragged a writhing body across the floor, the prisoner's wrists and legs tied tightly, and a cloth bag draped over their head. I sniffed the air, taking in the scent of the person's blood—the man's blood. I twirled my long purple curls around my finger, my eyes brightening as the prisoner was dragged closer and closer until he was pushed down to his knees—his rightful place.

My heart quickened as I let my hands trace his features over the cloth sack. A rhythmic pattern sounded from off in the distance, so familiar it now felt like a lullaby. It grew closer and closer, yet I still couldn't make out the words.

I let my fingers grip the edge of the bag, and I yanked it off him. Raw satisfaction teased every part of me as I took in his beautiful green eyes.

"Please don't do this," he begged, sweat and tears streaming down his face. "Please? Please!" he screamed out, his voice echoing around the room.

The lullaby grew louder before it became a lovely chant of Morgan's voice in my ears.

*"You're going to **KILL** him. You're going to **KILL** him. You're going to **KILL** him."*

I let out a small laugh before addressing the man by name.

"King Chadwick," I breathed out, so happy to see him grovelling before me.

Morgan's fearful eyes flashed in my mind, but I quickly pushed them away. My eyes met with Florence's through the encouraging shouts of the crowd, and he gave me a single nod, the light shining so brightly in his red eyes.

A pounding heart met my ears, and as I looked up, past the crowd, I saw myself clutching weakly onto the wall, only it wasn't truly me. It was the me with pink hair, curiously out of her mirror and here in the flesh. But there was no time to linger on the oddity as Florence's impatient tongue spat out, "Do it!" and my own tongue salivated over the thoughts of such a tasty meal.

So *without further ado, I gave both the crowd and my mouth the thing they wanted most—blood.*

I grasped onto Chad's head, tilting it firmly out of the way, and sank my teeth into his neck.

It was the taste I'd had so many times before, only this time it was the real thing, not a lousy blood duplication potion. I sucked up all his sweet blood until his body twitched before me, and I let it fall to the hard ground lifelessly.

*"You **KILLED** him. You **KILLED** him. You **KILLED** him," Morgan's voice called out, and then a strange high-pitched scream filled my ears—one I had only ever heard at Loxley Lair—and I opened my eyes with a start.*

Jade Austin

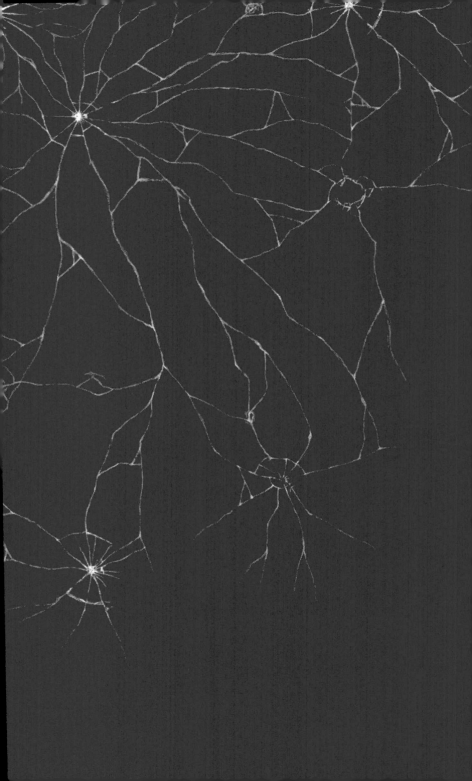

Chapter 37: Ginny's Prophecy

My arms swung out, crashing into a hard surface. Glass shattered against the bedpost. The shards tumbled to the ground with a splash, and small vibrations added to the mix as something soft landed amongst the mess. But all I had eyes for was Chad as he stared back at me, his dazzling emerald eyes wide with shock, but dancing with life—so much life.

My breaths competed with my heartbeat, both travelling at the speed of light with no relief in sight. Chad's quivering hand drew near to caress my heated cheek. The pulse of his blood ticked as the vein in his wrist flew closer to my mouth. The fresh memory of draining the life out of him pierced my mind. Before I knew it, fear forced me out of bed and against the stone wall of our room.

"Don't come near me!" I shouted, wincing at the mixture of shock and hurt that played across Chad's features. "It's me. I saw it. It's me who will KILL you. Mallory was right. She was right all along. You're not safe. I'm not safe," I pleaded.

But my pleas didn't cause him to shrink away. They only drew him in closer.

"It's all right," he said, his voice cracking on the words as he stood from the far side of the bed. "It was just a nightmare—a bad dream. I can ease your mind."

He began rounding the foot of the bed to get closer. His hands were poised upwards as though warning me he wouldn't hurt me, but that wasn't the problem. I was the problem. I was going to hurt him.

I retreated further against the wall, trying to become one with it, but as my shoulder met the corner of the two walls, I could sink back no further. I was trapped. There was no chance of fleeing if his blood tempted me as it had only moments ago.

My fingers tingled, and we both peered down at my hands, realising as one that I could disappear and go far away from here—anywhere to protect him from me.

"Don't go," he said quickly, casting his eyes back to mine. "Talk to me, Azalea," he begged. "Tell me what you saw."

His footsteps halted as he took in the fear in my eyes.

"I watched your death," I told him, choking back the tears that threatened to fall. "I felt as I drained the life out of you with my teeth, and tasted your blood on my tongue. I've seen clips of it before, short scenes your aunt sends me, but this time I saw the whole thing. You *can't* come any closer or the dream may come true."

He shook his head, not believing I was capable of such a thing. "You won't hurt me," he said. "I know you, Azalea. You would never let yourself do that."

"But I wanted to!" I yelled out, and he flinched from the mere force of my words. "I wanted to drain every drop from you, and not because I was thirsty." I closed my eyes to focus on the ingrained memory—to understand the strange sensation I had never felt until then. I could see it so vividly—feel the way my lips curled as I removed the bag from his head. There was no doubt in my mind what I was going to do to him, and the way I had looked at Florence—like I yearned for his approval...

"Perhaps it wasn't you," Chad broke in, intercepting my thoughts. "Perhaps it was the other you from the mirror."

My eyes squinted at him angrily, my mouth parted in bitter disbelief. "The one you cast aside as a portal trick?" I looked at the floor, too slow to avoid witnessing the stark penitence on his face as the blood drained from his cheeks, but I didn't care about his shame. "No," I said to the ground. "She was there too, watching as I did it—probably shocked that I was the one to do it. And the rest of the red-eyed beasts were cheering me on, especially Florence."

"Florence was there?" Chad asked, dumbfounded I hadn't mentioned it earlier. When I nodded down to the floor, he continued eagerly. "Then perhaps he plans to use another potion on you—one to make you love him again, or to confuse you—" he sputtered out, anxiously trying to grasp the puzzle pieces and form them together.

"I didn't feel love or confusion," I told him firmly, "just an overwhelming sense of duty and pride that I had completed my task of **KILLING** you." I winced as the word came off of my tongue again.

"Why don't you start from the beginning so I can understand?" Chad said gently.

I sighed, not wanting to relive it, but knowing it was inevitable, especially if I didn't inform him of everything. "I was at some dark castle," I began. "There was a crowd, and Florence was there, but I wasn't upset. It was like I knew what was coming. They dragged you in, and I could hear Morgan screaming at me. I saw the Azalea with *pink* hair in the distance, but it wasn't her that attacked you, it was me—purple-haired me. There was a bag over your head, and I took it off so I could suck every drop of blood out of you."

Chad swallowed hard. "And you're sure it was a vision, and not just a dream?" he asked delicately, a last shred of hope rather than the doubt of my truth.

I nodded my head. "It was definitely a vision, only this one ended differently from the others." I looked up at him, furrowing my brow. "There was a scream at the end—one I've heard before while living at Loxley Lair. You see, I don't think it was your aunt who sent this vision. I think it was Ginny."

"Ginny?" he asked, confused.

"Yes. Ginny," I said firmly. "You've seen her before. She's O'Brien's banshee."

"I thought banshees only prophesied the deaths of their family members," he countered, running his hands through his hair as though it'd help him think straight.

"I know," I said, exasperatedly tossing my hands into the air. "O'Brien once told me that she said he'd be dying well before his time. He thought he was the last person in his line, but perhaps he was wrong."

"Well, it's not like he and I are related," Chad insisted. "I'm not Irish."

"You told me your father was a mortal, so he's not tied down to the British Caster line. Are you sure he can't have a relative or two by the surname O'Brien?"

"No, I can't be sure, because I've never met him," he said simply, but something on the edge of his tone suggested he didn't want to speak more on it.

I swallowed hard, almost tempted to take a step towards him, but not daring to risk it—not for the lost look in his eyes or the slowed pace of his saddened heart.

"So perhaps you are related," I pressed gently. "For all you know, you could be the next to inherit Ginny's protection," I went on, but the only response that met my ears was a thoughtful silence.

I studied the shattered glass on the floor to distract my troubled mind, and to give Chad time to think. I focused on the way the dim lights were cast upon the glass, through the small puddles of water it cradled, and then all the way over to the flowers it had abandoned. Beautiful pink azaleas lay strewn amongst soft orange roses and green bells of Ireland. I marvelled over their mystical beauty, but then my cheeks flushed as I realised the day's date.

"Happy Anniversary," Chad whispered softly, his lips forcing a comforting smile.

After all the bloodshed in my dream, it was impossible to return the sentiment. I let out a hollowed breath, incapable of coherent thoughts or feelings other than the dread for what was to come—dread and misery I would produce.

Chad aimed his hands towards the broken glass and scattered flowers, taking the opportunity to glance in my direction, afraid I'd flee as soon as his attention was off of me. Then emerald smoke trailed from his fingers and around the mess on the floor. The fragments of glass melted together to form an elegant vase once more, and the fallen petals reattached themselves to create a lovely bouquet of flowers. They landed gracefully in his hands, and he inched towards me—the charming gift his only shield for what I was destined to do to him.

"They're beautiful," I told him, my body tensing more with every step he took in my direction. I held my breath so that I could stop smelling his blood lingering beyond the fragrance of the flowers, and I let my eyes meet his.

He studied me with sorrow and worry. His eyes travelled back and forth between the two of mine as though he longed to help me.

"I suppose there's only one thing that could truly soothe your mind then, isn't there?" Chad asked. His feet stopped their journey towards me, but his body twinged, itching to move closer, to reach out and touch me. "Let's go to Loxley Lair and speak to this Ginny O'Brien. Perhaps there's a way around all of this so your dream never comes to light."

Chills covered my skin as his words attempted to warm me, but my eyes peeled away from him to stare at the flowers. Avoiding the dream seemed too good to be true, but if anyone knew whether it was possible, it would be Ginny.

I dressed quickly, ignoring the clothes I had left out for our date, and going straight for the wardrobe. My fingers trembled as they tore a random dress from its hanger, and worked to replace the pyjamas I was wearing. Tears threatened to fall as pieces of the dream forced their way back into my mind. Guilt stabbed at my heart for the bitterness I had shown Mallory when these same images had plagued her day in and day out. She had seen me take Chad's life countless times, and I had only gotten mad at her for her pain. Regret began to brew as I thought of the silence I had given Chad in the days prior—wasted time when he might not have much left.

When I deserted the wardrobe, I fled directly to the bathroom, avoiding Chad's worried gaze. And once I was dressed fully, I forced my fingers to pry the bathroom door open so I could take in the very man I had just **KILLED**.

Chad's eyes swept down my dress, taking it in with a pale face.

It was black. The very dress I had worn to Detective Harrison's funeral as though we were headed off to Chad's.

"Perhaps we could not lose all hope for me yet, my love," he said gravely.

I watched as his throat bobbed, and I cursed my distracted mind for picking such a morbid outfit.

◌

"O'Brien, we need to speak to Ginny," I announced, skipping all greetings or means of formality.

O'Brien stared at me from his spot in the lounge at Loxley Lair. I could hear the creatures around us taking bated breaths, watching me speak through chattering teeth as I tried to force bravery into my tone but failed. I avoided their eyes as they waited. Grasping onto Chad's hand, I tried to focus instead on his strength—the hope he managed to possess in such a dark situation.

"All righ'…" O'Brien said slowly, confusion and trepidation worn plainly on his face. "Ev'rything all right, pet?"

"I don't believe so," I told him honestly. "I think Ginny sent me a vision, only the vision was of Chad's death, and I need to speak with her to find out more."

O'Brien's face paled at my words, and his gaze flickered away from mine as though he feared something like this would happen.

I exchanged glances with Chad before kneeling down in front of where O'Brien sat. "You wouldn't happen to know why Ginny's prophesying Chad's death, would you?" I asked gently, studying his face for clues. "Is it possible that you and Chad are related somehow?"

But O'Brien shook his head, his eyes still cast away from mine, down at nothing. "Naw," he said firmly. "We're not related. I'm the last of my line." His eyes flew up to look back and forth between Chad and me. "Ya see, banshees don't just disappear when the las' of us die ou'. Naw, they keep goin', lost forever if they have no one to follow, 'nd I didn' want that ta happen to poor Ginny." His eyes were haunted by his sudden realisation. "So I told her she should go ta you two when my time was over—help you two survive all this—only she's not meant to get visions of you so soon, not unless I'm supposed to—"

He couldn't finish the rest of his words, but we knew precisely what he was going to say. O'Brien's days were numbered, perhaps far fewer than he had anticipated, even beyond the warnings Ginny had given him.

I patted his knee, not wanting his time to be over so soon, not when he had such a kind-hearted soul.

381

"I thought you told me once that banshees can see your death to help you prevent it," I tried, using the most hopeful tone I could muster. "Perhaps, Ginny can help us avoid these deaths."

"Naw," O'Brien said, forcing a soft grin on his face. "Not for me. She said I go out as a hero," he reminded me, "'nd I think I'd rather prefer that to a never-ending, meaningless life as a vampire." He let out a small chuckle at the morbid humour of it all. "But for Chad, perhaps there's still a chance."

With that, Chad helped me back up, and O'Brien stood up straight. He clasped a firm hand onto Chad's shoulder.

"Let's go figure this all out," he told Chad bravely. "I think we're all goin' ta need some luck in this war."

An echoey scream bounced through the lair, crashing against the stone walls and straight to us.

"Ah," O'Brien said, his usual chipper tone returning to his voice. "She mus' know you're here."

We followed the shrill screams and draining cries across to the ballroom, and then off to one of the dark halls, filled with holes for the sleeping undead. Within each hole was a dark casket for the older generation of vampires who dwelled at Loxley Lair. They lined the corridor I had only travelled down once, during my tour with Charity, and were just as eerie as I remembered. Eventually, the corridor led us to the source of the screams, and the banshee's mouth shut as soon as her dejected eyes met mine.

I felt my body turn to ice as I took in her grey, sullen features, the way no life flickered in her eyes.

"Ginny," I said, letting go of Chad's hand and drawing closer to the floating woman. "You've predicted O'Brien's death," I forced out, my heart aching at the thought of my friend's passing, "but is it possible you've seen another death? Someone who isn't your descendant?"

Ginny slowly lifted her chin and dropped it back down, but there was no curiosity in her grey eyes, just a sense of knowing. She could feel exactly why we were here.

"You saw my vision," she said, her voice echoing like the nightmare itself, and I exchanged dark glances with Chad.

O'Brien leaned forwards, waiting with a wary heart to hear more of her vision.

"So is it true?" I asked, taking an eager step towards her. "Is that really what's meant to be?" My hands were trembling, even through the fists I clenched them in to try and stop the quakes.

"Yes," she breathed out. A death sentence in itself. Her eyes met Chad's and she cocked her head to the side, studying him before her eyes flickered over to me once more. "He will die a hero's death."

But her words did nothing to alleviate the pit in my core. Dying a hero was no excuse to leave the earth early. I had seen Chad's death with my own eyes—felt every moment—but that couldn't be the end. It couldn't happen that way.

"No," I spat out, without any more thought. "There has to be something—some way to stop it from happening," I insisted, but the banshee shook her head at me, her weightless hair trailing slowly from side to side.

"There's nothing to be done," she told me, the same look on her face as though she was trying to read me.

I huffed, frustration beyond anything I had ever felt coursing through me. "Then why send me the vision?" I asked her between gritted teeth. It was hard not to yell—to tell her she was wrong or insane. "Why show me something I cannot stop?"

Her stare bored into me as she waited to answer, as if the anticipation would calm me. It did the opposite. "Everything will happen the way it's meant to be," she said simply, and I just about blew up.

I walked towards her, ready to cast some sort of solidifying charm on her so I could rip the deceased head off her shoulders, but Chad magically appeared next to me, and before his smoke cleared, his hand was caressing my face. A warmth spread through to my cheek, my head, and my whole body as he stared right into my eyes, calming me down instantly with his magic.

"O'Brien, Ginny," he said without taking his eyes away from mine. "Thank you for all your help, but we must be going."

And with that, our feet left the floor and touched down a second later back at Castwell Castle.

Everything blurred around me. As Chad's warm fingers left my skin, the feelings came rushing back at a speed only a vampire could go. I couldn't tell what room we were in, or what was happening other than the rising sensation of fear, anger, and pure desperation inside of me.

"She's wrong," I told him, feeling the storm crash from every angle inside of me. "She's wrong, you're not going to die, and everything is going to be fine," I declared firmly, but there was no positivity in my voice, just sheer stubbornness.

Everything will happen the way it's meant to be.

I rolled my eyes. What codswallop. What bullshit. The red tears fell, clearing my vision.

"We'll think of something," Chad offered. He reached his hands out to hold me, but I just swatted them away before pacing back and forth.

"If we can see it, we can stop it. When she's wrong, you'll be safe. It's that simple. We just need to keep you away from anyone who has it out for you," I told him, completely disregarding the look in his eyes, the sadness I would not accept as truth. Turning back towards him, I said, "If you die, I can just reverse it. Teach me. Show me how to do the time bubble on command."

But his return was void of any hope. He shook his head, doubt setting in. "It would have to be done instantly—without hesitation. And what if you're—unable to do it? What if you're—"

My heart sank. He didn't even have to say it. His aunt's continuous screams said it for us. "What if I'm the one who does it?" I finished for him.

His shoulders fell and he let out a heavy sigh. He pitied me as though I were the one who was going to die, not him.

"I mean," he went on softly, placing his hands on my shoulders, "what if you're under a spell or something that forces you to do it?"

I stared back into his green eyes, taking in his dark lashes, his nose, his mouth, everything about him, everything that I loved. "Then we could have someone as a backup. Your aunts could do it. We could tell them our plan, tell them it wouldn't truly be me doing it—"

Chad's face seemed to sadden even more, and he let out another breath that sounded just as melancholy. "Neither of my aunts have time reversal as a power. Magic works in mysterious ways. Some have strengths others could only dream of. I have time bubbles whereas Aunt Morgan has visions of the future."

"Then we'll find someone who can do it, and we'll have *them* as a backup," I insisted. "What about your guards? One of them is bound to be able to do it."

Chad closed his eyes for a brief moment, as if gathering strength. "It's not a very common gift. And some who do have it can only do it in small bursts. Even *I'm* lousy at it and I've been practising for most of my life."

"Then who?" I asked, and his sad eyes told me precisely the answer. Lili.

Of course she could. She said she could produce time bubbles the first time I had ever met her. And Chad trusted her, even though I still couldn't bring myself to do the same.

I glanced away from Chad, knowing what had to be done, and if it meant saving his life, I'd do anything.

"All right," I told him, meeting his gaze once more. My voice cracked when I realised it meant she'd have to be around more—near enough to reverse it. "Tell her," I forced out. "Make her promise to do it if—" I let out a guilty breath, "—if I can't."

I couldn't take the pressure that weighed down on my heart, so I sobbed, releasing as much of it as I could. Before I knew it, I was wrapped up in Chad's arms, shaking both of us with my sorrows and squeezing him back tightly. Crimson tears soaked into his shirt, and I closed my eyes, reminded of all the blood I had taken from him in my dream. Only, it wasn't a dream. It was the future, and it was undeniably me.

"I just can't lose you," I choked out, terrified to be this close to him, yet too weak to pull away.

He leaned back from me, taking my chin in his hand and tilting it up so I could no longer avoid those dazzling eyes of his. They studied mine, going back and forth before they scanned my lips.

"And you won't lose me," he told me calmly. "We won't let it come to that."

I nodded, almost believing him, and his lips met mine—soft, passionate, and caring. Not an ounce of angst, just love. For once, I had Chadwick all to myself, body and soul. But as fate would have it, the moment was short-lived.

Chad's lips grew cold against mine. Stiff. Worried. His heart quickened, and when I opened my eyes, he pulled away. His face had grown dark with concern.

"Something's happening," he breathed out, and my heart froze.

His gift was the present, he had told me, and something was slithering against his talent, alerting him.

His phone began to ring, but he let the song play without glancing its way. There was nothing they were supposed to call him for. Not today. Not on our anniversary. Not unless the world was set aflame.

Chad's hand moved in an arch and a large screen appeared before him. The ringing stopped and resumed a second later. Still, he made no move to answer it. The answer would come from the telly, I deducted anxiously, not from *her*. For who else would be calling?

The screen flickered to life and chaos ensued upon it. Buildings as tall as the sky crashed down to the pavement. People screamed as they ran for their lives, and a reporter spoke through her tears in a language I couldn't understand.

"What's happening?" I let out through a ragged breath. "Where is this? Is this live?"

"Japan," Chad said quietly, his body as rigid and frozen as my own. "We have to help them."

The screen zoomed in on a massive pile of bodies, towering on top of each other, while a horde of red-eyed vampires drained the last of the blood. Standing on the dead bodies as though they were merely a gravelly hill under his feet, was none other than Florence.

I looked around and took in our bedroom, grounding myself to where I was. We needed to move fast. We needed help. We needed an army, yet so few had joined our side.

Hydie, I thought, projecting my thoughts as loudly as they would go. *I need you to come to my bedroom. There's an emergency and I need you to watch Noel and Leon.*

On my way, she replied, and a moment later I pulled the door open as her footsteps drew nearer. Her eyes widened when she took in the destruction on the screen.

"Connor," Chad said urgently, using a hand to almost grab his voice from in front of him and then cast it outward.

His voice travelled through the halls, bouncing diligently off the walls until I heard Connor stir from far away. The sound of rustling paws against pearled tiles met my ears, and then he came skidding across the room towards us. His werewolf form quickly transformed back to his human one, and between pants for air, he asked, "What? What's going on?"

But we didn't have to answer. His eyes grew wide as he took in the screen, all the destruction that roared out at us.

Another explosion went off on the broadcast, and I looked up at Chad in horror.

"What do we do?" I asked.

But it was apparent he was just as lost for a solution as I was. Shaking his head, he muttered, "I dunno."

"Can we make it there?" Connor asked.

"Not in time," Chad said with regret. "There's a mirror that could take us close, but I've never been to that city. We couldn't transport there. We'd have to travel the rest of the way on foot."

Denial flowed through me, forcing words from my lips. "No, there's got to be something faster."

"I've never been there before," Chad insisted with wide eyes.

"Perhaps some other witch or wizard has?" Hydie asked, squinting her eyes hopefully.

"Either way, we're going to need holy water—a ton of it—and more recruits," Connor chimed in.

"To Loxley Lair?" Chad asked, turning to face me.

"No—Ypovrýchio Kástro. All the holy water is there for extra precautions," I said guiltily, knowing it was a detail I had failed to inform him of amidst my silent treatment.

He gave a nod, staring down at the ground as though accepting the small punishment for his previous behaviour, and he took hold of all our hands before whirling us off to the underwater castle.

Green smoke swirled around us, the ground disappeared from under my feet as it had so many times before, and while my body went with it, my mind was jerked to a place far away. My spirit drifted in a dreamlike state over mountains, and valleys, and lakes, and seas, and then all I could see were a set of terrified brown eyes. The fear that coursed through those young eyes pulled me, tempting my body to follow it. My feet touched down onto carpeted floors, snapping my mind back into place, but the pull was still there and stronger than ever.

We appeared before Abigail and Cristin. They were sitting on the floor of a playroom, laughing and entertaining the children with toys, but as soon as Abigail saw us, the smile she wore vanished.

"What happened?" she asked anxiously, but all I could feel was the pull as it tugged me towards the mysterious brown eyes from my vision with an urgency I had only ever felt with dreams of my sister, Noel and Leon, and when Florence was near. But Hydie and the children were here, and Florence's eyes were not brown.

Hydie quickly went over to the children, bending down to them with a warm smile. "Fancy a snack while we let the adults talk about boring stuff?" she asked sweetly.

Noel and Leon got up eagerly and followed Hydie out. I could feel Noel's wise eyes on me before she left, but I couldn't bear to return her gaze, not when I'd be putting Abigail and Cristin in danger by taking them with us.

Chad flicked his wrist, producing the floating screen once more so the broadcast could explain the devastation unfolding. The images were worth thousands of horrible, torturous words.

Thirty seconds of watching brought on a new panic. Abigail flew out the door, returning nearly instantly with jugs of holy water. The fierce look in her eyes read she was ready to go—ready to go protect the city against Florence's rage. But with all the urgency and anxiety that swirled in the air, my eyes flew to Chad, so ready to find a way there, and the memory of his cold, dead body flashed before my eyes.

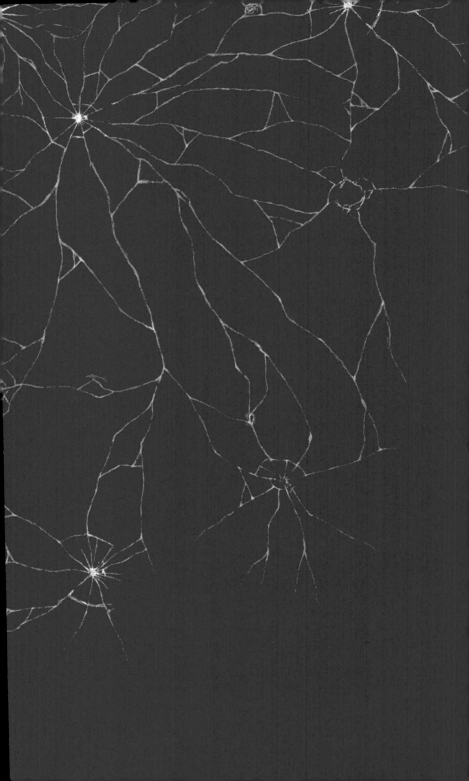

Chapter 38: The Proposition

*N*o," I breathed out, and Chad's brave face melted into confusion. I turned towards him to face him head-on. "Chad, you can't go. There are bound to be more vampires there. Florence is there," I said, refusing to be close to both of them. Ginny's prophecy could not come true. "We'll go without you. Eyeron will know where I am," I said, dangling the icy bracelet from my wrist. "He'll send Icaron, and hopefully others to track me there, and they'll help. Then you can send your guards and more people from Loxley Lair. You're a king," I told him sternly, in case he had forgotten. "You're the most valuable piece. Get your guards to protect you. You need to go into hiding."

"I'm a king," he repeated stubbornly. "That means I need to fight, not hide." His teeth gritted against each other as he grasped onto the handle of one of the jugs of holy water.

My brows rose with the pure fear that boiled up within me, and I closed my eyes, not knowing how I could possibly convince him not to come.

"Chadwick," I told him, my voice cracking on his name as everyone around me stirred impatiently, and the pull of the child called me. "A banshee just told us you were going to die. You need to stay."

I ignored the gasps around me as the others took in the news we hadn't told them earlier, and I begged Chad with my eyes to listen.

"It's my duty," he explained, not budging.

I let out an infuriated growl. "I don't give a shit about duty, I'm going without you," I declared through gritted teeth. "You're not going to die over this. I won't allow it."

"And how are you going to get there without me?" he challenged, throwing his hands into the air, but the pull called to me, stronger this time. I could feel it. It would take me there. "Neither of us has ever been to Japan. We can't just transport there. We could take a dragon, but even then it might be over by the time we get there. Either way, standing here arguing about it isn't doing any good."

But I wasn't merely arguing for argument's sake. I was saving his life.

I could feel it—the tingle, the strange twinge of magic as it crept within me. I hadn't ever been to Japan. It was too far to transport there, but something within me knew that wouldn't stop me.

"There's a child there, Azalea," Noel said, appearing in the doorway. All our eyes flew over to her tiny body, her eyes locked in a milky-white trance. The flicker of her eyelids broke her concentration, and her suddenly clear eyes met mine. "You have to save her like you did with us. She'll lead you there."

The pull. Those youthful brown eyes.

I nodded, smiling at the brilliant girl before turning back to Chad. "Go to Lili. Tell her what we found out, and tell her she has to protect you," I told him firmly before snatching the jug from his hand and walking over to Abigail, Cristin, Connor, and the rest of the holy water. Defiantly and fervently, I grabbed onto them, ignoring the unease on their faces.

"I'm not going to let you all risk your lives without me," Chad insisted, not daring to take a step towards us.

"I'm afraid you don't have a choice," I replied, biting back the fear in my throat.

I didn't know how to stop Florence. I didn't know how to fight knowing I had made a hole in Chad's pride. But those things weren't important. I wasn't going to put him in harm's way. I refused to lose him. I loved him too much.

"And if I refuse?" Chad spat out.

"Then with any luck, we'll have taken care of the situation before you arrive," I said simply.

And with that, I let the pull take me, and we were gone.

Not a second later, our feet crashed into the hard rubble that littered the chaotic street. The indigo sky crashed with violet lightning. I couldn't process all that was happening through the screams. Thousands of people were pushing past, shouts and cries in their foreign tongue that could only mean panic. The ground shook beneath us, cracking around our feet, and as I exchanged looks with Abigail, Cristin, and Connor, their eyes mirrored the same fear that had settled into mine. How the hell were we going to stop this?

A familiar swishing sound came from beside me, and none other than my persistent boyfriend appeared, his eyes locked with mine. No words came from his lips as he stared at me in shock, his chest rising up and down in an attempt to catch his breath. I furrowed my brow at him, but time evaded us. I couldn't ask how he had arrived, how he had turned up here when he hadn't been near us enough to grab hold and tag along, because at that moment, there was a giant screech. A dark shadow engulfed us, and we looked up to see a tall building, a hundred stories or more, falling towards us.

Without a thought of the consequences, of all the mortals around who would see, I covered my face and cast out a shield to protect the lot of us. Shards of glass and brick attempted to puncture my protective charm. I stumbled back from the weight of it, but my purple disk clashed with a green one, alleviating some of the pressure. The two disks seemed to morph into one. As the heavy fragments of the building ricocheted everywhere, I leaned into the chaos, turning my head and squinting my eyes as Chadwick pushed against his own shield.

"It's too heavy," he grunted, working hard to fight against gravity, but the building was too large. "We'll have to set it down as gently as we can."

I did as he said, and together we slowly, painstakingly lowered the mass of concrete, glass, and steel to the street, careful not to crush any of the frantic citizens. But there was no pause granted to us after the structure seemed to settle to the ground. Instead, another building began to fall. Only, my reflexes were much quicker this time. Drawing my arms back to summon all the power I had, I pushed it all towards the building. Magic in the form of purple liquid shot out at the structure like a fire hose, propelling the building in the opposite direction. The structure righted itself once more, its exterior walls sealing themselves back together, and I dropped my powers with a relieved breath. Yet everything was still coming undone.

It was all happening at once. My brain struggled to keep up with the chaos and screams. Abigail and Cristin sped around, grabbing whoever they could to move them away from the wreckage at speeds only our kind could go. Connor collected the jugs of water and ran towards the sound of teeth tearing into human flesh and the smell of blood, while Chad pushed every drop of green magic into keeping the buildings surrounding us from falling.

A pull grasped at the centre of my chest, yanking me violently towards it, but this was not the pull I had felt moments before. This one was rough, familiar, and held a force filled with lust, not innocence or fear.

My eyes flew to Chad—distracted and completely careless of his own safety by following me here. It would be reckless to follow Florence's pull on my own, without backup or added protection, but the others were busy. Chad wouldn't have had time to tell his guards where we had gone in the seconds it took him to follow us, and I didn't know if Eyeron would bother sending his men. As I took Chad in, the nightmare flashed across my fluttering eyes, and I knew it would be deadly to bring him with me.

So I ran.

I ran full speed between the toppling buildings, pushing against the rabble of screaming people, right to where the pull led me, to the centre of all the chaos. And there he was, leaning against a brick wall, wearing a smile just for me.

Without waiting for his fine greeting, I sent a harsh stream of vibrant violet. His movement to avoid it was swift, thoughtless, and as I sent bolt after bolt towards him, I realised that in my months of training, he too had been practising his escape from my wrath. He moved with such incredible speed. I tried to focus my eyes on trailing him—focus my magic on demolishing him simultaneously. But after at least thirty futile blasts that only worked to crumple the foundation of the buildings beside us and the alleyway we stood in, Florence remained unscathed.

He disappeared from before me, only for his voice to creep along the back of my neck. "I have longed to see your face, Azalea," he whispered.

I spun around and came face to face with the man who had started this whole nightmare. My body tensed for a heartbeat at the memory of his breath on my neck, just long enough to take in his red eyes as they shone brightly in the moonlight, and the crimson blood that dripped down him, soaking his clothes as though he had swum in it.

All at once, my body released the frozen hold that the memory of him had placed over me, and my arms flung out. They crashed into his chest, sending him catapulting into the wall that stood behind him.

"Florence," I breathed out. It had been so long, and even though I yearned to **KILL** him, I couldn't help but wish the absence between us had been longer.

"I'm so happy you've arrived," he said, his face contorted with pain and a different type of longing as he peeled himself out of the cracks in the wall. His words were sincere and broken as he spoke, as though love and sadness were feelings he was truly capable of.

But I refused to freeze. I would not let him cause any more destruction in this world. I couldn't tell if my force had contributed his own blood to that on his clothes, but the thought of his death occurring at that moment would make it impossible for my latest nightmare to come true. And that hope drove all the strength within me.

I sent violet ropes after him like hungry snakes seeking out their prey. They pulsed from my fingers, weaving around the rubble on the ground, twisting and curving, tracking his motions with the aim to **KILL**. But the damned vampire was quicker.

Florence grabbed my wrists from behind, slamming me into the side of a building, causing my magical ropes to retreat from the shock. There was a brief series of clicks and then everything turned white. My head pounded from the impact of being smashed into the wall, and as he held my palms against the building and away from him, I felt cold around my wrists. The smell of metal seeped into my nose, and as the white began to clear from my vision, I looked up to see silver handcuffs trapping my hands. The warmth of his hold contrasted against their cool feel, and the sight of them left my brain a muddled mass of confusion. Florence's body pushed against me viciously. Red liquid weighed down my eyelashes as a trail of blood trickled down, and I batted it away.

The building I was held against was crumbling thanks to me. If I forced out more magic through the palms that were pressed against it, surely it would fall, making me no better than the monsters who had torn down the others. I prayed there weren't any humans left inside it in case tearing it down was my only option of getting away from the man who had me pinned.

"I have yearned to see you," Florence groaned into my ear. The smell of iron on his hot breath plagued me as he moved his cheek to press against mine. "I have done *so* much to get your attention—all of it for you—but you've forced me to hide away."

I struggled against his strength, moving wildly, but he had grown stronger in his absence. My body's energy focused on the vampire part of me, healing the wound on my head.

"Let go of me, Florence," I panted, putting all my force against him, but he was just too strong.

"I will *never* let go of you, Azalea. I created you, and I will hold onto you for as long as we both shall live," he promised, the texture of smooth silk in his voice. "You don't know what I've been through—what I've done to deserve you. I want you to know who I am so you can see me!"

"I know who you are, Florence," I spat out, disgusted by every part of him, "and you'd *think* the son of Hitler would be wise enough to learn from his father's mistakes."

"Oh, but I have," he breathed out with a dangerous laugh. "I've learned from every single one of his mistakes, including his biggest mistake of deserting me. I've also learned a great deal from his enemies—how to make a statement. That's why I'm here."

My lungs heaved for air. I had wasted so much energy on a fruitless attack. I needed to regain as much as I could. Keeping my lips shut against the questions I longed to ask him, I loosened my tense muscles and listened to the sounds around me. My ear scraped against the gritty texture of the wall as I tried to hear past it. The creak of the building signalled its hold was failing. There were screams from far away, the sound of machines within, but there were no people inside.

Florence took my stillness as an opportunity to recapture my attention. As the gash in my head closed, he tightened his grip on my hair and smashed my head against the wall once more. A searing pain shot through me, travelling as fast as the cracks that spread up the tall office building.

White stars blurred my vision, but as I closed my eyes to deal with the pain, Florence went on.

"I'm here," he continued brashly, through gritted teeth, "because *you've* been watching me. You've stolen most of the gnomes' mushrooms to keep me in hiding. I couldn't go anywhere without your precious witch-boy spying on me with those stupid cameras. So I had to stay underground. But I thought of something so terrible it was great. You steal my mushrooms, then I'll create my own, just like they used against my father's allies in the war. Only, this one will make theirs look insignificant by comparison."

My eyes parted, braving the white stars as they dissipated, and I felt the wound on my head heal itself once more. "What the hell are you talking about?" I asked through the daze, cursing my inability to regain the strength in my body.

"I have a proposition for you," he cooed into my ear. "Come away with me, finally be my wife and conquer this world with me. *Or*," he taunted, "watch as I detonate an atomic bomb so powerful, it'll obliterate all the islands of Japan. Every single person here will die, all because of your inability to give in."

My heart froze and my energy weakened with it, too broken to fight. And then I understood. The mushroom cloud over Hiroshima, Japan. He was going to recreate it, only worse, because of some unjustified obsession over me and the father who abandoned him.

Chad's voice sounded from somewhere in the distance as he shouted my name. It met my ears like a song. The desperation to call back to him was met by his death flashing before my eyes, and I blinked away the bad memory with my jaw hinged tight. I couldn't call back to him. I wouldn't.

"Ah," Florence breathed out softly, his head tilting against mine to the sound. "Your stupid *prince* is calling. But soon he'll perish along with the rest of them. If you don't come with me, that is."

I gritted my teeth against the bitter chill Florence sent creeping up my spine. He would not take me prisoner or destroy the country. I wouldn't allow it.

"How silly of me not to invite you to the coronation," I countered with as much snark as I could muster, "especially since you were so busy mucking things up elsewhere, but Chad is actually a king now, and he's more pure and powerful than you'll ever be."

Florence's movements were quicker than a whip as he grasped my hair, slammed my head against the wall, and then pinned my hands again, all in one swift motion. White light blinded me once more. My scream echoed through the night, mixing in with the others, but through it all, I heard another sound, a small breath, and I felt the fearful pull of the child reining me in to help her.

She was there. The child was watching. And Florence was too distracted by his desire to notice her. I just needed one small distraction to get the bloody bastard off me.

"How about I do you one better, then?" he snarled viciously into my ear. "How about I announce to the whole world that people like us exist if you don't come with me tonight? I've had to fight to be chosen my whole life, and finally I'm winning. It doesn't matter that your witch-boy is a king. I've found followers who worship me like a *god* and believe in everything I stand for. They want the world to know what we are—to fear us! I nearly have everything. But there's still one thing missing, Azalea. It's always been missing, and that's you. I need you. I would *die* to have you."

"Think you could die a bit faster then?" I stabbed at him, but he pressed his lips roughly into my cheeks as he ignored me, speaking into my skin as his anger rattled both of our bodies.

"Come with me or they all die," he reiterated, and there was no longer any part of my body that chills hadn't conquered.

I heard the scrape as a trembling hand picked up a rock, the terrified breaths. My palms were ready to use my magic, they were eager to attack, but I had to time it perfectly. I couldn't screw this up.

Gathering all the courage I had, I turned my head, pressing my cheek further into his, and spat out, "I think I'll choose another option entirely, thank you."

And the child smashed the rock into Florence's head.

The smell of his blood drifted into my nose like a savoury treat as I turned with incredible speed, pushing him back in his split second of shock after being hit over the head. I cast my hand towards him, ready for my long, purple rope to shoot out at him—twist its way around him—lock up his limbs. A deep hurt flashed across his features as he fell to his knees, but his eyes brightened as soon as they took in my handcuffed wrists.

There was no magic.

No purple.

No rope.

No power.

Panic washed over me like a tsunami as a cruel laugh escaped Florence's lips. I thrust my hands towards him again, but no magic came out. My eyes flew over to a little girl—ready to grab the rock from her and use it on him as she had—but as soon as my eyes landed on her, my jaw fell.

The same brown eyes from my vision met mine. She was older than Noel by perhaps a few years, but my attention was immediately drawn away from her young, beautiful, tan face, and down to her legs. All eight of them to be exact.

"You're—you're a jorogumo," I gasped, taking in the hairy texture and fluidity as she stepped back on legs I had only seen on one other person. She was like Charity.

"Who the *fuck* is she?" Florence asked, crumpling further to the ground as the blood from the attack oozed down his head. He blinked as his eyes moved out of focus, and his palms scraped against the coarse ground to catch his fall.

The girl's eyes shifted nervously between Florence and me, the rock still raised in her hand, ready to use it again if she needed to. Fear was engraved in her eyes, and as I studied her with a rattling mind, I decided she was much too young to face Florence any more than she already had.

"Thank you," I breathed out to her. "I've got this now. Run and I'll find you when I'm done with him."

She simply stared, her heart pounding out of her chest, blinking at me.

I closed my eyes to steady my own heart. Of course she didn't understand. We didn't speak the same language. I'd have to deal with Florence and hope she'd have the sense to shield her eyes from the violence she was far too young to see.

My attention and rage returned to Florence as the crack in his head took way too long to heal. I remembered this. I remembered his body was stronger and quicker than mine, but something in his vampire genes was making his healing process slower than my own. And if speed and strength were not on my side, I could use this as his weakness instead.

I sprang towards him, ready to **KILL**. The chain between my hands crunched into his throat as I pinned his body down to the ground. My knees trapped his flailing arms. Air escaped his mouth, and I pressed the chains harder against him, relishing in the way that the promise of death brought panic to his eyes.

"What are these cuffs?" I screamed at him. "How are they blocking my magic?"

Florence's chokes and gags were barely audible amongst the girl's panicked screams. Her Japanese words spewed into the chaos, and though I prayed she would leave so she wouldn't witness it, her eight feet stayed rooted to the ground.

I pressed the chains deeper into Florence's neck as he wrangled underneath me, the crunching of bones meeting my ears. There was an intensity in his red blood as it began to pour out of the gash I was creating in his neck. I knew he wouldn't be able to answer me like that, but still, I drilled him with my questions.

A blast of fire crashed into my back, and I fell on Florence's face as the heat seared me. My forearms collided with the rubble, catching my fall. As my body worked to heal the intense burns in my back, I forced my lungs to work by listening to the strangled, gurgled sounds of Florence's lungs beneath me. His misery fed me strength.

Just as the wound on my back fully healed, I rolled off of him, and a blur of motion sped towards us. When it halted, I stared back at the version of myself with pink hair as she knelt down beside Florence and the pool of blood that had come from his neck. I watched as Florence struggled for air—as his eyes met mine and widened—as he reached out towards me, knowing she was going to pull him away. And in the blink of an eye, both of them were gone.

I pushed off of the ground, staggering as I stood, and looked over at the screaming jorogumo. Yet I had no time to soothe her trembles before the pink-haired Azalea reappeared in the alleyway, free of Florence's weight, but I could still smell his blood on her stained dress.

"You," I gasped, staring at what could only be described as my reflection. But there was no mirror or dream to accompany her this time, just her taunting pink hair.

The tiny jorogumo took off at a run when she set her wide eyes on her, and I fumbled to understand any of it.

"What? Did you think I was a myth?" the twin asked with a ridiculously light laugh that didn't fit the situation. "But aren't we all?"

I clenched my jaw tight, balling up my hot fists as they lacked the magic I needed. "Where did you take Florence?" I asked.

"Eager to see your betrothed so soon?" she asked, tilting her head at me curiously as she smiled so brightly that it had to be true joy. "He has been dying to kiss those lips of yours."

"Been there, done that," I spat out, and I was not going to be forced into doing it again. "Now tell me where you took him," I yelled. "He deserves a death that only I can give him."

"He said you always talked so kindly of him," she jested with a high-pitched sarcasm, "and now I finally get to see it all in action. He talks so fondly of you too. Well, I mean of course he does. He bloody loves you, doesn't he? Confess, you felt *something* those times he kissed you, love potion aside."

"Confessions are best left for the sinners," I sneered back, finished with her sadistic games. "I will never feel anything but hatred for that man, and if you don't tell me where he is right now, I'll **KILL** you just to get you out of my way."

"Oh, I'm not too sure about that, Azalea. You think I don't see you flinch every time you say the word—when you let talk of **KILLING** roll off your lips?" she taunted, and her lips curled into a satisfied smile, too sinister to be my own. "You're too afraid."

Her words held too much truth behind them—too much certainty that she could read me with ease. I shuddered at how well this stranger knew me.

"I'll **KILL** him," I emphasised, "*regardless* of any reservations I have about the matter."

"Let's not let *him* hear your blatant disdain for him, shall we? I'm the only way he gets satisfaction these days, if you know what I mean," she said suggestively.

I cringed as a vision of them in bed crowded my view—their naked bodies coated in sweat from their passion—a body too similar to my own.

Run.

Don't cry.

Just get away.

The familiar thoughts made their encore, and the woman nodded as though she could hear them too.

"That's precisely what you should do," she whispered. Her feet began to travel their way around me, closing in on her prey as ice trailed down my spine. "Run. Save who you can, but know you can't save them all."

My heart faltered. Blood drained from my cheeks.

"Florence isn't even here to know my answer," I reminded her, true panic coursing through my veins at the last-ditch effort to stop Florence's insane plan. I held my chained hands out in front of me. "What if I decide to go with him so he doesn't carry out his plan?"

But she smiled before winking at me. "We both know you won't go," she said matter-of-factly, and my heart fell with my sinking shoulders.

They were going to do it. They were going to destroy an entire country and tell the world we existed. And for what? For me?

"I have *nothing* to offer him," I insisted pathetically, but there was no use shielding the fear from my voice. "I could never make Florence as happy as he seems to think I would."

She merely shrugged as her eyes dropped to the ground and then back up to mine. "He seems to think differently," she said simply. "Either way, your paths will cross again, and I think you'll give in next time. Especially after our *next* little chat."

"Our next chat?" I asked dumbly.

"Yes," she cooed before turning it into another laugh. "You and I. Come see me in the mirrors when you're ready for a bit of information."

"Information?" What information would I so eagerly want from her?

"Yes," she replied grimly, "something that's been bothering you—something about your king."

"Chad?" I asked, more confused now than before.

"Yes, but for now you should *run*," she reminded with intensity as she pounced towards me.

My fists balled with tightened fury, so fierce as they pulled against the chains that dug into my wrists. Strength coursed through me as I ignored the pain—ignored the smell of blood as my arms fought against their hold. The clank of metal sounded through the air as the cuffs broke and then skittered against the uneven ground.

A look of awe flashed across the woman's face, as though impressed by my strength. Her eyes flickered down to my wrists before glancing back up at me. I cast a ball of purple flames at her, but she flicked it away as though it were nothing more than a piece of dust.

"*Don't cry*," she said, mocking my sadness, and I threw another flame but it, too, was flicked aside before she bounced joyfully along to the words, "*Just get away*."

It was a game. A fucking game to her.

Then she disappeared to God knows where.

I stood alone next to the crumbling building, lightning rippling against a pink sky, threatening everyone below. Thunder pounded through the air. Chad's voice shouted out for me again as the world shook beneath my feet. And the small girl, wherever she had gone, pulled me to her, harder than she had before.

I could feel every part of my body, my skin, my muscles, my bones, all of it, ticking like a timebomb, and I ran as fast as I could towards the pull. It took seconds to find her and wrap my arms around her as I kept running, eager to follow Chad's voice as it reached out to my ears like a siren's song. I finally saw him, huddled together with Abigail, Cristin, and Connor, panting with their empty water jugs, the sizzling remains of someone evil by their feet.

Relief swept over their faces as I pulled to a stop in front of them, but their eyes all widened as they took in the legs of the girl who was clutching onto me so fiercely. Yet there was no time to explain.

"You all have to go," I told them, forcing the girl to let go of me as I thrust her into Chad's arms. "I have to save—"

The girl screamed, reaching out for me as tears began to stream down her face. Chad's face screwed up into a frown, but as he opened his mouth, the ground shook again, and a bright white light blinded me. I felt Chad and the girl clutch onto me, and I squeezed my eyes shut to block out the light. Through the void of colour, I heard a terrifying explosion. My feet lifted from the ground before crashing with such force into a slick surface.

"Wait!" I called out, but it was too late.

Everything was gone.

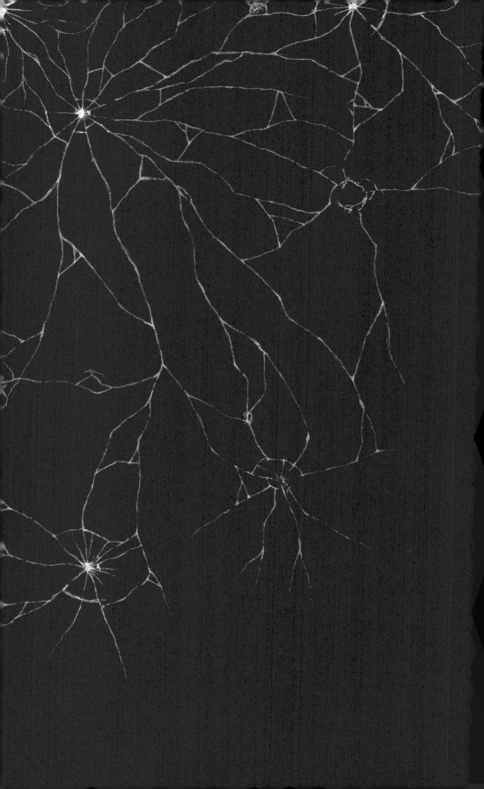

Chapter 39: A Mushroom in the Sky

S ix sets of feet collided to the ground in a hurry, nearly causing us all to topple to the shimmering marble floor. With my body competing against my mind for balance, my adrenaline-fueled body won and my brain was left in shambles.

The force of the pull snapped into place as the weight of the child jorogumo was transferred back into my arms. She wrapped her small arms around my neck so tightly that I couldn't breathe, but I let her cling to me. I couldn't bring myself to release her fragile form. Her mass of legs dangled down awkwardly as I held her, unsure of how to properly grasp her as she choked out the tears that mixed with her screams.

Everything around me went out of focus as a blur of red tears begged me to unleash them. There was so much movement, so much sound as my friends exploded with worry and confusion.

"What the *fuck* just happened?" Connor asked, his voice a mix of anger and fear.

"An explosion of some sort," Cristin struggled.

"But all those people," Abigail cried out.

"I had to get us out of there if there was any hope of surviving," Chad said, pacing back and forth with such fire in his eyes, the gears in his mind working hard to comprehend any of it.

"We have to find out if there are survivors," Connor insisted. His eyes were wide with urgency.

"There's absolutely no way anyone could survive a blast that—" Cristin began.

"I'll search for it," Chad interrupted, pushing his hands aggressively through his hair. "There have to be some cameras still intact for us to see what the bloody hell's going on."

But I knew exactly what was going on. Florence had blown the island right off the map, just as he had promised. All because he knew I wouldn't go along with him.

I blinked and the room came into focus as my crimson tears fell. Bile bubbled its way up my throat, and I swallowed against it, clutching the girl tighter in my arms. Florence was going to pay for this. He was going to die a most painful death, and I was going to be the one to do it. I had to. But first, I had to go back.

My body shook against the ground, remembering the quakes as though we were still in Japan. The girl in my arms was running her mouth at a thousand kilometres an hour, foreign words flowing out like a burst pipe. Her country, her people, all gone in the blink of an eye, and I was just standing there.

Without warning, my nerves combusted. The flip from a still body to a completely berserk one was switched, and I lost control of everything.

"I'm going back," I screamed, bending down to the floor in an attempt to pry the screaming child from my neck, but somehow my fierce, uncontrolled movements couldn't pull her off of me. My eyes flew up to everyone else, all of them staring straight at me with wide eyes, all except for Chad who apparently hadn't heard me. He furiously flicked his wrists and a screen appeared in front of him. His fingers worked frantically, swiping across it over and over, searching manically with a pounding heart through nothing but black and white static.

Through the child's screams and Chad's overpowering thoughts, I had to make him hear me. "I have to go back!" I shouted, momentarily giving up my fight with the traumatised child. "You shouldn't have taken me back with you, Chadwick. I could've stopped it. I can undo it like I did with my father's death, I can—"

Chad looked over at me with a horrified expression on his face, his fingers pausing in mid-air before running over to me and kneeling in front of me, begging on his knees. "Azalea," he said with a crazed look in his eyes—a look that suggested it was a horrible idea. His trembling hands felt along mine as he pleaded. "You can't go back there. We don't know what he's done. It's more dangerous than ever."

"But I *do* know what he's done," I told him. "He's activated an atomic bomb, worse than the one detonated in Hiroshima. He's trying to get back at his father by re-enacting the biggest move made by his enemies, so please," I begged, trying to will my arms to be gentle as I pulled the child away, "take her off of me. I have to get back there and reverse time. I can fix all of this."

My voice had risen with each syllable, a direct correlation to my anxiety, to the point that the child was now choking back her sobs, no longer screaming in my ear. I had to go. I had to go immediately, not waste time in a hidden, underwater castle.

Chad's face fell and his eyes shifted from a sickening fear to full-blown pity. He leaned in closer to me, placing his head against mine to try and calm me.

"That's impossible, my love," he whispered, and I closed my eyes as I took in the feel of him against me. "No witch or wizard is powerful enough to do that. It cannot be done."

I shook my head, determined to prove him wrong. "You told me I couldn't transport all the way to Japan, but you were wrong," I told him. "You've got to be wrong about this too."

"All right," he said carefully, running his hand along my hair. "Let's say that I am wrong and you get there. The aftereffects of an atomic bomb are too strong for a body to handle. *Even* for a vampire or a witch," he pressed when I opened my mouth to interject. "They tried back in the forties, and there was nothing anyone could do. You could get there, and it could take all your strength away from you."

"Then I'll use a protection potion," I tried.

"That bloody potion doesn't protect you fully from the sun," he said with a pleading tone. "It'll do ruddy shit at protecting you from this."

A shuffling sound filled my ears, and I looked over to see Cristin's arm wrapped around Abigail, stroking her arm up and down comfortingly as both they and Connor looked back at me with the same pitiful faces. It enraged me.

I fought the sobs in my throat with words I knew weren't true. "No. No, no, no, no, no. It *can* be done. It *will* be done. You shouldn't have taken me back here with you." My ramblings swept out like a chilled wind, biting every inch of me with a mad frost, but it didn't stop me. "You should've left me there, and I could've saved them all."

But again Chad shook his head, my mind shattering against his stubbornness. "As much as I believe in you and all the strength and goodness you possess," he said lightly, "it simply can't be undone."

My lungs started to capsize as the truth crashed into me. It sent me plummeting even further into the ground, sinking me as though the will to survive had vanished from every bone.

The girl's legs crumpled with mine. She let out a sharp cry. Chad placed a hand to the girl's cheek, and a soothing green smoke swirled into her.

"It's all right," he cooed sweetly, like a lullaby in her ear. "Everything will be okay," he told her, but they were lies whispered in a language she couldn't understand.

It would not be okay. None of this would ever be okay.

Something in Chad's soothing tone caused the small jorogumo to nod at him, and her grip gradually loosened around my neck until she fell into his arms, lulled to sleep by his spell.

Chad lifted my chin away from her so my eyes were level with his. His nostrils flared as the air went in, and his lips formed a tiny O as his breath exited his mouth, coaching me to follow along—to tune out the screams of the dead that were engraved in my head, to block out the sight of the blinding white light. My chest rose up and down as I stared back into his sturdy green eyes, grounding me to this moment.

"Abigail, Cristin," he said, his eyes never drifting from mine as his lips moved, helping me fight against the fire I held inside. "Take the girl and find a bedroom for her."

They nodded. Cristin lifted the girl's body out of Chad's arms, and he and his wife fled deeper into the castle with pounding hearts. Connor stood panting somewhere next to us, but all I could do was stare into Chad's eyes as he slowly stood from his knees, pulling me up with him. His hands interlaced with mine.

"I have to search the cameras and try to find any signs of life in Japan, in *any* of it," he added, hope nonexistent in his voice. "But I need you to keep breathing. Can you do that for me, my love?"

I nodded into him as I slowed another breath from rushing through my lips. I could do that. I could do that for now. But for how long? I didn't know. The screams kept forcing their way back in, but my breaths hushed them down. I looked out of the castle windows to the ocean around Ypovrýchio Kástro and focused on the movement of the water to guide my breaths.

"All right," I let out.

Chad placed his hand against my cheek and kissed me on my brow. "Good," he breathed into me, and he let go.

He and Connor stared back at the fuzzy screen, and it magically worked its way from station to station, to hopelessly blank station. A hundred black and white storms and nothing more.

Abigail and Cristin came back downstairs, closely followed by Hydie.

"The children are all asleep," Hydie announced, taking in the worn faces around her and the splatters of blood on my skin. "What happened—"

A deafening, high-pitched sound cut her off, bouncing along the walls as the light from the screen grew brighter. Chad yanked his phone out of his pocket, its screen equally as bright, and I realised the sound was coming from both electronics.

Our eyes flew around as the lights throughout the entire hall flickered before clips of the destruction in Japan flashed as a montage: buildings falling, people running for their lives, the pavement cracking, piles of dead bodies, lightning across the pink sky, a mushroom cloud billowing, and the obliterated remains of a country as it sank into the sea.

The air left my lungs as I took in the horrific sight. They had done it. They had destroyed an entire nation without batting an eye.

The screen zoomed in to achieve a better view of the sunken city, and then it flickered again, this time landing on Florence's smirking face.

Blood no longer spilt from his neck. In fact, there was no wound in sight. His clothes were also rid of the blood he had stolen from others, and the look in his eye told me he no longer feared death—but revelled in it. My fingers slid towards my palms against the marble floor, eager to grip onto reality, but in truth, Florence was very real, and that thought frightened me even more.

My eyes flashed from Chad, to Connor, to everyone to see if it was just my nightmare to behold, but all of their faces were illuminated in the screen's light, and beneath that, they had all gone ghostly pale. Chad's phone mirrored the large screen—Florence's shining eyes in their bright red hue, and the vampire's smile. My attention went back to the telly as I watched in disbelief. Florence's lips parted, and his familiar smug voice erupted out.

"Now that I've got your attention…" he said, his voice lingering in a joke no one would ever condone. His satisfied smile clung to his lips, and flashes of his vulgarity blinded me before his next words broke the traumatic spell he always held over me. "By now you've all seen the power I possess, as it is being broadcasted to every screen in the world. And although I've done much more than this, I must say, this is my greatest accomplishment *yet*."

A chill ran up my spine from the way he said, "yet", as though there was so much more in store.

"I've destroyed an entire country to get your attention," he continued, speaking loudly out to the world, though it felt like he was speaking directly to me, "so I don't think I'll have to elaborate when I say I'll do much worse if you don't listen closely."

He leaned in towards the camera, and instinctively, I leaned back. I could smell his breath—it haunted me as though he were in the very same room—but he wasn't. He was somewhere far away, threatening the world as he had threatened me so many times.

"Now this may come as a shock to all of you, but I am what most refer to as a vampire," he said, pausing sadistically for a dramatic effect.

"And many of you will choose not to believe this, but my fellow creatures and I are very determined to make you believe in every single one of us: vampires, witches, and so much more. We exist, and we will no longer stay hidden behind your fears and urges to destroy those whom you don't understand."

I couldn't tear my gaze off him. I couldn't believe this was happening before my very eyes, or even in my lifetime. The thought of mortals knowing about us was unspeakable. Someone's teeth chattered in the room, hearts pounded, and I could smell the fear seeping out of their pores, but I couldn't look away from Florence's red eyes.

"I think it's time to come clean about something else too. As luck would have it, I'm responsible for **KILLING** the daughter of the Prime Minister of Britain," he went on. "In my defence, I didn't know who she was when I **KILLED** the whore, but thankfully, I've had the most scrumptious witch by my side, helping me this whole time."

A shimmer of pink appeared beside him along with none other than my face.

I couldn't move an inch. I was paralyzed. The world was watching—witches and mortals alike were seeing my face and associating me with the **MURDERER**.

"You see, with the help of this little lady, I destroyed an entire chain of islands, and I will not hesitate to destroy each and every person who tries to fight against us, because creatures like us will soon rule over the lesser humans. We cannot be stopped. Isn't that right, my Azalea?"

I could not think. They were framing me. My heart froze solid as he said my name—as he lied to the world about who she was—as he used me to break the trust I was beginning to form with the Casters.

The woman gave a bright, toothy smile in return as she trailed a finger from one of Florence's shoulders to the other. He closed his eyes, delighting in the feel of it, before staring intently into my soul.

"You'll be hearing from us very soon," he said in a hushed voice, before the image of the two of them was replaced with the black and white storm and ear-piercing static.

There were no words to describe what they had done—not evil, not **MURDER**, not massacre. Nothing was enough.

And although there was no death painful enough or worthy of Florence, something snapped inside of me. I was no longer afraid. I wouldn't hesitate to slit Florence apart piece by piece. I wasn't afraid to place him in the ground, or light him up alive, or any of it. I was going to kill Florence, or I was going to die trying.

Shakes of fury rattled my body. I blinked at the fuzzy screen and suddenly I was back on the floor with Chad in front of me. He was down on his knees, putting his soothing hands on either side of my face. His magic raced to calm me, placing a foreign peace within my head as his strange, panicked words clashed against the smoothness of his magic.

"Listen to me, Azalea," he said with wide eyes, staring into me as if I were the only person in the room. "We will fix this, I promise you. It's all part of our list. We've *got* this. You saved your sister, you saved the children, and now it's time to kill that son of a bitch," he told me fiercely as his magical hands gripped onto my hair and pulled my forehead against his. "I'll find proof that the witch on the screen wasn't you, and we'll rally against him. I just need you to keep fighting. I can't do this without you, my love. You are stronger than him. You're stronger than you've ever given yourself credit for, and you *can* do this," he said so intensely that I believed him. He placed a powerful kiss on my lips that sent a rush to my numb heart, but as he leaned away from me, his green gift of serenity started to falter until his skin left mine, and the calm was all but a faint memory.

Chad's chest rose up and down fervently as he stood up, his eyes still focused on me as though praying I wouldn't break, but all the worries, pain, and sorrow came flooding back to me at once. I felt the crack deepen, elongating and slithering through me, only stopping when it pierced its way towards my icy heart. His eyes tore away from mine to address everyone else in the room, but as he did, the crack knocked against my heart, urging it to let in. I tightened my core to try and push it away. I couldn't afford to break right now—to let Florence shatter me. I couldn't let him win.

"I'll issue a royal mandate to forbid any Caster from leaving their home. Pray that the Night Crawlers and any other beings the mortals once deemed mythical follow suit. If everyone lays low while my soldiers and I force Florence and his group to stay out of the limelight, then we stand a chance at the mortals thinking the vampire and witch charade is all just a cruel hoax to deepen the loss of Japan."

Connor's nostrils flared as the heat from his fear washed over him, but he gave a brave nod.

"The Loxley Coven wouldn't have heard the news yet," Abigail said, her voice trembling through the terror-filled hall.

"I'll tell them," Chad announced. "I'll bring Charity and Leo here to look after the young jorogumo, but we have to be careful with who we trust. I'll bring the rest of the coven to another castle of mine, and then I must meet with my aunts to sort out the rest."

Abigail and Cristin clung tighter to one another as they nodded back at him. Hydie wiped away the tears that had fallen down her smooth cheeks.

"And Azalea," Chad said, turning back to me so suddenly that chills spread over my entire body. The sound of his anxious heart pounded against my eardrums as it slammed into his rib cage so violently that I thought it would break through. His breath entered his lungs in rattles, and then he said, "No one is to leave this castle—not to feed, not to hunt, not to do anything," he instructed firmly before his brows furrowed in concentration. "No one," he stressed. "Especially not you."

It was his final plea, in a voice so soft it sounded broken as panic radiated through it. His nostrils flared as his eyes begged me to listen. The wind from his green smoke pushed me backwards before it stole him away.

Shortly after, he arrived with Charity and Leo but then disappeared for the entirety of the night.

And I wept through the pain that pierced my seizing chest as the deaths of an entire country weighed down on me—the crack spreading its way around the entire perimeter of my heart, waiting for the moment it would burst.

Jade Austin

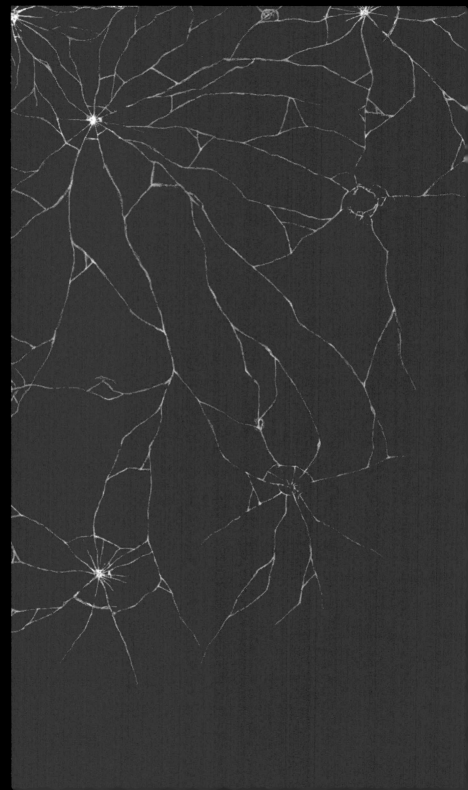

Chapter 40: Breaking Slowly

The next day, I woke to an empty bed, a fearful pull tugging me from my nightmare of red eyes and ominous, billowing clouds. My fingers felt along the walls, grounding myself to the present as the bumpy texture tickled my skin until the pull led me to her. When her brown eyes met mine, the small jorogumo ran towards me, her eight dark brown and hairy legs scurrying closer as she rushed to hug me. But even as I held her tight to me, running my hand along her silky black hair, the world was hushed with a dark, gloomy veil. Death hung over us all, obstructing our hearing, destroying our hope, and silencing our prayers.

I knelt down to her, forcing a brave smile on my face as I spoke, wishing to soothe her trembling legs with my voice as Chad had. "I want to introduce you to someone special. Someone like you."

She frowned at me through the haze we both felt but let me take her hand so I could lead her down the corridors. Charity's nervous fidgeting and pacing steps sounded from inside the room, and Leo answered the door.

I watched as Charity's worried brow smoothed, and her arms fell to her sides. She took in a breath as though it were the first time she had been graced with fresh air in a long time, and she walked over to the little girl, sitting on her human knees to humble herself.

"Namae ha nan desuka?" Charity asked the girl softly.

The girl clutched onto me tighter, not muttering a word.

"Perhaps if you showed her," Leo whispered, the side of his face pressed against the edge of the door as he leaned into it, watching with saddened patience.

Charity nodded and then, taking a deep breath, the bottom half of her body slowly changed forms, twisting and turning until she became the most mesmerising sight. Her legs had multiplied, lengthening and bending into a crouch. The skirts of her dark dress morphed into a textured, fur-like hair that coated her eight legs, and she bowed her head to the tiny girl, who loosened her grip around me.

The little spider girl looked up at me with fascination laced into her sunken eyes, and I nodded at her encouragingly.

"Kana," the girl said back to Charity, and the larger jorogumo breathed out a happy sigh.

"Kana," Charity repeated quietly. "What a beautiful name."

Over the course of the next few weeks, we stayed, hibernating and hiding in the underwater escape. I watched as Charity spun web after web, flinging it down to her spidery legs and casting webs across the walls to try and entice Kana. I watched as Leo practised his Japanese to help her feel a sense of home, and I marvelled at Noel and Leon as they tried to ease her into playing with them. But try as they might, Kana stayed silent in the underwater castle. I knew it was going to be a long time before anyone would be able to coax her from her shell. She was lost, empty, and void of everything she had ever known. Her eyes gave little life, hope, or insight into her mind as she watched them attempt to mend her aching heart, but I was happy for their efforts, as my heart, too, sat shipwrecked at the bottom of the ocean.

When Kana finally showed silent signs of accepting her new life—relaxed shoulders and the hint of a smile—I retreated into my own shell. My temporary bedroom was the only sight I could bear to see. The bomb had destroyed my urgency to fight, and a deep depression weighed me down, pressing me into the bed.

On day two of my confinement, Chad slept next to me for six hours, holding me tightly until he had to leave again. I hardly got any sleep as I memorised the pattern of his troubled breaths, and then when he left, sleep took me only for the nightmares to sweep in.

On the third day, I locked the bedroom door and didn't make a single peep when people came by to check on me. I didn't want to talk. I didn't want to tell them how I felt—how heavily the guilt weighed down on me. Their breaths would be wasted trying to convince me it wasn't all my fault.

By day five, I had nearly become one with the ocean. I watched for hours as the translucent blue lights danced across the floors, while doing nothing else but wallowing in self-doubt. I couldn't undo any of it. I couldn't undo it, or fix it, or wish it all away. All I could do was try to block it out.

On day eight, I paced back and forth across the blue floors, pounding on the thick glass that led out to the ocean, screaming and crying about how unfair the world was. But not even my strengths as a vampire or powers as a witch could break down the wards that kept us in the underwater prison. And nothing could break down the depression that consumed my mind.

In the middle of day ten, Chad slept next to me for the shortest time yet—two hours before he left and his side of the bed went cold again.

And by day fourteen I was hollow.

Empty.

Hydie knocked on the door for the third time that day, but I could tell by the breaths on the other side that she wasn't alone.

"Azalea," she said softly, her hair brushing up against the door as I sat on the opposite side. I was my own barricade. I didn't need useless furniture to feel protected. "Please come out," she pleaded. "You need to at least drink something," she tried, but the usual silence greeted her in my wake.

I heard her steps retreat slightly, then I jumped as heavy fists pounded against the door along with Connor's growl.

"Azalea," he said, his voice hammering as powerfully as his fists. "Come out right this instant," he demanded, but I simply chewed my cheek in response. I couldn't bear to face them.

There was a rumble and the tearing of fabrics as he shifted into his werewolf form. Hydie gave a stifled yip as the heavy weight of his body came crashing against the door again and again to try and break it down. I stood up, detesting the feel of the door as it shook against me, and purple magic flowed out of my hands and along the entire length of the wall, smothering the noise—the perfect soundproof barrier. I crawled into the bed, knowing the nightmares would eat me alive once I closed my eyes, but part of me didn't care. At least in my dreams I could feel *something*. Anything was better than this.

I didn't know how long Connor or Hydie stayed outside my door, and it didn't matter as long as I couldn't hear them call for me.

I forced my eyes to stay open, but the nightmares no longer waited for my slumber. They ran freely through my mind, casting images of the innocent people as they scurried helplessly through the streets of Japan, terrified as we deserted them. Soon those images faded and were replaced with Florence's red eyes, and then Chad's lifeless body as his blood trailed down my chin.

I wasn't sure how much time had passed before Chad appeared near our temporary bed. A questioning look played across his face as he took in the purple seal along the wall, but I shrugged at him before turning away. He didn't need to worry about my sorrows. He didn't need to know my fears. He didn't need to know the anger that sometimes crept through me at the thought that he had taken me away from the falling city and convinced me I wasn't strong enough to go back and save them all. No. He had far too much on his plate already.

My voice whispered in my mind, reminding me for the hundredth time that day of the words the other Azalea had mentioned—the information she claimed to have about Chad—information I didn't hold. They were words she said to try and tempt me, to lure me to the mirrors hidden in the attic of Castwell Castle, no doubt so she could break me. But little did she know that I would break before finding her again in that tallest tower, and in a far worse way.

I closed my eyes, hoping to be away from Chad as I so often was, but he rounded the bed and knelt before me. His fingers gently traced over mine, lulling me off to the sleep I didn't truly want, but a question slipped off his tongue, spreading chills through my body.

"You know there's nothing we could've done, right?" he asked, but the question that was meant to comfort me broke me down further.

Yes. There *was* something I could've done.

"You would've killed yourself trying to reverse time on such a grand scale," he told me, but I shook my head as a sob forced its way out of me.

"He told me if I went with him, he wouldn't out our existence to the world," I admitted, forcing the words out of my clenched throat. "He promised that if I came along he would spare all their lives."

Chad's breath snagged on its way out, and I could feel his muscles tighten with the news, but it only lasted a brief second before he placed himself on the bed beside me. His warm arms wrapped around me, and he nuzzled his head against my neck.

"Florence is a liar, Azalea," he whispered into my ear. "He'll say anything to get a hold of you, but you must fight, my love."

I nodded into him out of habit, but I didn't know if my heart was capable of fighting anymore.

He lay on the bed next to me, humming a song as he stroked my arm. "I'm so sorry I've been away, but I think something about our presence out there is keeping Florence and his army hidden away. He's been silent, but I can't tell if it's a blessing or a curse," he told me, and shivers wracked through me as I thought of the worst. It was definitely a curse.

"But I've been thinking a lot about Kana," he started again, "and the way she was clinging onto you after the bomb went off. I thought it might help to erase her memories so she wouldn't have to face so much pain, but it's not fair to decide that for her, or for anyone. It got me thinking about our row at the pub, or—after the pub at least." He pulled back to look at me, and I frowned as I waited for his explanation.

His body straightened, pulling back from mine so he could reach into his pocket. A soft thump sounded as he sat something onto the bed. His phone.

"Text him," he said, and I closed my eyes to fight away the vision of Wyatt's hazel ones. "Text him, or call him, or go see him," Chad insisted gently. "You were right. I have no idea what it's like to live without a memory, and it isn't right for me to keep you from finding out more about yourself," he decided. "Perhaps it could cheer you up a bit to find out who you are."

I turned away from him, a look of indifference masked across my face, but internally I was screaming. I didn't need his permission to phone Wyatt, and the thought that Chad believed he was the only thing stopping me from doing so infuriated me. But how could I think about my past when all those people would never see a future?

Right now, I didn't want answers to my past. I wanted a way to undo all the deaths, and my stubborn mind wouldn't let it go. I wanted answers as to whether or not producing a time reversal that grand was possible. If Lili could do it with her extraordinary powers that Chad's aunts boasted about—if she was capable—wouldn't she already have done it?

The world was an abyss, dark, hollow, cold. And as I struggled to wrap my mind around the attack for the thousandth time, my brain seemed to shut down, and I was swallowed by the hollowness. The sight of Chad's blood on my lips pierced through me once more, and I remembered the plan we had begun to lay out, right before this whole mess erupted.

"Just stay safe," I reminded him, a heavy breath falling from my lips. "You have to make sure your witch protects you."

I heard the tiny sound of his eyes shutting, and he pulled me into another embrace, now cradling me from behind. "Please don't call her that," he said sadly. "She's not mine, nor do I ever want her to be."

I didn't so much as shrug in response. I had no energy to debate the matter. As long as she kept him safe from me or whoever was destined to murder him.

Another fortnight passed within the blink of an eye, yet simultaneously dragged on treacherously slow. The prickles that had numbed my mind and body slowly transformed into a vengeful urge to know more—to know why—*how* they had done it, and what hideous event was next.

Chad's elongated absences stung, and loneliness swallowed me whole. Visions of the mortals rioting up in the world above were my company. The idea to help Chad with whatever he faced on land transpired but diminished time and time again. There was simply no energy to save a world that hated me—one who thought I was the woman on the screen that had killed those innocent people. Our best chance was for me to stay hidden deeper than I had been before.

A war within me clouded my judgement, and the idea of finding the answers I longed for consumed my conflicted mind. The battle always travelled down the same path, winding its way into a circle before arriving at the same location time and time again. The path was blurred. We were all in uncharted territory, not knowing what to do next, yet through the fog, I could hear her voice—my own voice—whispering the one possible source of answers.

A pull tugged at me, speaking straight to my soul. A song pushed at my feet, yanked at my arms, and screamed against my eardrums. It called to me, begging me to eat the forbidden fruit and visit the attic to talk to the woman with my face. I longed to reach into those mirrors—to demand answers. But what lies would she spew? What half-truths or secrets would she use as kryptonite?

Those questions didn't act as roadblocks, but stepping stones. My anxiety took hold of my throat, choking me until I forced out the cloud of purple smoke and transported myself all the way to Castwell Castle, right outside the door to the dark, mysterious attic and its hall of mirrors.

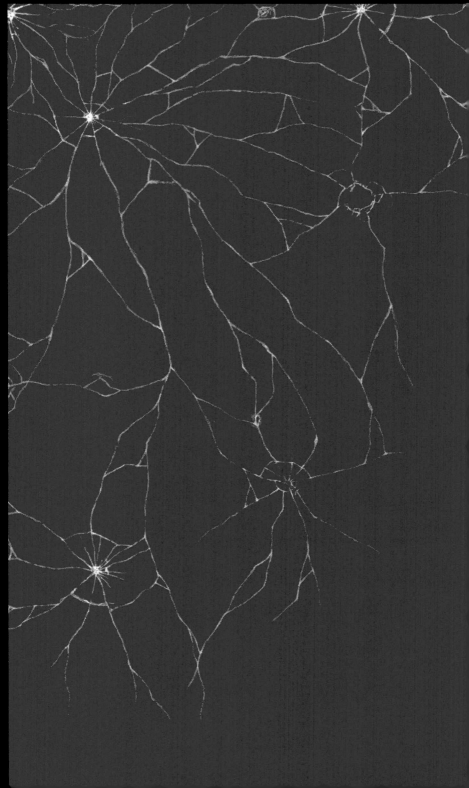

Chapter 41: Information On Your King

I fought the urge to turn back, to transport straight into my temporary bed, to stick to my promise of staying underwater. Instead, I reached for the circular latch—yet it moved on its own. The door screeched open slowly as though it had been waiting for me to arrive. Oh, how predictable I had become.

The mirrors drew me in, and I gasped when I caught sight of my reflection. Not because it was *her,* but because I hardly recognised myself. My face was gaunt from weeks without blood. Dark shadows circled my red, thirsty eyes, and my skin was so pale it looked as though I were the walking dead.

"Over here," a familiar voice whispered.

I turned around with incredible speed to examine the mirror behind me, but this time, the reflection was no longer under my control.

A satisfied grin curled her lips as her eyes dropped down, studying my shrunken curves, my pale skin, the cheeks that once looked healthy with a golden-brown colour but were now dulled with grey. Her glowing skin and twinkling eyes only further confirmed the transformation my body had gone through.

"Fancy seeing you here, although I am surprised it took you so long," she cooed, and I cringed at how light her tone was. I knew the dark things she was capable of. "You look dreadful," she said, a cheerful hop in her words, "so either war is not your strong suit, or you've just been let in on the secret. Which one is it?"

I shook my head, refusing to fall for her trickery. There was only one reason I was here, and it was not for the information she told me I'd find by visiting her. "I'm not here for your game," I told her firmly. "I'm here for different information."

"Not here for my game?" she asked with an exaggerated gasp, her hand flying to her chest. "Azalea, the game is only just beginning. It would ruin all the fun to stop now."

Fun.

How could she describe the event as fun? She was soulless.

I closed my eyes and tried to push away her words, but it was no use. She was always in my mind, dancing her way around, manipulating me.

"Tell me why you blew up an entire country," I demanded fiercely, reopening my red eyes. "Why did you take all those lives?"

"To make a statement," she let out. Her voice was raised, but the happiness behind it seemed to falter. It was as though she was reciting lines she had heard over and over again. "To show the world how much power we possess, and tell them that we aren't willing to stay hidden anymore. That it's our time to rule."

"Then why have you stayed quiet in the weeks after?" I asked.

"We're steeping the tea, brewing the fear. Pretty soon the mortals won't know what to do with themselves. They'll come out of their holes, and it'll be our time to strike again. They'll make a nice collection for the vampires. Don't you think? Fresh blood always on tap?" she asked, and my stomach fell at the thought of more human slaves.

They had to outdo everyone, didn't they? The Downy Coven, the entire Second World War...

"Now," she started up again, "I'm dying to hear if you know the information your king has been hiding from you." I gave her a blank stare, and she gasped, fake shock radiating off of her like a foul stench. "Don't tell me King Chadwick still hasn't told you."

Every part of me seized up. It was bait. Meaningless bait I shouldn't fall for, but I was tempted. It slowly drew me in like a piper's song until she could see it in my eyes. I wanted it. I needed more.

"Told me what?" I spat out between gritted teeth, hating every bit of my lack of self-control.

"All the little things he's been up to these past few months while he's been away," she hissed, the light sparking behind her eyes once more.

"He's been working to catch Florence," I growled.

"Ah, yes, that and... other things," she hinted. "Things that would put you in worse shape than you already are, if you knew. If that's even possible," she said, looking me up and down as though I were complete rubbish.

Her eyes flicked over to some point beyond her shoulder, a smile creeping on her face. *Florence.* He was close. Too close but not quite there. "Ah, it seems we're out of time. If only there were a hall of mirrors we could meet at, share our dirty little secrets over a glass of wine. But maybe you're bigger than that. Perhaps you're so confident in your relationship that you're strong enough to ask him yourself." She gave a shrill laugh that made me want to throttle her. "Then again, we both know you're not."

My body trembled as I spewed out words Chad had spoken before. "Anything he hasn't told me is for good reason." Words I was so unsure of and longed to be true. "I trust him with my life."

"And what about your heart? Do you fully trust him with that?"

The intoxicating wink she gave next forced acid up my throat.

"Whatever you need to tell yourself, darling," she said with a humour only she could feel. "Well, I must run, but since you're so curious, I suppose I can leave you with a quick image. They do say a photo's worth a thousand words. Perhaps a short clip will help you realise your true path in life."

She disappeared without another word, only to be replaced by something much more horrifying. My knees buckled as I took it in, my shoulders tensing. Every mirror turned to a scene of Chad standing in a room with Lili. There was an intense look in both their eyes, and suddenly Mrs Prophecy was leaping towards him, attaching her lips to his. Her arms wrapped around him and a knife stabbed into my heart. He didn't back away. He didn't peel the leech from his lips. Instead, after a painfully brief moment of shock, he leaned into her, deepening their kiss. His hand caressed her arm, and the dagger twisted in my heart.

I squeezed my eyes shut and covered my ears to block out their sounds, but the thousands of images of them snogging were ingrained into my skull. He was kissing her. He was kissing her how he had kissed me thousands of times, before Wyatt or Japan or any of it, and she was enjoying it. I was going to be sick. I was going to die right in that room if I didn't get out of there.

I opened my eyes and twirled around in a circle, but I was surrounded by their faces. He pushed his lips further against hers, and then the vision started over on a loop with her diving back into him, and him letting her.

The door to the attic was nowhere in sight. Shivers racked through me, and my body shook from fear. I was trapped. There was no way out. My eyes shut again, but nothing I did seemed to void out the scene. The image had a mind of its own and a voice that screamed out at me. So I screamed back. I screamed so loud that the glass of the thousand mirrors shattered—right along with my heart.

Jade Austin

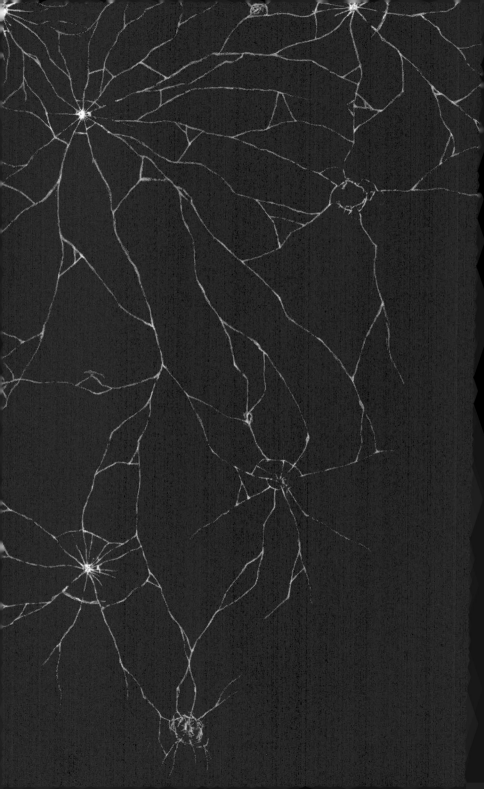

Chapter 42: The Interrogation

G lass rained down on me, scraping against my skin, tearing it apart as my heart crumbled to nothing.

This couldn't be real. This had to be a trick. I wouldn't believe it until I heard from him, but the seconds ticked by like a bomb, and the more I stood there, dripping in blood, the more I couldn't convince myself it was a lie.

Adrenaline crashed into me, and I took hold of it tightly, transporting to our bedroom within Castwell Castle. My body was so weak from transporting and not drinking, but it worked hard to push out the shards of glass that pierced into my skin. Piece by piece, they clattered to the ground of our bedroom, crunching as I stepped onto them.

I ran down the stairs and through twists and turns and corridors until the muscle memory alone led me to the potions room. My nose pulled me the rest of the way to the potion I needed, and I ladled spoonful after tiny, pathetic spoonful of Chad's blood into a large wine glass before tossing the ladle aside and drinking deeply from the cup.

The last of the blood dripped onto my dress, and I wondered what the hell I was going to do next. I couldn't track him down at his aunts' castle looking like this. I couldn't wait for him to come back to Ypovrýchio Kástro for all my friends to hear me self-combust through my screams. No. I'd wait for him to find me here so we could have a nice, proper conversation about whatever the fuck it was that I just saw.

Taking one last serving of the blood duplication potion with me, I held on firmly to the wine glass and transported to our bedroom. The bed we had laid in so many times together was cold from the weeks we had slept hidden at the castle under the sea. It was as empty as my heart. But over the course of not thirty minutes, the void filled with fury and bubbled over the second he popped into our bedroom amongst a cloud of green smoke.

Chad's face was racked with worry as he looked towards the empty bed and the shards of bloodied mirror on the floor. Then he threw his eyes around the room to try and find me, but my body was strewn across the chaise, lounging in a half sitting, half lying position as I watched his green eyes finally land on me. I swirled my finger around the blood within my glass, casting a warming charm on it, but the sight of him there made the blood begin to boil. Placing my finger into my mouth to lick it clean, I watched as his face moulded into the relief of finding me, morph into surprise as his eyes shifted up to mine, and then settle on fear as he took in my expression.

Good, I thought as a satisfying twinge of pleasure overtook me. Fear was exactly what he should feel.

My mouth struggled to hide a cruel smile as my eyebrow arched upwards.

"What?" I asked, feigning innocence. "*Should* you be frightened? Ready to admit just what it is that you've done?"

His eyes flashed over to the glass I was holding and his throat bobbed. Slowly, he moved his feet towards me as though I were a snake that could dig my venom into him if he moved too quickly, but he was wrong. I was much worse.

"If you're mad at me, I don't think drinking my blood is the right course of action," he suggested, attempting a soothing voice. But I threw every ounce of ire I felt towards him with my eyes, and he halted his advance. What a smart man.

"It was either the blood duplication potion or straight from your neck," I said testily.

"That's not funny," he warned, tilting his head, years of hard labour carved into his features.

"Ah," I replied quite seriously, "but it wasn't intended to be."

"And do you 'intend' to tell me what I did to upset you?" he asked, folding his arms—an unwarranted defence that infuriated me even more.

"No," I spat back firmly, setting my glass down on the floor before my violent grip could crush it. I stood up to try and get level with him, yet he still towered over me, even from steps away. But I held strong. "I want *you* to tell me."

He ran his fingers through his hair, his face coated with even more exhaustion than usual, and his eyes widened in disbelief. "I just showed up at Ypovrýchio Kástro to find an empty bed, completely freaked out that something had happened to you, and now that I've found you alive and well and *not* torn to shreds by Florence, you expect me to randomly guess what it is I did wrong this time?" he snapped.

But I had no room in my bleeding heart to feel guilt for scaring him, so I took a threatening step towards him and growled, "If you have to 'guess' what it is that I'm so livid about, perhaps now is a brilliant time to open up and admit all of your dirty little secrets—get them all out at once."

"Dirty little secrets?" he asked, gawking at me as though I had gone mad, but he didn't know the half of it. I was past mad, or sad. I was devastated.

"Yes, *Chadwick*, and if I were you, I'd hurry, because taking a bite out of that pulsing neck of yours is becoming more and more appealing."

"Azalea," he pleaded, pain and pure stress flooding out, "I don't have the time or energy for this game. Please, just tell me what I did right this instant, or I'll—"

"Or you'll what?" I countered. "Go back to her and do it again?"

It was as if I had stolen his breath. He puffed out any air he would have used on a retort, and part of my consciousness drifted into his like a cloud of invisible smoke.

The kiss.

His mind had unlocked itself, whether from the shock of such an accurate accusation or something else, but it slapped into place like the unwanted truth it was.

Tears pricked my eyes, but I tilted my head up stubbornly and swallowed the acid that had crept up my throat. "That's exactly it," I told him.

He froze at the realisation of his mistake, but then grimaced at my own obvious anguish.

"Azalea, I was going to—" he started.

"You were *not* going to tell me," I snapped back at him, feeling exactly what he was going to say before he could say it—before he could *lie*. "I can feel the lie behind your words. I can *feel* it, Chadwick. If I hadn't found out on my own, you would've taken those words with you to your grave. Hell!" I exclaimed, almost laughing at the irony of it all. "You still haven't said it. Not out loud anyway. So say it," I dared, stalking closer to him and shoving my finger into his chest. "Say it and let me hear it from you."

As I went to shove my finger into him a second time, a stream of magic shot out at him. A life's worth of training kicked in as he deflected it, casting a small shield as protection. With his other hand, he grabbed my wrist.

"It happened," he let out softly, his volume hovering below a whisper, his tongue doused in regret. "But she's the one who kissed me."

"Don't. You. Dare." I was shaking. My voice quivered, giving away the weak coward that hid behind my firm, fiery stance. "I saw it. I saw your hands all over her, and I don't give a shit who 'started' it. You went all in."

With each syllable came a jab at his shield. The green shimmered in the light, sparking against the immense weight that my single finger put upon it. His eyes were a pool of sadness, but where my emotions gave my magic strength, his gave him a weakness.

I could push past it, I could blast right through his shield, and probably would if I didn't get away from him. Or worse, I could explode him like I had done to my father, blast him into a million bloody, twitching pieces. And who knew if I would be able to replicate the time bubble again? I fought to restrain my strength the best I could, but I couldn't help wanting to hurt him. I was furious, utterly livid, and I was broken.

"Azalea," he breathed out, using most of his strength against my wrath. "I don't know how you found out, but—"

"*That's* what you're worried about right now?" I asked furiously. "*How* I found out. Well, I'll tell you what. That should be the least of your worries right now because—"

"Fine!" he interrupted desperately before I could spew out my threats. "But it was a mistake and it—"

"Cannot be undone," I finished for him, pushing against his shield. "And don't tell me that you told me and then got my permission to produce a time bubble to make me forget, because that's horse shit."

Chad shook his head grimly, his lips shut as no clever evasions came to the surface.

The rest of my hand itched to join in against his shield. Purple cracks sprouted along the green dome, spreading like wildfire, and fear encroached his eyes. I had to stop. I pushed off of him and crossed my arms, clasping my hands into tight fists, struggling to keep in my magic.

"It happened," I huffed out, "and you didn't tell me, and that's really fucked up."

I needed to leave. I could feel my purple powers swirling inside me, close to forcing their way out. I found out the truth. As much as I had wanted it to be a horrid trick, a lie, it was the truth, and I couldn't handle it. If I stayed, I was going to hurt him, reversible or not.

He tried to step towards me, but I gritted my teeth and gave him a look that strongly advised against it, and he hesitated.

"At least let me explain," he tried, but I wanted to rip off his head. I could feel my eyes turn back to red, regardless of all the blood I had just drank, and my chest rose with anger and fell with panic.

430

"No," I said defiantly. "I think that's all the listening I can manage for today."

And I disappeared.

I landed next to the lake on the grounds, surrounded by the cloud of my purple smoke, the cold air biting me. But Chadwick was on my tail. He was next to me in an instant, and I backed away from him as sparks of panic flew from my hands, which were thankfully cast down at the ground.

"How did you do that?" I asked frantically, trying to force my magic down. "How'd you find me so quickly?" Was I truly that predictable? He couldn't just follow me when I transported. Yet apparently he could.

He let out a careful breath, seemingly weighing the odds of angering me further. "It's called tailing," he said. "I can hold on to part of the magic you leave behind and use my own to get pulled with you. It's how I was able to follow you to Japan. Now let me explain what happened—"

"I don't want you to explain," I screamed out as jets of my magic blasted into the ground, threatening to rise towards him. "I want to be on my own. Away from you."

He looked down at the holes my magic had made in the ground. I didn't want to admit that leaving was for his own good. I just wanted him to leave me be, but he wasn't listening.

"It was before us," he spat out before I could vanish again, but it didn't make sense.

"You didn't know her before you met me," I called out, screaming over the buzz of electricity that was streaming out of me.

"I know! I know," he said quickly, closing his eyes and furrowing his brows as he gripped the ridge of his nose. "What I mean to say is it was before we were officially together."

"When exactly?" I countered, clutching my fists shut again, but nothing was helping. "Because if I remember correctly, you met her in your month away with your aunts, *after* our first kiss, right before—"

"The ball," he breathed out so low I wouldn't have been able to hear him if I didn't have my superb hearing.

"Yes," I breathed back, "when we—"

My stomach dropped. That night. I remembered it so well. The night I had wanted to leave after his aunts put a frog in my throat and embarrassed me in front of all the Casters there. The night he had followed me, convinced me I was all he wanted, all he needed. He didn't need some girl in a prophecy who was meant to be with him. And that same night, I had given in. I had let him. We had...

My powers finally eased down and I reined them into my sad fists. "So let me get this straight," I started again, refusing to let my feet advance towards him, regardless of how furious I was. "You kissed me—

refused any of my attempts to stay away from you in order to keep you safe from Florence, but you insisted we stay 'at least' friends so that you can run off and snog the girl you convinced me was part of an unfulfillable prophecy? You looked me in the eyes the night we got together and told me she didn't exist, that she was a myth, all while knowing you had just gone and snogged her? And then you turn around and shag me at your ball? How long after? Weeks? Days? Hours after seeing her? You *knew* she existed, all while you had already kissed her and clearly had some connection with her!" I screamed.

I didn't know if I was asking him or telling him at that point. I was just confused and torn.

"You told me you didn't want to be with me," he said softly, as though I might explode if he mentioned it too loudly, but his words bit me.

"Of course I said that. It was to save your life—to save both of us from getting hurt and because we both knew you were meant to be with someone else. And it turns out you had run off with her—snogged her and clearly enjoyed it. So why come back to me? Why try to win me over if you already had her? Was it too easy for you? Was I the tougher one to win so you went for me instead? This is bullocks. That's what it is," I decided. I couldn't take it anymore. My magic was going to explode within me. "Stay," I told him firmly, and I transported to the forest right outside of Loxley Lair.

But of course he didn't listen. He tailed me again, immediately going in to explain.

"You didn't want me," he said, misery ringing through his voice, but it was just another bite. "I was trying to get over you and Lili—"

"Don't you dare say her name," I snapped, and I could feel my fangs elongate, my eyes turn redder. He was too fucking close. My chest wouldn't stop pounding and neither would his. I could almost taste his blood as it teased me among my heartache. He needed to stay away or I was going to do something I'd regret for the rest of my morbid, eternal life.

I transported to the alleyway by the library, the alleyway by the pub, to the wood outside Downy Lair, to anywhere I could think to throw him off, but he kept following, spitting out words I could only hear fragments of. Then without thinking, I landed in the gardens outside his aunts' castle, and he was quick to frown when we got there. Not that he had any right to frown.

"Look, I don't know if she's in here," I told him sharply, my eyes burrowing their way into his as I stepped towards him with heat in every step, "and I don't really want to know, but perhaps you should try to 'get over' me with her again." His words, not mine.

And then I ran. I ran fast and far using the other part of me, the part without a single trace of magic for him to track.

I wanted to mean it, I did. I wanted him to go explore whatever side of him was so drawn to her, thanks to fate or that damn prophecy, but as soon as I was away from him it all truly began to sink in.

I fell down to the ground of some unknown forest, completely lost in more than one sense. We had gotten past the idea of the prophecy coming in between us, or at least I thought we had, but now... I couldn't unsee them. It was vastly different from him seeing Florence and me kissing. He hadn't been under a spell. He had kissed her of his own free will.

Rain began to fall, reminding me of how cold and cruel the world could be. There was no love within it, no warmth, no happiness—only heartache, frost, and death.

Abigail's words seemed to pound through my head, reminding me I always had a home at Loxley Lair, but right now she was wrong. I couldn't go to the lair, or Ypovrýchio Kástro, not the library, the pub, our bedroom, or anywhere else. There was nowhere I could go where Chad wouldn't find me. No one I could turn to without him showing up moments later, but I couldn't risk it. Not for my heart. Not for his own safety. Not for the war.

I had felt this heartache before. Felt this low, this empty in the pouring rain. But deep within me, this familiar feeling triggered something, and as I got back to my feet, they led to a place I somehow knew I'd been before. Through the woods, through the cities, hiding from the glow of the moon and city lights and losing myself in the shadows. I vanished my blood from my dress, and when I finally arrived some thirty minutes later, I knew precisely whose door it was before my knuckles rapped against it. Before footsteps approached from the other side. Before it creaked open and I stared into his hazel eyes, bright and surprised, but very happy to see me.

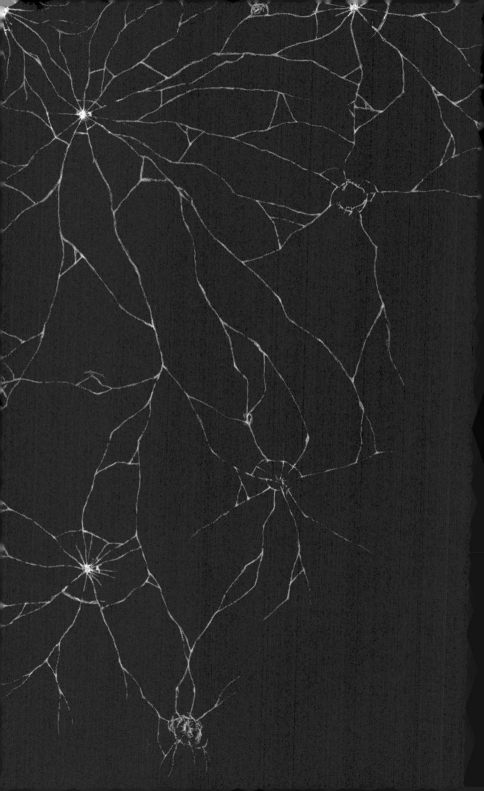

Chapter 43: I Could Give In

Warm air burst out of the flat, enveloping my drenched skin and dress as Wyatt stared back at me, blinking the sleep out of his eyes as though he was nearly sure I was a dream. "Azalea," he breathed out, the smell of amber liquid and sleep floating off his breath. "What are you—You're soaking. Are you hurt? How did you—" But his mind overcame the lingering sleep, and his eyes grew wide as he realised just who I was. "You were on the news—"

"That wasn't me," I told him quickly, shaking my head furiously. "I know how it must look, I do. But I'm being framed. This woman with my face has been haunting my dreams. We heard what was happening in Japan, and went to help, but it turns out the woman is real. She's like a twin I didn't know I had, or something, but all I know is that I didn't kill those people. It was all her and that man, Florence."

Wyatt let out a long breath as his eyes shifted back and forth between mine, eager to catch up to it all. After a slow blink and a forced swallow, he nodded at me, and I let out my own breath of relief. He believed me. If that didn't speak to my character of whoever I was before, then I didn't know what would. How much did he know of who I was—who I truly was besides a witch? He was ready to believe anything I said. He trusted I was a witch, he had hardly second guessed that I had lost my memory, and now this.

"Can I stay here for a bit?" I tried quickly, falsifying a smile across my lips, one I hoped would keep my bloody tears at bay. Tears that would frighten him and reveal the other part of me that I wasn't ready for him to know, especially with how Florence had portrayed all vampires. My lungs fought to take in a deep breath but rattled against the frosted air. "You see," I went on politely through my shivers, "it's dreadfully cold out here, and I need a place to hide away for the night, if that's all right with you."

"Your mate or—boyfriend, I suspect," he started, his face furrowed with confusion, "does he not believe you or something?"

Or something. Something like that, I thought miserably, but I shook my head. "He was with me when we were trying to help everyone. He knows it wasn't me, but we had a row," I told him, hoping that would be enough. "And I can't go home just yet."

"Did he do something to you?" he asked urgently, taking a step out into the cold. "Did he hurt you?" His voice was as worried as his hands as they reached out to grasp my arms, to check I was all right, but I pulled out of his reach, taking a half-step further into the chilly night. I didn't want to be touched. I just wanted to sit and warm up.

"No," I said firmly. "No one hurt me. I'm fine, I'm just—" *What was I?* I thought as the anxiety from lying built in my chest. I tilted my head, taking in the feel of the warm air escaping from his home as I stood sopping wet on his doorstep. I swallowed to buy more time and then looked up at him once more. "I'm just cold," I said, lifting my shoulders pathetically, and I was. I was so fucking cold I couldn't think. Chills wracked my entire body, shaking me violently. My jaw clenched, fighting off the chatters of my teeth, and my core ached from the instinctive tightening of my muscles.

"Of course you are," Wyatt said, promptly grabbing my arm to pull me in. The door clicked closed behind me, and he immediately began rubbing my arms to heat them. This time I let him. The heat was slow to return—so dreadfully slow that it ached on evermore. I needed the heat. I needed it so desperately.

I took in Wyatt's face as he worked to heat me up, so familiar, yet so foreign. Lines of worry painted his face, and he looked up to meet my eyes.

"Let's get you changed into some proper clothes and then you can tell me everything," he said, immediately rushing past a futon and over to a set of drawers. The wood scraped against its tracks as he pulled it open, and then he began rummaging through it.

I frowned at the drawers as I took in the room for the first time in this life. The walls hovered in closely to the few items of furniture the space would allow. Clothes and bits of trash cluttered the floors and surfaces, bits of spoiled food from the tiny kitchenette wafted into my nose and churned my stomach, and the clatter of his rummaging clawed at me. He took out some articles of clothing and stepped in front to try and hide the swipe of his arm as the random items on the dresser swiftly replaced the clothes he had just taken from it.

As soon as he caught me staring at him, I could smell the blood as it rushed up to his cheeks. "I am so sorry about the mess. I've been a real ruddy wreck lately to the point I haven't done anything, and that's not like me. You know that's not—" He stopped, his fingers flying up to the bridge of his nose, his eyes shut, and he shook his head. "Well, perhaps you don't remember," he corrected, "but here." He shoved a t-shirt, socks, and a pair of scrunched up pyjama pants into my arms before his hand pressed against my back to lead me towards one of the very few doors in the place. "Change in the loo and then we'll get you warm," he insisted, and as the door slammed behind me, I realised I hadn't seen a mortal move so fast.

I held my breath as the smell of an untidied bathroom crashed into me. It was just as cluttered as the rest of the house, and I wondered just how much of an emotional rut he was in to let it get this bad. The sound of frantic movements came from the other room. A few trash sacks were fluffed open, and more items scraped against the laminate kitchen surfaces and sloshed down into the bottom of the sacks.

Looking down at my rain-soaked clothing, I began to peel it all off me, all the way down to the knickers I had to roll down my wet, frozen legs. After slipping on the dry clothing, I carefully placed my underwear against my dress and fought to fold them inside of the fabrics in such a cramped bathroom without knocking my elbows against the confining walls.

I heard the cold air rush in through the front door as I exited the bathroom, just in time to see Wyatt placing three stuffed trash sacks outside in the rain. He closed the door behind him and jumped slightly as he took me in.

"Do you want a drink?" he asked, grabbing out two glasses, but he quickly shook his head and placed one of them back. "Of course you don't," he let out quickly, shoving two cubes of ice in a glass and pouring what smelled like bourbon until it settled near the rim. "You never were much of a drinker with how sloshed your father always was. You don't mind if I drink, do you?" he asked as he raised the glass into the air and it threatened to spill.

My stomach, which was still clenched from the cold, lurched up a bit at his words—the way he knew me more than I knew him. It was as odd as talking to Hydie—both people who knew my past self better than I ever would.

Tiny droplets trailed down the side of the glass and mixed with the salty perspiration on his hands. The smell of the liquor was more nauseating than the rubbish now that most of it sat outside, but I placed a faux smile on my face. "Of course not. I'm the one intruding on your space. There's no need to ask me if you can have a drink."

He let out a short, quivering laugh before placing the glass to his lips and drinking several gulps of the reeking liquid.

"I know I shouldn't be, because of the circumstances, but I'm really glad you're here," he said, staring into my eyes. "Nervous as hell, but so very glad," he added softly, and my lungs paused their hard work as my heart squeezed past them to become a lump in my throat. His lips parted again as he examined my face closely. "You hadn't called and everything you told me, your accident, your memory—well, it was a lot. I thought perhaps you didn't want to remember me, and that's why you hadn't called."

I bowed my head, avoiding his eyes, too afraid to look at them. "No, that's not it at all," I replied quickly. "I've just been through a lot the past few weeks, and I'm not handling it very well, to tell the truth." My voice tapered off. *Death.* How could anyone handle all those lost lives with grace when grace for such an unspeakable act was not deserved? Especially when I could have stopped it all.

"And then I saw the news report—or more like the news invasion," he said, deep in thought as he swished the drink in the glass. Ice collided with the sides of it before his eyes flew back to mine. "And when I saw your face, I didn't know what to believe. I knew it wasn't like you. It couldn't be you, at least not in the right mind."

I studied him carefully, my hands gripped tightly around the wet fabrics of my dress as I waited to see what he'd think of the whole situation—what he'd think of me. I didn't have words to comfort or work things out in my own mind, much less his, so the silken fabrics grounded me to the present. They kept me in London, away from the island that had gone up in smoke and was no more. But the moment of being separate from the tragedy didn't last long.

"Vampires…" he said, his voice trailing off in disbelief. "You always wondered what other creatures existed alongside witches, but I can't believe it's real—no one can." Finally, something he wasn't so ready to believe. "I mean, the whole world is terrified. People *say* they don't believe it, they insist there must be another explanation, but after all the deaths that man on the news is responsible for, after the destruction of that entire country, how can anyone find doubt in his words?"

I nodded as guilt weighed down on me. I should have killed Florence. I should have tried to kill him any chance I had, since the first moment I laid eyes on him and found out he was the one who changed me into a vampire. None of this would be happening right now if I had.

"It's insane," I told him.

"Yeah," he agreed, staring far off into the distance. "Yeah it is."

I watched anxiously, taking in the way he sipped at his drink and worked through the information in his head. Insane was the most mundane way of putting it.

"Here," he offered, suddenly snapping out of his daze. He set his drink on a small table beside his bed, took the wet clothes from my hand, and put them in a plastic bag. He placed the bag on the floor and then folded the futon up into a sitting position. "Have a seat," he insisted, plopping down a smidge away from the middle, and propping his arm along the back of the sofa as though he was about to sit next to an old friend.

I sat against the metal armrest, as far away from him as I could without seeming rude, and studied the way he watched me: familiar, kind, patient. The shadow of memories washed over me.

"Were we good mates before…?" I asked him timidly.

"Ah," he said, glancing down at the floor and rubbing the back of his neck. "We were more than mates. We were sort of in love."

"Sort of?" I quipped, encouraging him to explain more.

He laughed before smiling up at me. "All right," he gave in, "we *were* in love, I just didn't know if that's what you'd want to hear right now, with all you're going through. I don't want to add to any raw feelings you might have."

But I gave him a weak smile as a thousand emotions flooded me. "Don't worry about what I want to hear," I told him firmly. "I don't think I could handle any lies right now. I'm just looking for the truth."

He nodded before looking away again. "Well, we were definitely in love."

"Is that how you know what I am?" I pressed on, not allowing myself time to wonder more about my feelings towards him, forgotten or not. "Did I tell you, or did you find out?"

"A bit of both actually," he laughed, leaning forwards to rest his elbows on his thighs as the memory played in his mind. "We were chemistry partners, and you were always ruddy crap at it," he explained softly, and the faint memory of how I created my password brushed gently across my mind. "But there was one day when you thought no one was looking and you sort of—held your hands out towards the beaker, and the chemical reaction started working properly. You thought I wasn't looking, but I was always looking at you. I couldn't help it. I was infatuated with everything about you—the way you'd laugh over an experiment gone horribly wrong, the way you'd furrow your brows at me when I so easily memorised the periodic table, your brown eyes," he said, lingering in the memories before he met my blue eyes and gave me a curt smile.

He leaned back against the futon, his hand along the top of its frame once more, such a short distance away from me, and let out a small laugh. "But things are different now," he said with a shrug. "I kept asking you questions about how you had made it work, and after a while, you let me in on your secret. You told me you were a witch, and that your sister and father had powers too. After that, it became *our* secret."

I let out a deep breath. Now it was my turn to soak in all the information.

"And I told you about my father?" I asked, remembering a remark he had made earlier about his drinking habits.

He nodded. "Yeah, a right arsehole, he was," Wyatt said, drumming his fingers against the cool metal frame. "But I take it you got out of there? That was your sister at the pub, wasn't it?" he asked, hope dancing behind his eyes as he gave me a warm smile. "She's the spitting image of you. I thought she was still too young to be hanging out there."

I let out a laugh, and it felt so foreign coming up my chest and through my lips. I hadn't laughed in weeks. "No," I said, shaking my head. "She's eighteen now, believe it or not. We all wanted to get out one last time before the curfews started, and that pub is a very special place."

"How so?" he asked, and I was glad that a bit of positivity stayed in his tone as he said it.

"Well," I started, folding my legs up underneath me, "Chad, my boyfriend, opened the pub and then he gifted it to our mate, Connor," I told him, doing my best to make light conversation in such a dark time. "We used to go salsa dancing every Sunday," I offered, not really knowing why I was divulging such random information, but saying it anyway. It seemed like one of the only times in my past that was happy. The thought of it sent a bit of warmth amongst the cold I still felt.

Wyatt stared deeper into me, really trying to assess my features as he asked, "Every Sunday until he hurt you?" His flat, matter-of-fact tone caught me off guard, and the smile slipped from my face.

"No," I replied immediately. I felt my brows furrow as I looked away from his intent stare. "No," I started again. "I told you, he didn't hurt me."

But he shook his head at me. "I know that look, Azalea," he insisted, and I looked back at him as his eyes pressured me to tell the truth. "He may not have put his hands on you, but he did hurt you."

I stared back at him as his fingertips moved along the fabric of the futon, and I listened to the sound of it scraping against his skin. My tongue pressed against the roof of my mouth as I considered it—considered telling him everything that had left me shattered. But I settled on the latest one that had sent me right over the edge.

"He kissed someone else," I let out, not daring to look away from him or I'd chicken out. I resettled myself on the futon, shrugging it off as my tone lightened to downplay it all. "It's said," I started mystically, "that he's supposed to marry someone else, and after our first kiss, it sort of got to me. I avoided him. Well," I went on, "it turns out that he met the mystery lady in my short absence, and he kissed her." It felt ridiculous saying it out loud, like I was unjustified in my anger, and maybe I was. "I shouldn't be upset," I said with a sigh, "but he didn't tell me. I had to find out from someone else, and that's the part that really tore me up."

Wyatt nodded, biting the inside of his cheek as his eyes squinted in concentration. Then without notice, he scooted in towards me, his fingers tracing their way along the side of my face. My breath hitched in my throat, and my heart was pounding, desperate to escape. But his heartbeat was slow and steady as his soft skin played against mine.

"I'm really sorry," he whispered, the scent of the drink on his breath causing me to turn away from him, but he took his other hand under my chin to pivot my face back to him.

My eyes flickered back and forth between his hazel eyes, and I couldn't breathe.

I could kiss him.

I could give in to Wyatt, let his lips bring me comfort. But that wouldn't be fair to either of us. I didn't remember the love I felt for him. And as much as I wanted to get back at Chadwick, that was the wrong thing to do. The bloody wizard was right. I'd had no claim over him when he kissed her, or she kissed him, or whatever the hell had happened. I had literally ignored his letters because I knew he should be with her, even if I didn't know she was with him at the time. He had every right to go test things out and see if she was his destiny—every right. I'd still resent him for it for the rest of my life, but I could probably find a way to forgive him. To keep it from me, on the other hand, well, that I could never excuse. But either way, I could not kiss the man in front of me.

I let my eyes wander away from Wyatt, and a disheartened air left his lips. Time seemed to stretch on as he slowly leaned in and kissed the top of my head. As he wrapped me up in his arms, his body told me that my silent decision not to give into temptation was all right, but I could almost feel his heart crumble as he held me against him. Perhaps it was good that I didn't remember our past together. Perhaps that knowledge would have made me give in.

Sobs attempted to choke their way up and out my throat, but I clutched onto him, accepting his warm embrace as I forced them back down. I couldn't let him see my blood tears. I wasn't ready to tell him about that side of me. Not yet. I just wanted one night to forget what I had become.

"I'm tired," I told him softly.

I felt his jaw move around uncomfortably before he leaned back from me.

"Of course you are," he whispered, and as he nodded, his lips formed a smile that didn't reach his eyes. "We should get some sleep." He gave my cheek one last graze with his fingers before his face scrunched up, and he looked around the tiny studio flat. "I—I don't really have a big place, or a sofa, or anything," he let out awkwardly, his hand rubbing the back of his neck as he avoided my eyes. "This futon is all I got, but I can sleep on the floor if that makes you feel more comfortable."

"Oh. No," I said quickly, furrowing my brows along with him as I realised what he was saying. "No. That's truly not necessary. I woke you up, and you were very nice to keep me, but perhaps I should be going now," I told him. It had been a bad idea to come here in my current mental state. My shattered heart ached to be healed, but spending the night with another man was not the answer. Especially when he didn't have a sofa I could camp out on.

I stood up from the futon, but Wyatt grabbed my hand and gently tugged me back to him. I fell softly beside him, my legs brushing up against his, and my cheeks warmed in embarrassment.

"It's three in the morning, Azalea," he said, fear coming out in his tone. His face flashed with worry as though he couldn't believe I was considering going back out there. Rain crashed against the windows, and the thought of the cold air was enough to make me shiver. He shifted in his seat, begging me with his eyes to stay, and he swallowed hard before his lips parted again. "And the last time you left here and went out into the pouring rain was nearly the last time I ever saw you again," he recalled, his eyes haunted by the memory, and Florence's red eyes burned against my retinas.

That night. I had left here in the middle of the night, and had been changed forever.

Wyatt's soft fingers ran along the back of my hand, easing me back to the present. "There are sick, sadistic creatures out there—*killing* people, Azalea, and curfew is in effect," he said in a pleading tone. His eyes were wide with worry and his heart started to pound again. "It's not safe," he stressed.

I looked down at the pyjamas covering my skin and my soaking wet hair. I could transport, I could, but I was void of the strength or willpower to go. And where the hell would I go anyway that would be away from Chadwick?

"Okay, I'll stay," I decided, and Wyatt's brows rose ever so slightly in surprise. "But you were perfectly comfortable in your own bed when I got here, so I'll be the one sleeping on the floor," I insisted.

"Nonsense," he said with a warm smile, and he squeezed my hand happily. "I won't try any funny business, I promise," he added sternly, "but maybe it's best if you get some of my body heat. Your hand is still freezing," he said.

From all the blood flowing anxiously through my body and overwhelming my mind, I forgot he was still holding my hand. My eyes travelled down, and I let out a nervous laugh as I slid my hand out of his. Yet I nodded nonetheless.

I was so cold.

Wyatt pulled me up so he could lay the bed down flat once more, and my mind screamed at me that this was the wrong thing to do. He fluffed a blanket out flat, and the gust of air sent more shivers down my spine.

"That was always your side," he explained cheerfully, pointing to the side against the wall, and I grimaced at the thought—my side.

I crawled over to it as though my muscles had taken over, not allowing my brain to process what I was doing, and laid down. It was as though the world moved in slow motion as Wyatt crawled in next to me, lifting the covers over both of us, but as visions of Japan, the mushroom cloud, and all the dead bodies crept back into my head, I pushed every thought away. All my emotions drained out slowly until the hollowness pierced through like a sting against my ears. Wyatt was faced towards me, his forehead pressed up to mine, and he gently rubbed my arm to get the blood flowing properly again.

I didn't notice as my muscles loosened from all the tension of the night. I willed all the fears of another nightmare to creep away from me. And just as Wyatt's arm stopped moving against mine, when his breathing slowed to a light snore, and sleep was about to take me, a loud pounding on the door shook me to my core, and I sat upright.

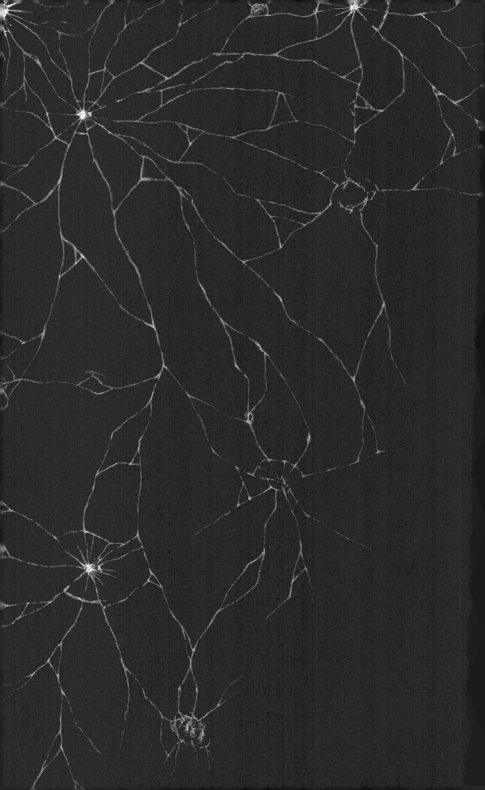

Chapter 44: A Waking Nightmare

I watched in horror as the door crashed open, slamming into the wall beside it, green smoke dissipating in its wake. Wyatt jumped up and out of the bed just as Chad crossed over the threshold, but it was too late. Chad abruptly halted, and his eyes travelled back and forth between Wyatt and I. Thoughts and triggers contorted his face into different expressions as I sat there completely mortified, cursing the world for letting him find me like this.

I scurried off of the futon and jumped to my feet, careful not to show off my vampire speed, but it hardly mattered. Wyatt stood with his chest heaving, his mouth ajar as he gaped at Chad.

"How—how—" Wyatt stammered, but I cut him off.

"Chadwick," I greeted, somehow out of breath as the quickened beating of my heart clashed loudly against the pounding of theirs. "This is *not* what it looks like," I insisted, but the cliché phrase was shredded to bits as he looked down at what I was wearing—Wyatt's pyjamas.

Fierce eyes gazed back at me as Chad's brow rose, baiting me to tell him more lies, but it wasn't a lie. I hadn't done anything with Wyatt, at least not anything incriminating.

When my flustered brain couldn't grasp onto any words that would rectify the situation, Chad spat out through gritted teeth, "Grab your things. We're leaving this instant."

The power and ferocity of his demand forced me to grab the sack that contained my soaked dress, fear shaking me to the core. I had never seen him like this. I had never seen such anger emanate out of every pore of his body. I moved towards him, ready to leave the dreadfully awkward situation, but just as I was making to pass, Wyatt grabbed onto my arm and pulled me into him.

Chad's eyes ignited with fire as Wyatt frowned at me and said, "No."

No? I repeated in my head as a bit of blood rushed out of it. *This is a nightmare. Please be a nightmare.*

"Perhaps we could speak in private," Chad growled out, but Wyatt held on tighter.

Casting a threatening look back at Chad, Wyatt insisted, "How about you go shove your requests up your arse?"

Apparently, his front door being magically banged open had caused him to be fully awake and stubborn as ever. He rolled his shoulders back and opened his mouth to say more, and I recoiled at the horrid possibilities of what he might say.

"Azalea told me all about you—going off to snog some girl and then lying about it," he said, and I cringed so tightly, right as Chad dropped his scowl to stare back at the man who held me, his face purely aghast. "Now leave her alone so she can have some peace and quiet away from you," Wyatt finished angrily.

My body was frozen in horror. It was a nightmare, a trainwreck, a disaster, all at once.

"Azalea," Chad tried again, anger resonating through his voice as he ignored Wyatt and shifted his heated eyes back to me. "We need to talk. Now," he added, but a realisation set in, and my muscles ceased their urge to walk towards him.

Wyatt was right. My brain needed peace and quiet, and perhaps I wouldn't be able to find that here, but I was definitely not going to find it by going with Chadwick.

"No," I said for myself, shrugging off Wyatt's grip and hugging the sack of clothes to my chest. I could feel the cold from the wet fabrics seeping through the sack, all the way to my skin, but the quiver that shook me didn't stop me from refusing him. "I don't want to go with you," I told Chadwick, my voice neither firm nor frightened, just some pathetic, confused mix between the two.

Chad shifted his weight between his feet as his strong posture broke, and he diverted his gaze down to the ground. "Azalea," he tried again, a bit of his usual softness towards me shining through. "Something urgent has come up and I need you—"

"No," I spat out again, much more fiercely this time. I didn't want to talk to him. I didn't want to hear anything he had to say. I just wanted to sleep and get rid of this chill going through me. "Figure it out yourself," I demanded. "I'm not going with you."

His eyes returned to my outfit, teeth grinding together roughly at my response, but this time I didn't care. Let him think whatever he wanted. I didn't give a shit. Let him wallow as I had.

Chad blinked, his expression stubborn. His eyes broke their intense hold on my body to look over at Wyatt, whose stance was just as furious as before. Wyatt's feet shifted from the pressure but his scowl at Chad remained, clearly unaware of the powers he possessed, or his high title.

When Chad's darkened eyes landed back on me, they lightened, and he tentatively opened his mouth. In a much softer, secretive tone he told me, "Eyeara's family is backing out of the alliance," he said pointedly, careful not to reveal their race in front of the present company. The tension and hate within me simmered down, and I closed my eyes as another one of my fears became a truth. "They saw the news," he continued, "they saw your face, and they won't accept that it wasn't you. They think they can detach themselves from the rest of the world to stay hidden, but we can't win without them and all they're capable of. I need you to come with me and convince them otherwise."

Tears rushed to my eyes but I blinked up at the ceiling to rein them all in.

I didn't want to go. I didn't want to face all the things that had forced me to shrivel up into my dark hole, but the stubborn feeling in my gut told me I had to go fix things. Perhaps I was too damaged to be made whole again, but there were still lives to save and a war to fight—one I couldn't hide from, as much as I desperately wanted to.

I turned into Wyatt, to thank him for his company, the roof over our heads, but his shoulders fell in disappointment.

"You don't have to go," he tried, his words carrying a strength I didn't feel within myself.

"I'm afraid I do," I told him, guilt sinking in my stomach. I had unintentionally disappeared from his life before, and I could look around his flat to see the stress that it had caused him; the mess, the drinks— Was that all my doing? I looked back at him, giving him what I hoped was an optimistic smile. "But I promise I'll come back," I offered lightly. "I just have to take care of some things first."

Before my rattled brain could process his motions, he placed an arm around my waist and pulled me into him. His lips brushed against my ear as he spoke, not low enough to be a whisper. "I'll always have a place for you, Azalea," he told me, and I froze, knowing he was speaking loud enough for Chad to hear. "A place in my heart, in my home, and a bed if you ever need it."

My back was stiffer than a board as he said it—his heart—his *bed*. Why couldn't he have just whispered that whole bit? Or better yet, left it unsaid?

Then he placed a light kiss upon my temple. I just about died from the sound of Chad's teeth as they scraped together fervently, his arms held carefully behind his back as if to secure them away from the destruction they itched to cause Wyatt's face.

As I walked over to Chad, he didn't even look at me. He glowered straight into Wyatt even though his hand moved to wrap territorially around me, gripping onto the t-shirt I wore as though he wished it was Wyatt's neck. "Pleasure meeting you," Chad growled out with absolutely no pleasure in his tone.

"The pleasure was *all* mine," Wyatt said slyly, raising his brows in some sort of masculine threat that made me want to tear both of their heads off.

Fucking pricks.

Chad narrowed his eyes and gave a sarcastic grin as we were engulfed in his green swirls, and before I could utter a word of goodbye to Wyatt, we were gone.

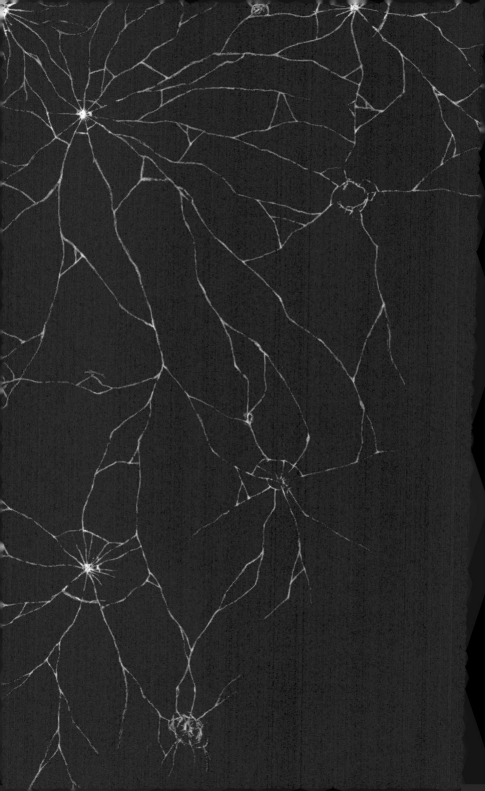

Chapter 45: I'm Still Shattered

O ur feet landed against frosted dirt and leaves, and I barely had time to look around at the woods and wonder why the hell we were here instead of wherever the bloody elves were before Chad opened his mouth, words spewing out like water crashing down from the tallest waterfall.

"Before we go to the elves, we need to talk."

Ah. So that's why we were here. So he could ambush me with questions that had no place in this moment of time—no place in the grand scheme of things. I was enraged.

Not only was he derailing our mission, but he had also made a right fool of himself in front of Wyatt, and gone and used magic in front of him. It didn't matter that Wyatt already knew I was a witch, or that the world suspected we existed, but now Chad was just willingly showing off his powers?

I took a deep breath, reining in my own powers and mentally preparing myself to keep them controlled as he began another row. "Let me make this very clear," I enunciated, inching closer to his face, not bothering to mask the fury still radiating through me. But I felt my magic swish calmly, bending to my will to keep it inside of me. "We will talk when I say I'm ready," I told him firmly, taking a threatening step closer to him, and he flinched. "And if you try to push me into any conversation with you that does not directly involve the war, I will leave, and you can sort through this whole mess on your own. Do you understand?"

Chad chewed his tongue, his lips sealed shut, but a battle raged behind his eyes, keeping him from agreeing. "But Azalea—" he tried.

"No," I shut down. My stomach gave a heave as I took in the deep stress that creased his face. I didn't know how long I could be around him before I lashed out again, so I took his arm and muttered, "Hurry up before I change my mind."

"I didn't cheat on you," he spat out instead, his tongue slipping on the words as though they were hard to get out, and I flinched at the sharpness of them. "We weren't exclusive. Hell, you weren't even bloody talking to me when it happened. I—"

"Oh, piss off!" I hissed, fully aware of the situation we had been in but still incapable of overcoming it.

I tightened my hold on his arm, urging him to transport us, but he wrangled his arm from my grasp before pulling away from me.

"I can't," he insisted fervently. "I can't do anything until you've heard me out, Azalea," he pleaded, his green eyes looking anywhere but at mine as his hands waved around chaotically. "I couldn't sleep, I couldn't eat, I couldn't think, and then all this business arose with the elves, and I knew I couldn't rectify the situation without you," he spat out quickly, a crazed rush pulling the words out of him. He slid a step back from me and took a few heaving breaths before continuing on. "I wanted to give you space, or whatever you needed, but I can't do it, Azalea. I need you. I had to find you. I—"

"How *did* you find me?" I interrupted, fury building up inside of me. "Did you follow me?"

"No," he said quickly, but it didn't ease the heat that was corrupting my insides. "I used a tracking spell," he let out, a quiver radiating out of his throat. He took a small green purse out of his pocket, the same purse he had once given me.

I rolled my eyes. He followed me with a fucking purse, but we couldn't get an item off of Florence to track him down? How could the world possibly work in such a ridiculously unfair manner?

His eyes flickered down to the pyjamas that still hung loosely from my body, and a bit of fire returned to his eyes before he looked back up at me and snatched the sack of clothes from my hands. His eyes bored into mine with a glare as he reached into the bag, retrieving my dress from it with angry hands, but a small article of clothing fell out as the dress unfolded. I closed my eyes, a bit of horror biting at me as my knickers touched the forest floor.

When I opened my eyes, Chad was staring down at them, the tempo of his shoulders performing an accelerando in time to his quickening breaths.

He left his chin pointing down towards them as his eyes flashed up to mine, and chills prickled along every inch of my skin. His nostrils flared, his eyes narrowed, and he growled out at me, "If there is anything you'd like to admit on your part, now would be the time to do so."

Fear coursed through me. I knew exactly how it looked—exactly what accusation he was casting out at me, but I didn't like the way he said it. Rage swept into the mix and gradually outweighed the fear. He stared at me, waiting for me to admit something, but unlike him, I had nothing to admit. Nothing had happened between Wyatt and me. Chad had no right to make such an accusation after the truth he had kept from me.

Magic flickered at my palms, but I closed my eyes. I took a deep breath in through my nose to ease the sparks. I warned the power within me of the impending row and willed it all the way down until it ceased to light my hands. If I could mentally prepare for it, I could keep it at bay. But apparently my moment of meditation took way too long for Chad.

"Fine," he growled before he threw his hand towards me, and green magic flung the dress and underwear at me violently before forcing the clothes to sink through my skin, and suddenly I was wearing the dress again. Water no longer soaked the fabrics, and instead, they were warm. The pyjamas were left crumpled in his hand. Fire ignited them as he leaned into it, the glow of the flames reflecting in his eyes as the clothes turned to ash. He flicked his wrists, extinguishing the fire as he threw the ashes to the ground and scowled at me. "You want to be mad at me for letting her kiss me before we were officially together? Then I'm allowed to be livid and hurt by you sleeping with another man when we *were* a couple."

I took a step back from him, but my voice didn't portray my fear. Instead, it conquered it, turning it back into anger. "Don't say it like I had sex with him," I hissed back, letting the red consume my eyes. If I had to fight down my magic and force my fangs back to protect him, at least my red eyes could portray my anger without hurting him.

"How would I know whether or not you did?" he bit back, birds in the trees flying away at the sheer volume of his shouts. "You were fast asleep next to him, in his clothes. And then I come to find out that you can't even keep your bloody knickers on around—"

"Really?" I growled out at him. "You think I'd sink even lower than you? Well, I didn't. I wouldn't dream of sinking so low, I—"

"So you're telling me you didn't even think about having sex with him?" he asked, throwing his hands up accusingly as though I were incapable of withholding my urges against an ex. "Your body refused to be intimate with me. Perhaps it'd be perfectly fine shagging someone else."

"Oh, fuck off," I screamed, unable to care who heard us yelling at this point. Screw the curfew, screw getting caught, I was furious. "I didn't think about doing that so don't put those words into my mouth," I demanded.

"You are lying," he enunciated. "And if, by some small chance, you didn't think about it, he sure was. He was thinking about all sorts of things he wanted to do with you. All the things you two should 'do again' according to him—"

"What do you mean he was—"

"Azalea," he cut off, pure aggravation running through his tone. "Tell me if you two did anything—"

"Why should I owe you the truth when you kept a secret from me for a bloody year?"

"Tell me or I'm going to—"

"To what?" I asked, rage brewing through me like magma. "Threaten me? Tell me I can never see him again? Slip me some truth potion when I'm least expecting it? What?"

"No!" he insisted, his voice a crashing avalanche. "Tell me or I'll completely lose it," he cried out. All anger vanquished from his stance as his shoulders fell and his lips quivered. His eyes fell to the ground, agony shining in them. "I wouldn't—I—"

I could hear his insides breaking, but I was already beyond broken. I had moved on to something far worse. Either way, he couldn't afford to travel that far down. The world couldn't bear his sorrows when it depended so wholly on his every command.

"I didn't have sex with him," I admitted a bit softer than before, but still stubbornly. "Nor would I have, even if I wanted to."

He swallowed before looking down to the ground. "And did anything else happen?"

"What?" I snapped, apparently unable to play nice long enough to get back to our mission. "'Anything else' like what you and Mrs Prophecy did?" I asked, meaning to be snarky and cruel, but the words just crumbled my insides even more.

"Yes," he admitted, and the truthfulness made my stomach plummet unexpectedly. He was still unable to look at me. "Did you two kiss?"

Part of me wanted to lie so he could hurt as badly as I did. Part of me wanted to invent an image of the made-up scene so I could play it on an infinite loop in *his* head, but I knew it would be wrong. Instead, prepared my tongue for the truth. At least the better side of me could contain my magic, my thirst, and my tongue. Sometimes.

"No. We didn't kiss," I let out, and I watched his shoulders relax ever so slightly before the urge to make them tense once again consumed me. "But I wanted to," I added truthfully, and his green eyes shot up at me. My throat clenched at the hurt that ran through them. Being the coward I was, I looked away from him. "I wanted to find that missing part of me, to ruin your heart, to feel something other than the hollowness and pain that's been haunting me. But I didn't," I said quietly, lifting my shoulders helplessly.

He let out a staggered breath, portraying the pain behind my words, only it didn't make me feel better as I had predicted. I felt much, much worse. There was no joy in hurting the ones you loved. There was no satisfaction, no savoury revenge, no fix to the situation—only more heartache.

I shook my head, not waiting for his words. I was too cold to bear them. "Let's go," I told him, walking deeper into the woods as though I knew where we were going, though I didn't. I didn't know where to go, or how the rest of this bloody situation would turn out.

The crinkle of frosted leaves crunched underneath my feet, but no footsteps followed me, only a saddened voice that floated to my ears.

"I should've told you," Chad breathed out, his voice so low and hushed as the sound of the air struggled to enter through him. "I should've told you right away, but I was so scared I'd lose you again."

And he would have.

A flood of guilt crashed into me, but I shut my eyes to will the waves away. Sadness soothed the heat behind my eyes, morphing them back into their blue colour.

Of course he was scared. I had refused to talk to him after our first kiss. He had written letter after letter, all that I pushed away with silence. He *should have* gone and kissed her, especially since there was the possibility that she was the woman from the prophecy. How could he let fate slip away from him when it was so readily in his hands? I pushed him to do it. If he had told me he kissed her when I came to his Valentine's ball, the rest of that night would never have happened. *We* wouldn't have happened, and I don't think I could handle the thought of all my memories with him being erased—all those happy memories and the light he brought into my darkened world. I wouldn't erase him for anything. But to keep it a secret? He was right. He should have tried.

I let the flood of emotions wash away his words as I turned back to face him. He was still exactly where I left him, not an ounce of the bravery or confidence that usually straightened out his kingly frame.

"Chadwick," I started hopelessly, "my father broke me down so deeply as a child that not even a memory potion could undo the trauma. And when Florence came along, he took every last bit of joy that I had." I raised my voice as pain and sorrow fled out. "Slowly, I was starting to heal—to fight for a better life—and you helped me with that *so* much, but what happened in Japan sent a crack into me, and I broke once again.

Finding out that you lied to me for an entire year finished the damage. It completely shattered me, and Chad," I breathed out, "I'm *still* shattered. Right now, I don't feel like there will ever be a way to piece me back together again."

His jaw moved around, aching to say something, but he kept his lips locked shut. My shoulders shrugged off the importance of everything between us to focus on what truly mattered.

"Let's go talk to the elves and work at saving the bloody world," I let out softly. "Then we can focus on whatever it is we have or *don't have* between us."

He winced at my words, and his eyes fell back to the dirt floor for a fraction of a second before they pierced back into me. Emerald green winds swirled around him. He reappeared right in front of me, his arm wrapping around my waist, his lips centimetres away from mine as his warm breath caressed my chilled face.

"All right," he said, straightening up his back as his fingers tightened onto the side of my dress. "But just know that I'm going to spend the rest of my life trying to make it up to you," he finished.

Determination coursed from his eyes to his voice, but I didn't have time to piece together my thoughts. My breath caught as his green smoke whirled around us, and once more, we disappeared into oblivion.

Jade Austin

457

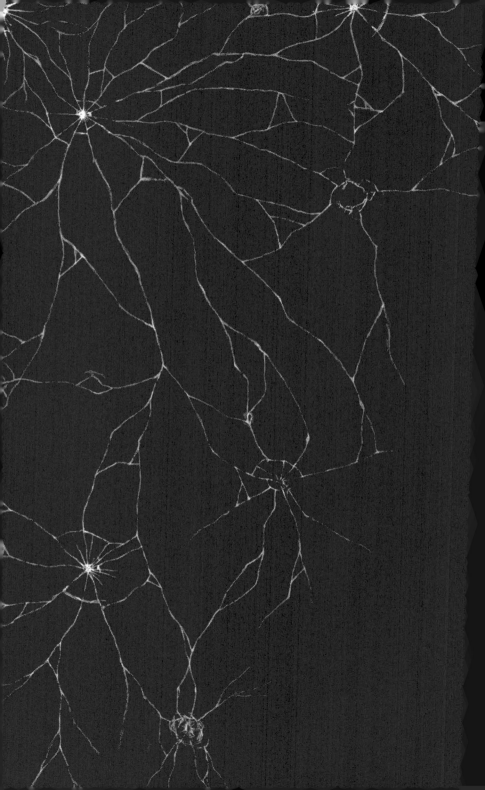

Chapter 46: The Purple-Eyed Beast

My feet stumbled against rocky terrain. The trees that had just surrounded us were gone, leaving nothing to block the chilling wind from blasting against us. I stood on my toes as it froze me to my core, closing my eyes as my hair and dress blew violently into Chad. A fierce roar echoed through the air, and the hot breath of a massive beast filled the frigid night. I clutched onto Chad's shirt and shuddered as I took in the sight of five enormous dragons.

My eyes flew to Chad, who studied me closely, and as much as my stubborn, furious mind wanted me to let go of him, my terrified hands didn't dare.

"What the hell are those?" I asked before I could catch such an obvious question from slipping through. I scrunched my eyes shut, hoping the dragons would disappear. "I don't mean *what*, I mean *why*. Why are we standing in front of a bunch of bloody dragons?" I yelled out, and one of the beasts roared again. I shrivelled further into the madman who brought me there in the first place.

Chad's arms tightened around me, and I cursed my apparent fear of dragons, wishing I didn't have to cling to the person I wanted to see *nearly* the least in the entire world. He was ranking in the bottom four. First was Mrs Prophecy, my least favourite by far, and then Chadwick, Florence, and the spiteful *other* me were throwing hands to compete for the next lowest ranking.

"Remember how I told you that some magical realms had very specific ways to allow others to enter them?" he asked, shouting over the dragon as he continued to hold me tight. "Well, to visit the elves, we must travel by dragon."

My upper half leaned away from him so quickly to question his sanity, but he merely nodded his head towards the beasts.

"Go on," he nudged. "Look."

I stood higher on my toes and peeked out from above Chad's shoulder, gripping tighter as I took them all in. A score of Chad's guards surrounded the dragons, looking quite small compared to the creatures. There were no chains or ropes to hold the creature down. Instead, the guards' magic swirled together like a rainbow. The dragons tangled together in a great mass, all sorts of patterns and markings along their scales, but one in particular stood out the most.

I stared at the dragon, right into its huge, vibrant purple eyes. White scales cascaded their way down its massive body, all the way to its spiked tail. It was everything I thought a dragon would be from the moment Chad told me they existed; fierce, fiery, and elegant, but most of all, this dragon was familiar. I had seen it many times before—memorised every scale, the way it slithered around without a care, and the way it played along Chad's bare chest and travelled around to his back as I ran my fingers along it. The outline and features of this dragon were identical to—

"Your tattoo," I breathed out, and he nodded against the side of my hair.

"See?" he asked softly, knowing he didn't need to shout for me to hear him. "You already know this dragon. You know her character and how playful she is. She'll keep us safe."

My eyes travelled up to the night sky. The thought of such a height made my stomach lurch.

"Oh no, no, no, no," I insisted. "I can't. I *distinctly* remember telling you that I was meant to stay firmly on the ground—not on a ship, not in the air—on the ground. I can't do this."

Chad tilted his head down at me in a very stern but encouraging way. "Yes, you can," he told me firmly.

Tentatively, I nodded back, using his strength to believe in myself. His green magic swirled around us, and suddenly, we were rocking back and forth atop the creature that towered the equivalent of three stories high.

Chad was positioned in front of me, grasping at the dragon's reins as it twisted around. Wind swept up my skirts, which were awkwardly hiked up so I could properly straddle the creature. I wrapped my arms around Chad's chest to stop myself from falling off, and swallowed hard.

"Perhaps I should ride with one of your guards," I suggested, disapproving of the close proximity to Chad.

He let out a sad sigh. "I'm afraid it'll just be us visiting the elves," he replied, shifting his weight in the saddle. "It'll be less intimidating this way. We don't want to upset them further. I'm afraid you'll have to hold tight to me, unless you'd like to attempt flying one on your own."

I grumbled soundlessly to myself, knowing that wasn't a viable option. Of course I couldn't fly a bloody dragon.

Looking down at the guards to distract my uneasy nerves, I asked, "What are they doing to the other dragons?"

"Calming them," he explained, "or at least trying to. Dragonhide is thick. It takes a large amount of energy to use magic on them." He placed his arm over my hands to secure them in place. "We should travel fast before the sun comes out."

I let out a soothing breath, hoping I wouldn't get motion sickness in the sky. How long would the journey take?

"Where exactly do the elves live again?" I asked with quivering breaths.

"Antarctica," he replied simply.

"Right," I said firmly, but in all honesty, I had completely forgotten that's where Eyeara was from. "How long will that take?" I asked in horror. There was no way we'd get all the way to the southern pole before sunrise based on our current timeline.

"Dragons have ways of travelling faster in the skies. There are magical portals they can take us through. It'll still take a few hours, but it's the only way we can enter."

A few hours? *Fantastic*, I thought bitterly.

I shivered against the winds. As though he could feel my pain, Chad's hand shimmered with green, and I was instantly warmed.

"We're ready for you, Saga," he said, carefully running his hand down the hardened, shimmery scales, and even though I was most definitely not ready, the dragon took off into the sky.

My stomach lurched, and my arms instantly tightened around Chad's core. I wouldn't have been surprised if I crushed a rib or two. When he didn't writhe in pain, I couldn't help but realise that there was a sense of bitter disappointment in my heart. He let out a strangled laugh as the wind rushed around us, wings beating heavily as we soared straight up, and the white dragon with purple eyes took us further and further into the sky.

We flew through misty clouds, protected by Chad's warming charm until we reached a spot where the night air was so clear that we could see every star the sky had to offer. Saga, the dragon, shifted her balance so it no longer felt as though I would fall off of her, and then she zoomed through the air with an ease that took away some of my fears.

Up ahead was a blurry mass of circles, hardly visible to the mortal eye, but when I focused on their shimmering pattern, I figured it must be one of the portals Chad had spoken of. I closed my eyes as we breached the entrance, and when I opened them a second later, the beautiful stars returned to view.

Chad looked over his shoulder at me with a warm grin. "How are you doing back there?" he called out.

The stubborn part of me buried my head against his shoulder blade so he could no longer see me. "I'm fine," I called back to him, wishing desperately not to talk. "Just tired."

He didn't ask me anything else. After about half an hour, my stomach started to unclench, and I began to enjoy the brisk air that seemed to magically clear my troubled mind.

We soared through several portals, over mountains, above the Sahara Desert, and across the stormy seas. After what must have been hours, the purple-eyed beauty dipped down several kilometres, leaving my stomach back up in the clouds. My eyes focused on a massive cluster of ice, and my breath left my lungs as I marvelled at the sight.

A palace made of ice waited down below, and as Saga curved around in a large bend, I was able to take the structure in from nearly every angle. The walls were made of waterfalls that had frozen into place. There were lights from within shining through the walls, casting a soft blue glow against the early morning navy sky. Icicles cascaded down the towers, shining brightly and giving off the effect that the castle was moving.

Chad steered Saga to the ground near the entrance. Her long wings beat heavily against the air as she hovered, and then her strong legs thundered down onto the floor of ice. Green magic swirled around us, and suddenly my feet were on the slippery surface, Chad's arm around my waist to steady my landing.

I slid away from Chad and ran my fingers gently along Saga's scales to thank her for our safe journey. *Perhaps she isn't so frightening.* But just as the thought entered my mind, her belly glowed with orange fire, and she growled out towards the palace. She lowered her body protectively, ready to strike if need be, but Chad patted her leg to calm her. His eyes were trained on the palace, too, as he took a step in front of me.

My eyes followed theirs. I watched as the light blue wall of ice nearest to us shifted, but it was only a second later that I realised what was happening. At least fifty figures, their colour nearly identical to the icy palace behind them, marched towards us, draped in frozen armour. Bearing shields of ice and icicle-like spears, they approached us menacingly. My heart stopped as they halted their step two metres from us. Saga smashed her tail against the ice threateningly, yet the frosted elves were unfazed by the heat of her breath and her fire.

"King Eyeron is expecting you," a guard in front announced. His nearly translucent eyes bored into Chad's, and a puff of air escaped my lips.

Chad's muscles tightened against me, and he growled out, "Splendid," at the irritable news. "If only I had a bloody charm bracelet to warn me about *him*."

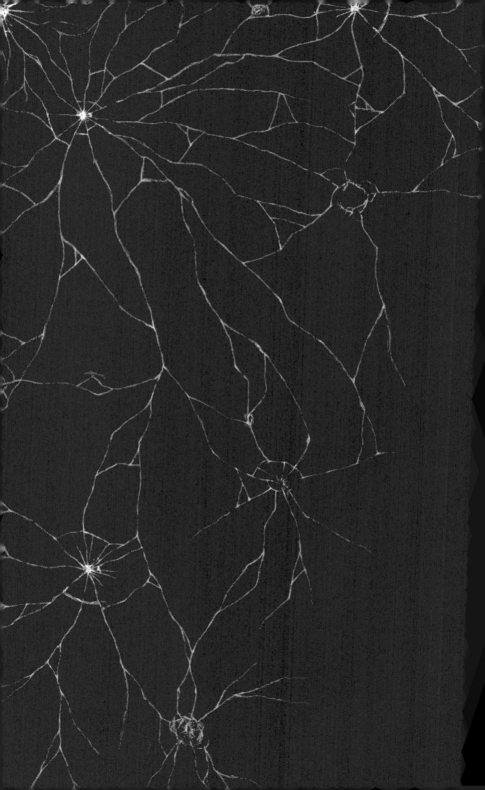

Chapter 47: The Cowering King

A quarter of the blue guards led us through a set of tall, smooth front doors, while another quarter followed closely behind, sandwiching us in between them. The rest remained outside to stand guard. A long, thin hallway trailed at least a hundred metres to the next door, and as the main entrance shut behind us, it shuddered the palace with a heavy thud. It felt as though the walls were closing in on us.

"The king and his council are waiting in the throne room," an elf guard reported.

Chad nodded firmly, his face relaying indifference, but I could read the fury in his eyes.

The doors flew open and King Eyeron scrutinised us as we all filed into the enormous room. He sat upon an overly large throne of ice, which I was mildly surprised didn't melt from the heated glare he gave us. Next to him, on a much smaller throne, was who I assumed to be his wife. Icaron and the rest of the council stood on either side of them, and as the guards dispersed themselves along walls, Chad led me bravely to the centre of the room, his shoulders held back in their usual kingly stature.

I scanned the room, anxiously looking for alternative exits, but apart from the doors we came in, there was no way out. My eyes took in every tense body in the room, every guard along the walls, until I saw Eyeara. She leaned against the frozen wall, her body looser than the others, and she gave me a friendly smile before a thunderous voice interrupted the small reunion.

"We're all quite confused as to why you're here, King Chadwick," the elven king sneered, not even bothering to fake a customary greeting. "I believe I've made my stance quite clear, or have you gone deaf *and* ignorant in your time flocking with vampires like her?" he hissed, his eyes flickering over at me for only a second.

Just as lovely as the last time I spoke with him.

"You must reconsider," Chad demanded, his voice just as powerful as the elf seated in front of him, if not more so. "You're cowering, and your fearful retreat is going to give victory to their side."

"I missed the part where that's my problem," Eyeron jeered, and I was ready to rip his head off.

I looked over at Chad, wondering when I should step in, cursing the idea that we had fought over our relationship rather than making a steady plan. But Chad was already pouncing back at the insult.

"It will *be* your problem when the rest of the Casters are captured or dead, and Florence seeks you out," he roared.

"And who's going to tell him how to reach us?" Eyeron snapped. His voice continued to grow with his thunderous rage. "Or is this bloodsucker not as pure as you claim she is?"

"You'd do well not to insult her in front of *your* king," Chadwick warned, but Eyeron hardly let the threat faze him.

"We've already heard of her alliance with her creator," Eyeron went on, "yet you bring her here, into my house, and continue to threaten me. I'm no fool. I know she can't be trusted. I know how weak she makes your judgement, and I'm not falling for it."

I couldn't take it anymore.

"I am not the woman from the news, regardless of whether or not she shares my face. Which is something you'd know if you had sent your men there to help," I shouted, gesturing towards Icaron and the others at his side.

"We had more important things to do than follow after you," the elf replied bitterly.

"More important?" I countered, not believing he could belittle millions of deaths. I grabbed the topaz and silver chain around my wrist, yanked it off, and threw it down by his feet. His eyes glowered as it slid across the icy floors, but I didn't care. It was useless. The chain had done what it was meant to do—imprison me. It was never meant to gain their trust.

I squared my shoulders to the sheepish king. "If you saw the woman with my face, then you saw what those vile creatures did to an entire country," I pressed. "What's more important than saving all those lives? Do you feel no remorse?"

"My duty is to the elves and nothing more," Eyeron bit, leaning back in his chair as if he needed no other explanation.

"So when they come here and kill your wife and daughter right before your eyes, do you wish *us* to brush it off?" I asked. "Should we let them tear you all to shreds and not lift a finger about it?"

"You know," he said, his voice shifting to calm, a smile spreading on his face, "there was once a time we thought this alliance would be bound by blood. By marriage," he added with a smirk, "but that's not the case now, is it?"

Chills prickled down my back and my eyes flew over to Eyeara. Her eyes darkened as she took in her father, and when I looked back at him, I wondered how elf blood tasted compared to a mortal's.

He gave a chilling laugh before continuing. "We're free to make our own decisions as you're free to make yours. I don't see what the problem is."

"The problem *is*," Chad chimed in, "that it's morally unjust. Queen Aria," he started, taking a step towards the second throne. The queen flinched at her name but met his eyes with kindness. "You must see how erroneous all this is. Come to the aid of those who have fought by your side for centuries—helped your species stay hidden from mortals. We've placed wards, portals, and protective spells for you. We're a team. It's not as though we've done nothing."

Queen Aria's eyes darted nervously to her husband as she opened her mouth. "Perhaps we could consider—" she started, but Eyeron cut her off with a growl.

"Aria," he barked, spit spraying out from his mouth, "'Perhaps' nothing. We're not helping any side that keeps bloodsuckers, and that's final."

"This is ridiculous," Chad shouted at Eyeron, his voice loud and powerful as it crashed into the frozen walls. "You have the power to hear and see the truth, you're just flat out refusing to do so. Have Eyeara show you the truth. Listen to *her* if you won't listen to me."

Eyeron stood from his throne, apparently unable to bear our company any longer. "We will not be fighting," he snapped simply. He turned on his heel and began walking away from us, the rest of his council following in suit, but his arrogance sparked something in me.

I took a step towards him and screamed, "How can you plan to sit back and watch millions more die just because of your prejudices?"

The elven king turned back to me so quickly. The whites of his eyes had turned stark black, and he screamed out, "You have put our lives in danger by merely being here." A wind stirred within the room and my heart pounded. Even his council members seemed to quiver. "Now, it's time that you've left us alone. We will not be joining you in any war, and that's final," he called out, his booming voice bouncing off the ice at every angle, crashing into me like slaps across my face.

"But—" I tried.

"Out!" he demanded, and I jumped at the severity of the threat his voice carried, as though terrible things would happen if we resisted his command a second longer.

He turned and stomped towards the smooth wall behind him, half the guards, his council, and his wife forming an organised line behind him. The impertinent king waved a hand, and the wall shimmered, swirling to form a doorway, and he walked through it without another word.

The rest of the blue guards marched in towards us, and beads of sweat congregated above my brow. Chad's hand folded its way around mine. My eyes flew up to his, but he didn't return my gaze. Instead, his eyes were trained on Eyeara, watching her as she leaned calmly against the wall. Without a word, she broke his eye contact with a blink and began walking out towards the door we had come in through.

"I'll show them out," she announced loudly.

A rush of frigid air blew past the princess, split into two paths around Chad and me, and forced the guards back roughly. There were echoey thuds as their bodies smashed against the walls. Then the gust of wind turned abruptly to push Chad and me from behind, and we stumbled out into the long, claustrophobic corridor. The door slammed shut behind us, and I jumped once more from the precision of her power.

The tall, slender elf strode fiercely down the hall. Chad tugged me along after her until she halted almost randomly, and turned to face the wall. The same shimmer her father had made danced along the wall until it, too, opened up into a doorway, and she turned to smile at us.

"Sorry about him," she said, and I blinked through the daze, wondering what the hell was happening. "He'll get what's coming to him soon enough," she said, her smile sincere.

And she walked through the magical doorway, apparently expecting us to follow.

Jade Austin

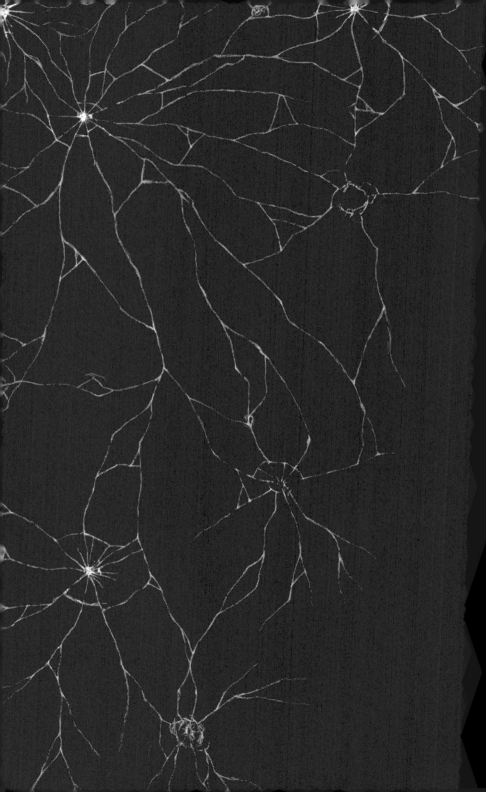

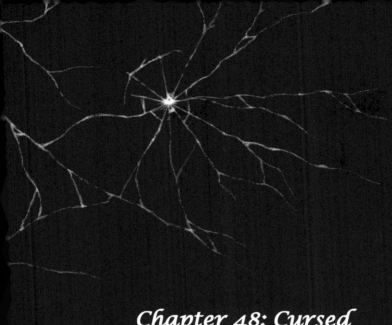

Chapter 48: Cursed

*P*rincess Eyeara marched elegantly through thin corridors, down slippery spirals of stairs, and beneath sharp stalactites of ice that blended into the ice walls around us.

"I'm a bit of a soul reader," she said without turning her head to face us. "And your soul is screaming for help." Her words chilled me, and although I couldn't tell whether she was talking to me or Chad, her piercing blue eyes flickered towards mine, and my question was answered. "There's a blockage of some sort," she went on as she neared a wall and stopped abruptly in front of it. She turned to face us, and my stomach leapt as Chad and I pulled to a halt. "I felt it the night of the coronation," she admitted, "but now it feels different."

Without warning, she pivoted back towards the wall and used her elven magic to make a door appear. After inspecting the corridors around us to ensure we hadn't been followed, she pulled the door open, and we spilt into the room after her.

The ceiling of this new room towered high above us, a spectacular frozen chandelier hanging low and sparkling with a magical blue glow. Everything, from the vanity to the large bed, was made from frozen blocks of ice, beautifully carved with extravagant details. I stood open mouthed as I took it all in, my warm breath leaving me as a cloud.

"I need a tear from you, Azalea," Eyeara announced urgently, and I closed my mouth to turn around and face her.

"A tear?" I asked, dumbfounded.

She gave an apologetic smile prior to nodding. "Yes, I'm afraid a tear is the only way to find the answers." Her eyes left mine again but slowly returned, and in a very gentle voice, she said, "I'm going to have to search your mind, sift through memories until I find something dark. But I promise it'll all be worth it in the end."

Eyeara stepped towards me carefully, her feet sliding soundlessly along the slick ice, seeking permission with her steady gaze. I nodded, granting her access, and allowed her fingers to travel up my neck, through my long curls, and curve around my head as she held my mind in the palms of her hands.

"Close your eyes," she said softly, "and open your mind."

With a steadying breath, my lashes met and all I could see was the light blue ice. A wind pushed against it and a spiralling flurry of snow blew through, twisting until faint sculptures of ice peeked through the storm. They came closer and closer, gliding smoothly as if enchanted, until I could make them out for what they were.

Two sisters laughing behind their shield of azaleas and hydrangeas.

A book of magic being read under the cover of white sheets.

A first kiss shared between a woman and the man she loved.

The smooth texture of Chad's hand as he reached towards me, descending the stairs of his garden, begging me not to run away.

Pulling me past the fountain.

Holding me tight.

Me demanding him for the kiss he promised he wouldn't give again unless I asked for it.

But as soon as our lips met, a black dot appeared. It grew larger and larger until the ice figures were covered in darkness—a memory tainted.

My eyes scrunched against it—willing the black to shrivel back to where it came from—but it only spread faster until the whole scene was coated in the despair I felt so heavily in my heart. And then, the black ice cracked and shattered into a million tiny pieces, piercing me just as the mirrors had done in the hall.

My eyes burst open. My lungs heaved for air as though I had been drowning, but there was no black—only the icy blue bedroom that had surrounded me before.

I heard the breaths of Chad and Eyeara, synchronised my pounding heart with theirs, and blinked quickly as something heavy trickled down my cheek: a tear.

My eyes shifted over to Chad in embarrassment—ashamed to let him see me so weak when I needed my strongest shield against him. I should have fought away the sorrow and cast it to burn in a fire, but it was too late. Chad's breath quivered as he took me in. Guilt washed over his features, and his hand lifted ever so slightly to reach out towards me, but then tightened into a fist to fight its ascent. I felt a twinge somewhere inside me, but I couldn't fully tell if the lack of his touch made me feel better or worse.

Eyeara's hands fell slowly out of my hair, and her long blue finger reached out towards my eye. Her soft skin brushed against my bottom lashes, and I closed them to ground myself to the feel. The wetness on my cheek transferred to her finger, and her cold breath grazed my face as she sighed.

"Just as I suspected," she whispered.

I opened my eyes to look at her finger. Atop it sat a single tear, only it was not crimson; it was black.

"Sorry about that," she said sincerely, and I forced a half smile.

A frosted breath left her lips as she blew on the tear, and wisps of black smoke surrounded us. Hundreds of scenes danced in slow motion around us, filling the room with a cacophony of sounds, none discernible to my ears. And with another frosted blow from Eyeara's pale blue lips, they were all gone.

"Someone's very envious of the life you have, Azalea," she noted. "So much so that they've used dark magic to interfere with your well-being."

Chad edged forwards, concern etched heavily on his face. "What does it all mean?" he asked fearfully.

But Eyeara's eyes stayed glued to mine. "It seems you've been cursed—several times over," she said mystically, and my jaw tightened as I waited for her to reveal more. "Cursed to fear things—to fear words—to try and stop you from feeling certain emotions. But those spells you've broken on your own."

I cast my eyes to the ground as I felt exactly which things she was referring to. It wasn't so long ago that I had feared blood. I had cowered from the colour red and pushed away any chances at love as they all screamed out at me to stay away. And to kill—that was my latest fear—severed by the passion I found to put an end to Florence. But I was *cursed* to fear those things?

The sound of Eyeara's parting lips drew my attention back to her. "The curse that still lies within you, however, is stronger—perhaps given to you in the form of a potion to truly harbour its effects. *This* one you can't break on your own," she told me firmly.

"And that curse," I started, stepping in closer to her with an eager mind. "What is it?"

She looked towards me thoughtfully but her pale eyes seemed to sink through me. "A memory curse," she breathed out, and I felt as a puzzle piece from my shattered heart locked back into place.

My memories. All stolen. All trapped away.

I opened my mouth to ask more, but Eyeara's eyes flew over to Chad with a dark intensity behind them.

"In order to get anywhere," she told him fiercely, "you're going to have to get *everything* out in the open." Her words pounded against me. Chad's eyes fell to the ground, insistent upon fleeing from mine. From the corner of my eye, I could see Eyeara turn to me, and her gaze pulled me in like a powerful, heavy force. "And you," she said, her soft, mesmerising voice luring me in further. "You're not accepting your full power. To win, you're going to have to open your mind to everything it's been trying to push through to you. But before you do anything else, you're going to have to break that curse and get your memories back."

A line of chills played along my spine as a million thoughts flooded in, violently washed away by the hurricane of emotions that swarmed in and took their place. I couldn't think. I couldn't feel anything but the need to know more.

"How do I break it?" I asked, praying with all my might that she'd have the answers I had yearned to find for so long.

"That part will be easy, more or less," she added, her eyes flickering over to Chadwick before they made their way back to mine, and I had a dark feeling it was going to be less "easy" and more of the other part.

My chest compressed in on itself as her soft lips parted, and words flowed out like the lyrics to a song when the wordless melody had been stuck in my head for an eternity. "You're going to have to find Baba Yaga," she said, and the tension that had been floating aimlessly around me crashed into my soul.

I was going to find my past.

But a vicious, invisible entity, separate from myself, crashed unwillingly into my consciousness. Heat and fury radiated through it, halting any hope from spreading in my chest. The entity's anger swirled into a storm and then morphed into fear before a voice sounded through echoes in my head.

Shit, it cursed ominously into the night.

But its terror instantly gave me the strength I needed. It told me I was one step closer to killing Florence. And I was so bloody ready.

I'm Still Shattered

THE JOURNEY OF THE STORY

I began writing the "I'm Still Alive" trilogy back in 2008 when I was sixteen years old. I had always planned for them to be the books that would get me out of poverty and onto better places. I'd get a movie deal and act as the main actress. Boy, a girl can dream!

One of my favorite parts of being the author of this series is hearing from my readers. They message me their favorite parts, ask questions, and share their excitement for the next installment. I nearly cried when a reader reached out and thanked me for including manananggals in the story, as her culture is so rarely included in fantasy novels.

If you're interested in finding out some fun facts, Abigail's full-length story, and other deleted scenes, please visit the "I'm Still Alive by Jade Austin" group on Facebook. Feel free to follow me on TikTok and Instagram @jadeaustin09.

Please leave a review on Amazon and Goodreads. It would truly mean the world to me.

Enjoy!

ABOUT THE AUTHOR

Jade Austin resides in the scenic *Pacific Northwest* with her husband *Will*, her brilliant son *Cooper*, her dog *Frodo*, and they have a beautiful baby boy on the way! *Currently*, *Jade* teaches middle school mathematics but in her free time she enjoys writing, reading, and anything *Harry Potter*. *After* facing homelessness as a child and being raised by a single mother, she greatly prides the life she has come to live. *Her* writing goal is to give young women, especially those of color or living with *PTSD*, anxiety or depression, the opportunity to see themselves in a novel, have an escape through fantasy and a pathway to a better future.

ACKNOWLEDGMENTS

Without my readers pushing me, I wouldn't have made it to this point. You believed in my work when it felt no one else did. You kept me going and for that I owe you so much.

Special thanks to Samantha Ziegler and Zian Schafer for all of your encouragement, support, and brilliant ideas. Getting to know you both has added so much joy to my life.

Thank you to Finished Fiction for your supreme editing skills, time, and beautiful suggestions. If anyone needs a dedicated editor, follow her on Instagram @finishedfiction.

Thank you, Rebecca Kenney at RFK Cover Design for the amazing cover. I didn't know it was possible to love a cover more than I loved the first book's cover, but you've blown me away.

Thank you, Mom, for believing in me and being my biggest fan.

Thank you, Will, for not only taking over housework and taking care of our son so I could write, but also for helping me survive the worst morning sickness of my life. What would I do without you?

And thank you, Cooper, for all the morning snuggles and love you've given me! Your sweetness, smarts, and creativity are some of the things that make Mommy so proud of you!